MW01032168

Healing of the Heart

A Shumard Oak Bend Novel - Book 4

Heidi Gray McGill

Heidi Gray McGill Books LLC

FUSING FAITH
AND FICTION™

Although in-depth research was done on the historical aspects of this story, the author has taken artistic license with the writing.

All scripture is taken from: Holy Bible. King James Version, Bible Gateway, https://www.biblegateway.com/versions/King-James-Version-KJV-Bible/

Ray Pritchard, "Top 100 Motivational Quotes," QuoteFancy.com, QuoteFancy, 2024 Update, https://quotefancy.com/quote/2332443/Ray-Pritchard-May-you-be-filled-with-the-wonder-of-Mary-the-obedience-of-Joseph-the-joy

PUBLIC DOMAIN HYMNS:
Robinson, Robert. "Come Thou Fount of Every Blessing." Hymnary. Accessed April 4, 2024. https://hymnary.org/

Palmer, Ray. "Lord, My Weak Thought In Vain Would Climb." Hymnary. Accessed April 4, 2024. https://hymnary.org/

Palmer, Ray. "My Faith Looks Up To Thee." Hymnary. Accessed April 4, 2024. https://hymnary.org/

Oakey, Emily S. (attributed to), Bliss, P. P. Bliss (Author). "Jesus Loves Even Me." Hymnary. Accessed April 4, 2024. https://hymnary.org/

Wesley, Charles. "Jesus, Lover of My Soul." Hymnary. Accessed April 4, 2024. https://hymnary.org/

eBook ASIN: B0CW34Q3VR
Paperback ISBN-13: 9798324120719
Imprint: Independently published
Publisher: Heidi Gray McGill Books LLC

Cover design by: Erin Dameron-Hill

Printed in the United States of America

Dedication

Armilda "Amy" Kull Kress
January 2, 1923 – April 15, 2016

Grandmom, as she was affectionately known to her grandchildren and me by marriage to her grandson, was a beautiful woman with a challenging past that molded her into a no-nonsense woman.

In 1938, at sixteen, Armilda defected from Estonia with her sister Agnes and brother Viktor, fleeing to Germany at night without her parent's knowledge. She learned the local language and worked for the railway. After the war, Armilda met American Army Lieutenant John A. Kress. Armilda spoke no English, but John knew some German and her heart language of oranges, silk stockings, and coal. They married in May of 1945. John returned to the US to report to his duty station, while Armilda and Gary, their firstborn, followed with other war brides and children on a voyage that likely took up to fourteen days by sea.

Armilda learned her third language, English, when she arrived in the United States. One of my favorite memories is how Grandmom would confuse words. She once asked me to get her the shredded knife rather than the serrated knife. A family favorite was her rendition of "Guantanamera," the Cuban patriotic song. She'd sing, slightly off tune, "One kind of meadow...," and we'd all chuckle.

If you live in the South, you know what No-See-Ums are. These tiny flying insects are challenging to see. Grandmom dubbed them See-Me-Nots, and she never changed her mind about their proper name.

Grandmom's love for her family was evident in her ability to bring joy through her unique sense of humor. She had a knack for inserting words we thought were Estonian into everyday language, and we later discovered she had made these up. Her youngest child, Carol, will tell you it is awkward when your friends don't recognize the word "glersy" for "armpit." Grandmom's playful nature and quick wit always made us smile.

Grandmom was not just a woman of resilience and humor but also a regal and stylish presence. Despite her humble beginnings, she carried herself with the grace and elegance of nobility. Her understanding of making something out of nothing, overcoming adversity, and hard work was deeply instilled in her three children. She was always dressed to the nines, and her collection of shoes and hats could rival that of Macy's.

Although I based the character of the same name in Healing of the Heart after Grandmom, she was never a nurse. Her idea of medicine was prune juice for internal injuries or Windex and a wet paper towel for external injuries—well before it became famous in My Big Fat Greek Wedding.

Contents

Chapter 1

T eddy lifted the frame of the wire-meshed boarding house door to keep it from squeaking. The new invention allowed air to flow freely but did not permit one to enter or exit unnoticed—at least not this door. Like her exhausted limbs, the tight hinge moaned at the belabored action, pushing against Teddy's hand in its desire to announce her arrival.

"Theodora Morse, I'm certain you are well aware your rent is due today promptly at five?"

Teddy jumped, letting go of the frame and allowing it to make a satisfactory clap back as it went back into its hold. Teddy's exhaustion made it difficult to lift the edges of her mouth into a smile. Widow or not, Mrs. Jones ran her establishment like a proper business. She may disapprove of Teddy working nights, but the woman deserved respect.

Teddy forced the muscles in her face to cooperate. "Yes, ma'am." She'd perfected the action of serving the hoity-toity upper class at *Les Madeleines*. Serving others was a gift, but it became a chore between twelve and four every day. She much preferred her night job as a nurse at the hospital.

Mrs. Jones humphed. "No rent, no evening meal."

Teddy didn't have the energy to argue. If she wanted to stay on track with her savings, she could pay the rent on time, but it would mean another skipped lunch. "Yes, ma'am. I'll have it to you this evening."

The woman's curt nod before leaving had Teddy taking a deep breath, using only her diaphragm. Thank the Lord she was not required to wear a corset. It would take forever to remove, and all she wanted was to plop into bed and succumb to some much-needed sleep.

Corsets were ridiculous contraptions. They kept a woman from being a full, productive member of society. The ladies at *Les Madeleines* were perfect examples of the effects of a too-tight corset. She couldn't afford to get herself all riled up before bed and forced the rapidly increasing heat of her blood to cool.

Sleep. That was all that mattered. Teddy lifted her heavy feet toward the bed waiting on the second floor.

Three girls came bounding down the stairs and into the foyer, each with their eyes on the retreating Mrs. Jones. Teddy loved her roommates but felt slightly agitated, knowing they'd each had a full night's sleep, breakfast, and were off to start their day. Teddy scolded herself. These girls were more than roommates. They were friends. The thought caused a smile to form on Teddy's weary face.

Each girl was unique. Alone, they were disastrous, but together, they made a good team. Where Josephine led, Merriweather followed. And Birdie's pessimistic melodrama was counteracted by Teddy's positivity and ability to find a solution to any problem.

Josephine's sharp tone and overly loud volume filled the foyer. "Did she fuss at you again?"

Teddy didn't have time to reply before Birdie blurted, "She has it in for you. A day late for rent one time, and you'd think you were a criminal."

Merriweather's soft tone and sigh followed on the heels of Birdie's confrontational tone. "Losing her husband so young to the war and having the responsibility of a boarding house must be difficult on her."

Teddy mentally rolled her eyes, but her expression remained the same. Mrs. Jones had to be in her late fifties. "She simply reminded me it was due at five."

"She never reminds us." Josephine's words bordered on impolite.

Birdie tied a scarf under her chin, covering a grease stain on her collar. "I can't stand here and talk all morning. Unlike my workfellows, I'm never late. Somebody has to set the example." She picked up the sides of her wrinkled dark blue cotton skirt, a motion she must often do if the permanent grease stains were any indication.

The screen door creaked, then slammed, making Teddy's weary body flinch. She removed the pins from her nurse's cap, rubbing a sore spot where one had dug in all night.

"Your hair is so pretty, Teddy. All soft and wavy. I have to cover my dirty mop with this old thing. I hope to buy a new scarf with this week's pay." Merriweather lowered her gaze.

"You look very pretty in your yellow scarf, and it makes your face glow. And you wouldn't want to stand out at the Harrison mansion."

"Oh, no. I tuck this away as soon as I arrive. Mrs. Harrison wants us all to look the same and makes us wear ugly caps that fully cover our hair." She attempted to tuck one limp strand back into the tight bun that pulled at her already-constricted features.

Josephine picked at her chewed nails. Why couldn't the girl see how nasty a habit it was? A simple metal nail file would do wonders, as would a nail brush for her cuticles. Teddy rubbed the pad of her thumb over the smooth curve of her well-kept nails. Maybe she'd get a nail care set for each of her roommates for Christmas if her funds would stretch that far.

Teddy ached for a hot bath to soak her tired feet and hands but focused on her roommate. "You haven't worn that dress in a while. What are your plans for the day?" The question had Josephine masking her expression even as she hid her hands behind her back. She placed them on her low bustle.

"Oh, the usual. I'll see you girls this evening. Don't be late with rent, Theodora." She dragged out Teddy's given name with the same tone Mrs. Jones had used. Her laughter followed her and her full skirt out the front door.

"What's the usual?" Merriweather asked, then put her petite fingers over her mouth. "Oh, shame on me. It should be none of my concern, though I never have figured out what she does for work."

The hall clock chimed seven thirty, and Teddy felt her body wilt. She should have been asleep by now.

Merriweather reached for her friend. "Have a good day, Teddy. And don't let those high society ladies get under your skin. If they knew how hard you worked, they'd be kinder."

"I doubt that, but thank you." Likely, the ladies she served didn't have any inkling of what actual labor was. Teddy watched as Merriweather primped a moment longer in the mirror.

Merriweather glanced at the clock. "I really must go. Make it a good day, Teddy. And get some rest. I don't mean to sound like a mother hen, but you are working too hard." Merriweather leaned in and gave Teddy a hug that nearly squeezed all the air from her lungs. "I snuck a biscuit from breakfast and put it on the desk," the girl whispered before letting go.

"Thank you." Teddy meant it for more than the words of concern and the biscuit. She looked forward to that hug every morning. It was a gift from her friend that started, or technically, ended, Teddy's day right. It reminded her she was real, tangible, not just a server girl at the ladies' lounge who needed to remain invisible or a nurse at the hospital, which often required the same, especially in the presence of a doctor.

"Thank you," she whispered again, though Merriweather would not hear her over the *clip-clip* of her heels on the wooden porch.

The heavy *clop-clop* of the sturdy heels of her more serviceable shoes echoed in the enclosed stairwell to the shared room. She longed for pretty things but knew practical would have to do for now. She'd make her wardrobe and shoes last, no matter how ugly or out of style they were. She closed the bedroom door behind her and let her cares fall from her shoulders. It was her favorite time of day, and she had the room all to herself.

Even though the bed called her name, Teddy lit a match and watched the flame in her desk lamp come to life. She replaced the globe and stared as the light illuminated the room. Perfumed air and the smell of sulfur melded. The single chair squeaked as she pulled it from the desk and plopped into its hold. Her Bible was within reach on her bottom bunk, and she ran her dry hands over the soft leather, taking care not to break off the worn edges.

"Lord, may the words I read today invade my whole being and transform me. Enlighten me with your words as if they are new. Make them a part of me so I may share you with someone I come in contact with. Help me be a light to one who lives in darkness and an encouragement to one whose flame is burning low."

Pages crinkled, and the bookmark keeping her place revealed Psalm thirty-four. Teddy lifted her hand to her unladylike and ever-widening mouth. Her eyes watered with the yawn, and she raised her gaze to the morning light from the single, soot-covered window. Dimness and fatigue made reading difficult, but Teddy was determined. She scooted her Bible closer to the lantern. "Let's see what you have for me today, Lord."

"I will bless the Lord at all times: his praise shall continually be in my mouth. My soul shall make her boast in the Lord: the humble shall hear thereof, and be glad. O magnify the Lord . . ."

Thud, thud, thud. "Miss Teddy, you in there? Miss Teddy!"

Teddy's hand flew to her mouth in an attempt to keep the scream that wanted to escape inside. Whatever could be so urgent? She didn't smell smoke, but fire was the first thing to cross her mind.

"Goodness, what's all the fuss, David?" Teddy's heartbeat did not match her calm tone or steps and increased when the boy's flushed face was before her.

"Miss Teddy, I know it's your Bible time, but Cook cut her hand real bad. She dun ruined a loaf of bread."

Her time with the Lord and sleep would have to wait. "Extinguish my lamp, please, David, while I fetch my things. And shut my door behind you." Teddy grabbed her medical bag with shaking hands and hurried out the door.

"Yes, ma'am."

She heard the familiar click of her door as she hurried down the stairs and into the kitchen.

Cook, a portly woman in a too-small apron, sat on the potato-peeling stool, her back against the wall. Only one of the three legs showed under her girth. Her round knees peeked out from her skirt, and she cradled her hand in their folds. Her raised hem revealed stockings pooled around swollen ankles.

When Teddy entered, Cook looked up and feigned a smile, though the tense lines around the woman's eyes didn't relax. "Oh, good. The doctor is here. I'm so sorry to interrupt you, dearest." Red oozed from the cloth surrounding Cook's hand.

"I'm no doctor, but you'll likely only need nursing." Teddy's heart raced as she unwrapped the soiled apron and skirt and examined the laceration. The sounds of something boiling matched the noises in her ears as blood rushed through her veins. Teddy worked to calm her racing mind. She'd need a level head and steady hands.

"So silly of me." Cook's voice wavered.

Teddy forced a calm tone. As if she'd donned her nurse's cap, she covered her racing adrenaline and began giving orders. "David, please pull that crate over, and get Cook's feet up. Thank you. Please start another kettle or two of water. This dress is going to need washing when we're through."

"Yes, sir, I mean, ma'am, Miss Teddy."

Teddy washed her hands, then laid out her supplies. Cook's thumb would require several stitches, but the most critical concern was cleanliness. She bathed the wound, talking through the process as if this gray-haired woman were a child.

"Let your arm rest on the table while I stitch this up." Teddy moved in swift, practiced motions, tying off the last stitch moments later.

"All finished." Teddy washed her hands and began cleaning her instruments. "Keep that hand above your heart, or it will throb." Teddy replaced the items in her bag and pulled the woman's skirt down farther to cover her ankles. "Let's get you changed, then for the next hour, you'll sit here with your feet and hand raised and direct David to do your bidding."

"Doctor's orders?"

The sparkle in Cook's eyes soothed Teddy's nerves. "Nurse's strong suggestion. David is a capable young man, and you're a fine teacher. I'm certain whatever you are preparing for the evening meal will be spectacular as usual."

Cook leaned closer. "Well, Cook's strong suggestion is you take one of the cookies I made with a cup of coffee up to your room. You didn't make it back in time for breakfast again." Cook's whispered words settled over her like one of Merriweather's hugs. Softer, but it still took her breath away.

Teddy helped the woman stand and ensured she was steady on her feet.

Cook blew a quick stream of air through the space between her front teeth. "I hurt my thumb, not my legs. I can change myself, though I might need help with the buttons."

"Of course." Teddy opened the door off the kitchen into Cook's quarters and closed it behind the woman as the back door opened.

Light surrounded David's matted hair. Tufts stuck up from the back like a poorly made thatched roof. "Since you said the water was for laundry, I set the wash kettle up outside. I only filled it half full since it ain't wash day."

"How smart of you, David." She wanted to suggest that he wash his clothes while they were still on his body but kept silent. Dirt may cover the boy's face and hands, but his smile shone brightly.

Teddy heard bubbles popping in the pot and checked to

ensure it wouldn't boil over. "You go on, and continue with your chores. I'll clean up here. Then you can be Cook's helper."

"Think she'll let me have a cookie?"

"I'll put in a good word for you." Teddy did her best not to laugh as the boy bounded down the stairs and out of sight into the side yard.

The unusable loaf of bread went into the slop bucket at the side of the stove. The chickens would eat well today. Teddy used boiling water and soap to clean the countertops. Cook had taken her advice and used a wooden board for cutting meat, but eggshells sat in a pile directly above the slop bucket. Her eyes closed as she took a deep breath. Nursing was one thing; teaching was another. She doubted she'd ever help the older woman understand the importance of keeping a clean kitchen work surface.

"I'm not decent. Can you lend a hand?" Cook peeked out from the crack in the door of her room off the kitchen.

Teddy's heart clenched when she looked into the woman's pain-filled eyes. "Absolutely. Give me a moment to hand your soiled dress to David."

The boy must have heard her, for he appeared on the back steps with arms stretched and eyes closed to take the load. "I'll get this soaking, then be right in." He peeked one eye open and fixed it on the cookie jar before he left.

Cook's back was all that showed through the slim opening. Teddy reached for the button at her neck, securing it first, then opening the door a bit more to tie on a clean apron.

"Thank you, dearie. That David is such a helper. Would you stir the pot? I can't have the bone broth ruined. We're already down one loaf of bread." Cook's voice shook.

Teddy stirred the pot again, then helped the woman adjust

her skirts to sit. David reappeared, pushed the crate forward, and helped lift the woman's swollen ankles.

Teddy knew Cook would have good care with David nearby. "If you two can do without me, I'll head back upstairs. I believe David's earned a cookie." Teddy winked at the boy, who wiggled like an excited dog.

"Thank you, sweet girl. You're a godsend." Cook's head tilted. "And you, young man, deserve two, as does Miss Teddy. Crawl up there, and grab the tin."

With coffee in hand and two molasses cookies tucked in her pocket to add to her drying biscuit, Teddy allowed her heartbeat to slow to the cadence of her steps. With the adrenaline rush gone, she was bone weary and hoped she could make it back up the flight of stairs.

Teddy's Bible lay open, but she couldn't focus. She savored each bite of the biscuit and cookies, chasing them down with a sip of the dark brew until all was gone. Her bed called to her, and she'd have considered crawling in fully dressed, but she needed her nurse's uniform ready for her evening shift.

The soft cotton of her nightgown caressed her, snagging on the dry skin of her fingers. Her skin was as rough as Josephine's nails. The whipped beeswax felt heavenly as she coated her tired hands, rubbing them like she had the back of a child in the night, lulling the patient to sleep. She lay back and continued to massage, moving up her tired forearms.

Rap, rap, rap.

Teddy could not identify the sound or where it was coming from.

Bang, bang, bang.

"Miss Teddy, wake up. You'll be late. Didn't you hear the hall clock strike eleven-thirty?"

Sunlight fought through the soot-covered window. Teddy bounded from the bed.

"Thank you, David." She called toward the closed door. Teddy wasted no time changing into the out-of-style service uniform. Her shoes needed a good polish, but it would have to wait. She tied the laces, then did her best to focus her tired eyes on the form standing in front of the full-length mirror.

Her hair was a mess. The neat bun she'd so painstakingly put her dark, unruly mop into before last night's shift now hung limp and to one side. Waves of loose strands stuck to her damp face. A nine-hour night at the hospital and less than three hours of sleep caused wisps of brown to curl around her face.

"I could use a miracle, Lord." Her fingers worked through the tangled mess. Her brush pulled the strands into a chignon that was barely passable, but it would have to do. Teddy had not a moment to lose and rushed down the stairs straight into the arms of a man.

Chapter 2

"**O**omph." Thomas grasped the woman plastered against his chest. His arms steadied her. His hands remained on the puffy sleeves about her shoulders a moment longer than necessary before placing a proper distance between them. "My apologies. Are you all right, miss?"

A pair of dark eyes stared up at him, then blinked. The woman increased the distance between them and tucked a wayward strand of hair behind her ear, her shaking hand mimicking the fluttering in his stomach.

His finger and thumb rubbed at the coarse hair just beginning to show on his face. The scent of lavender reached his nostrils, and he rubbed his fingers together as he lowered his hand, remembering the soft feel of the sleeve's fabric.

She offered a slight smile. "Quite."

"Quite?" Thomas had no idea to what she was referring.

"You asked if I was all right. I apologize for not paying attention to where I was going." Her doe eyes dropped, and she tucked the same lock of chestnut hair once more behind her ear.

"Looks like you know exactly where you are going, just in a hurry to get there." Thomas ran a finger under his collar and cleared his throat. "It was my fault. I wasn't paying attention as I entered. Honestly, I'm not exactly certain if I'm even at the right place."

Dark, sunken circles under the woman's eyes had Thomas pushing away the urge to diagnose.

"Who is it you're looking for?" The woman's gaze flicked to the wall beside her.

Thomas patted his breast pocket, then stuck his hands in each side pocket before pulling out a piece of paper. It was upside down, and he couldn't read his handwriting. The woman followed his every move, making heat fill his cheeks. "The matron of the house?"

The tick of a clock filled the silence as she stood before him like a statue. She blinked and brushed at the white apron over her plain dress. Her mouth worked as if forming words, which finally came forth.

"Mrs. Jones. Yes, right." She angled her head, but her eyes stayed on his. "Mrs. Jones, you have a visitor." The slight lift of her lips made his respond in turn. "I beg your pardon, I'm late for work, but she'll be right with you. Good day, and I pray you find whatever you're looking for."

Thomas stepped aside to allow her through the front door. His fingers rubbed together as if he still felt her firm arms under her sleeves. This was a young woman used to hard work. Thomas swallowed the lump in his throat as the door shut behind her.

He took in his surroundings. It was a far cry from his rural home in Shumard Oak Bend, Missouri. A wide staircase, which the woman must have come down as he'd entered, was flanked on either side by two rooms.

Nothing but the scent of fresh bread and something meaty felt familiar about this place, yet Thomas felt comfortable. He ran his fingers over the smooth wood of the piece of furniture before him. Familiar or not, Thomas needed to acclimate to this new world before classes started in a few days.

A large mirror graced the foyer's wall, and he took in his appearance, running a hand through too-long hair. He pushed his jaw out and blew up at the ever-wayward strand of hair threatening to cover one of his eyes. Two and a half weeks of train soot covered his traveling suit, and he brushed at the front of his jacket, upsetting a knickknack on the foyer table. He steadied the piece and took two steps back.

Well-loved books showed from behind an ornate glass-paned cabinet. He squinted to see the titles behind the wavy glass and sent up a silent prayer that there would be a room available here. It was the last place on Fourth Street and Judge Pennypacker's list of potential boarding houses with excellent reputations. His benefactor had suggested Thomas stay within walking distance of the university and the hospital.

Thomas straightened as an older woman entered. Her aged fingers slid over her graying bun. With squared shoulders and a lifted chin, she carried herself with an air of authority.

She wiped her hands on an intricately embroidered apron tied loosely at her thin waist. What other man would notice such things? If his mother hadn't made him sit and learn the fine art of sewing under Delphina's tutelage, he might not have been so good at stitching up man and beast. Thomas did his best to make the laughter wanting to escape look like a pleasant greeting.

"Might I help you?" Her terse tone held suspicion.

"I hope so. I'm Thomas Shankel. Judge Horace Pennypacker, my benefactor, recommended this establishment. I'll be attending medical school and need room and board."

The woman's posture relaxed, as did her taut features. She smoothed her apron and put on a cordial smile.

"Well, with a reference such as that, I own this fine boarding house. You can call me Mrs. Jones."

Relief settled over Thomas as he shook the woman's offered hand. If there were an immediate opening, he could get his belongings and the judge's man, Douglass, could go home. Only God knew how much it was costing Thomas to have the man at his beck and call all morning.

Mrs. Jones entwined her fingers and placed them over her stomach as if getting ready to quote the Sunday oration. "We have one room for two dollars and forty-five cents a week. Rent is due upfront and is not refundable if I am forced to terminate our agreement for unsavory behavior." Her earlier smile gone, Mrs. Jones removed her spectacles and held Thomas's gaze.

Thomas pulled air into his nose at an even pace and relaxed his facial muscles. He'd need part-time work or something to earn extra money during breaks to help cover the cost. Perhaps purchasing only one new suit for important functions rather than two would stretch his funds. Whatever it took to become a doctor, he'd do it.

Mrs. Jones replaced her glasses, but her eyebrows remained raised in anticipation of his response.

"Yes, ma'am. I agree to your terms."

She peered over the rims. "I do not abide by drinking, carousing, or having visitors in your room, and I strictly adhere to the Sabbath."

Thomas wondered if the congregants of the large stone churches he'd passed would be the same as the fellowship of believers who met back home in the clapboard structure that also housed the school. Brick and stone seeped warmth from a body. Would it do the same for a soul?

"You'll receive two meals a day. Breakfast is on the sideboard between six and seven in the morning. We do not serve lunch. I serve the evening meal promptly at five-thirty in the dining room."

Thomas followed her gesture toward the ten chairs surrounding the cloth-lined table. He felt a pang of homesickness but pushed it away, replacing it with the excitement of this new adventure.

"With you being a medical student at the university and a friend of Judge Pennypacker, I'm sure we can work something out to keep your meals warm if you don't get in until after dark."

His earlier enthusiasm turned to dread, and the eggs and biscuit from breakfast roiled in his gut. What was he getting himself into? He could have studied back home under Robin instead of coming halfway across the country. As a medicine woman, she knew as much as he ever hoped to learn at medical school.

But God had called him. That reminder and his purpose to serve others calmed his nerves once more. He focused his attention back on Mrs. Jones.

"If you'll follow me, Mr. Shankel, I'll show you to the available room. I cleaned it this morning."

Thomas obeyed, following the click of Mrs. Jones's footsteps as she crossed the gleaming floors covered by well-worn rugs that were nothing like the rag rugs at home. No matter how tidy, dust motes floated in the light, streaming in from the parlor windows just off the foyer.

Fresh lemon oil greeted him as he ascended the stairwell

behind his potential new landlady. The hall was dim, with only a shaft of light coming from the round window at the end, positioned over two hand-painted signs indicating the lavatory and bathing rooms. Two doors on his left matched one on his right. The door at the end of the hall held a small vine wreath with a pink bow tied to the bottom edge—a woman's touch.

Mrs. Jones cleared her throat, pulling his attention from the feminine decoration. "I rent all my rooms to men, except for that one." Her gaze was stern.

Had she known his mind had immediately drifted to the doe eyes of the woman he'd met earlier? Perhaps the woman lived in that room but surely not alone. He knew the East was more progressive, but Mrs. Jones did not seem like someone who would allow a single lady in a boardinghouse full of men. Could the female boarder be married?

His fingers tingled as he rubbed his chest, and he felt something akin to butterflies take up residence. Staying out of her way was a good idea. He could not afford the diversion of a woman. No matter how beautiful.

"You'll mind our rules, and we won't have any issues like the man I gave leave to yesterday." She peered at him over her glasses.

Thomas gave a single nod. She seemed to accept this as his consent of her rules.

"This west-facing room is vacant." A keyring jingled, and the sound of Mrs. Jones opening a door pulled his attention to the room directly across from the door with the wreath.

"You are responsible for cleaning your room, but I'll wash your furnished sheets and towels every two weeks. You can do your personal laundry on the opposite week, but you'll need to sign up for a time slot."

He'd done his fair share of household chores, thanks to his mother and Delphina. There was no such thing as women's work on the ranch. He hated laundry day more than any other, but he could hold his own. Would he have time with his school schedule?

"No smoking in the room. We have a lavatory and a bathing room to the left outside your door. Learn the habits of those here to determine when you might use the facilities. My patrons have been with me for several years and have their routines." Her clipped words bounced off the stark room's walls.

Mrs. Jones continued speaking, but Thomas focused on the single window. Although clean on the inside, streaks of soot covered the outside. His chest constricted as his gaze focused on a wall of brick from the home on the other side. No sunlight made its way through the panes. Cold enveloped him even in the suffocating heat of the room, and he longed for a breath of fresh mountain air.

He took a step back toward the hallway and worked to swallow the bile rising in his throat. He loosened his top button and drew in a slow breath. The scent of lemon refreshed his resolve, as did the memory of his parents reminding him to keep his focus on the Lord and the gift given him. He worked to straighten his spine. He could do this.

"I'll take it," he blurted.

"Very good, Mr. Shankel. That will be two dollars and ten cents for the remainder of this week." Her hand splayed open, revealing a simple gold band on her left ring finger.

Thomas felt for his wallet and produced the required funds. "I'll have my things brought up straight away."

Mrs. Jones took the coins and placed a key in his hand. He stood in his new home, missing Missouri's view and fresh air more than ever. Several hooks lined the walls opposite a bed larger than his back home. On the side wall, a sizable rectangular mirror hung over a well-loved dresser, its paint marred and missing like a beloved toy. It was more suitable for a woman's finery, but he was thankful for it.

He wondered if the winters here could be any colder than Missouri. He'd only seen a fireplace in the parlor but hoped the room directly below also had one and would warm his room.

Thomas stood before the mirror and gazed into the disfigured form before him. Two panes of glass had been wedged together to make the oversized mirror. It was an honest reflection of how he felt—disjointed, with half of his heart in one place and the other standing here.

A small desk and chair sat under the window. He'd need oil to fill the lamp. A deep sigh escaped. "Lord, make my funds be as loaves and fishes."

For the next two years, he'd have to rely on the Lord to meet all his needs. God had proved Himself true in the past. He'd do it again. Light feet carried him outside, where Douglass patiently waited. "It looks like I've found lodging. Would you mind helping me carry my things?"

Douglass stepped from the conveyance. "Of course, sir."

The men each handled one end of two rectangular crates, one on top of the other. Thomas repeated his steps from earlier, taking care not to mar the floral wallpaper in the hall.

"We should have made two trips." Thomas strained as he shifted to lower the crates without dropping them. The sound of wood on wood echoed in the room.

"I'll get your other two bags and something to open those crates, Mr. Thomas."

At least they'd progressed to using first names after

spending an entire morning together. Thomas hung his suit jacket on one peg, then reached inside for his wallet. He needed to settle up with Douglass when the man returned.

"Here you are, sir." Douglass placed the bags on the floor.

"What do I owe you for your kindness today?"

"No charge, sir. I work for the judge. He pays me a fair wage."

Thomas wondered if that wage was the same as the one the skeleton of a waitress from breakfast received. Two coins clinked, and he offered them and a handshake to Douglass. Confusion clouded the man's dark eyes.

"Douglass, I'm not familiar with customs of the East yet, but I know a good man when I see him. No matter your position, it would be my honor to call you a friend." Thomas moved his hand closer.

Douglass dipped his head slightly and shook the offered hand but refused the money. "I'm honored. You keep that. You're going to need a new suit of clothes." The man flashed a large white smile, slowly lifting his gaze to meet Thomas's.

"I'm hoping this suit will work for school if I can beat it hard enough to remove all the soot. I'm afraid I'll have to forgo a second to get whatever is in style for social events and services. According to the sign I saw in the window of a tailor we passed, prices are a bit higher in the East than I'd expected." Thomas knew his current suit was out of style, but it was clean and fit well. It was the better of the two he owned.

"You're gentry now, Mr. Shankel."

"Thomas, please. My station hasn't changed."

"You step through those university doors toting the judge's name, and you'll see what I mean. Now, you'll be needing one suit for parties, another for church, and one for school. Judge

Pennypacker uses Wanamaker's on Market Street, but I know someone who can make you what you need that's just as good for less than what it costs the judge."

His schoolteacher had suggested Thomas wait to purchase attire until after he'd arrived. Acquiring what he needed for a lower price sounded like a gift from above.

"Thank you. I'll take you up on the offer. I have a few days before classes begin. Perhaps I can meet your tailor tomorrow? Where will I find him?"

"It's a woman. My wife. She's busy during the day, but if you have time this evening, I can pick you up at seven." Douglass fidgeted, but his gaze remained firm.

"Perfect. I'll watch for you. Thank you, Douglass."

"Let me get those crates open." The man wedged a bar under the lid. The sound of nails creaking filled the room as they left their hold in wood. "You need anything else, Mr. Thomas?"

Old habits must be hard to break. At least the man wasn't calling him Master Thomas like the slaves on the plantation had called him when he was a boy.

"If I do, I'll let you know this evening. I can unpack on my own."

He bid his first friend in Philadelphia good day, then reached into the open crate and pulled out the wrapped drawing of the friend he'd left behind. The pencil strokes by his little sister's hand lay behind clear glass. He searched the barren wall and found what he was looking for. A single nail stuck out from the seam of peeling wallpaper.

Serafina had captured his and Gabe's roughhousing as if the two were still in motion. Gabe's brawny arm encircled Thomas's neck. The smiles on their faces would have lit the room back then. Thomas ran his hand over his face, feeling the tense muscles under his palm.

Life wasn't fair. He was following their dream while Gabe was attending classes at The Missouri School of Mines and Metallurgy in Rolla, Missouri.

"Lord, why is there so much injustice?"

The ache of home had him searching for writing supplies. The chair squeaked as he sat. He'd send a letter to let his family know he'd safely arrived and provide his new address. And he'd enclose a note of encouragement for Gabe.

Chapter 3

August, 1871
Teddy

"**H**ave you seen him?" Birdie's breathy words held a hint of wistfulness. It felt overly dramatic to Teddy, unlike the girl's naturally stoic nature.

"Who?" Merriweather's gaze roamed the room as if a man would be in their private quarters.

Teddy watched as Merriweather gave up the search and removed her shoes, tucking the laces inside before placing them in their proper place under the bed. "Exactly, Birdie. Who are you talking about?"

Birdie gave a satisfied smirk, knowing something the others didn't.

There was the Birdie she knew. Teddy massaged her tight shoulder muscles and held in a sigh. She didn't want to play the game Birdie had started. She'd had a miserable day at *Les Madeleines*, starting when she'd spilled water on one of the tables. One would have thought she'd poured scalding coffee on the woman's silk dress.

Birdie huffed when no one asked for more information. "The new tenant. He's across the hall. Tall, dark, handsome, and the most startling blue eyes." She flung the back of her hand over her forehead and gazed up to the window before looking at Teddy, winking and exhaling a theatrical dreamy sigh.

"Who has blue eyes?" Josephine came in and bent to untie her shoes. The bustle of the dress lifted, then two shoes flew out from the skirt, landing haphazardly under the bunk.

"The new tenant," Birdie and Merriweather said in unison.

Josephine snorted. "Well, if he's living here, he's not rich. He's fair game, ladies. I have no interest. My Mr. Tall, Dark, and Handsome will be able to provide for all my needs." She wiggled her eyebrows, and Merriweather gasped.

Teddy would settle for self-sufficiency and providing for her basic needs. Being dependent on a man for anything was not what she desired. She enjoyed working and loved nursing, but scrimping and saving to buy her own home was still a distant hope. It would be several more years of daily sacrifice until she could realize her dream.

"All I want is babies." Merriweather's sigh had Teddy rolling her eyes again.

Children would be the one thing she'd miss. They weren't possible without a husband. Well, technically, they were. Birdie interrupted Teddy's thoughts with a loud snort.

"I'm not having kids," Birdie said. "They're just trouble and cost too much."

Merriweather sucked in a deep breath. "Birdie, children are a gift from the Lord. You can't decide if you have them or not."

"But you can decide if you keep them." The wry smile that crossed Birdie's lips garnered the desired effect.

Teddy reached for Merriweather's arm and lowered her to the chair. Birdie missed the glare Teddy shot her way before changing the subject. "I believe I met the gentleman. I ran into him this morning."

"You ran into him. Sounds like you." Josephine crawled up onto her top bunk, legs splayed with her skirt tucked between them.

Was that dried dirt on her hem? They'd had no rain in recent days. Josephine closed her knees, hiding the discoloration. She tucked her arms around the sides as if to hold her knees together. Josephine stared at Teddy, her eyes daring her to ask.

Teddy was too tired to play this game as well. "Yes. I ran into him, as in literally. I was almost late for work." Time to change the subject. "What a day. All those ladies talked about was how important the corset was to a proper lady's attire, the size of the bustle, and whose hat had the best feathers. They keep the milliner happy."

Birdie plopped onto Teddy's bunk and pulled her down to sit beside her. "Milliners and hunters. Now, there's a job. Back home, I could hit a duck from a thousand yards with my Old Reliable. Wouldn't be much left of him, but I'd a got him. Would've signed up for the army if they'd let me." Birdie positioned her arms as if holding the rifle and sighted on a bird flying past the window before jerking as if she'd fired.

Josephine shooed the make-believe gun away and took over the conversation, her boisterous voice making it impossible not to pay attention. "It's ridiculous these hats they wear. I saw a picture of a whole peacock on a hat in *Harper's Bazaar*."

Merriweather perked up. "Where did you get a copy of that magazine? I love looking through them, but by the time I see one, it's woefully out of date."

Teddy scrutinized the woman on the top bunk. Josephine was hiding something. She watched her shrug, closing the conversation.

Birdie picked at a loose string on her stocking. "Stupid, if you ask me."

Merriweather patted Birdie's hand. "You'll make that hole worse. Take it off, and I'll mend it while we wait for dinner. And it's not stupid. If I had money, I'd wear the finest dress with the biggest bustle. But I'd never put a bird on my head."

Teddy marveled at the back-and-forth weaving as Merriweather worked her magic on the stocking. Where had Merriweather learned such needlework? Teddy knew how to darn but was mesmerized by the fluid, over-under motion.

Teddy knew these roommates as she saw them now but didn't know much about their pasts, except for Merriweather, who had willingly shared. The lives Josephine and Birdie had led before were mostly a mystery.

Dong. Five thirty. Birdie thanked her roommate and replaced her stocking as the others put on their shoes for dinner. Josephine's stomach growled, making Merriweather giggle. Teddy hoped whatever smelled good would be enough to hold her over until morning. Meat was still expensive after the war, and Mrs. Jones and Cook worked hard to stretch it as far as possible.

Smells of roast, potatoes, and freshly baked bread filled the hallway.

Josephine breathed in deeply. "Mrs. Jones is pulling out all the stops for her new tenant. Now I'm intrigued."

Merriweather smoothed her skirts and hair before squaring her shoulders. She might be meek and mild-mannered, but Teddy knew the girl was hunting for a husband. Teddy planned to stay out of her way. A man was the last thing she needed. She wanted to focus on her career, not the needs of a man who required a woman. Let him hire a maid.

Teddy gripped the handrail harder than necessary as she descended the stairs. Being on her own would be challenging but not impossible. If she could ever get to that point, she'd prove it to those who thought her one spoke shy of a solid wheel.

The men rose as the ladies entered. Mr. Ferret pulled out a chair for Merriweather. The rest of the men settled themselves and continued their conversation.

Teddy tried to keep her focus on the portly man, who was new to the establishment and whose name she could not conjure up, sitting beside their newest resident as he continued the conversation the ladies had interrupted.

"The Harvard Summer School is going to bring more internationals every year," the man said.

The new resident nodded politely but did not engage the man on his right.

Teddy had known immediately who her friends were discussing when they'd mentioned his eyes. Even at this distance, the blue shone like sapphire under intense light.

Josephine kicked her under the table. "Birdie wasn't kidding. I may be back in the game after all."

Teddy's eyes grew, and her finger lifted to her mouth. Did the woman not know how to whisper? Mrs. Jones entered and took her place at the head of the table. Chairs scraped the floor as the men stood.

"Gentlemen, please be seated." The woman's erect frame didn't bend even when she bowed her head. "Bless this food, O Lord, and the hands that have prepared it." An unnecessary but ever-present sigh ended her prayer.

Teddy heard a strong amen above all the others from the other end of the table. Could the new resident be a believer?

27

She watched the man more carefully, not that you could tell the status of one's heart by their manners.

Mrs. Jones passed the plate of thickly sliced bread. "A special welcome to Mr. Thomas Shankel, the newest addition to our table and home. Judge Horace Pennypacker, Esquire, one of our town's most outstanding gentlemen, recommended my establishment." The woman's pride made her sit straighter if that was possible.

"Thank you for your hospitality and this fine meal, Mrs. Jones." Mr. Shankel put butter on the side of his bread plate.

Teddy glanced out of the corner of her eye. He was handsome, but his hairstyle was outdated, though the lock that fell over his forehead complemented his strong jaw. His suit was also several seasons out of date, if the length and size of the collar were any indication. But even though the fabric was worn in places, it appeared clean as if recently brushed. A slight yellowing showed under his collar, but the pressed shirt showed only signs of wear, not neglect. It would not have traveled well, so he must have done the pressing on his own.

Silver clinked on china as conversation flowed easily. Teddy listened but never commented as the men discussed the classes offered at The Harvard Summer School. When they began debating President Grant's signing of the Ku Klux Klan Act, swallowing became difficult. She'd address the portly man and suggest a change of subject, but his name still escaped her.

The man continued, not noticing the discomfort of his fellow dining companions. "It might empower the federal government to protect the civil and political rights of individuals, but I've seen some of those wanting to do the protection, and I'm not sure this is going in the right direction."

Birdie spoke with her mouth full. "Some protect better than

HEALING OF THE HEART

others."

Mr. Shankel's fork clattered on his plate. He placed his palms on the table. "Mrs. Jones, wherever did you get such a fine cut of meat?"

The woman beamed. "I have my sources. Judge Pennypacker's name carries a great deal of weight in this town. Please help yourself to more." She dabbed at the corner of her mouth with her napkin.

Teddy captured Mr. Shankel's gaze as he searched the table and thanked him with a quick nod for his help in changing the subject. "Might I pass the potatoes? They are especially creamy this evening," she offered.

His lips pulled in for the briefest moment, causing dimples to form. Teddy felt a pang for what could not be. She desired a career over marriage. Not that she wondered if Thomas was available. But those blue eyes that remained on her sparkled, causing her heart to beat unnaturally.

"Thank you."

It took Teddy a moment to realize his words were in response to wanting the potatoes. She lifted the bowl in front of her and passed it down the table. She didn't miss the movement from Mrs. Jones, who looked as if she may have wiggled in her seat from the praise.

Mrs. Jones folded her hands in her lap. "Mr. Shankel, would you mind telling us a bit about yourself and what brings you to the City of Brotherly Love?"

"Thomas, please. Mr. Shankel is too formal."

Teddy marveled at the effect he had on Mrs. Jones. The pink that flushed the woman's cheeks made her harsh features soften.

"I'm originally from Edgefield, South Carolina, but I've lived most of my life in Shumard Oak Bend, Missouri. I start classes at the medical school next week to earn my doctor's degree. There's not much more to tell."

The portly man piped up. "Good. Good for you. Will you remain here to practice after graduation?"

"My home and family are in Missouri. I plan on returning and using my skills to help those in my community."

Merriweather leaned in to see their new resident. "What an honorable goal." A pretty flush covered Merriweather's cheeks at her boldness.

Mrs. Jones looked from Merriweather back to Thomas. "Yes, very. Have you visited our fair city before, Mister—I mean, Thomas?"

"This is my first trip east since I was five, ma'am. I'm afraid I know little of city life."

Mr. Ferret's high-pitched nasal tone had everyone turning in his direction. "I'd be happy to show you around and help you get your bearings." The man shrank back into himself as if surprised he'd made the offer.

"I'd be much obliged, Mr. Ferret."

"Reggie. Please call me Reggie." The man looked as if the words had been painful to speak.

Mr. Shankel looked at his watch. "Perfect, Reggie. I have an appointment this evening, but perhaps tomorrow?"

Teddy furrowed her brow. An appointment, already? And in the evening?

Josephine kicked her under the table again. "Don't judge a book by its cover."

The woman's whisper was embarrassing.

"Do you like to read?" Mr. Shankel's voice carried in their direction—his focus on Josephine. "Pardon me. You know my name, but I do not know yours."

"I'm Josephine Blake. It's a new age. Please call me Josephine. Read? Not particularly."

One never knew what would come from Josephine's mouth, so Teddy jumped in. "We share the room across the hall. This is Merriweather and Birdie. I'm Teddy. And yes, first names are fine."

A burst of air came from Mrs. Jones's nose.

"It is a pleasure to meet you, ladies. Please, call me Thomas."

Teddy breathed a sigh of relief as the others around the table introduced themselves by their first names and shared where they were from and what had brought them here. The portly man's name was Crocket. Teddy suppressed a giggle. His shape, like the large earthenware jar, would help her remember his name. Conversation flowed as Mrs. Jones poured coffee and served thick slices of butter cake.

The sweet cake's crispy edges were Teddy's favorite. She loved the hint of vanilla in the crust, but tonight, the thick layer of vanilla-flavored, buttery filling was a delight on her tongue.

Thomas sat back in his chair, his hand resting on his stomach. "Did you make this, Mrs. Jones? I've tasted nothing quite like it."

"I'll give your compliments to our cook. She leaves at five each day for another position. Perhaps you can check in on her tomorrow. I understand she had a nasty cut this afternoon."

Mrs. Jones did not mention Teddy or her involvement,

not that she would have. The woman frowned on Teddy's choice of profession, saying a young, single woman had no business being intimate with a man. If you could call cleaning excrement and wounds intimate, she didn't want to know more.

"I'm not a doctor yet, Mrs. Jones. But if she'd like for me to look at the injury, I'd be happy to do so tomorrow. I do have some training from a local medicine woman."

Mrs. Jones's eyebrows nearly reached her hairline. A knock sounded at the door, and the matron excused herself, returning moments later, those brows now lowered into a scowl. "Mr. Shankel, you have a visitor. He will remain outside until you are ready to leave."

Thomas's polite tone did not match the new crease between his eyes. "Thank you. Meeting and dining with each of you this evening has been a pleasure." His gaze scanned the table, ending with Mrs. Jones. "I don't know how late I will be. Is there a curfew?"

Josephine snickered under her napkin.

"I lock the doors at ten, Mr. Shankel. But mind the company you keep. This town may be called the City of Brotherly Love, but it isn't wise to wander the streets after dark."

"Yes, ma'am. Thank you for that kind bit of information." His chair creaked as he stood. "I bid you all goodnight."

Teddy wondered who might be at the door. Perhaps a traveling companion, but why would Mrs. Jones require the visitor to remain outside? She wished the slurps of coffee and tinkle of silver would silence so she could hear if it was a man or woman.

Not that it mattered. She wasn't interested. Her goals and dreams required her to stay focused. Merriweather, or

Josephine, for that matter, could have him.

Crocket interrupted her thoughts. "Reggie, be sure to take Thomas to the grave of Benjamin Franklin at the Christ Church Burial Ground. He can throw a penny on the grave. Good luck, you know. I've thrown my fair share."

"How'd that work for you?" Mr. Ferret asked.

"I'm still waiting on the right woman to slow down enough to feel the push of fate in my direction."

Josephine leaned in, her voice blessedly quiet for once. "Fate probably saved the woman by pushing her off a cliff."

Teddy used her napkin to cover the laughter that escaped. She didn't believe in fate, but if she did, she'd certainly not leave her future in the hands of someone who'd tossed a coin on a grave.

Chapter 4

August, 1871
Teddy

The tightness in Teddy's throat made it difficult to breathe. Her eyes burned but remained focused on the misshapen cracks in the street. She slowed her steps, causing a hurried passersby to swerve and curse.

The weight of Teddy's legs matched the heaviness in her heart. She worked to remain upright while climbing the boarding house stairs. The railing assisted in her labored ascent.

Smells of bacon, eggs, and something sweet assaulted Teddy's senses, and she moved more quickly up the interior staircase and into the lavatory. Her gut roiled, and she lost the remaining contents of last evening's meal into the porcelain bowl.

Splashing water on her face, Teddy allowed the droplets to meld with the tears streaming from her red-rimmed eyes. The mottled mirror added to the distressed look of the image peering back at her.

Teddy clenched her teeth to keep her quivering jaw from opening. Her heart leaped at a knock at a door nearby.

"Ready, Thomas?"

Teddy slowed her breathing at the familiar whine of Mr. Ferret's voice and the creak of a door in the hallway.

"Thank you, Reggie. I'm excited about our adventure today. Let me grab my jacket."

Thomas's voice was smooth and friendly and helped steady Teddy's nerves.

"I have our day mapped out," Mr. Ferret said. "We'll be back in plenty of time for the evening meal."

Teddy could practically see the movement in Mr. Ferret's body from the excitement in his voice. She eased her back against the wall and thought she heard a tinge of laughter in Thomas's reply.

"A good plan is always prudent."

She closed her eyes at the click of the door, thankful neither man had mentioned needing the facilities before leaving. Their two sets of footsteps grew quieter, but she remained behind the closed door for a few more moments.

Peeking out, she tiptoed to her room, then threw herself on the bed and let the tears flow freely.

Teddy struggled to catch her breath. She rubbed at her throat, desperate to relieve the tension. Her damp skin caused her to shiver even though the still air of the room remained warm.

Standing, she shook her hands as if to let go of the last remnants of what she wished was a dream, then wrapped her hands around her shaking body.

It wasn't a dream. Dr. Whitaker had moved beyond his flirtatious words and touched her. She squeezed harder, wanting to remove the feeling of his hand on her waist where it had trailed down her backside.

Why didn't she wear a corset like every other respectable female? She was respectable, wasn't she? She might not be of the upper or even middle class, but she was a good girl. There had been no acceptance of his verbal advances. Right?

Teddy paced the small space, replaying every seemingly harmless comment from Dr. Whitaker and some outright lewd ones. Not once had she batted an eyelash or let a smile cross her lips. She had given the head physician no encouragement. After the initial shock, she'd ignored the remarks and remained stoic, earning her a few names she did not appreciate.

Surely, she had not aided the behavior.

She needed her nursing job. If she changed shifts, she would not receive the few extra cents of pay for working the late-night hours. A different shift would also make it impossible to keep her second job at *Les Madeleines*.

Teddy swayed and grabbed the desk chair. She would have to avoid him. Perhaps another floor in the hospital had openings.

"How unfair." Teddy balled her fists and pushed them into her hips. "I love my patients and am good at what I do. Why should I have to change? He's the one making unwanted advances."

Teddy sank onto her bed. The deep breath was welcome, but it cemented what she already knew. Teddy had no recourse. Dr.

Whitaker was an esteemed physician and prominent man in the community. Most nurses would swoon at his advances.

Teddy's gaze shot up to the window as if it would provide clarity. Were there other women being subjected to what she was experiencing? The previous ten hours played in her mind. She pulled her lips in and flopped back on the mattress. She would pay closer attention.

But first, she needed sleep. "Lord, please. Let me sleep."

The hall clock's chime carried up the stairs. Was it time to get up already? Teddy wiped at her crusty eyes. She needed to hurry so she'd have time to put something in her empty stomach. Teddy removed her wrinkled deep blue nurse's uniform and hung it, hoping it would be wearable by the evening. A hairpin that had pushed into the nape of her neck from her cap begged to be released. She removed each pin and brushed the waves of her hair; the motion calmed her nerves.

"Lord, I didn't get my Bible time in yesterday or today. Forgive me. Help me know what to do about . . ." Not wanting to speak her offender's name aloud, Teddy placed several hair pins in her mouth. God knew, even if she didn't utter a sound.

She twirled her unruly locks, trying to capture each wayward strand, then secured the mass at the back of her head. It wasn't the latest fashion, but if she wanted time to eat before work, she had to make it the priority out of her choices. A simple updo would have to suffice.

Teddy didn't enjoy seeing the puffy eyes looking back at her in the small room mirror. She rubbed whipped beeswax over the dark circles, then added some to her dry lips. Coffee. That would at least give her the energy to make it through the next hours.

The stairs creaked under her weight as she descended. She willed herself to forget the ordeal she'd been through.

"Hi, there, Doc."

Teddy's hand flew to her chest. "Oh, David, you scared the living daylights out of me. And you know I'm not a doctor." She lowered her hand and winked at the boy.

"I know, Miss Teddy, but it suits you. Are you headed to that uppity lunch place?"

Teddy loved this boy's forthrightness. "That I am, but I was hoping to have a cup of coffee and maybe a biscuit before I left."

"Come on. Cook said one loaf of bread fell. She was going to feed it to the chickens, but I snagged it."

Teddy wasn't sure if he meant it had fallen on the floor or hadn't risen well, but his conspiratorial tone and movement toward the kitchen on tiptoes had her following.

David reached under the table, pulled out a basket, and produced a loaf that looked as if someone had put a finger into the center before placing it in the oven. The red tip of David's nose made her wonder if it had been him.

"You can have it. I got extra eggs this morning," he said.

"Thank you." Teddy sat and sliced the bread, then slathered room temperature butter over the soft center.

David placed a mug of coffee in front of her.

"You didn't have to do that. Thank you." She slid the remainder of the loaf in his direction.

"I know, but I figured you'll be serving all day. Might be right nice if somebody did it for you." The tips of his ears matched his nose.

"That is very thoughtful." David consistently surprised her. The boy was of school age but worked all hours at the boarding house. She watched the muscles in his arms flex as he carried in the wood for the stove, then he swept the mess he'd made out the door and off the porch. He'd had good training.

Teddy leaned back in the chair even though it wouldn't do to be caught in the kitchen. Her fingers rubbed at her temples, and she felt a curl loosen.

"You okay, Miss Teddy?" Worry twisted David's naturally congenial expression.

"Thank you for your concern, but I'm just tired." Teddy forced a smile.

"Yeah, your eyes are all puffy. Mrs. Jones gets those dark circles. She uses powder to cover them up, but it don't do no good."

Teddy had never considered the life of their boarding house owner. Besides the evening meal, the woman did most of the cleaning. Maybe Teddy should approach her about working here to ease some of the woman's load, though Teddy doubted the matron could match her fifty cents a day at *Les Madeleines*.

The door off the kitchen opened, and the disheveled hair of Cook appeared. "Thought I heard voices. Just taking a beauty rest. Been up since before dawn."

David opened his mouth to say something Teddy knew would not be appropriate, so she said, "David was being quite the gentleman this morning and served me bread and coffee."

Cook smiled like a proud mother and winked at the boy. Teddy watched as David's cheeks took on a new hue.

The woman turned her way. "You're looking a little peaked, dear. Did you not sleep well?"

Teddy's chair scraped the floor. She didn't want to talk about it. She put on a practiced smile. "I slept, just didn't get the same beauty rest as you." David's brows furrowed, and Teddy nearly laughed.

"It's you that needs checking on. How is your thumb?" Teddy held out her hand, but Cook flicked it away.

"Nonsense. I'm keeping it clean." She lifted the soiled bandage.

"So I see. Let me just take a peek. You'll be doing me a favor; otherwise, I'll worry all through my shift."

Cook narrowed her eyes and didn't look like she believed Teddy, but she obediently sat on the long bench and offered her injured thumb. Teddy unwrapped it, applied a salve mixed with comfrey around the edges to keep the area soft, and replaced the bandage with one from her pocket.

Cook put her other hand out. "Good as new. Now, give me that soiled bandage, and I'll wash—I'll have David wash it up."

"Thank you for breakfast, David. I appreciate your thoughtfulness. I've got to run. You two have a marvelous day." Teddy took one more swig of coffee, then made an uncharacteristic move and gave Cook a quick hug. She turned to David, but his eyes went wide, and he scooted out the door.

Cook wiped at the corner of her eye with the hem of her

apron. "Well, isn't that a delightful gift? Thank you, dear."

Teddy could only nod. Her feet felt lighter as she walked across the foyer and into the humid air of the August afternoon.

Silver tinkled against the signature pattern of *Les Madeleines* china. Teddy watched as napkins raised and lowered as if dancing, while the ladies patted at their pursed lips and non-existent crumbs. The stuffed, straight-backed chairs were no match for the spines of the young women sitting in them.

Teddy stood against the wall and watched every movement, anticipating any need. She refilled water glasses, replaced pots of tepid tea with hot ones, and kept the crumbs at bay. Emmaline Whitaker, whose neatly coiffed blond hair should still be in long, cascading curls, was the leader of this clutch of women, even at sixteen.

The small, almost indistinguishable movements of Emmaline's eyebrows and lips gave away the girl's true feelings on whatever the others were discussing. Her father had mastered showing manufactured emotions and covering up real ones. Teddy watched in amazement as Emmaline's fingers, so like her fathers, tapped once on the tablecloth. She'd witnessed Dr. Whitaker do the same. It was an indicator many new nurses missed before receiving the wrath of the physician.

Teddy's nose itched, but she did not twitch as Miss Whitaker's pert one wrinkled when the dark-haired debutante to her right took a larger-than-appropriate bite of a flaky pastry. The girl's hands looked boorish compared to

41

Emmaline's slender fingers, which moved to her lap and tapped twice on her napkin.

Teddy's tall frame often commanded respect when in her nursing uniform, but the piercing blue-eyed stare of Miss In Charge was all it took for the underling to put her fork down and swallow the bite with difficulty.

Teddy had been on the receiving end of such a look from similar but more masculine eyes. An involuntary shiver moved through Teddy's body. She scrunched up her toes, then spread them as wide as they would go in her clunky shoes.

Quiet settled over the group as if Emmaline had conjured it. A practiced smile showed a hint of straight teeth without causing early wrinkles to form in the girl's flawless skin.

The only piece of Emmaline Whitaker that didn't match her frame was the volume of her champagne voice. It was light and bubbly when it should have been soft, yet everyone within three tables knew what she was saying. Exactly as the girl desired.

"My father, the Doctor William T. Whitaker the third, has taken on a new group of students."

Whether or not they'd finished with their meal, the girls set down their forks and listened with rapt attention. Teddy waited for each girl to nod before removing their plates and sweeping the tablecloth clean.

"Daddy says I may have first pick this year." Emmaline ran her slim fingers over the chain at her neck and pressed the locket to her creamy skin. "I suppose I'll be the first of our little circle to marry."

It took all of Teddy's willpower not to roll her eyes at the girl's light sigh.

A mousy girl with sleeves big enough to clothe another human leaned in from Emmaline's left. "Have you considered what you will wear when you meet them?"

Emmaline flicked her wrist. Teddy steadied the teapot, then continued pouring into each cup around the table. She watched as Emmaline drew the attention of each girl as they anticipated her answer.

"After my coming out, Mother ordered a new fall wardrobe. Madame Molloy measured me last week." Emmaline looked over the rim of her cup at the responses of the others until the first dropped her gaze, then she set her cup on her saucer without a sound.

A girl in a frock made of something between drapery and furnishing fabric kept her head down. Teddy felt for the girl. The sign of weakness would fuel the cruel side of Emmaline.

"Opal, dear. We all know your family's assets in South Carolina suffered in the war. No one will hold it against you if you have to wear the same things you have for years."

Teddy breathed out slowly. The others at the table did not catch the slight, but they also didn't notice the napkin balled up in Opal's fist in her lap. Each girl gave a nod of agreement or a look of pity to support their leader, but Opal kept her head down, seeing none of it.

"What you are wearing now is at least the right color. All the ladies' magazines say rich, dark colors are en vogue this fall. Though the fabrics will be more plush. I've chosen an emerald satin brocade, a crimson velvet, and an embossed blue as deep as a stormy sea. Mother said I had to have it, no matter the price, when she saw how it accentuated my eyes."

Teddy refilled tea and brought a plate of petit fours, doing her best to ignore the discussion of the three-dimensional effects of bodices, bare shoulders, and ridiculous adornments on hats.

A stately woman approached the table, and Teddy moved farther into the wall.

"Good afternoon, ladies. What a delight to see the next generation keeping the traditions of our station."

Emmaline stood and offered her hand to the woman. "Aunt Pauline. I didn't realize you were in town. When did you arrive? Father will be pleased to see you."

"I doubt that, but thank you for your kindness. I arrived just this morning."

"You'll stay with us, won't you?" The little girl in Emmaline peeked out from beneath the polished exterior.

"Not this time. I'm staying with . . . a friend."

These girls were too naïve to catch the pause. Teddy smiled at the thought of a skeleton in the Whitaker family closet.

Chapter 5

August, 1871
Thomas

Thomas could almost reach out and touch two of the four walls of Douglass's home in a single turn. It was no bigger than a mining shack and as poorly insulated and lit as a slave cabin, yet the tight quarters felt like a familiar hug. The smells of home-baked goodness, sweet fruit, cinnamon, and baked pastry wafted in the warm, dry air, making his mouth water.

A large woman with a smile to match reached for his hat and hung it on the peg just inside the door. "Welcome to our home, Mr. Shankel. My Douglass tells me you're in need of a suit."

Thomas returned the slight bow of the robust woman and looked to Douglass for introductions.

"This is my beautiful wife, Harriet Douglass, and your new tailor, or seamstress, I should say."

Her silver hair and white teeth sparkled in the firelight. Thomas returned an amiable smile.

Douglass tapped the wooden chair beside him. The straight lines against the curved upper back cradled the man's hand. "You care for a cup of coffee and a piece of pie?"

Thomas took in the simple table and two chairs at the end of the short two feet of counter and patted his stomach. "Thank you, but no. I ate more than my fill at the boarding house."

He needed to change the subject. Thomas was never able to tell a lie. Meager funds were typical after the war, and he'd take nothing from these people. "So, Douglass is your last name?"

"One and the same. Only name I have. You might change your mind about pie in twenty minutes. I'll keep the coffee hot. Roasted the beans myself. We don't need any fancy Arbuckles' Ariosa coffee here." Douglass winked.

The man's dark hand brushed against his wife's lighter, scarred one as he walked to the stove. The woman's cheeks took on a deeper hue. Longing filled Thomas with a desire for a relationship where meanings and conversations passed through simple touch.

The tape measure and the chalk in Mrs. Douglass's hand wobbled as she directed Thomas to the small area close to the fireplace. She tightened her fist around the items, and the slight tremor stopped. "Mr. Shankel, you come stand here."

Thomas noted her swollen knuckles and crooked fingers and moved in the direction she pointed toward. "Please, call me Thomas."

"Alrighty, but you'll be calling me Harriet."

The coffee pot clattered against the single-burner iron cookstove. Douglass's bones creaked as he plopped into one of the kitchen chairs, whose joints made no noise.

"Oooph." Air escaped Harriet's tight lips as she crouched

low. Thomas stood still as the woman pulled at his pant leg.

"You need my help over there?" Douglass offered.

Thomas followed the slow tilt of Harriet's head even as her eyebrows reached for her hairline. Laughter bubbled from deep within him at the woman's expression. He coughed to keep from embarrassing himself in front of the two he hoped would soon be his friends.

"Don't listen to a word that man says. Doesn't know the threading side of a needle. Now, let's see what we got here."

Thomas watched as Harriet's gaze lingered a moment longer on her husband. She stuck the paper and pen in her mouth as she stretched the tape measure in one direction, then another. Thomas hoped she wouldn't swallow them because of the smile she tried to contain.

He followed her instructions, keeping his feet a foot apart, lifting and lowering his arms as requested, and keeping his chin up. His eyes roamed the home. The fireplace warmed and shed light on the kitchen and parlor, which were the same. The firelight cast shadows as Harriet crouched, stood, bent, and took notes. He diverted his eyes from the chicken scratch on the paper and the narrow bed in the room behind the open door.

Thomas focused on the sounds of passing carriages, raucous male laughter, and the howl of a dog as they whistled their way through the single window. Even if he felt uncomfortable having a strange woman so close to his person, this home was a haven from the outside world. The sounds on the street reminded him of the growth in the town of Shumard Oak Bend, and the calming crackling of the fire felt like the comfort of home.

Thomas ached to lower his arms but did not flinch. He focused on the knots of the pine floor that appeared to move in the flickering light.

Harriet stood and measured his arms and neck, then tapped his tired shoulders. "You can relax. I got all the measurements I need." She scribbled several notes and numbers on the edge of the now-damp magazine page.

Wood scraping the floor pulled Thomas's attention to the right. Douglass poured a mug of steaming liquid. "You'll be sorry if you don't taste this pie. 'Sides, I'd enjoy the company. That wife of mine will spout numbers to herself for the next half hour." Douglass placed two plates of pie on the table.

The well-worn wood of the high-backed chair was soft in Thomas's hand as he sat. The earthy, almost smoky smell of coffee rose from the brown ceramic mug, the liquid dark and inviting. "Thank you." Thomas eyed the slice of pie on the table. Light caramel-colored fruit peeked from beneath a golden crust. Thomas used his fork to lift a flake as light as air.

"Can't beat Harriet's pie crust," Douglass said. "She makes do with pears for the filling for now, but you wait until apple season. Mmm mmm, that's one good pie. Woman knows how to make a pie with zucchini, too; yes, she does. Didn't even know it weren't apple until she told me."

Thomas took a bite. The grainy texture of the soft pear complemented the crisp crust and sweet juices. "Zucchini pie?"

"When you got an overabundance of the squash in the heat of summer, you've got to get creative. She is that and much more."

Thomas followed the man's gaze to the hearth, where

Harriet sat by the fire's light, reading her notes. Their forks clinked on the heavy stoneware.

Douglass wiped his mouth. "You got a girl back home?"

It was as if Douglass had read his mind, where his thoughts focused on home. "No, sir. No time and fewer options."

"You were looking a little far away. Missing your family?"

"Yes, sir. I suppose I am. Them and my best friend, Gabe."

"Always good to have a friend. Tell me about home. Who all are you missing?"

"Well, there are my parents. My little sisters, Cecelia, who is thirteen, Serafina, who's twelve, the eleven-year-old twins, Esther and Ruth, and Patricia, who just turned nine." Thomas paused slightly, checking his math.

"That's a pile of girls." Douglass took a swig of his coffee.

Thomas fully relaxed. "My brother, Charlie, and I are the only boys, and he's married with his own child now. It's a girl."

"Lots of family to miss."

Thomas felt the familiar pangs of homesickness. "What about you? Do you have family nearby?"

"Oh, some cousins scattered about, but most of our family on both sides is gone. The Lord never blessed us with children, but then, I supposed Harriet had her fill taking care of me." Douglass winked at his wife, who made an *mm-hmm* sound in response through a closed mouth. "Who else you missing?"

Thomas drew in a deep breath. "Miss Martha and Henry. They were a big blessing in helping me get here. She was my teacher and is Judge Pennypacker's daughter."

"Well, I'll be. I didn't make that connection, but now that you mention it, I remember Miss Martha going out west to help her aging aunt. How's Miss Martha getting along?"

"Fine. I grew up calling her Aunt Martha. She was our schoolteacher until this year." The coffee scalded his tongue and reminded Thomas to quit rambling.

"Seeing as you made it into medical school, she must have been a mighty fine teacher. She taught me my ABCs before the law allowed it. I didn't have a choice but to learn. She was a force to be reckoned with, even as a small child."

Thomas let out a slow breath. He could name most of the townsfolk of Shumard Oak Bend. They all felt like family, like Moses, Delphina, and their daughter, Mary Ellen. "I plan on returning after graduation and setting up a practice. It will be a long two years, but it will go by quickly with the Lord's help."

Douglass beamed. "Good to know you're a fellow believer."

"Yes, sir. Since I was six. My Grammie helped me hear God's voice and obey it. I guess I still am. Obeying His voice, I mean. At least, I hope being here and attending medical school is God's purpose for me." Thomas's knee bounced under the table, causing his coffee to slosh in his mug.

Douglass reached his hand out for a well-worn Bible at the table's edge. "Psalm ninety verse seventeen." He didn't open the book but quoted from memory.

"And let the beauty of the LORD our God be upon us: And establish thou the work of our hands upon us; Yea, the work of our hands establish thou it."

The crackle of the fire and Harriet's murmurs of agreement filled the room.

Douglass continued, "Thomas, knowing the Lord's will is mighty tough. To gain that wisdom, one must pray for divine instruction and plead with the Lord for knowledge. You have to want to be taught by the Holy Spirit, and seek Him in everything, whether good or bad. You spend time on your knees long enough and stay clear of claiming any merit of your own, and He'll direct your steps in due time."

Thomas felt his head move in agreement, but in his heart, he could not understand why God had not allowed Gabe to walk this path with him. They'd dreamed of opening a practice together.

Harriet accepted the chair Douglass now stood behind. "You men save me a slice of pie?"

"Of course, darlin'." Douglass placed his work-worn hand over his wife's. "Mr. Thomas, we best be getting you back. My wife gets up earlier than I do, but I'm the one needing more beauty rest."

"You're still as handsome as the day I married you." Harriet's eyes softened as she gazed at her husband.

The creak of Thomas's chair on the wood floor felt intrusive. "Thank you both for your hospitality. The pie was delicious. My Aunt Aideen would have loved for her crust to be that flaky."

"It's the apple cider vinegar. Just a splash now, but it makes all the difference. And you're most welcome. I'll have your Sunday suit ready for you to try on by Saturday." She looked at her husband for confirmation.

"I can come get you Saturday night, same time, if that works for you," Douglass offered.

"Thank you, I'd be most grateful." Thomas yawned, immediately embarrassed at the unexpected sound. "Pardon me. I'm more tired than I realized."

Douglass's hand on Thomas's shoulder made the last of the tension he'd been carrying release.

"Young man, you've had a busy day. Let's get you home."

Harriet placed her hand on her husband's other forearm and whispered, "Come straight back, Douglass."

The parting kiss Douglass placed on his wife's hair was familiar, much like how Thomas's mother had said goodbye right before he'd boarded the train east.

"I'll hurry back," Douglass said. "Don't you worry none."

Harriet did not offer the hand still hugging her husband but dipped her head. "It was a pleasure meeting you, Thomas. We'll settle up on Saturday."

"The pleasure was all mine. Thank you both for your hospitality." Blessed cool air greeted Thomas, and his eyes took little time to adjust to the darkness of night. His mind went over the home's interior as he climbed aboard the conveyance. The home had no lanterns. They'd used the small fireplace to provide light. And nothing on the walls but the splash of fabric over the two windows provided color. Yet he'd felt right at home.

Neither man spoke as they maneuvered through the streets. Even at this hour, people milled, mainly with a stagger. No lamplights lined the narrow street, but Thomas could still make out the rows of small houses and a large brick church, distinguishable only by the wooden spire and cross lifted high above the single-story structures surrounding it. Lights ahead let him know they'd arrived at the edge of Center Square. The city bustled with men in dark clothing, but no skirts rustled near the shopping areas.

"Mr. Thomas, you be mindful when walking back and forth from school to that boarding house of yours. Even in daylight, you're likely to meet some . . . Let's just leave it at that. You mind your back in this town."

Thomas understood, though Douglass's words felt foreboding and caused his heart to pick up speed. "I suppose humanity is the same everywhere, but thank you for the warning."

The street widened and larger, two- and three-story structures came into view.

Douglass pulled on the reins and slowed the horses in front of the boarding house. "Whoa. Here you go. If you need me, come by the judge's place. Don't be trying to find your way to my home. It's not a good place for a white man of your standing to get lost."

Thomas didn't need the lamplight to see the concern in his friend's eyes. He dipped his head once. "Thank you for your care. Good night, Douglass."

"Night, sir."

Thomas labored up the three steps to the door. No lights shone in the front windows. He fumbled with the key, the unfamiliar action reminding him he was not truly home.

The door creaked, as did the floor. A sly smile inched

the side of Thomas's mouth higher. He might not be used to locking and unlocking doors, but he was familiar with sneaking in and out. Gabe's dark eyes and ever-present, broad smile shown in his mind. Thomas removed his shoes and tiptoed across the polished wood.

The chime of the clock had him scrambling to catch his falling shoe. Would that constant *tick-tick-tick* keep him up all night? Thomas kept to the outside edge of the steps where it would be least likely to make noise and slid his feet across the well-worn path down the hall.

Light shone from the crack underneath the door with the wreath, but not enough to help him see, so he could unlock his bedroom door. He fumbled twice before hearing the click.

No matter how tired he was, he needed a bath—and not like the ones he'd had over the past weeks of travel. The hall was quiet as he tiptoed into the bathing room. Tepid water, warmed only by the day's heat, came out in a steady stream as it slowly filled the tub. They'd added indoor plumbing to their home out west, but their tub wasn't nearly this deep. It would take time for the water to rise enough to get a good soak in this one.

Water splashed as Thomas sank into its depth and shivered as his back connected with the cast iron. He couldn't afford to fall asleep here, so he briskly rubbed and scrubbed, dunking his head underneath to remove the last remnants of soap.

Rough cotton scratched his skin and smelled of tobacco with a hint of lavender. The combination made his stomach flip. The nightshirt he placed over his damp head reminded him he'd need a haircut soon. Another thing Martha had suggested he wait to get until he'd arrived. He'd ask Douglass whom the judge used, then snickered, wondering if Harriet used her scissors for that as well. He'd do just about anything to save a penny.

Murky water swirled down the drain, and Thomas cleaned up after himself before blowing out his candle. A toilet flushed, as did his cheeks. He was in his bedclothes, and someone was in the lavatory next door. Dark brown eyes and unruly chestnut waves clouded his already blurry vision. Thomas put his ear to the wood, then heard the creak of the one next door and light footsteps padding across the floor. When a second door opened and closed, he hustled back to his room in the darkness.

Habit had him in front of the mirror, combing his hair from his eyes, even though it was too dark to see. The sheets were cool on his skin as he slid beneath their embrace. The mattress sagged, pulling Thomas into its center point. He'd need to fix that, but he only desired sleep and sweet dreams tonight.

The women he'd met at dinner had all been nice enough, but Teddy had seemed like one who'd know how to skip rocks and climb trees. The one Reggie seemed to like, Merriweather, he thought was her name, probably preferred dolls and dancing.

Dancing. Thomas felt his pulse quicken. He was used to Shumard Oak Bend summer socials and barn dances but did not know what to expect here.

"Lord, I'm out of my element and need your help. You are a God of grace and mercy, so I'm asking you to send some my way. I can hold my own in the classroom, but I'm going to need divine intervention to figure out the rest."

Douglass's words from earlier floated through his mind. He yearned to gain the wisdom only the Holy Spirit could provide. He wanted to be teachable and seek God in all circumstances, even in how to adapt to this new lifestyle. Thomas crawled from the bed and knelt, his knees poking out from under his nightshirt.

"Lord, I need your help. It's one thing to keep up with those I'll be competing against in the classroom, but it's another thing altogether outside the university walls. Direct my steps, Father. I want to represent You well."

Thomas climbed back into bed, exhaustion taking over, but not before uttering one more prayer.

"And be with Gabe, Father. Heal his heart."

Chapter 6

"**L**ooking good, Thomas. Looking good." Douglass brushed the shoulder of Thomas's new suit.

Thomas buttoned the front of the jacket and bent his arms, testing out what he expected to be a constricting feeling, but the fabric gave with each motion.

"Mrs. Douglass—" Thomas started.

"Harriet," she scolded.

The woman's eyebrows moved up toward the gray strands poking out from beneath the front of a mob cap like what Grammie and Aunt Aideen had worn a decade ago. He wanted to hug this woman, but he found his side pockets with his hands instead.

"Harriet. I've never had such finery. And thank you for the shirt. Aunt Martha would marvel at these stitches."

"Who do you think taught her?" A tinge of color graced the woman's cheeks even as she smiled.

Douglass pulled his wife close. "Fine job as always, my dear. Thomas, where are you going to wear this one?"

Thomas ran his fingers over the wings of the jacket's pressed collar. "Service tomorrow morning. Then there's a gathering of new students at the Whitaker home on Monday evening. Maybe I should wear the charcoal gray one for that?" Thomas felt overwhelmed at the list he'd received of mandatory social functions.

"This morning coat is all the new fashion but is considered casual attire in the circles you'll be swirling in." Harriet held up a deep charcoal gray wool. "Now, this frock will work for social occasions. The satin waistcoat of this suit rivals any other out there." Harriet's flush deepened.

"No one sews like you, my dear." Douglass turned his attention from his wife to Thomas. "Young man, you need a respectable hat."

Harriet reached for a box on the kitchen chair. "And shoes. Pointed-toe boots may work in the wilds of Missouri, but you're a city boy now. Open it."

Firelight glinted off the shine of the black shoes. The squared toe looked foreign and expensive. The ever-increasing knot in Thomas's stomach tightened. He ran his fingers through his hair. He likely also needed a haircut—so many expenses.

"Now, son, don't you be fretting over cost." Harriet ran her fingers over the soft leather. "There's a story behind them shoes. They came to me in payment of a sort. I couldn't imagine what I'd do with them, and I certainly didn't need them. Figured the Lord had a plan. Well, he did."

The soft thump of a wooden heel on the floor drew Thomas's attention. He stared at the shoes she'd placed before him. "Mrs. Douglass—Harriet, I can't accept these without giving you payment. Tell me what they're worth, and I'll gladly compensate you."

"There'll be none of that." The authority and finality in Douglass's tone was clear even as the lines around the man's eyes softened.

Neither the action nor the words did anything to clear the tension in Thomas's gut. This family had less than he did. He was young and capable. A few extra work hours each week on top of classes were doable if he could find work to accommodate his schedule.

Harriet placed the second shoe on the floor and scooted it closer to Thomas with her foot. "Try them on. If they fit, well, then, you'll know this is from the Lord. It's no gift from me."

His Adam's apple felt stuck in his throat, and he worked to swallow it down. He'd be able to refuse them if they didn't fit. He removed his boot and slid his stockinged foot into the supple leather. Softness wrapped around his foot like a well-worn riding glove. He removed the second boot without thought and looked down at the oddly shaped shoes that felt like a second skin.

"That's what I thought. God's done it again." Harriet's words were a mixture of awe and fulfilled expectation.

"I can't—" Thomas began.

"Oh, yes, you can. Don't be telling God what you can and cannot do when He's been planning on those shoes fitting your feet from before I even knew what to do with them. God works all things for good and knows what you need before you need it." Harriet's hands moved to her hips as she spoke.

Thomas had enough history with the Lord to know God

sometimes worked this way. He'd just never been the recipient of a gift such as this. A mist clouded his vision, and he reached into his back pocket for his handkerchief, only to realize it wasn't there.

"My wife's got that covered, too." Douglass placed a small white cotton square in Thomas's hand.

Thomas's thumb moved over the letters *TS* embroidered in a thread of pale gray the color of Grammie's eyes. Whether overwhelmed from the kindness, pangs of homesickness, God's provision, or worry about how much all these items would cost, he didn't know, but tears threatened to form. He forced his spine straighter and clenched his jaw.

A firm hand gripped his shoulder. Embarrassed by his emotion, Thomas swiped the soft cotton square across his eyes. It smelled of lavender and sandalwood. He inhaled deeply, allowing the fragrance to calm him, then worked to clear the tightness from his throat. "How much . . ."

"That's my wife's department. She's got it all written down. You try on the other suit, and I'll get the coffee on. You can discuss figures over a piece of gingerbread cake."

Thomas missed the man's touch immediately.

Harriet helped remove the suit jacket he wore and gave him a nudge toward the open bedroom door. "Go on, now. I need to make sure the second pair of trousers is a good fit. And change that bow tie for the white one on the bed. White ties are what all the men are wearing these days at formal events."

Thomas obeyed and then looked in the mirror. He ran his fingers over the fitted garment that flared at the waist. His fingers tripped over the buttons trailing down the torso, pulling his eye to the hem that reached just above his knee. His gaze traced back up to his now-squared shoulders. If he didn't speak, perhaps he could pass as one of them. Panic crept into his increasingly knotted gut. What was he doing? He didn't know how to maneuver in high society. He was just a farm boy from Missouri.

Thomas picked up the handkerchief and breathed deeply of its calming scent. It would impress Robin, or Singing Bird, as he'd first known her, that these easterners knew lavender's value in calming nerves. She'd have added bergamot, but the sandalwood grounded him with its manly scent.

Knock, knock. "Thomas, you need help with that tie?" Harriet asked.

"Yes, ma'am. I could use some assistance." Thomas unlatched the door and handed her the white tie. Chin lifted, he allowed her deft fingers to lift his collar and work the tie into a large knot before returning the cotton of his shirt to its former state, where it hugged the white fabric of the tie.

Harriet stepped back, her head tilting and perusing him from the shoes up. "My Douglass is right. You'll be needing a proper hat." As his mother would have done, she moved the wave of hair hanging over his left eyebrow and allowed it to fall back into its natural position.

Thomas watched a sheen cover her deep brown eyes. She pulled her lips in and swallowed.

"Douglass, take this boy to Fareira's, then get him to the barber when you've finished. Thomas, don't you let Mr. Fareira's workers talk you into something fancy. You go with a simple, factory-made felt, not one of last season's tall top hats. Choose a modest one. You don't want to draw more attention to yourself than you already will." Harriet stared at his eyes.

Thomas knew his blue eyes often caused people to take an over-long look in his direction. But he assumed Harriet meant more than the color of his eyes would cause him to stick out in a group of Philadelphia elites. Nervous energy found its way to his toes, and he drew them in, then spread them freely in his shoes. He willed himself to calm down, then realized Harriet was still speaking.

"An opera hat might serve you well, but a Wellington style should do just fine. Fareira's should have plenty of those in stock."

"Yes, ma'am," he choked out.

Harriet cocked her head again, but this time with a furrowed brow. She seemed to look straight into his heart. She nodded once, then clenched her jaw, flattening her lips into a thin line.

"Coffee's ready," Douglass called from a few feet away.

Thomas could use a cup. "Let me change, and I'll be right back." The soft *clip* of Thomas's new shoes followed him to the bedroom. He laid the three-piece suit, tie, and crisp shirt on the bed, smoothing the wrinkles. His old clothes felt familiar and worn, but surprisingly, they weren't as comfortable as the formalwear he'd just removed.

Rows of shelving wrapped around the upper wall, starting a foot below the ceiling. Stacks of fabric from blue to brown to black lined the bottom shelf like a storm coming in over the horizon. The middle shelf looked more like a rainbow after a storm, and Thomas marveled at the variety of colors and textures. Clouds lined the top shelf, from rough white cotton to creamy pale yellows, some with a sheen reflecting the last rays of sunlight through a westward-facing window. Threads in every color competed for space with some baskets of notions and tins he expected held buttons.

Memories of sitting on the floor with Delphina's button tin and stringing buttons together while she sewed filled his mind. Memories were a gift he cherished. The smell of coffee and the spicy tang of ginger and molasses greeted him when he opened the door.

Douglass offered Harriet a chair. "Come, dear. Let's enjoy a few moments of rest and your fine cooking."

He offered Thomas the other. Thomas shook his head. He'd stand.

"Now, son, I made me a special chair just this week, hoping you might come regular-like." Douglass pulled a three-legged stool from underneath the table.

"You know how to handle a piece of oak." Thomas ran his hand over the smooth wood.

"Ah, nothing but a little sand, linseed oil, and a whole lot of elbow grease." Douglass's words sounded like it was nothing special, but the upward tilt of his chin and the square of his shoulders let Thomas know he appreciated hearing the compliment. Thomas allowed the man the privilege of sitting on the fine piece of furniture and took the chair across from Harriet.

Thomas ran his fingertip along the edge of the smooth tabletop and marveled at the workmanship. Even though the table showed much use, it had aged gracefully. He lowered his hand to his lap, and Harriet did the same. A contented sigh escaped her lips that curved into a smile as Douglass placed a dark piece of cake dusted in powdered sugar in front of her.

"Thank you," Harriet said.

There was no endearment, but there was a tenderness in her words. How Douglass served his wife, even before a guest, spoke to Thomas's heart. He waited until Douglass had taken his seat and Harriet had taken her first bite before he poked the tines of his fork into the spongy dessert.

The smooth texture of fine flour melded with the bite of strong molasses. A plump raisin complemented the strong taste of ginger. He closed his eyes and took in the mixture of flavors and textures. A contented sound escaped his lips as his fork toyed with another morsel.

"Sour cream." Harriet pointed to the cake on Thomas's plate with her fork.

"Excuse me?"

"The secret ingredient. Sour cream. Sometimes, I use buttermilk, but sour cream keeps it moist longer. Not that it lasts long in this house." She winked at Douglass.

"You are a fine cook, Harriet. And seamstress." Thomas placed his fork on the side of the empty earthenware plate and wiped his mouth. "I'm not sure I can afford you, but I'd like to settle up." He attempted a laugh at his hurried words, but it sounded forced.

"Now, before you go getting all worked up about price, I want to tell you a story." Harriet nodded a thanks as Douglass cleared the table. "During the war, my employer vowed to pay us in any way he could. Those whose husbands were serving and had children got the first choice of whatever Mr. Talbot had to give. Sometimes, he had items he'd traded for, like dried fruit, beans, and produce. Other times, it was eggs and venison from people settling up their accounts. But he always paid us workers."

Harriet sipped slowly, her hands grasping the mug as if to soak in the warmth.

"My Douglass and I needed little. We worked a garden out back and canned, and the Pennypackers were good to us. I knew those other worker's families needed the food more than we did, so I asked to be paid in notions. One week, Mr. Talbot would give me the ends of the bolts. Other times, he'd give me a few spools of thread and a box of buttons. Those shoes were one payment."

Harriet took a sip of her coffee before continuing. "Douglass added shelving in our room, and I've been stockpiling. Someday, I may have enough to start a little shop right here in South Philly. Black folk and immigrants need clothes, too. There's no reason they can't have good quality. Why, I could sew for all types of working-class folk from South Street to the Delaware River, and all the way to the Schuylkill River. Wouldn't that be something?"

Douglass beamed at his wife, shaking his head with every word she uttered. "If anyone can do it, you can."

Thomas marveled at the woman's attitude and aspirations, as well as the strong support of her loving husband. The cake settled more easily, and he took a swig of the strong coffee.

Harriet continued, "So, you can pay me for my time and the white fabric I needed for the tie, but you won't be giving me a cent more. God provided, and I aim to honor His faithfulness with a bit of my own. Now, if you want to send some business my way, I won't turn that down."

Harriet pulled a torn edge of a magazine with figures written in the margin from her apron and slid it across the table. Her finger tapped the figure at the bottom twice before returning to her lap. The figures blurred. Although it was still a fair amount for the price of labor, it was nothing compared to what he'd expected.

"Thank you," he choked out. He wiped non-existent crumbs from his lips before replacing the napkin, then pulled his wallet from his coat pocket. The new federal bank notes crinkled as he placed them before Harriet. His last feelings of concern and stress dissipated. He'd have enough for a hat and haircut, with a few dollars to spare from his clothing allowance. Warmth filled his belly, releasing the last of the tension.

Douglass clapped his hands on his knees. "Day's a wastin', but before we head out, it would be an honor to pray with my new friend."

The warmth of earlier spread, and Thomas pulled in a cleansing breath. God had blessed him beyond measure, and he sat in awe of His goodness.

Chapter 7

August, 1871
Pennsylvania Hospital
Teddy

"There you go, young man. Is that more comfortable?" Teddy assisted the bony shoulders of her most trying patient to his resting place. Gray and white strands feathered across the pillow, blending into the crisp linen.

"Young man? I'll have you know I'd have snatched you off your feet and kissed you senseless by now if I were still a young man. A woman as pretty as you has no business working in a place like this. You should be home raising babies."

There were so many things wrong with every one of Mr. Zingle's inappropriate statements. Maintaining professionalism and being kind wasn't hard for Teddy; moving fast enough to stay away from the old man's hand—and keeping from rolling her eyes—was.

"I'll be back in an hour to check on you." Teddy nearly reminded him to get some rest but didn't want to hear the quip he'd likely say in response.

Armilda stood at the end of the hall, clipboard in hand, her pencil moving across the page. Her friend didn't have any issues with patients. Her thick Romanian accent, soft and melodic, yet somehow slightly monotone, came across as no-nonsense. Add her steely gazes to her sturdy bone structure and ramrod-straight posture, and Armilda had no trouble keeping patients from running roughshod over her. Not even Dr. Whitaker bothered the beautiful nurse.

Armilda pointed the tip of her pencil toward Teddy's forehead, making small circles with the tip. "Those lines in your face will become permanent if you don't unfold that brow."

Teddy repeated the statement in her mind before finally realizing Armilda meant she should smooth out her face. She used her right hand to rub at her temples, the action helping to steady her nerves and release the creases her friend continued to point at.

Armilda slid her pencil into her smooth bun. "Ah, Mr. Zingle. He can be a handful, but he doesn't bother me. I'm happy to cover his care, if you'd prefer."

"I'm fine. He's just a degenerate lecher." Teddy watched confusion flit through Armilda's eyes as if the woman was processing the comment. "You know, an old fuddy-duddy." Armilda's head cocked slightly, and Teddy simplified her word choices. "Let's just say he should know better."

"True. Fuddy-duddy?" The words spoken in staccato tempo with Armilda's rounded lips in a tight circle made the word sound more like foody-doody. The last of Teddy's tension evaporated.

"Ladies." The head nurse tapped her toe on the tile floor.

Teddy held back a giggle, thinking about how the

tapping might reverberate all the way up to the woman's ample backside, causing her to look like an excited puppy. The head nurse cleared her throat.

"Yes, Miss Rutherfordton. We were discussing a patient. We've settled the issue." Teddy's clipped words mimicked the responses she once had given as a war nurse responding to a superior officer.

"If you have time to talk, you aren't doing your job." The woman looked over her spectacles at Teddy.

"Yes, ma'am," Teddy responded. When the woman turned, Teddy looked at Armilda. She was as relaxed as before, pencil back in hand, filling out paperwork. Nothing seemed to bother the woman. Dr. Whitaker wouldn't dare speak inappropriately to Armilda, but what of the other nurses?

Teddy considered her shift-mate a work friend, but they'd never done more than enjoy a break together on the rare occasion they'd had the opportunity. Should she speak to her about what was happening?

As if thinking the man's name had conjured up the devil himself, Dr. Whitaker walked through the door, a young man at his heels. Oxygen evaporated from the hall. Teddy fought for breath. She glanced at Armilda, who gave no acknowledgement of either man's presence.

Dr. Whitaker bypassed the beauty and moved toward Teddy, barking orders to the harried man, who furiously made notes, his face firm in concentration. Teddy fought the urge to take a step back. Instead, she pushed her clipboard up and out as if trying to position it better in the dim hall light.

Even from this distance, she smelled Dr. Whitaker's

potent scent. She didn't like that it affected her. The strong cologne should repulse her, but it smelled of money, power, and freedom, all wrapped up in a carefree life of trips to the ocean in summer and the mountains in autumn. Things as unattainable as the moon.

"Do not let him get to you," Teddy whispered. The words strengthened her resolve. She turned her back on the men and marched from the frying pan back into the fire, as her late mother would have said.

Thankfully, Mr. Zingle's eyes were closed as she slipped behind the curtain to his bed area. His breathing was steady, and Teddy pulled the wool blanket up to his neck. He may be a miserable patient, but God had created the man in His own image, and even he was precious in God's sight.

Teddy refilled Mr. Zingle's water and placed the cup within the man's reach for when he awoke. Asleep, he could be any child's sweet grandfather. Crow's feet creeped out from beneath his bushy eyebrows. His dry lips vibrated with each intake of breath, which resembled a grumble on his exhale.

She felt Dr. Whitaker's presence before she heard him. He sidled up next to her, much closer than necessary, and took the chart from her hands.

Teddy remained still for several moments, eyes trained on the slow rise and fall of the patient's chest. She could be strong like Armilda. She remained firmly planted until she could stand it no more. Putting on her sternest nurse's expression, she whirled around, ready to face the man she would not allow to take advantage of her any longer.

He thrust the chart at her. She took it and felt his fingers graze her hand. She stifled a shiver and focused on the man still writing furiously behind Dr. Whitaker.

Dr. Whitaker turned to the man. "Don't just stand there; we have more ground to cover."

Teddy turned her focus on her patient and waited for the sound of two sets of shoes to leave the partitioned area. Though it was small enough that she could easily see the entirety of its contents in one quick scan, she double-checked the area. Teddy peeked her head outside the door and saw the polished shoes of the young man following coat tails, leaving the same way they'd come. Armilda looked up long enough to shrug one shoulder, her graceful neck tilting slightly toward the closing door. Teddy returned the gesture, breathed a sigh of relief, and moved on to her next patient.

"How are you this evening, Mr. Pane?" Teddy knew the man would not verbally respond. Extensive surgery to his jaw made it impossible. The man blinked once. "Good. Let me check your vitals, then I'll let you get some rest." Her hands still shook from her encounter; staying busy helped.

Any surgery carried risk, but this hospital had adopted the research of the Hungarian doctor Ignaz Semmelweis and understood the importance of cleanliness. And thanks to new advances in anesthesia where chloroform replaced ether, she dealt less with the trauma side of what patients endured during their procedures.

Though she experienced the occasional death of a patient, most individuals improved daily after surgery with her ministrations. Post-surgery care was her favorite floor to work on. Patients were more likely to die during an operation than after, which had not been true during the war. Gangrene had often set in, killing even the healthiest soldiers.

"Rest well, Mr. Pane. I'll check on you again in an hour." Teddy smoothed her apron before stepping around the curtain and into the next patient area. "Miss Lily, you're supposed to be sleeping." Teddy moved to the child's bedside. "Are you in much pain?"

Dampness clung to her limp, dull hair, but the girl's eyes were bright as she attempted to nod. Teddy felt her forehead for fever and breathed a sigh of relief.

"Miss Lily, cleft palate surgery is difficult, but you've had good care and are recovering nicely." Teddy checked the girl's pulse and blood pressure, then used a damp cloth to wipe away the tears. She smoothed the hair clinging to her temples.

"It isn't quite time for your medication, but I have something that might help." Teddy pulled the vial from her apron and kept it hidden in her hand. She pulled the stopper and placed a drop of the liquid on each temple. Lily closed her eyes and inhaled.

"Lavender is my favorite for moments of stress." Teddy replaced the stopper and lifted the blue glass to the ceiling light. She'd need to refill it soon. The bottle sank to the bottom of her apron pocket, and Teddy rubbed her fingers together, spreading the calming scent.

A buxom woman entered. "Sorry, Miss Teddy. I done needed to visit the . . ." The woman dropped her gaze.

Teddy smiled at the dark eyes and familiar face. "Not to worry, Mammy. I know that straight-backed chair isn't the most comfortable place to sleep. Can I bring you anything?" Teddy would get a scolding if she provided for this child's personal caregiver, but she couldn't help but ask. The woman had been by Lily's side throughout surgery and these many weeks of recovery.

"No, ma'am. The Davenport family takin' care of me and my Lily." The woman patted a basket beside her, then lifted a quilt square to her lap.

"What beautiful handiwork. Don't let the doctors see those stitches, or you'll make them jealous." The color in the woman's cheeks deepened as she dipped her head. Teddy turned her focus to her patient. "Miss Lily, you try to get some rest."

Teddy refrained from leaning down to kiss the girl's forehead. Her nursing duties required her to squelch the desire to do more than the hospital permitted, even though she'd already broken the unwritten rules by sharing her personal lavender with the girl. She moved her finger over the girl's forehead lines, willing the child to relax. Mammy hummed a low, haunting tune. Teddy felt the skin relax, even though the girl's tears did not.

The *clop* of Teddy's heels on the tile floor reverberated in the open expanse of the large convalescing room, making the mewling sound of Lily's crying more pitiful. Teddy leaned against the outer wall and made notes, checking the time on the ticking hall clock. She watched the second hand move up the left side. Lily would get medicine for her pain in one more hour.

Teddy checked and charted patients, cleaned the floor from one patient's retching, assisted with bed pans, refilled waters, and restocked supplies. Her feet ached. She may have time to sit for a few minutes while the moon was still high if she didn't give into idleness—or fear. Snores and moans crept from behind the heavy curtains that hung from the ceiling, allowing patients some privacy, but little sound barrier.

Teddy looked at the door at the end of the large room. Dr. Whitaker was likely home with his family, sipping an expensive port and smoking a nasty cigar. None of this week's patients required additional after-hour visits from the man. Teddy felt her body relax.

It was well past sunrise, and her heart felt light even though she'd worked an extra half hour. She thanked the Lord for the extra funds and the strength to endure her hardships as she walked home. She'd not stood up to the man, but she had faced him. Not in her own power—she knew, but she'd allowed the Holy Spirit to work in her place.

There was a spring in her step even though she was tired. Teddy whistled the tune she'd taught the children during Sunday School the week before. The lilting, catchy refrain formed on her lips, and she sang as she walked.

I am so glad that Jesus loves me,
Jesus loves me, Jesus loves me;
I am so glad that Jesus loves me,
Jesus loves even me.

Teddy entered the quiet boarding house, hurrying to her room. Today, nothing would keep her from her Bible time.

Chapter 8

"Quite the spread, wouldn't you say, Thomas, my boy?" Judge Pennypacker's drink threatened to leave the confines of the fine crystal as his finger trailed down the food-laden table. His other hand rubbed his extended belly.

"Quite." Thomas had only nibbled at his sparsely filled plate. Why would someone put cucumber and soft cheese on such a tiny piece of bread? And no one needed to tell him the fish eggs in that bowl were called caviar. He'd gutted enough fish in his life to know that portion went to the hogs.

"The olives are my favorite. Dr. Whitaker has them imported from South America or some such place. Fascinating —the variety." He popped a light brown orb into his mouth, worked it around, then spat the seed into his hand. "Just look at that." Flesh still clung to the seed now pressed between the man's thumb and finger.

A small green olive rolled across Thomas's plate. "Unique." He caught it with his thumb, and it squished under his touch. His already-nervous stomach quivered, and he grasped the plate even harder, feeling the pit beneath his thumb. He itched to rub his free hand on the back of his neck or step outside into the last hours of daylight to enjoy the breeze.

The judge's face softened. "Don't borrow trouble, my boy. Each day has enough of its own."

Thomas shifted from one foot to the other. "I'm not like them."

"They are a might different, but they put on their pants one leg at a time, just like the rest of us. I didn't grow up here either. Did you know that?"

Thomas turned to face the man, giving him his full attention.

"Virginia is my home. When you meet the love of your life, you'll go to the ends of the earth to be with her. It's my Clarissa who has the Philadelphia heritage. Mind you, I come from good stock, but like you, I knew more of horseflesh than gooseflesh, if you get my meaning."

Thomas felt his shoulders begin to relax.

"You'll learn to speak the unspoken language soon enough. You focus on those grades, and prove yourself. It worked for me. Well, marrying up helped a good bit, too. You're as smart as the next boy. What counts is in *here*, not on here." The judge moved his finger from his temple down his bulky frame.

Not a single patron of this party looked like him. The poised and elegant women wore smiles that never faded. The men carried themselves with confidence and familiarity. Thomas felt out-of-place amid the silk dress coats, top hats, and gold pocket watches hanging from elaborate chains.

The judge leaned in close to Thomas's ear. "Let's talk of brighter things. The food is good, but have you seen the dessert?"

Thomas flinched when the man pointed in the opposite direction of the dessert table. A bevy of young ladies, dressed in flowing gowns, flitted fans in front of their downcast eyes as if desiring to attract attention but not wanting to see the result.

The olive he'd let go of slid off the plate when the judge nudged his arm. A small, dark-skinned man whisked in from nowhere and picked it up from the elaborate rug, then melted back into the woodwork before Thomas could give his thanks.

The judge leaned in. "Most eligible ladies in Philly. Each comes from a prominent family. You'd do well to snag the eye of any one of them."

Only one pair of eyes looked his direction. Her gown was more refined than the others, the blue fabric mimicking the movement of water, and suitable for dignified women much older than the girl appeared. It bordered on the edge of showing womanly curves yet remained modest. Multiple shades of blue layered into its graceful drapery while showing off her slim waist.

The dress was not like the practical, ankle-length dresses his sisters wore for working, but rather, a more graceful length that just cleared the floor and left a sensible amount of fabric trailing behind her. Even though her ensemble was tasteful and lady-like, the girl had an air of danger about her. She did not portray the coquettish behavior of the other girls hiding behind their fans but stared blatantly at him.

His Adam's apple constricted his airway. He jutted his chin forward, running his finger around the inside of his collar and loosening the white knot deftly tied by Mr. Ferret. At least his tie was right. He rubbed his damp palms with his handkerchief and returned his focus to his companion.

"Nice suit, by the way. Excellent quality. More suited for Sunday service, but well made. I believe a narrowed waist such as that might be a fashionable look on me. Did you go to Wanamaker's?" Pennypacker used his plate to point to the frock coat Thomas wore.

Thomas didn't know how to respond or if the man was in earnest and was thankful when Dr. Whitaker interrupted and offered his hand.

"A pleasure to see you again, Mr. Shankel. It's an honor to have you in the program. I hope you are adjusting to the civilities of this fine city?"

Thomas didn't like the insinuation in the man's words but forced a smile. He shifted the plate to his other side and shook the hand of the man who would be directing his steps for the next two years. "Philadelphia lives up to its name. I truly have experienced the brotherly love it claims," Thomas offered.

The man held his gaze and his hand a moment longer, then tipped his head as if receiving his comment as acceptable.

Judge Pennypacker lifted an empty plate. "Dr. Whitaker, what a fine party. The food is excellent, your home is lovely as always, and your gardens are exquisite. I only wish my wife could have accompanied me this evening. My compliments to your wife and staff."

"Thank you, sir," Dr. Whitaker replied, not inquiring as to the reason Mrs. Pennypacker had not attended. "It's an honor to have you again in our humble home."

Humble? Thomas gazed up the winding staircase that was wider than the original structure of his home back in Shumard Oak Bend—and more elaborate. Its deep mahogany wood banister circled to the second floor, where earlier he'd seen more food and smartly dressed men lingering in another large ballroom.

"Have you been upstairs yet, Mr. Shankel?" Dr. Whitaker's gaze followed Thomas's up the stairs as the sounds of stringed instruments playing "Beautiful Dreamer" flowed down.

"Oh, yes, sir. Thomas, please, sir." The nerves in Thomas's stomach reached his mouth.

Dr. Whitaker's expression did not change. "I heard you stitched up your boarding house cook's hand the other day."

Thomas furrowed his brow, then remembered. "Oh, no, sir. It wasn't me. I checked in on her at Mrs. Jones's request, but there was nothing else for me to do. Miss Morse, another boarder, is a nurse. She was the first available and handled the emergency quite well, I'm told."

Something odd flashed across the man's face when Thomas mentioned the nurse. A bead of sweat ran from his side temple into his collar, but he didn't move to wipe it away.

"Well, I'm sure you'll be the first available next time. You said in your application you learned your stitching skills from your aunt, was it?"

"Yes, sir. Judge Pennypacker's niece." The other man's extended belly protruded even more with pride at having been mentioned. "Aunt Martha considered sewing skills useful to me as well as my sisters. I didn't enjoy it as a child, but it came in handy on the farm. I've stitched my fair share of man and beast."

"You consider yourself the local doctor of sorts?"

Something in the man's tone made Thomas pause. He felt he was being tested, and the answer he provided would set the stage for the next two years.

Pride is a sin.

"No, sir. The unlucky individuals I helped had little choice. I believe my prayers did more good than my meager ministrations."

"Well, we all know prayer has its place." Dr. Whitaker placed his empty glass on a server's tray and took another. "See you bright and early, Thomas. Mrs. Levesque, what a pleasure to see you this evening." The man changed his attention and conversation, dismissing the two, and walked away.

Thomas wondered if he'd passed the unwritten examination.

"I'm headed to the desserts—the edible ones." Pennypacker laughed and wiggled his ring finger. "Care to join me?"

Thomas followed the man but had no desire to eat. He wanted to get out of the line of sight of the lady who had yet to divert her gaze. She was lovely, with loosely woven braids of golden hair wrapped around the contours of her head. Unlike the older women present, she did not wear a hat, further showing her creamy complexion. Women of the West who spent time outside working alongside their family in the fields or in their gardens had darkened and freckled skin; this young woman didn't look like she'd know the proper end of a spade unless it was on a playing card. Thomas felt the first smile of the night cross his lips, and he diverted his gaze from the women.

A group of what he guessed to be fellow students came down the staircase. Low whispers and quick glances toward the young ladies made the fans matching their gowns move faster. He'd need to meet his colleagues at some point but couldn't muster the energy tonight. He needed to be in the classroom where he'd be on equal ground. In this setting, he was at a direct disadvantage.

A mousy fellow brought up the rear, like a runt of the litter trying to keep up with his pack. The man's discomfort shone on his clean-shaven face and averted gaze. Thomas's heart went out to him.

"Judge Pennypacker, would you excuse me? I should meet up with my classmates."

"Of course, my boy." The man's words were hard to decipher through his full mouth of pastry.

Thomas placed his partially eaten plate of food on the tray of a passing servant, doing his best to make eye contact with the man. Hired help in the East certainly was not the same as in Missouri, at least not in this household.

Making his way to the crowd of young people, Thomas caught the eye of the student he hoped to meet. The man's gaze darted left and right from widened eyes, and the student fidgeted with something in his hand.

Thomas slowed his step as if approaching a scared animal and moved to the man's side. He'd need to bend over to speak if he didn't want to be overheard. The student was several inches shorter than his almost six feet, and Thomas could see pink skin through his thinning hair. Thomas lowered his voice and his head.

"I'm Thomas Shankel. Are you a new student at the university?"

Thomas thought he heard an audible gulp. The man stood like a statue—not even his thin hair moved in the breeze from the onslaught of ladies' fans.

"James. Jimmy. Jimmy Reeves." The name came out like a squeak.

"Nice to meet you, Jimmy. It's warm in here and difficult to hear over all the noise and music. Would you care to view the gardens with me? I've yet to have an opportunity." An awkward silence filled the space between them. Thomas peered out of the corner of his eye to see a barely perceptible nod, then followed Jimmy's quick steps through the crowd to the doors leading out to the veranda.

Jimmy continued across the wooden porch and down the steps. His shorter legs moved at a pace that increased Thomas's heart rate. He'd been passive on the train, but not knowing what he would talk about once they stopped was more the cause of his sweating palms than lack of regular exercise.

Jimmy finally slowed and gave a quick glance back toward the house once he'd reached the manicured edge of a fragrant shrub at the edge of a row of trees. Shade covered the area and offered relief from the warmth of the evening.

Thomas quietly followed Jimmy along the edge of the small thicket until it opened into a large grassy area with stone benches.

"Summersweet Clethra," Jimmy said. "In Latin, *Clethra alnifolia*. It's also called sweet pepperbush. Do you know plants, Mr. Shankel?"

Thomas took a deep breath, inhaling the spicy scent of the white flower. "Thomas, please. I'm not familiar with this plant but know a good many in Missouri."

"I believe Dr. Whitaker plans his party every year around the flowering of this species. It only blooms for four weeks of the summer between July and August. We've caught the tail end of it."

Thomas must have looked as confused as he felt. Jimmy showed the first hint of a smile.

"Yes, I am a new student in the medical program at the university, but I've lived here all my life." Jimmy pointed to the other side of an enormous sculpture of a rider in hunting gear atop a magnificent horse. "Over that hill is my home. Our families have been friends for generations."

Jimmy's fingers on his right hand caught Thomas's attention. A coin passed between each tip, then returned. The motion fascinated Thomas, and he pulled a coin from his own pocket.

"How do you do that? Will you teach me?"

Pink tinged Jimmy's cheeks and spread quickly to his neck and ears, but Thomas didn't back down.

"It's a bad habit." Jimmy put the hand with the coin in his pants pocket.

"It's fascinating. Please. I could use a diversion." Thomas looked toward the house, then at Jimmy.

An exhale from Jimmy that mimicked moments of frustration from Thomas's mother almost made him laugh.

"There's a bench over there. Let's sit, and I'll show you. If you're sure." Now it was Jimmy's turn to look back at the house. "You need to be relaxed to do it correctly."

The cool stone felt good, as did sitting. His shoes were comfortable, but Thomas had been standing for hours. He focused on Jimmy's fingers, then the coin that looked as if it bent over the man's slim knuckles as it moved from left to right, then disappeared, only to start over again.

"First thing is to relax your hand." Jimmy's voice was quiet, and Thomas leaned in to hear over the sound of the fountain and birds flitting in and out of the overhanging red maple trees.

Thomas placed his coin on his middle finger and balanced it between his knuckles. "Like this?"

Jimmy smiled for the first time, causing dimples to further accentuate his baby face. "That's a good start. Push your thumb against your index finger, and it will be easier to get the coin started. Now, pinch the coin between the ring finger and the pinkie." The coin moved fluidly over, then under Jimmy's hand before returning to the starting position.

"Anticipate the motion of the coin. Let it slide through your fingers and catch it under your palm with your thumb. Then slide the coin back up to the side of your index finger, and do it again."

Jimmy pointed to Thomas's next finger getting ready to touch the coin. "Here, try this larger piece. It's easier to learn with. Good. Good. Keep your palm parallel to the ground. Only use your fingers."

Thomas focused intently on the piece, following Jimmy's

directions and feeling empowered to conquer this new skill by Jimmy's encouragement.

"I did it," Thomas trapped the coin in his aching fingers. "Where did you learn to do that?"

Jimmy's now-bright eyes and broad smile waned. "Nervous energy, I guess."

"What type of tree is that?" Thomas pointed to a yellow-leafed tree, hoping to once again see a spark in his new friend's eyes.

Jimmy popped up from the bench. "Oh, come see. It's a ginkgo biloba. The only species of the genus. Truly a one-of-a-kind tree." Thomas hurried to catch up.

"Its common name is maidenhair tree because of the unique shape and color of the leaf in the fall. They originated in China, but my great-great uncle, John Bartrum, planted the first one on his farm here in Philadelphia in the late 1700s. Ginkgoes drop their leaves all at once, rather than gradually."

Jimmy's animated tone did not match his gentle touch. His fingers slid over the silky green leaf with the tenderness Thomas had often shown a newborn chick. Thomas turned when he realized Jimmy was no longer speaking.

"Sorry. I'm boring you. We should head back to the house."

"No. I was thinking about how I feel about new life on the farm. Where did you learn so much about trees?" Thomas inquired.

Jimmy studied him for a moment as if making a decision. "Trees, flowers, weeds, all plant-life. I wanted to be a botanist, but my parents had other ideas. So, here I am." The coin resurfaced.

"You'd like my friend Gabe and his mother, Robin. They taught me about the healing plants, but I know little about common flora." Thomas wished Gabe could be here now, learning alongside him.

"Is this Robin a nurse?" Jimmy stopped his slowed steps to the house and turned to Thomas.

"Medicine woman. Her Arapaho name is Singing Bird. She's the closest thing to a physician we've had in our town for many years. When I graduate, I plan to return and open a much-needed practice in my hometown of Shumard Oak Bend."

Jimmy's eyes took on a dreamy look. "I'd like to travel west. I've seen drawings of the great sequoia and redwoods, but it's the cacti I'd like to see. How anything can grow in the desert and produce a bloom, I can't fathom."

"I've had my fair share of run-ins with cacti and it's no fun pulling out the spines."

"Glochidium."

"Excuse me?" Thomas squinted his eyes as if it would help him decipher what was being said.

"The hair-like spines. Typically barbed. Cactus glochids easily detach from the plant when touched and lodge in the skin, causing irritation upon contact."

The muscles in Thomas's cheeks lifted. "Jimmy, I think we're going to be good friends and, I hope, study companions. You retain information like few others."

Jimmy returned the smile. "I'd like that. Only, I'm not sure being smart is all I'll need to graduate." His steps slowed as Jimmy led the way up the path to the veranda.

"I've seen the skill in your fingers. You shouldn't have trouble there." Thomas mimicked the quick motion of a coin in Jimmy's hand.

"That's not it either. It's the problem of fitting in. I've gone to school with a good number of these fellas all my life, and I'm not like them. In family heritage I am, but . . ." Jimmy's words trailed off.

The sinking feeling of earlier hit Thomas's stomach hard enough that his hand flew to his belt buckle. If it took more than smarts to be the top of his class, and if this Philadelphia socialite didn't fit in, how did he think he ever would?

Chapter 9

August, 1871
Les Madeleines
Teddy

Teddy poured tea and wiped crumbs from the table before pressing her back against the ornate wallpaper of the dining area wall of Les Madeleines. She squeezed her fingers into her palms until her nails might draw blood. Listening to these socialites recount every word and look from the evening before made her toes curl.

"Emmaline, everyone fawned over you. You'll have first pick, of course, so you can choose whomever you like," the girl to Emmaline's right said.

The table of girls, their mothers' well-meaning influences showing in their posture, waited for Emmaline's response. They may not be aware of the power play going on, but Teddy had to restrain from rolling her eyes. For Emmaline to place her focus on one man meant she'd drawn the boundary line, and the others could fight amongst themselves for the remaining eligible residents. By not claiming her prize, she kept them in limbo.

Emmaline crossed her hands in her lap and tapped one index finger in time with the tinkling piano keys emanating from across the room. "I simply do not have enough information to decide. Looks are one thing, but they're not always a good indicator of ability. Whomever I choose, he'll be top of the class."

"Surely not Jimmy Reeves," the wide-eyed blonde to Emmaline's left asked.

Emmaline's condescending glare had the girl shrinking back in her chair and lowering her now-quivering chin. "Adeline, dear, Jimmy isn't even on my dance card."

The girl stammered in her apology. "Forgive me. I . . . it's . . . he's by far the smartest."

Emmaline breathed in and released a practiced sigh. Not too much, just enough to show her displeasure, which again set the girl in her place. Teddy watched the exchanged glances, noting who felt shamed at likely having had the same thought as the girl, and who considered themselves superior and sided with Emmaline.

The drama that took place between sips and sighs was enough to gag a snipe. Teddy resisted the urge to laugh. These ladies may be educated in the arts, languages, and how to catch the most eligible bachelor, but they would be the first to have the wool pulled over their eyes when snipe hunting in her neck of the woods.

Nostalgia tugged at Teddy's heart. Not homesickness, since she didn't miss the chaos of her siblings, but the companionship of family where understanding occurred without speaking. She missed the carefree days of childhood.

Teddy relaxed against the wall, releasing her balled fists. She'd grown up in what many called the best poor man's country in southeastern Pennsylvania. Her family members were hard-working farmers, tending the land and mining it of its bounty. The well-known Morse family name had become less spoken in the last ten years.

Eight siblings, all girls, and not a one of them with more desire than to marry. Except her. Her sisters only wanted children and to farm pieces of their own land, which Daddy sold to the new sons-in-law with new last names. Teddy loved the land, the animals, the freedom to walk for hours without encountering another soul. But the freedom that provided meant giving up another type of liberty.

Teddy wanted to provide for herself, to prove she was capable of more. She'd found her calling during the war and known nursing would be her way out and her path to independence. Her dream was now a reality, but her wages were not enough to live beyond the confines of the boarding house.

"Miss Morse, is there something wrong with the wall you appear to be holding up?"

Teddy sprang to attention at the harsh whisper. "No, ma'am. Sorry, ma'am." No further words needed, Teddy resumed her duties. She slid between broad skirts and flounced sleeves, pouring tea and replacing morsels her family barn cat would turn up his nose at.

The girl across from Emmaline placed her napkin beside her plate, the sleeve of her yellow gown grazing the raspberry jam at the edge of the fine china. "I met all but one of the new students. They say his name is Thomas Shankel. Not a family name my father recognized."

"Caroline, you asked your father about him?" Emmaline's voice was low and controlled, but her finger began its familiar tapping in her lap.

Teddy allowed the water to leave the spout slowly, never taking her eyes off the flow.

"Of course. If Daddy is going to provide a dowry for my hand, he wants to know what he's getting in return."

Teddy flinched, her concentration broken, when a green sleeve lengthened with creamy lace moved toward the flowing water. Teddy used her cloth to wipe the spill from the saucer.

"Opal, please be mindful," Emmaline said. "You might soil your American-made lace."

Opal lowered her gaze and withdrew, but Teddy suspected the girl didn't grasp the slight intended to elevate Emmaline by diminishing her companion.

A *tsk* escaped the mouth of the girl to Emmaline's right. "My father is close friends with Judge Pennypacker, Mr. Shankel's benefactor." The girl paused as if this were new information to which only she was privy. "My father said Thomas Shankel comes from a wealthy landowner and cattle farmer out west," the girl added, her chin jutting forward and lengthening her neck.

"Missouri." Emmaline recaptured the conversation. "The family owns most of the town." Her eyes darted toward the lowered head of the girl to her left.

"Shumard Oak Bend," Adeline whispered the necessary information.

"The town of Shumard Oak Bend. Strange to name a town after a tree, but I suppose if you own the town . . ." Emmaline's voice trailed off as if bored with the conversation.

Teddy marveled at the boldness of the girls and their

affinity for gossip. She knew Thomas came from Missouri, but wealth? He didn't act or look like he had more than a few nickels to rub together.

Caroline dabbed her handkerchief at the stain on her yellow sleeve, spreading it. "If my father would allow it, I'd go to university myself."

Silence blanketed the table with unfamiliarity. Teddy's stomach muscles quaked for the girl, holding in the breath she dared not release.

Emmaline's finger picked up speed. "Whatever for?"

"Whatever for? Independence. I loathe the idea of marrying only to schedule teas, attend church socials, and fulfill other ridiculous obligations."

"If you're married, you'll be fulfilling more duties than are on your social calendar," one of the six offered, making a few blush and go wide-eyed, and the rest look confused.

Emmaline made a feminine but distinct *ahem* deep in her throat. "Inappropriate, Louisa."

"Inappropriate? Sounds like my kind of table talk. Hello, ladies." A tall, regal woman placed her silk-gloved hand on Emmaline's shoulder while the fullness of her skirt invaded the table space.

Emmaline's now-clasped hands flew to under her chin. "Aunt Pauline. What a pleasure to see you again. When you didn't come to the party last night, I feared you'd returned to Virginia." A wide smile created dimples and made her usual haughty tone impossible to maintain.

The woman's chin lowered to her shoulder. "I believe

to speak of why I was not in attendance would be . . . inappropriate discussion." She winked at the saucy girl who'd made the comment earlier, then focused her sly smile on each of the girls at the table, ending with her niece.

"Would you care to join us, Aunt Pauline?" Emmaline scooched her chair over, pushing the fabric of Adeline's dress out of the way as if it was bothersome.

"You distinguished ladies don't want an old fuddy-duddy ruining your fun." The woman glanced at Teddy and gave a barely perceptible nod. Teddy pulled a chair from an empty table and placed it near Emmaline.

Emmaline patted the chair. "Please, join us. I've yet to hear why you're in town." Emmaline focused her full attention on the woman.

Teddy marveled at the transformation of the leader of the pack. It was as though she was a child sitting at the knee of a beloved aunt who promised a bedtime story.

"I came to visit an old friend and will stay with her until winter. Then I'm thinking of heading to the Carolina coast for some warmer air." The woman pulled at the tip of each finger on her glove, exposing long, slender fingers with short nails filed and buffed close to the skin.

"Miss Whitaker . . ." Caroline began.

"Please. Keep me young for a bit longer and call me Aunt Pauline."

Caroline's head swayed with the extra weight. Was everything about status and connection?

Teddy made space on the table and added a place setting,

then poured tea from a fresh pot. She'd become accustomed to not being seen and blending into the wall and found it easy to tune out the chatter on most days. But not this day. She was all ears and soaking up the conversation, but it was the woman's pinched features that made Teddy pay closer attention. Was she in pain? A headache, perhaps?

As the girls oohed and aahed and asked questions of her travels, Teddy watched the overly animated answers of the woman. Light powder covered the dark circles under her eyes. Her hat sat lower than fashionable, showing only the ends of her lackluster hair. The deep red bodice of her gown bunched in places as if the dress had been made for a much larger woman. Emmaline's Aunt Pauline looked more tired than ill, but something wasn't quite right.

Teddy knew eavesdropping was improper, but she needed something in her arsenal against Dr. Whitaker. Whatever was going on between him and his sister may be the one thing she could use—

Teddy blinked. Shame on her. What an ungodly thought. She should focus more on the needs of Emmaline's aunt and how she could pray for her.

There was something in the woman's tone and forced smile that Teddy recognized but couldn't distinguish. She chanced a glance at Miss Whitaker's slim fingers, which moved constantly in her lap as she spoke. Surely this practiced socialite wasn't nervous amidst girls several years her junior. Perhaps her hand motions provided clues like Emmaline's and her father's signature finger-tapping.

Teddy moved silently around the table, keeping her head down but glancing again at the fidgeting hands on red silk as she rounded the table. That's when she saw it. A ring of exquisite filigree. A large stone twirled around and reappeared on Emmaline's aunt's left hand as she twisted it over and under. This was no Miss Whitaker. And the woman wasn't nervous. She was grieving.

Adjusting her stance, Teddy placed herself in a position to grab surreptitious glances. Aunt Pauline placed a butter cookie on her plate, then took a small bite. Her mouth worked but did not swallow, as if the fragment was too dry. She sipped her tea, holding the cup with both hands and leaving it near her mouth a moment longer than needed.

Caroline monopolized the conversation with something that required the girls to lean in. She held the attention of all the girls with her whispered words. Teddy moved around the table until she was next to the aunt.

"Ma'am," Teddy whispered without making eye contact. "May I get you anything else?"

The woman didn't hesitate. "Orange juice. With a heavy dose of spice." She turned slightly. "Do you understand?"

"Yes, ma'am." Teddy glanced at the clock. Two in the afternoon and Aunt Pauline wanted alcohol? But who was she to judge? The bartender did not seem surprised at her request, and Teddy placed the etched crystal filled with orange liquid on the table without the girls even noticing.

The woman's napkin fell to the floor, and Teddy grabbed it, prepared to offer a new one, but Emmaline's aunt reached for it, grasping Teddy's hand. She gave a light squeeze, then released it, placing the cloth back over her lap.

Teddy stood against the wall and replayed the exchange in her mind. Had it been intentional? A thank you of sorts?

She performed her duties and perfunctorily filled teacups and replaced the three-tiered tray of finger sandwiches, scones, and sweet treats. Lingonberry and raspberry jam, lemon curd, and Devonshire cream sat in small crystal dishes with miniature silver spoons sticking out from the thick condiments.

The sweet smell of jam and tart lemon curd wafted through the air. Aunt Pauline lifted her napkin to her nose and mouth, placed it on the table, and pushed her chair back.

"It has been a delight having tea with you ladies. Emmaline, it is always a pleasure seeing you. I must be on my way," the aunt said.

Teddy offered her arm as Miss Whitaker moved to stand. Teddy adjusted her stance to accept more force than what she'd expected, then adjusted again with the quick release of the hand on her arm. Miss Whitaker gripped the back of the chair and smiled down at her niece with pinched features.

"When might I see you again, Aunt?"

The hope in Emmaline's eyes made emotion swell in Teddy. She hadn't seen this side of Emmaline, who was still a girl, yet had been thrust into society as a young woman.

"We'll make that happen soon, darling." But there was no commitment in the words or promise in the tone.

"Emmy, I promised Mother I'd be home by three. She hired a new French tutor for me after dismissing Madame LeBlanc. It was a pleasure spending the afternoon with you all." Opal said, her finger awkwardly pushing a stray strand of thick, dark hair behind her ear. Her almond-shaped eyes followed Emmaline's aunt as she stood. Each girl offered a polite smile.

The moment Opal reached the door, Caroline leaned in slightly, threatening to add a lemon curd stain to the lace of her bodice. "I heard Madam LeBlanc started courting a Southern sympathizer."

Adeline's petite hand flew to her high neckline. "What a tragedy. They'll need to move south like the rest of the carpetbaggers."

Louisa looked as if this wasn't new information. "I heard he's a scalawag with political aspirations."

Emmaline placed her napkin on the table, signaling the end of the meal and the current thread of conversation. "Opal's family should have hired better quality in the first place, and then they wouldn't be dealing with this issue now. Monsieur Aubert has served our family for two generations. He taught my father and Aunt Pauline and now teaches me."

"Your aunt didn't answer why she isn't staying at your home. It isn't like you don't have room. When was the last time she visited?" Caroline's tone bordered on insolent. Her lifted eyebrow made the wisps of Teddy's hair on her neck lift.

Emmaline tapped a pointer finger in her lap but never gave away a hint of emotion. "Caroline, I know you're naïve, but mystery can be a woman's best weapon."

Teddy snorted and covered her mouth and faked a cough. This girl wielded words like a sword, and stitches might be required if the conversation continued.

Caroline conceded the win and placed her napkin on the table, but she never broke eye contact with Emmaline.

"Will there be anything else today, Miss Whitaker?" Teddy asked, hoping to keep whatever the female version of a duel was called from happening.

Emmaline's finger slowed. "We were just leaving."

Teddy lifted the tray from the ring at the top.

Caroline huffed. "I was just asking a simple question."

"My dear, everyone's entitled to ask ridiculous questions once in a while, but you abuse the privilege." Emmaline stood, the others hastening to follow. "Enjoy the rest of your day, girls."

Teddy stood holding the tiered tray like a lantern, illuminating the remark. She knew she should close her mouth but remained statuesque. Had Teddy said such a thing, her mother would have washed her mouth out with soap at the rudeness. Someone giggled, and Teddy pulled herself together.

"Shall I put this on your father's tab, Miss Whitaker?" Teddy questioned without making eye contact.

"Yes. I suppose I am today's hostess and would never want to shirk my duties."

Teddy didn't need to look up to see the martyred look on Emmaline's face. Her breathy words were image enough.

When the girls were all out of the way, Teddy cleared the table. She hated wasting food, but there would be happy hogs somewhere outside of the city. She longed to scoop up the remaining lemon curd and pop a scone into her mouth. Working two jobs and saving every penny didn't seem worth it some days.

Each girl who'd sat at the table she now cleaned would likely never know the difficulty of deciding between a week's worth of meals and a new pair of shoes.

"What's got you in a huff?" another server asked as he wheeled a cart to the table and placed the stacked plates on it.

"Nothing a few of these scones and a crock of lemon curd wouldn't cure." She offered him a smile. "Do you think they realize how pampered they are?" Teddy whispered so the other patrons wouldn't overhear while pointing her nose toward the flock at the door.

"Honestly, I don't believe they ever think. Period. Most of those girls couldn't form an argument to save their lives."

He hadn't heard the cutting retort Emmaline had formulated, seemingly without thinking. The girl was smart, but she wouldn't be winning any awards. Teddy followed her coworker and the cart he pushed, a pile of used napkins and the soiled tablecloth in her arms.

The man turned to her. "What time does your shift end?"

The back of Teddy's neck prickled, and she slowed her steps. "Um, now, but I'm headed to my next job, Sam, so I really —"

"Perfect. Meet me out back in ten minutes."

Sam's wink and smile made Teddy's stomach drop. She didn't have time for a relationship, and she certainly didn't want to hurt any feelings, but there was no time to argue. He'd left her standing in the hall, arms full.

Teddy dreaded the conversation but would rather tackle the difficult now instead of setting the man up for disappointment later on.

The weight of the back door matched Teddy's mood. Smoke assaulted her as Sam blew out between his yellowed teeth.

"Good, you're here. This'll cure what ails ya. Have a good rest of your day." Sam handed Teddy a box of pleated paper with the lid tucked in, then took long strides away from the building, smoke following him and evaporating into the humid air.

Teddy glanced around, but she was alone. What had just happened? She opened the box to find a dollop of lemon curd in one corner and three broken scones. The smile that formed felt good, and she sighed contentedly.

"Thanks, Lord. A sweet treat as a sweet reminder that not all of humanity is bad, even if they still need You."

Chapter 10

August 1871
University of Pennsylvania Medical School
Thomas

"We meet again." Thomas stepped aside from the opening door and allowed Teddy to enter the boarding house. Water dripped from her overcoat.

Teddy removed her hood, and loose strands peeked out from beneath her nurse's cap. "Just not as forceful this time."

"It seems we both know where we're going. Let me help you with your coat." She turned, allowing his hands to reach over her shoulders and lift the wet fabric from her frame.

She turned back to take the coat, but he was already adding it to the growing tree.

Teddy adjusted her cap. "Thank you. You may know where you're going this early and dressed so smartly. I do not."

"You don't know where you're going? I'm guessing to bed." Heat rose in his cheeks at his teasing.

"No, silly, I don't know where you are headed so early this morning. And yes. A good night's sleep, or morning as it appears, is what I plan on doing."

Teddy's smile and easy banter made him feel comfortable in her presence but did not quell his nervousness. "First day of school. I feel like a child hoping the teacher allows me to sit next to my best friend this year." He forced a smile and put a hand over his quivering stomach.

"How exciting. I'd say you're ready, but I'm afraid you've forgotten something important."

Teddy's gaze moved to his head, and he touched the top, wondering if he'd forgotten his hat, which he knocked askew. Her laughter was like sunshine on this rainy day.

She reached her hand beneath the forest of coats and produced an umbrella. "You may want this. I didn't consult Mother Nature before I left for work last night." She took a handkerchief and wiped droplets from her face.

"Ah, yes. There is little worse than spending an entire day miserably wet."

"I can think of a few." Her fingers trailed down something brown covering her once-white apron.

"I'm not going to ask what that is." Thomas cleared his throat as the smell of someone's regurgitated meal reached his nose.

"What, you don't like this? Perhaps your first day of medical school will involve identifying and classifying all forms of . . ." She pointed to a few deeper stains, then lifted her pointer finger to her chin. "In fact, I've been told I'm a good tutor. Maybe, out of the kindness of my heart, I will let you wash it for me. You know, so you can practice the fine art of deducing the ailment from the aroma, color, and complexity of the stain."

"It sounds like you're asking me to identify a fine wine. Just so you know, I draw the line at tasting." He tried to keep the look on his face serious, but the quaking in his gut now felt more like fluttering butterflies.

Teddy laughed. "Enjoy your day, Mr. Thomas. We can discuss homework another time. I'd hate to make you late. I'll pray your first day of school is as exciting as primary school field trips and recess."

Her wink surprised him. He could not contain the smile that spread across his face, making his eyes squint. "You as well," was all he could get out as his gaze trailed her retreating form up the hall steps.

It took effort to open and secure the umbrella, but it wasn't nearly as much as it took to force his nerves to obey. Those pesky butterflies attempted to show themselves, and Thomas chuckled, remembering the apron. Until she'd dabbed it away with her hankie, the water droplet on her cheek had reminded him of morning dew on a spring flower. The ease with which they'd bantered this morning was like moments with his sisters, but he'd never felt unsettled in his stomach with them.

The deep sound of large bells tolling reached his ears, and he picked up the pace, leaving his musings behind. The students moved like ants approaching a prize sugar lump, then stopped at a formidable stone structure ahead. He was breathing hard as he took the steps to the medical building classrooms two at a time.

The smell of dampness and acidic vinegar, which had likely been used to clean the huge foyer, greeted him, as did Jimmy, who stood just inside the ornate wooden doors, reaching for the umbrella. "Here, hand that to me. The lecture hall filled quickly, so I saved you a seat. My driver dropped me off early. Obviously, yours did not." He took Thomas's coat and held the dripping fabric in one hand and the umbrella in the other, keeping them away from his polished shoes as water dripped onto the shiny floor.

"Thank you, Jimmy. I needed the fresh air and, obviously, a shower." Both laughed, relieving some of the tension under the weight of Thomas's messenger bag.

Thomas ran his hand over the leather, holding what he hoped was all he'd need for his first day of class. He stepped gingerly over the tiled floors, being careful not to slip. He followed Jimmy into a large amphitheater-style classroom. The backs of dozens of heads looked down toward the front where a large blackboard, wooden desk covered in haphazardly strewn papers, and an unoccupied chair waited for their owner to arrive.

Thomas followed Jimmy down several steps, then sidestepped over the other students' feet until they reached the center of the row. Most students had their heads down, and he didn't see any familiar faces. He breathed more easily once he had settled into the wooden seat and laid his paper and freshly sharpened pencils on his lap. Jimmy passed him a rectangle of wood with a clip at the top.

"I wondered if you'd been in a theatre-style classroom without desks," Jimmy said. "This clipboard will make taking notes much easier."

"Thank you." His dry throat made it difficult to say more. He pinched and closed the tight clasp on the clipboard, his bouncing knee causing his heel to tap. The person beside him took in a deep breath, not attempting to hide his irritation.

"You'll wear that thing out before we start," Jimmy chided.

Thomas willed himself to still, at least on the outside. There wasn't much he could do about the jumble of nerves on the inside—except pray. *Lord, may today be all field trips and recess—and a little learning.* A burst of air escaped his nose, and he wiped the back of his hand over his mouth.

The rustle of papers and scraping of shoes pulled Thomas's attention down to the front. The student to his left clapped as if he'd had a few too many cups of coffee to start his day. Thomas arose with the rest of the students as Dr. Whitaker stood at the front with a thin white coat over his morning suit. The raised hands of the commanding figure below quickly quieted the clapping of a few students.

"This, gentlemen, is a lab coat. Some of you will earn the privilege of wearing one such as this upon graduation. Similar to a priest's collar or a clergyman's garb, which I'm sure none of you in this room would care to wear, the white coat symbolizes professionalism and integrity. It signifies your commitment to caring for the sick and suffering.

"This jacket sets actual doctors apart from quacks, snake-oil healers, and medicine men who do not practice evidence-based medicine. Today, you begin your journey into the world of medicine. Forget everything you think you know, every wives' tale you were told, every Indian poultice you've read about. You are now a medical student, and at this university, we study the science of medicine."

The air around Thomas threatened to choke him. He ran a finger around the inside of his collar and hoped those around him would think the moisture was from the rain.

Boarding House
Evening Meal

Mrs. Jones wiped her mouth and placed her napkin on the table. "Mr. Shankel. You received a letter today. It's on the hall table."

"Thank you, ma'am." His eyes burned with exhaustion. Even the brisk walk home had not loosened the tension in Thomas's shoulders. On top of a full day of lectures, Jimmy had invited him to luncheon at the botanical gardens. Thomas had not expected the price of the meal to be so much for a simple fare of bread and boiled meat. He'd need to seek places to buy bread, cheese, and dried meat for his noon meal—or skip it all together.

Thomas listened to the animated chatter of his boarding house friends but didn't have the mental energy to take part in the discussions. He broke a piece of the crispy crust from the edge of the pie placed before him and stuck it in his mouth before everyone had been served. It was as rebellious and wicked as he'd been in a while. The first hour of class had focused on rules. Not that he would have trouble keeping them, but the reality, the magnitude, of what it would take beyond classroom studies made the crust turn to dust in his mouth.

Reggie leaned in. "Shoofly pie. Have you had it?"

Thomas put down his coffee. "I don't believe so. It certainly smells good. Anything with molasses is a favorite of mine."

Reggie pointed his fork to the head of the table, where

Mrs. Jones took the first bite, then used his utensil to cut off a piece from his plate.

Thomas eyed the crumbles on top and the dark interior. "Mmm," was all he could get out as he chewed the gooey goodness.

Reggie took a swig of coffee and leaned in. "I heard she won a blue ribbon for this recipe. I'm not one for sweets, but I love a good shoofly pie."

Crocket placed his fork on the dessert plate, already finished. "You know, shoofly pie is original to Pennsylvania Dutch country. That's probably why you haven't tried it. Now, in the northeast, they favor the Boston cream pie. Buttery cake with a layer of thick pudding all covered in chocolate. That'll get your tastebuds twirling. If you're from the south, I suppose pecan pie might be a local favorite. That's like nothing else I've ever had. Once when I was in . . ."

Thomas tuned the man out, scooped the last bite onto his fork, and let the flavors and textures meld in his mouth.

Thomas let out a contented sigh. "Mrs. Jones, I'm uncertain what other establishments feed their boarders, but you and Cook put on an exceptional spread. And your desserts never disappoint." Thomas realized he'd interrupted Crocket, but no one seemed to mind, except for Crocket. Several others added their agreement.

She dabbed at her mouth. "Very kind of you to say. Cook always prepares something for Sundays and Wednesdays because those were the days my husband enjoyed having dessert with his evening meals. Sunday, to celebrate the Lord's Day, and Wednesday because Mr. Jones said he needed a pick-me-up in the middle of the week."

"Sounds like a man with good taste," Thomas offered. "Now, if you'll excuse me, I have much to do. Thank you again for the lovely meal."

Thomas lifted his chair as he pushed it under the table. To some, he may be unsophisticated and lacking Philadelphia society's social graces, but he wasn't uncouth. Teddy met his gaze, and Thomas returned her smile.

The only mail on the foyer table was his. Thomas recognized his mother's familiar handwriting and held the note close as he climbed the stairs. He fumbled with the key to his room, plopping down and allowing the feather pillow to cradle his head.

He had a long night ahead of him, and he couldn't afford a nap, but studying could wait. Reading news of home came first.

My dearest Thomas,

Your father and sisters send their love, as do the crew. They are feeling the loss of your strong back and work ethic, but I think they only complain to make me feel better. I miss you desperately. Were it not for your clear calling from the Lord and your promise to return upon graduation, my heart might break.

We received word of a collapse at one of the mine shafts where Gabe works after classes in Rolla. Praise the Lord, there were no injuries. I wanted to make sure you knew he was fine should the news arrive in Philadelphia.

I need to get back to making breakfast, but I wanted to get something in the mail to you before the wagon headed to town for supplies.

  I miss you. Work hard, son. Honor the Lord in all you do.

    Much love, Mama

If his mother had been in the middle of cooking and had stopped to write this, his family likely would struggle to eat whatever she'd made. He'd had far too many flavorless or overly salty meals, and even ones where she'd used sugar instead of salt for the seasoning. He'd gladly eat one of those meals now.

"Time to get busy." Thomas did his best to focus on his reading for class but could not keep his mother's words from seeping into the crevices of his mind. Gabe working in the mines. His friend putting himself in danger every day in the depths of the earth.

"Lord." Thomas ran his fingers through his hair and leaned back in his chair for a much-needed stretch.

"Do your best for Me."

It wasn't that Thomas audibly heard God's voice, but more that the scripture he'd memorized over his lifetime surfaced and settled his heart.

"'Whether therefore ye eat, or drink, or whatsoever ye do, do all to the glory of God.' That I can do. Thank You, Lord. I can focus my actions on doing what I know You've called me to do. My focus needs to be on my calling, even though my heart aches for my brother in Christ. I leave Gabe in Your capable hands and the path he's chosen—or the one chosen for him. In all things, Father, I will worship You. In all things." He spoke the last words with resolve.

Thomas folded the letter and placed it in the side drawer, then turned back to page one in his *Basic Human Physiology* textbook.

Chapter 11

Late October, 1871
The Douglass Home
Thomas

"Welcome, Thomas. Please, come in, and tell us all about your classes." Harriet pulled Thomas in from the crisp morning air.

Warmth drew him in, both from the crackling fire and Harriet's smile. "Thank you. I apologize for not visiting sooner. Classes are quite challenging." Thomas removed his top hat and outer coat. He rubbed his hands together before offering one to Douglass.

Douglass gripped it. "Good to see you, friend. No apologies necessary for not getting by. Please, sit yourself down. I just made cocoa."

"Cocoa? What's the occasion? It looks like I'm interrupting something." Bits and pieces of nutshells covered the table.

"Shelling shagbark nuts. Makes some good-tasting milk." Douglass offered Thomas the chair and pulled the stool from under the table.

"I've not heard of shagbark nuts." Thomas turned the smooth meat over in his palm, then popped a piece into his mouth. "Hickory?"

"Exactly." Harriet swept her hand over the mess strewn across the table. "One of the best-tasting nuts but a pain to get out of the shell."

Thomas reached for a hammer. "How can I help?"

Douglass covered his hand. "Oh, no, you don't. You're a guest."

"I thought you said I was family." Thomas winked at Harriet.

Douglass cocked his head, a look of acceptance on his face. "Fine. If you want to help, pick up the pieces I send flying and grind them in this here bowl while you tell us all about your first months of school."

Thomas did as he was told, sorting through the chunks and bits of shell and nut meat, placing the larger pieces in a separate bowl. "There is so much to learn. The human body is fascinating. We spend most of our day in the classroom, then, once a week, we rotate in groups of four to follow doctors who are leaders in their specialty as each does his rounds. Dr. Whitaker isn't the only talented physician in Philadelphia. All of my professors are. They each have so much knowledge, and I'm trying to soak it all in, but it's hard. I'm thankful for Jimmy. He's my study buddy."

"Having a friend is important," Harriet offered.

Thomas wanted to say how the other students seemed to see him as the country bumpkin and didn't include him in most of their outside activities. Just this weekend, a group of them had gone to the opera. Not that he had the funds or the desire to dress up and sit through a performance in a language he didn't understand. Thomas didn't want to burden Douglass and Harriet, so he kept quiet.

"Is this Jimmy fellow a believer?"

It was just like Douglass to get to the important talk.

"We haven't yet had that conversation. He loves plants, though, and I bet he could tell you all about the tree these came from." Thomas turned the cream-colored shell in his hand.

"How about church? You being fed?" Douglass continued his questioning.

"Honestly? It's not what I'm used to; that's for certain. The preacher is a fine man and preaches the Word, but there's something missing. It's almost as if what a person wears and which row they sit in is more important than the condition of their heart."

Douglass nodded. "You make certain you study the Bible as much as those textbooks, and your heart will stay fed."

Harriet chimed in. "What about the boarding house? Are your accommodations suiting you all right?" She sounded like his mother, and he smiled.

"Yes, ma'am. I've enjoyed mealtime the most, and not just for the food I didn't have to prepare but also for the conversation. I don't have to think." Thomas laughed. "The other evening, we had a scintillating discussion about knitting. The women proposed teaching the men, so we'd have something to keep our hands busy during the winter. Crazy enough, every single boarder agreed, in exchange for teaching the women card games. Mrs. Jones nearly had a conniption until the group promised no money would be involved and all activities would take place in the parlor with her present."

Harriet's laugh was deep and throaty, reminding him of Aunt Aideen. A pang of homesickness replaced the joy of the moment.

"Have you heard from home?" It was as if Douglass had read his mind.

Thomas shook his head. "I received two letters from home but expected to hear from Gabe by now. Not a word. They're getting my mail—because my family wired me money when I realized I'd need more than I'd planned to purchase textbooks and equipment. I don't want to be beholden to them, so I'm seeking employment. Any ideas?"

"Work? Son, when do you figure you'll fit that in?"

"My Saturdays are mostly free, except for laundry." Thomas watched unspoken words exchange between his friends through smiles and a wink, and he wished he understood this language.

Harriet pushed back her chair and wiped her hands on her apron. She pulled three mugs from the cabinet, stirred the pot on the stove, then used a dipper to pour dark liquid into each cup.

"Here you go."

The mug was warm with sweet-smelling steam rising and calming his anxious heart. Douglass was right. Liquid sweetness melted in his mouth, reminding him again of home. He closed his eyes and thought of evenings spent in front of the fire drinking hot chocolate with his sisters.

"My mother can hardly boil water without burning it, but she makes the best hot chocolate. She always adds a pinch of cinnamon to it."

"Now, that's something I haven't tried." Harriet stood and pulled a cinnamon stick from the cabinet and a grater from the drawer. The smell of the spice mixed with the aroma of nuts and chocolate as it floated at the top of her mug. She gave it a swirl, then sipped. "Well, I do declare. Douglass, you're going to like this." She repeated the process for her husband, then offered some to Thomas.

"Might be my new favorite drink," Douglass said. "You'll have to let your mother know you shared her recipe. So, you're looking for work?"

Thomas watched an unspoken exchange again. "Yes, sir. I figure I have more time now than I will later in my studies."

"Pardon my forthright question, but is there something you're needing to purchase, or are you struggling to make ends meet with your rent?"

"A little of both. I want to do this on my own, and I'll need to purchase books each semester, along with a few other things. I don't want to choose between having a place to lay my head and having to borrow, rather than purchase a medical book I want to keep for future reference."

Thomas need not be ashamed in front of his friends. His family had the money, but he didn't want to rely on them for everything like his fellow students did. When he'd said he wanted to earn his degree to become a doctor, he'd meant both the hard work and the funds needed. It was important for him to do this one thing on his own.

"Well, me and Harriet were discussing this very thing the other day. It won't make you money, but it will save you time and sure would help us out."

"I'm listening." Thomas brushed the shell crumbs from in front of him and placed his mug on the table.

"Harriet here has forbidden me from getting on our roof, and we have some repairs needed. I can't rightly afford to hire someone to do the work, but I can get the needed materials. We could knock it out in a day if I served as your helper while you did the work. In exchange, Harriet will do your laundry."

"That's mighty generous, but I don't see how that will help me pay my bills."

"It won't, but working for the judge will. He's needing someone to fill in until Josiah's leg heals. I told Judge I knew just the man. It's mucking stalls and caring for the horses, but it's early morning every Saturday, and you'd still have your afternoons free to study."

"And I'll do your laundry with ours if that's all right with you," Harriet added.

Douglass smiled at his wife. "Now, it's not permanent, but I can pick you up on my way to the judge's house. I know you're skilled with horses, though not much skill needed in mucking stalls."

Thomas didn't have to think hard. He missed his horse and the physical labor he was used to. Already, his hands were softening. "I'll take you up on your offers. When do I start? Do I need to speak with the judge?"

"You let me handle the details. As for the roof, how does now sound?" Douglass winked. "I've already got the supplies."

It felt good to laugh. Thomas swirled the remaining liquid in his cup as if he was considering the request. The cooled chocolate was just as good as when it was piping hot. He placed the mug down and looked at Harriet.

"Today I'm working in exchange for laundry, but how will I pay you for the other weeks?"

Now it was Harriet's turn to let out a low chuckle. "Thomas, my man's been doing both his and Josiah's job for two weeks. Trust me. If he can come home and not be bone-weary, I count it fair trade for doing your laundry."

It may not be much, but it was a step in the right direction. Thomas felt the excitement of getting his hands dirty and breaking a sweat with hard labor. "It's a deal." He offered his hand to his friend. "And thank you."

"My pleasure. Let's get to work."

The men pulled the supplies and tools from the shed. Thomas climbed the ladder and thanked the Lord for clear skies and a slight breeze. Not having to climb up and down the ladder saved time, and the two worked together efficiently.

Thomas surveyed his work. His knees and back ached, but it felt good. He rubbed his forearm. It'd been a while since he'd swung a hammer.

Douglass called, "Only five shingles left. Will that be enough?"

"Save those for another day. I'm done here." Thomas started down the ladder. He'd be sore tomorrow, but the anxiety and stress he'd felt at the beginning of the day were gone, replaced with the satisfaction of a job well done.

"Thank you, Thomas. Let's clean this up, then I'll take you home. You don't need to be walking now that it's getting close to sunset."

Thomas carried the ladder and lifted it to where it hung above the shed door. Everything in the small space was as neat as Harriet's kitchen. He wouldn't need much room when he opened his clinic back home if he built shelving like this to keep his storeroom orderly.

The familiar pang of missing home settled in his gut. Every time he learned something new, he wanted to share his excitement with his best friend but knew it would only hurt Gabe more deeply than he already was.

Thomas said a silent prayer that Gabe was enjoying his metallurgy studies and able to juggle that with working in the mines and the farm. He reminded himself he'd given Gabe to the Lord, but as Thomas stepped from the shed into the waning light of evening, he knew Gabe would rarely see the same, being deep in the earth or in the classroom during both sunrise and sunset.

Douglass closed the door and stood beside Thomas. "You want to pray about what's on your mind?"

Thomas pinched the bridge of his nose. How did this man know the inner workings of his heart? "Maybe you should be the one in medical school. You're pretty good at diagnosing a problem."

"I just read people, and I'm guessing what you're feeling is more than just missing your family. How about we talk on the ride back?" Douglass placed his warm hand on Thomas's shoulder. "Let me say a quick goodbye to my bride, and we'll head to the livery."

They walked in silence down the street and borrowed a small carriage. The *clip-clop* of the horses' hooves on stone kept time with Thomas's heartbeat.

"You don't have to share, but if you need to get something off your chest, I'm all ears."

Thomas knew he could tell Douglass anything, but he wasn't sure what was really bothering him. "I'm not certain I know. Finances are weighing on me, but God has provided for all my needs, and your generous offer is an example of His faithfulness. My classwork is challenging, but I'm applying myself and studying hard. We haven't been told ranking yet, but I believe I'm doing well. I've made friends at the boarding house—and Jimmy at school." Thomas quieted.

"No lady friends?"

Brown eyes and chestnut hair swirled in his vision. He expelled a breath and shook his head to clear the swirling image of the woman from his mind and regain focus before reluctantly confessing that he had no time for a special lady friend. "No, sir. No time for that."

"Mm-hmm. What about your classmates? Are you fitting in?"

Thomas released another deep sigh. He didn't fit in. "I'm thankful for the suits your wife made for me. That's helped, but I can't compete with generations of Philadelphia's gentry. To be honest, I'm not sure I want to. I came here for an education, so I could return home and help the people of Shumard Oak Bend. I care little about which fork to use or words to say in particular settings. It's as if my classmates know all the right answers to questions I'd never care to ask."

Douglass's laugh caused the horse to sidestep. "Whoa, fella. Sorry about that."

Thomas couldn't tell if he was speaking to him or the

horse. "I try to be a part of their conversations, but most of the time, I don't have a clue what or who they're talking about. I've found it easier to be quiet. Unfortunately, that means they haven't gotten to know me—the real me."

"'And be not conformed to this world: but be ye transformed by the renewing of your mind.' That first part of Romans 12 is all you need to worry about, son. You focus on being who God designed you to be, and don't worry about meeting the expectations of the upper crust."

The horse slowed, and Thomas looked over to see light shining from the front window of the boarding house. The stress he'd let go of while working on the roof returned. He ran his hands over his thighs and pushed on his knees.

"Thomas, you be you." Douglass's firm tone pulled Thomas back to the conversation.

"I don't fit in here." Thomas sounded like a small child.

"Paul is clear and tells us not to chase pleasure, possessions, or status. There's no need to be like everyone else or fit in with Philadelphia society. Paul encourages us to be transformed, not by what we wear or what we say but by how we think. You don't need to fit in to be in the center of God's will. You keep doing what you're doing, and God will bless your efforts."

Thomas nodded and stepped down from the carriage.

Douglass tipped his hat. "I'll stop by on my way to the judge's next Saturday and give you a lift. Be ready at half past six. Oh, and remember your laundry. I'll take it home and return it to you Sunday after I drop the judge and his family back home after service."

"Thank you." Thomas meant the words for much more than he could express and hoped his friend understood the depth of the sentiment.

Chapter 12

November 1871
University of Pennsylvania Medical School
Thomas

"Who recognizes this?" Professor Holder pointed with his metal stick to the round, raised lesions on the child's lifeless body.

Unlike some of his classmates who looked green, working with cadavers was only difficult for him when the specimen was a child. Thomas raised his hand.

"Yes, Mr. Shankel?"

"Ringworm, sir."

"And you know this—how, Mr. Shankel? You've studied the latest findings of William Tilbury Fox?"

"No, sir. I had it as a child." Thomas flinched but schooled his features as his classmates snickered.

"And how did you contract this disease?" The metal rod now tapped against the man's palm like a schoolteacher's ruler.

Thomas used his diaphragm to breathe deeply and exhaled his answer. "Direct contact with an infected man or beast, sir."

"And you know this for a fact. You could prove this theory with scientific evidence?"

It wasn't a question. It was a challenge. Thomas could hardly say Singing Bird had shown him the circles on a deer he was skinning and explained how the fungus grew and survived in dirt, debris, and contaminated animal bedding. It was why they had hung the deer in the tree to gut and drain rather than in the barn. They didn't want to contaminate the chickens or horses with the ringworm fungi.

But how did he explain this scientifically? He must have waited too long to answer, for Professor Holder slapped his palm with the stick, bringing Thomas back to the conversation.

"I don't care if you think you know an answer. It matters not if you've had a personal experience, even if they incorporate an itch that must be scratched. I only care about facts. In this class, you will provide scientific proof for your hypothesis."

Thomas tuned out the professor and the whispered comments sent his direction. Like a child being scolded for speaking out of turn, Thomas swallowed the hurt at being put in his place. He respected his elders, especially a man as bright as Professor Holder, but the man had given his classmates more reason to see Thomas as less than them.

He felt a tug at his sleeve and looked over to see Jimmy point with his eyes. The class was leaving the exhibition area and heading outside.

Addison Blakeney stood preening on the lawn, his entourage looking at him. He spoke loud enough for all to hear. "Hey." Addison locked eyes with Thomas, index finger extended, aiming directly at him. With a deliberate motion, he lifted his finger to his temple, tapping it lightly before twirling it in a fluid, circular motion. "Way to go, plebeian. I think the ringworm settled in your brain."

Thomas bit back a response that would not please the Lord and smiled as he walked closer. "You may want to wash your hands since you touched the girl's toe."

Tendons stuck out from Addison's neck, and he blinked wide eyes that turned steely. "Listen, voodoo or medicine man or whatever it is you think you are. Even if you survive the program, no one will hire you. Not with your backwards breeding. Maybe you should stick with stitching up animals."

Two boys, one flanking each side, laughed at Addison's joke. Thomas didn't crack a smile. He knew how to deal with bullies. He'd stuck up for Gabe for all his growing-up years. It just felt different when directed to him.

"Enjoy your afternoon, gentlemen. And don't forget—" Thomas motioned as if washing his hands before sauntering down the university sidewalk as if their jabs had not affected him. Only, they had. He wasn't cut out for high society. Addison spoke more truth than lie. Thomas knew having the best grades wouldn't be enough, especially if he kept acting the fool in front of the professors.

"Thomas. Wait up." Jimmy rushed to catch up. "Don't pay any attention to those guys. They're jealous of your high marks on our last exam. What do you have planned for the weekend? I thought maybe we could study on Saturday."

Thomas hesitated, then continued walking. He hadn't told his friend about his job. But what was friendship if you didn't share important details? "I have to work on Saturday morning, but I'm free in the afternoon. Would you like to meet at the library?"

"I should probably show up to volunteer on Saturday morning as well. I give tours at the botanical garden. We've been so busy with schoolwork and all . . . but if you can be number one in the class and do it, I can, too."

"Number one?" Gravel crunched under his foot as he stopped.

"Yeah, didn't you hear a thing Professor Holden said? They posted grades in the hall. I shouldn't know, but I have a thing for numbers, and I saw yours once, so I know you are right above me. Addison and his cronies didn't need to look. I'm sure they were at the bottom."

Thomas worked hard, but so had all the students, especially Jimmy. He didn't seem the least bit upset about being second.

Jimmy took a step. "So, what volunteer work were you able to secure?"

Thomas didn't want to lie. He had volunteered to take Josiah's place until he healed. He just happened to be getting paid to do so. "Horses. I'm working with horses."

"Better you than me. I don't even enjoy riding. Those beasts know I'm afraid and take advantage of the situation."

Thomas snickered. "They're smart animals. Tell you what. How about we meet around one on Saturday? I'll need to change and wash up before we study, or you won't be able to stand me."

"You're at Mrs. Jones's boarding house, right? I'll have my

driver pick you up, and we'll study at my house. Unlike at the university's library, we'll be able to talk in my home library. And you'll stay for the evening meal. Mother and Father are in Europe, so it's just me. I hate eating alone."

Jimmy waved at someone in the distance. "Will you excuse me? That's my driver. Insolent soul, but he's been with our family since my father was a boy, and he likes to keep a schedule. See you Saturday," he called back as he hurried to catch his ride.

Thomas's steps felt lighter as he walked home since he knew he had something fun planned for the weekend. Not that his job wasn't fun, but the conversations he had with the other hands were about as lively as with the animals. The hands didn't seem to trust him and kept their distance. If Douglass was around, they spoke freely with him, but Saturdays were full of outings for both the judge and his wife, which kept Douglass busy.

On the farm in Missouri, everyone pitched in. Clint and Moses worked right along with the hired farm hands. When they took cattle to market, Charlie and Lizzy worked as hard as the cowhands and Mexican vaqueros they hired. Thomas and Gabe stayed behind when the rest went on the cattle drives to oversee their respective farms.

Thomas had been left in charge of the homestead since he was barely of age. Not that he was more capable, but each did their part. No one person was more important than the other. Each used their talents and experience to get the job done in the most efficient way.

Not in Philadelphia. Or at least, not in this neighborhood. Thomas hadn't experienced the difference in class nor the amount of pampering the elite required until now. They'd never survive in rural Missouri. He took the steps to the boarding house two at a time, his satchel slapping against his side.

The woodsmoke from the parlor fire wasn't enough to overshadow whatever smelled rich and spicy, like dishes the Mexican workers at home prepared for them on cattle drives. He immediately looked at the hall clock to see he was almost late for dinner. He heard sounds coming from the parlor.

Racing up the stairs like a child, he unlocked and opened his door. Not bothering to shut it, he flung his satchel on the bed, then tossed the hat and felt a twinge of accomplishment when it twirled on the top of the coat tree before settling. He wasn't as successful with his coat and picked it up and hung the neck on the peg sticking out.

"Hands," He said flatly to no one but himself as he surveyed his palms with a smirk and thought of Addison's reaction to his comment. He used the facilities and stepped into the hall just as the clock chimed. The men were still standing, allowing the ladies to sit first when he arrived. He squeezed in, making pleasantries with his new friends.

"Let us pray." Mrs. Jones folded her hands. "Bless this food, Father, and help us each to be thankful for Your bounteous goodness and favor. Amen."

Chatter and the clinking of dishes made Thomas's heart feel at peace. Rarely did he get a word in at home, especially on a school day when his sisters recounted their day in painstaking detail. Dinner with friends felt good. Safe. Familiar.

"Mr. Shankel. You received mail today. I left it on the hall table," Mrs. Jones said as she passed the bowl of sweet potatoes.

"Thank you, ma'am."

Thomas chewed and swallowed but could not have stated what he'd eaten. He was eager to hear from home. He exchanged pleasantries with those nearest him but could not get the letter out of his mind. Finally, dinner, dessert, and the never-ending story Crocket told came to a close.

"Thank you for a fine meal, Mrs. Jones. If you'll excuse me, I have a tremendous amount of studying to complete." Thomas pushed his chair back and stood, nodding to those surrounding the table.

The envelope was thick, as if it contained more than one page. Thomas hurried to his room, pushed the satchel out of the way, and plopped onto his bed. His shoes landed on the floor with a thud, and he curled his feet up under him as he and Gabe had done many times as boys.

His finger slid under the flap and carefully pulled the envelope open. He unfolded the papers, and a small piece slid out. A perfect representation of a downy woodpecker filled the sheet. Serafina had used charcoal to fill in a black tail, then drawn an outline of the bird's white outer tail feathers and classic black spots in perfect rows. If he let go, the tiny bird might flit away.

Rachel's familiar handwriting filled the page. *My dearest son,* she began. She'd been the woman who'd raised him from the age of five. But neither she nor Clint, the man he called his father, were his parents.

His head connected with the wooden headboard. Oh, how he missed home. They may not be blood, but they were family. Normal, hardworking people who loved God and country. People he looked up to and wanted to make proud. Thomas lifted the pages and continued reading.

My dearest son,

We pray you are well, enjoying your studies, and learning much. Robin asks daily if you've learned anything new and is convinced the university is filling your mind with all sorts of nonsense. Today she marched in with a basket of what looked like only weeds and announced that God had made everything we need to heal our bodies. What more is there? I can't argue with that, but thankfully I had just received your letter and told her how you are learning of ways to cure things that medicinal plants alone cannot.

I had to hand her the paper to read about the cleft palette surgery you witnessed. Your drawing was quite remarkable, and my heart ached for the child. Reading your descriptions once was enough for me. I'm not saying don't share what you are learning. Please continue sending such marvelous stories of advances in medicine. I just may have Clint read the letters first and tell me which parts to skip next time. What am I saying? I can hardly wait to read your letters. I burned supper the other night as I sat not two feet away at the table and devoured every word you'd written.

Thomas laughed out loud, knowing it would take much less than a letter from him to cause dinner to burn.

Your sisters are well. Each has enclosed a brief letter, so I won't spoil the stories they have to share. We hired a new hand. He's from Kentucky and moved his family west after the war. He's been a help to Moses. I'm not sure how old Moses is, but he is showing signs of living a life of hard labor. Since Preacher Hans is taking care of most of the ironwork in town, Moses is managing the field hands, so your father can focus more on the cattle business. Robin has done all she can for the man but cannot relieve the natural pain of aging.

If Moses was suffering now, how would he be in two more years? Thomas knew Robin would dig deep into her Arapaho knowledge to provide relief to their friend, but Thomas wanted to do more. The doubts that had plagued him earlier in the day about whether he would make it through his schooling evaporated with his newfound determination not only to maintain his position as the top student but also to secure the coveted internship position with Dr. Whitaker. He would learn more at the man's side than he ever could in a textbook.

When he set up office in Shumard Oak Bend, he'd care for all the ills of those he loved. Thomas lifted the paper with renewed fervor.

Gabe is not well.

Thomas froze momentarily, then pulled the paper to his face, as if seeing the words closer would help him read the meaning behind them.

He is melancholy without you. Pete and Robin say he will not return to his schooling. He didn't give a reason, but he now works double shifts mining lead in Rolla. He says they pay a decent wage and provide room and board. We prayed with the Mannings, not knowing what more to do. We ask that you pray for him as well.

I don't want to discourage you, so no more negative talk. We are proud of you and are so pleased to hear you have found a church home and godly friends.

We love you, sweet Thomas.

Rachel signed Mama with a large *M* while Clint signed his full name as if he were still signing a legal document as a US Marshal.

Thomas read the letter again before picking up Cecelia's letter and doing his best to decipher his sister's words. She had the worst penmanship but could best him with both gun and bow.

Oh, how he missed his sisters. He wouldn't even mind an evening around the fire listening to them chatter on and on about things that didn't matter, like the latest fashions and putting their hair up rather than leaving it in braids.

Were his sisters really that much different from the young women he'd seen at Dr. Whitaker's? Just because the Philadelphia dresses would never do for one of Shumard Oak Bend's Fourth of July celebrations, did their finery make them superior—or simply unique?

Thomas leaned his head back against the headboard, the spice on the meat at supper not settling well. He'd soon have more information to potentially answer that question. Dr. Whitaker's New Year's celebration was all the talk on campus. It seemed everyone wanted an invitation.

Everyone but him.

Chapter 13

T homas breathed in the smells of fresh-cut pine boughs as echoes of "Gloria in Excelsis Deo" filled the church. Although the practiced voices of the choir met his ears, the off-key monotone of the gentleman humming beside him made it difficult to worship.

His first Christmas away from home made him long for familiarity, which he sought in the pews of Philadelphia's First Presbyterian Church. But it wasn't the people, nor music, nor even the words from the book of common worship that provided solace to his soul—it was the thought of the Christ child.

"And suddenly there was with the angel a multitude of the heavenly host praising God, and saying…"

Thomas jolted in his seat, looking to the front where he expected to see the owner of the booming voice.

"Glory to God in the highest, and on earth peace, good will toward men."

Thomas resisted the urge to follow the actions of the children who turned to see the voice coming from the nave.

He willed his gaze to remain on the stained-glass windows depicting familiar stories of the Bible in an unfamiliar medium.

Everything in Philadelphia felt grander, more ornate, manmade. From the stained glass that pulled his gaze to the vaulted stone ceiling to the behemoth tubes of the pipe organ. Even taking part in the lavish pageantry of unfamiliar rituals felt overdone. Where was the crude horse's trough filled with hay and the rag doll or cornhusk baby Jesus of Missouri Christmas?

The minister's low voice did not match his slight frame, which was swallowed up in his clerical garb. "Would there be Christmas if Joseph had not fulfilled his purpose? Let us consider this verse from Matthew 1:20 that speaks of Joseph's response to the angels. 'But while he thought on these things, behold, the angel of the LORD appeared unto him in a dream, saying, Joseph, thou son of David, fear not to take unto thee Mary thy wife: for that which is conceived in her is of the Holy Ghost.'"

Thomas had never heard this verse used in a Christmas sermon. He steepled his fingers in anticipation of what he might learn.

"Consider what might have happened if Joseph hadn't obeyed the angel. Although God is sovereign and would have found another way, Joseph would have missed the joy of raising Jesus. If you were Joseph, would you have obeyed without hesitation? The Bible doesn't elaborate on Joseph's response, but he heeded God's call and stayed faithful to Mary."

Thomas rubbed the bridge of his nose between his finger and thumb. Was he moving forward in obedience as Joseph had done?

133

"This Christmas, consider the story of the birth of Jesus through the eyes of Jesus's earthly father. Stay committed to your calling despite external obstacles. Human laws cannot deter us from following divine laws. Like Joseph, commit to what God has called you to without looking back."

Thomas knew his commitment to become a doctor was firm, but was he allowing perceived expectations of society to keep him from fully immersing himself in the profession he knew God had called him to? He needed to be faithful in all things.

He bowed his head. *Forgive me, Lord. Boundaries set by men should never deter me from the path You've clearly set before me.* Thomas felt a weight lift from his shoulders but knew there was one more step he needed to take to walk fully in obedience.

Lord, I give Gabe to You. Fully surrender. I do not understand why You did not allow his path to be the same as mine, but I trust You know best. My future is in Your hands, no matter the consequences. Gabe must find his own way. Thomas remained in an attitude of prayer, the hum of the minister's voice in the background. He opened his eyes as sunlight streamed through the stained glass, creating a kaleidoscope of color over the wall.

The white sleeves of the minister's robe flapped as they reached toward heaven. "Let us stand."

Wood and bones creaked as congregants stood for the benediction.

"May you be filled with the wonder of Mary, the obedience of Joseph, the joy of the angels, the eagerness of the shepherds, the determination of the magi, and the peace of the Christ child. Almighty God, Father, Son, and Holy Spirit bless you now and forever. Amen."

The resonant "Amen" filled the room with a sense of unity Thomas did not feel. He remained in his seat, allowing the minister's words and prayer to take hold of his heart. He was in no hurry. Jimmy was not available to walk the botanical gardens as they often did on Sundays. The rest of the boarders he normally played games with had all gone home to family for the long holiday weekend.

Everyone had a place to go but him. Douglass had insisted he join them on Christmas Day. Thomas had refused, not wanting to interrupt their family time together. They'd agreed to celebrate early over lunch yesterday.

Harriet's gift to him of a new handkerchief and Douglass's of new pencils had felt lavish in comparison to his crudely made mittens for Douglass. They may have been heartfelt, but his first attempt at knitting, under the tutelage of the girls at the boarding house, had left much to be desired. Harriet had crooned over her gift as if the pad of paper had had gold embossed edges.

Judge Pennypacker stood at the end of the pew. "Thomas, my boy."

Thomas moved quickly to greet the man. "Merry Christmas, sir, ma'am." He smiled at the equally round woman he assumed to be the judge's wife.

"Stayed in the city for the holidays, I see. I guess it would have been too far to travel home. I apologize for not asking sooner. Do you have plans for tomorrow?"

Dr. Whitaker looked over the judge's shoulder, his gaze first on Thomas, then on the judge's wife. "That he does. It's a pleasure seeing you out today, Mrs. Pennypacker."

Dr. Whitaker's hand felt heavy on Thomas's shoulder.

"Thank you—" she started to reply, but Dr. Whitaker interrupted.

"My wife has instructed me to have Thomas join us tomorrow. You know I'd never want to disappoint her."

The man's hand remained firm, and Thomas wasn't certain if he should say something or remain the quiet pawn in this unusual match.

The judge lifted his chin. "Well, my boy, it's good to see you're well taken care of. Come, my dear. William, please give our regards to your wife and lovely daughter." He tipped his head to the man, then to Thomas.

The tension between the men decreased with each retreating step of Judge Pennypacker, but unease remained.

"Well, that's settled," Dr. Whitaker said. "Arrive tomorrow at two."

Thomas strained to get words past the tension in his neck. "In the afternoon, sir?"

"We're well past the age of Santa. These days, we wait for the ladies to grace us with their presence before enjoying the festivities. We'll have a late meal, so dress casually and bring your appetite—nothing more." He slapped Thomas on the back, then gripped his upper arm. "Farm work must be in your blood. I'd have expected you to go soft by now."

Thomas was uncertain if the doctor's words were meant as a compliment. He wasn't a wild horse to be tamed and bridled. Was that the expectation? Was he to conform to the mold of Philadelphia society—or perhaps the persona of a medical doctor? Unease filled Thomas as he watched the back of his mentor retreat into the light streaming in from the open doors.

Christmas Day 1871

Snow and gravel crunched under Thomas's boots as he made his way up the long drive to the Whitaker's stately mansion. Light shone from several upstairs rooms, and a curtain moved. He followed the evergreen hedge until the mansions' small stones turned into deep shades of gray flagstone, their haphazard pattern a jumbled mess—like his thoughts. An imposing lion's head stared over his head, not caring who he was or why he was there.

"Lord, help me not make a complete fool of myself." Today, it was more than saying or doing the wrong things. He was meeting the doctor's daughter. Until now, he'd avoided social gatherings not required of students where she might be present. If Joseph could do the difficult, so could he. His heavy hand rapped on the wooden door. He couldn't bring himself to touch the mouth of the lion knocker.

The door creaked, and a sentry figure dressed more for a formal dinner than battle took in the length of him. "Mr. Shankel?" No expression showed on the man's face, but at Thomas's nod, the man let him in, then took his coat. He held the scarf between his finger and thumb, as if it needed a good washing, before handing Thomas a square of cloth to wipe his boots.

The smells of roasting meat and something sweet drew

Thomas's attention down the hall toward the aromas.

"This way, please."

Thomas followed the toy soldier and watched in amazement as the man slid a large door into the wall, revealing a library with floor-to-ceiling windows interspersed with shelves of dark wood—full of hundreds of volumes of leather- and fabric-bound books.

"Thomas. Punctual as always. I like that characteristic in a man. Sit, please. Apéritif?" Dr. Whitaker offered as he gestured toward the leather chairs near the fireplace.

"No, thank you, sir." Thomas wasn't certain what an apéritif was, but since the man held a decanter and glass in hand, he was thankful he'd declined. The clinking of crystal and the roar of the fire sounded like music to his ears, and he soaked in the warmth surrounding him.

"I believe the last time you were in my home you had not yet familiarized yourself with our exceptional city. How are you liking it so far?"

"What I have been able to see is remarkable. The advancement in the East is quite astounding. I saw my first penny-farthing while walking here today. Quite the Christmas gift, though I prefer my horse to riding atop a contraption on two wheels."

Dr. Whitaker's index finger ran across the etching of his flat-bottomed glass as he settled into a leather chair. He gestured toward the other. "Please, make yourself comfortable."

Thomas's feet were as heavy as stone. A lump formed in his throat, and he wondered if Joseph had experienced such nervousness. "You have a lovely library, sir," Thomas managed to say, his stomach quivering. He was too nervous to sit. He steadied himself by holding onto the back of the offered seat before stepping over to the nearest bookcase. Running his hand along a shelf, he breathed in the familiar scent, trying to calm his nerves.

"I believe my daughter has read nearly every book in here, except for my medical journals and perhaps those written in Russian, Greek, or Hebrew. I believe there are one or two from Asia in there somewhere." His hand moved in a dismissive motion.

"Father, Mother says dinner is served."

A jewel of emerald green stood in the doorway, golden strands flowing over her creamy shoulders. He'd recognized her beauty before, but the foyer lights reflecting off her womanly features created an ethereal effect.

Thomas's mouth went dry, and he wondered if his heart was still beating until the increased pressure in his chest confirmed its rapid pulse. Blue eyes shone from beneath her long lashes, their depth pulling him under.

"Ah, yes, Emmaline, allow me to introduce Thomas Shankel," Dr. Whitaker said.

Her focus remained steady as she curtsied.

"Thomas, my daughter, Emmaline. You met at the Medical Student Welcome Celebration in late August, did you not?" Dr. Whitaker asked before draining the last of his drink and setting it on the side table.

"I did not have the pleasure of being formally introduced." Thomas's feet slogged through the tightly woven rug.

His boots threatened to trip him as he moved forward. Remembering decorum, he bowed, taking the beauty in from the floor up, ending at her sly and satisfied smile. Thomas blinked twice. "It's a pleasure to make your acquaintance, Miss Whitaker."

"Emmaline, please. I'm sure we're to be fast friends," she offered.

Light from the window made the gold flecks in her eyes dance, casting a spell Thomas could not break.

Dr. Whitaker offered his arm to the beauty. "Let's not keep your mother waiting. Shall we?"

Thomas avoided looking at the bustle in front of him and focused on the seascape hanging to his right. Evergreen boughs covered the marble top of an ornately carved wooden table on the side wall as they entered the dining area.

Candles lined the table, which would easily seat a dozen or more, but only four place settings graced one end.

Dr. Whitaker pulled out a chair for a stately woman. The deep red of her dress made the silver flecks in her otherwise golden hair shine. "Darling, this is Thomas Shankel, our top student. Thomas, my wife, Eleanor Whitaker."

"It's a pleasure to make your acquaintance, ma'am. Thank you for inviting me to your fine home."

"You are most welcome, Thomas. May I call you Thomas?"

"It would be my honor."

Dr. Whitaker assisted his wife, and Thomas moved quickly to do the same for Emmaline, then took his seat beside her. A gold-rimmed bowl sat atop a scalloped-edged plate. Thomas ran his finger along the blue flowers before picking up his napkin and placing it in his lap.

Extra forks, crystal, and plates swam before his eyes. *Commit. Don't let society's rules deter you,* he reminded himself.

A smartly dressed staff member kept his water glass full. Others brought creamy soup, roasted meat, herbed vegetables, light-as-air rolls that melted in his mouth, and a spicy meat-filled pastry that needed Harriet's secret ingredient. He could not imagine eating another bite and was thankful when a different server removed his dinner plate.

"My compliments to your staff, Mrs. Whitaker, for this exceptional meal." Thomas moved to place his napkin on the table when a server slid a slice of fruitcake in front of him.

Dr. Whitaker lifted his second glass of wine to his lips. "Did you know Europe outlawed fruitcake in the early 1700s?" He didn't wait for Thomas to finish chewing the nut-and-candied-fruit concoction. "They made them so sweet the country deemed them 'decadence incarnate' and considered them morally wrong to eat." The man's arm flung in a grand gesture as if on stage.

"William, don't be telling stories to this young man." Mrs. Whitaker's cheeks flushed slightly.

"Illegal, I tell you. But not this one. Dry as jerky. Another glass of wine to wash this down, Otis." Dr. Whitaker held his glass aloft to the awaiting servant.

Thomas focused on the spiced cake, moving bits around his plate and spearing a soft nut.

"Father, you and Mother have interrogated Thomas all

evening. I've not had a moment to get to know him. Would you permit us to play a game in the library while you two drink your coffee?"

Mrs. Whitaker's expression showed gratitude. "Marvelous idea, darling. Otis, coffee, please." She placed her hand over her husband's when he moved to speak. The motion silenced him.

"Thomas, do you play dominoes?" Emmaline stood.

Thomas followed Emmaline's lead and stood. "It's one of my favorites." He turned to Mrs. Whitaker and bowed. "Thank you again for a lovely meal."

"Our pleasure. You children enjoy yourselves. Your father and I may join you later."

Thomas had not been in the company of a young lady alone, especially one this beautiful. An additional worry crept through his veins until he saw one servant follow them into the library and stand near the door.

This time, Thomas took in the room's entirety. A family portrait hung over the fireplace with a much younger Emmaline. It was a lovely room, but something seemed off. "Where do you place your Christmas tree?" he asked.

"Father doesn't believe in celebrating Christmas." The *clink* of dominoes covering the table filled the room.

Thomas wasn't certain how to respond. "Do you not exchange gifts?"

"Father permitted the illusion of Santa Claus until I was eight, but I knew far before then that it was a made-up holiday."

"But what of the Christ child? The celebration of His birth. Your family attended service yesterday."

She waved her hand dismissively, like he'd seen Dr. Whitaker do many times. "It's not like we're heathens."

Something in her diverted gaze told him there was more to this story.

Emmaline checked the overturned dominoes to ensure they were sufficiently mixed. "Ready? I hope you aren't a sore loser."

This time, her downturned eyes served their intended purpose. He wouldn't go down without a fight, but he wasn't against making a poor tile choice to give her the advantage.

The clicking of marble tiles on glossy wood matched that of the clock over the mantel. Thomas scrutinized and strategized, giving his brain a workout until only one tile remained in front of him and two in front of Emmaline. Unease settled in his gut. He should have let her win. At least her points would be low.

Emmaline played a double, then her last tile. "Game. I win."

He turned his tile over. "You're a formidable player. I challenge you to a rematch."

"I have all night, Mr. Shankel."

"So, we're back to formalities now that you've bested me?"

"By the end of the evening, you'll be calling me Uncle." Emmaline turned the tiles over, and they shuffled them around. His fingers accidentally grazed hers, and she stilled.

"Father says you're in the running for intern at the rate you're going." She glanced toward the door. "Just don't tell him I said so. Is that why you're here? To earn his favor?"

She never looked up from her continued shuffling, then began choosing tiles. Thomas was too stunned to speak for a moment but regained his tongue. "I was not aware I was even in the top ten, and it certainly is not why I'm here." He did not tell her of the awkward interaction he and her father had had yesterday.

A slow smile eased the wariness on her face. "Two out of three. Winner chooses the next game."

Thomas won the second game. The pout on Emmaline's lips did not match the twinkle in her eyes. She was easygoing, with a hint of youthfulness still peeking out of her grown-up exterior, which he did not miss and worked diligently to avoid. His sisters still wore high necklines, mostly to keep the sun off their skin, but Emmaline's emerald green dress with its low, square neckline and band high above her waist made it hard to concentrate.

He recounted his tiles before setting them in order. "What other games do you have for me to choose from when I win?" Thomas didn't look up. He pulled his lips in to keep them from betraying his cool demeanor.

"Oh, I don't think it will be an issue."

She won, but he didn't care. Emmaline clapped her hands and bounced in her seat.

Thomas attempted to move the domino over his knuckles. It clattered to the tabletop. "You won fair and square. It's been some time since I've had such a remarkable opponent."

"I like that term. Perhaps we should play more often." A slight blush covered her cheeks.

Thomas had not courted a girl, but he was not ignorant of subtle hints. Myriad thoughts flew through his mind as they stacked tiles in the metal container. Being unequally yoked with a non-believer would certainly not be God's will. Perhaps they didn't celebrate the holiday for other reasons. Many believed the secular side of Christmas was pagan.

What if Joseph had not said yes? Was Emmaline the missing piece of the puzzle to get him into the crowd needed to succeed? Was this God's response to his commitment to go all the way in answering the call?

Could he reconcile the pull he felt toward Emmaline and her lifestyle with the calling and commitment to finish his medical training and return to Shumard Oak Bend? He was willing to step forward in faith and find out. Especially for Emmaline Whitaker.

Chapter 14

December 30, 1871
Teddy

S unlight glinted off the freshly fallen snow that crunched under Teddy's boots. Tree limbs bowed under the frozen weight. Horses trampled the falling white flakes into brown sludge, their traditional clip-clop more of a slurp-clunk.

Only two more days until the new year. She loved the holiday that meant fresh beginnings and held hope for greater things—new opportunities and friendships—like one with Thomas.

Her lips curved upward, though no one could see them under her scarf. The man was disastrous with knitting needles but could give all the boarders a challenge with games. She'd laughed until her sides hurt at his antics last evening during charades. How he'd thought they'd guess Spain's San Fermín Festival from his gyrations, she'd never know. They had at least gotten the animal correct.

Male friendship wasn't something she'd expected when she'd moved into the boarding house, but even Crocket's incessant storytelling had endeared the man to her. He was lonely, as they all were, and needed to find his footing in the group. As long as he steered clear of politics, his stories were quite interesting.

Light reflected off something shiny and pulled her focus to a shop window. Mannequins behind partially frosted glass sported the latest fashions for spring, the embellishments the only flora showing color amidst the currently muted pallet of whites, browns, and grays of the surrounding landscape, with the occasional green poking through.

One more year of wearing the same dresses, and then she'd add something new to her attire, like the small blue flower print on the child's yellow spring dress. It was oh so much more practical and fun than the layers upon layers of the woman's dress next to it and far less finicky than the white linen and lace next in line.

Did the designers and social setters expect working-class women to wear these styles? Was Teddy relegated to dime store catalog clothes, her siblings' hand-me-downs, or worse yet, the work of her own hands? She may knit, but she'd never mastered the tiny stitches needed to sew.

Each careful step toward the job she did not enjoy reminded her that by this time next year, she should have enough saved for a place of her own. Her spirits lifted at the thought until startling blue eyes with a forever wayward strand of brown hair threatening to cover one of them came to mind.

The blast of heat when she opened the service entrance to *Les Madeleines* matched her cheeks.

Her friend Sam whipped by, using his thumb to point toward the approaching manager. "Stay clear of that one. She woke up on the wrong side of the cage today."

The manager's no-nonsense steps and rigid form turned Teddy's way. "You're early for once. It's not quite eleven-thirty.

Help with the tea trays. Some oaf knocked over two this morning, and they need to be reassembled." The manager's abruptness and sharp tone deflated Teddy's mood.

"Yes, ma'am," Teddy replied. Teddy pulled her lips in, her cheeks hurting at the effort to contain her laugh. "Duly noted," she said to no one as she hung her items in the closet, changed out her shoes, and secured the hair loosened by her knit cap.

Memorized motions from two years of training made restocking the trays quick. Teddy looked at the reservation list and removed one place setting from her table just as she heard the unmistakable voice of Emmaline Whitaker.

The girl's words mingled with the tinkling of piano keys but still overshadowed the music. "I wouldn't have come at all in this dreadful weather, but I would never want to disappoint my friends."

Teddy recognized each girl as they moved to their places at the round table. She busied herself with replacing a poorly pressed and folded napkin. Mousy Adeline assisted Emmaline with her full skirts and bustle before sliding without notice into the seat to the leader's left. Teddy assisted the others with their chairs.

Opal wore another piece of drapery from a decade ago. It was missing a button at the very top, and the girl had done her best to cover it with her thick, dark hair. As long as she kept her chin up, no one should notice.

Caroline, who had chosen a dress the same color as the jam today, settled back in her chair, words already tumbling out. "We've just returned from Boston. Mother said you entertained a certain someone over the holidays."

Louisa turned and gaped, wide-eyed, first at Caroline, then at Emmaline. "Who? Do tell all." Teddy had pegged her correctly. The girl loved gossip, her now-narrowed eyes shooting daggers at Caroline, showing disapproval at not being the first to know.

Caroline opened her mouth to speak, but Emmaline's pointed look had the girl lifting her empty teacup instead. Caroline glared at Teddy as if the infraction was her fault, and Teddy moved quickly to fill the cup.

Emmaline placed a linen napkin in her lap, the signature pink of *Les Madeleines* clashing with the deep purple gown. Teddy moved her direction, finally pouring tea into Emmaline's cup, creating the perfect opportunity for the girl to keep her secret for a moment longer. Had Teddy not cared for keeping the job, she would have blurted the familiar name herself.

"Thomas Shankel," Emmaline admitted. "Father invited him for dinner, but I believe he preferred the after-dinner entertainment more than the exquisite meal."

Opal nearly spilled her tea as she looked up, horror on her face.

Caroline rolled her eyes. "Not that kind of entertainment, you ninny. They played games."

Emmaline's finger tapped in her lap. Teddy pinched her forefinger and thumb into her opposite hand. The sting kept her from telling Caroline to tread lightly. She was stepping on the sleeping dragon's toes.

"We played games—and not just the usual." Emmaline's eyebrows lifted and lowered in quick succession.

Teddy caught the implication even if the others did not. The scone she'd eaten upon arrival sat like a stone in her stomach.

"We lost complete track of time. He's quite the catch. Smart, handsome, and rugged in a way I find wickedly appealing."

"Emmaline." Adeline's whisper pulled Teddy's gaze to the girl.

"Don't be such a prude, Adeline. We did nothing improper, though I entertained the thought."

Giggles filled the air, taking all the oxygen with it. Teddy swallowed the rising bile. The discussion shouldn't affect her. Thomas was not in her future. He bridged the gap between classes. If Emmaline had any say, he'd soon be more a part of her world than the one where he currently lived.

No fingers tapped. No sighs escaped. Emmaline manipulated the conversation, allowing each girl only a few moments to share of their holiday travels, extravagant gifts, and eccentric family members. Teddy noted Emmaline did not mention her Aunt Pauline and wondered if Dr. Whitaker had invited his sister to the gathering.

Louisa wiggled in her seat. "So, did he ask you?"

Emmaline wiped her pursed lips. "Ask me what?" Innocence was not a characteristic she wore well.

"Emmaline Whitaker, you know perfectly well what I'm talking about. You've attended every event this season without a beau on your arm. Not that many haven't tried. Will you be attending the New Year's Eve soirée with Thomas Shankel?" Louisa's tone was terse.

Emmaline flashed a mischievous smile. "Ah, the resident sleuth. Perhaps I should start addressing you as Miss Pinkerton. As for Thomas, well, my dance card remains delightfully open."

Teddy felt like her eyeballs would fall out with the exercise they were getting. It would have been easier to turn her head with the volley.

Caroline lifted her cup in a mock salute, but she could not break the tension building between the two girls. "You've been taking lessons from your aunt."

Emmaline's steely gaze moved from Louisa and settled on Caroline, who broke eye contact and took a sip from the raised cup.

"I'm keeping it a mystery for your own good. None of us should settle. Mother warned me men can keep their secrets for only so long before showing their true colors. Besides, Caroline, unlike Adeline, who's had her sights set on Jimmy Reeves since primary school, you'd have loved and lost six men by this point. I'm merely keeping you from heartache."

Adeline kept her head low, the flush covering her cheeks, making her almost pretty. Louisa attempted to cover a smirk behind the tips of her splayed fingers. Caroline shoved a most unladylike bite into her mouth and chewed wildly.

Teddy could have taken the butter knife and cut through the unease between the girls. It was going to be a long shift.

Saturday evening

Merriweather leaned into Teddy's side, her dining room chair creaking and covering the whispered words. "Whatever's the matter? You've been somber all evening."

Teddy took the girl's hand and squeezed it once. Merriweather did not release the grip yet righted herself. Teddy squeezed again, hoping her thankfulness for Merriweather's concern shone in her eyes. "Later."

Mrs. Jones clinked her fork on her water glass. Voices quieted, and forks stilled. "I received word our blustery weather will continue through the night. With tomorrow being Sunday, I propose we hold service here in the morning." Her cocked head and raised eyebrows reminded Teddy of her mother. There would be no discussion.

Thomas spoke. "A lovely idea, Mrs. Jones."

"I'm glad you think so, Mr. Shankel. You'll give our scripture in the morning. Merriweather will lead us in song."

Merriweather blanched, and Teddy reached over and grabbed the damp, yet cool fingers of her friend and held on tight.

Mrs. Jones tapped the table near Merriweather's plate. "You will do just fine."

"I'll help Miss Merriweather with the music," Mr. Ferret offered.

Teddy looked from the pale face of her friend to Reggie's blushing one, then back to the head of the table. "What a wonderful idea, Mrs. Jones," she added.

The boarding house owner nodded once. "In the same missive, Cook let me know she cannot return this evening. Therefore, I also propose we make do for breakfast, then enjoy a larger than normal Sunday luncheon."

Birdie raised her hand. "I'm happy to help with that, ma'am."

Everyone stared.

"What? Just because I work in a factory doesn't mean I can't cook. I grew up on a farm. I kill 'em, clean 'em, and fry 'em up." Birdie snorted at her joke.

No one joined her.

Mrs. Jones cleared her throat. "Very well. You and I will prepare the meal."

Crocket placed his napkin on the table. "It would be my pleasure to prepare a dessert."

The boarding house mistress allowed her spine to relax. "That leaves Theodora and Josephine with clean-up duty."

Josephine moaned. Cool air rushed under Teddy's feet, and she wondered if David had opened the back door. Surely the boy was not out in the elements.

Mrs. Jones continued, not waiting for Teddy's agreement. "Since Cook is not returning until the weather clears, if you ladies wouldn't mind assisting with the dishes tonight, I thought I'd make hot cocoa for this evening."

Teddy's mouth watered. She couldn't remember the last time she'd had the creamy chocolate drink. Chairs creaked, and dishes clinked as the group assisted with cleanup.

"Thomas, would you men please ensure there is plenty of wood and prepare our evening entertainment?" Mrs. Jones asked.

Teddy pushed her way through the kitchen door. Perhaps she could liven up the after-dinner entertainment like Emmaline had. Whatever that meant.

Soapy water sloshed on Teddy's sleeve. She let the bubbles remain and watched them pop and melt into the fabric. It felt good being in the kitchen. The satisfaction of putting a dirty dish in the scalding water and watching it come out clean was soothing.

Merriweather rinsed and dried as Josephine put the items away. Teddy used her shoulder to bump playfully into her friend. Merriweather returned the gentle shove.

Merriweather's sweet voice added to the noise of the room. "You're feeling better?"

Teddy nodded. She didn't understand her feelings and wasn't ready to discuss them.

"I'm glad you don't have to work tonight. If we play charades, please be my partner. I always feel like such a dunce."

The pleading eyes of the girl made any remaining stress from her day evaporate. "To be honest, I'd like nothing more than to head outside and build a snowman."

"Oh, wouldn't that be delightful? Can we, Mrs. Jones?" Water dripped from the plate Merriweather held as she bounced on her tiptoes.

Mrs. Jones pointed at the pooled water. "Unless you prefer ice skating indoors."

If Teddy didn't know better, she'd say the woman showed a hint of a humorous side.

Merriweather squealed. "Here, I'll go tell the boys." She shoved the plate and towel in Josephine's hands.

Teddy dried her hands and polished the brass faucet, then dried the deep sink. She wiggled her toes in excitement. It had been years since she'd built a snowman.

Merriweather burst through the door. "They said yes, and the sky is so clear the moon will give us plenty of light." Her breathy excitement filled the room.

Mrs. Jones cracked a smile. "You children, run and play. I'll have hot chocolate ready for you when you come in."

Teddy didn't miss the sheen in the woman's eyes, nor the softness around her mouth. "Thank you, Mrs. Jones. Won't you join us?"

The woman shook her head. "My bones are too old for this weather. But I'll pull up a chair by the window. Mind you, remove your shoes before you come back in."

The terseness was back, but it didn't diminish Teddy's excitement as she buttoned her coat.

Birdie beat Josephine to the door. "Last one outside is a rotten egg," she exclaimed loudly enough for all in the house to hear. The door slammed behind them, slowing down Teddy's attempt to get outside before the men.

Crisp air seeped through Teddy's layers, and she stood trying to catch her breath from the biting cold. Teddy prayed the leather of her boots would dry enough for her to wear them on Monday. Dampness clung to her woolen skirt, making her look like the snowman her friends were building. Something hit her shoulder, and she turned to find Merriweather's already-red cheeks turn a deeper shade.

"Oh, Teddy. I'm so sorry." Merriweather stood with a wooden spoon in front of her, not even trying to hide the mock trebuchet.

"Impressive distance. With some planning, you could lob a snowball clear across the front yard. That gives me an idea." Teddy wiped the snow from her jacket and grabbed a handful, reaching deep to find the dense wetness.

Birdie smirked and did the same. "You thinking what I'm thinking?" Birdie squeezed the ball harder.

Josephine and Merriweather joined them. Their full skirts hid their growing stash. Teddy studied her roommates' faces. "Josephine, what are you planning, or should I say scheming?"

Josephine stepped beside the snowman, her back to the men. She drew three circles and a line in the snow, then pointed to each. "Snowman, tree, tree, porch railing. Four shields to their one." She pointed to the bottom-heavy snowman on the other side of the expanse.

Birdie's pile grew quickly. "I won't need shelter. I can hit a moving target at fifty feet. All I need is a solid weapon, and they'll be the ones hiding. The secret is to make them small and compact. Like this." She took one of Merriweather's snowballs and crushed it to half its size.

Josephine's laughter was deep and throaty. Her head cocked to her left, pointing to the three men lifting the last ball and placing it atop the other two. "This is going to be fun. Being the lone girl in a family of four boys has its advantages.

I'm guessing only one of those three knows how to throw."

Merriweather looked up. "Which one?"

Teddy could not hold back her laugh, even if it was at her friend's expense. "Let's strategize. Merriweather, can you throw?"

"Not well."

Her sheepish reply melted Teddy's heart. Had the girl never had a moment's fun? "Then you'll run supply. Birdie and Josephine, I'm certain you're more accurate than I am, so if you aim low and fire in succession, I'll just do my best to keep up. Ready? One, two, three."

"Snowball fight!" Merriweather yelled like an Indian raider.

Thwop. Thwack.

Two well-aimed spots on each side of Crocket's backside had him yelping.

"I've been hit. It's an ambush. Initiate alert status. I repeat, ini—"

Crocket's face registered surprise as another snowball hit his raised arm, making Teddy wish she'd visited the lavatory before heading outside.

Thomas hunkered down behind the base of the men's snowman, its head threatening to topple from its body. "Prepare to meet your maker, ladies." He came out from behind the creature, his arm already in motion. "Take no prisoners, gentlemen. This is war!"

Merriweather squealed and ducked behind the tree closest to the house. Teddy took over Merriweather's job behind their snowman, making and handing snowballs to the two markswomen. Snow flew in all directions, and she laughed so hard she plopped down and held her stomach.

Ding-a-ling. Ding-a-ling.

Teddy looked to the street to see if the fire wagon was coming over the snow-filled street. The noise increased, and the voice of a very stern Mrs. Jones pulled her attention to the porch.

"You'll have all the neighbors thinking there's a brawl going on in my front yard with all that racket. Head in. Your cocoa is ready."

One last snowball careened through the air. Thomas caught it. "You ladies could have shortened the war by a few years."

Birdie threw her empty arms in the air. "That's what I keep saying."

Thomas bowed low before Birdie and Josephine as they made their way up the steps behind the others.

Teddy gathered her snow-laden skirts around her and attempted to stand. An equally encrusted mitten reached down.

"May I be of assistance?"

That ridiculous lock of hair had fallen over his blue eyes.

Teddy tried to stifle her giggles. "Thank you. I'm afraid I'm a bit stuck."

"On three. One, two . . ." Thomas began counting, but Teddy couldn't resist. She let her mittens slip from her hands, and Thomas tumbled backward, tripping over the remaining weapons cache and landing on his backside.

Teddy burst into uncontrollable laughter, then squealed as a snowball hit her knee, spraying wetness across her face. "Oh, it's on now," she sobered, scooping up the snow to retaliate.

Thomas scrambled to his feet. "You do not know whom you're dealing with. Are you sure you want to do battle with the likes of me?"

Teddy scrunched up her face and sighed. She knew the moment he let down his guard. She felt the wooden spoon in her hand and flicked the snow on it into the air. The trajectory was off, and it smacked Thomas in the center of his forehead. She gasped as she watched his stiff body fall backwards.

Teddy scrambled to her knees and crawled to where the prostrate form lay. "Thomas. Oh, Thomas. I am so sorry. Are you hurt?" She touched his shoulder, then moved the remaining snow from around his eyebrows.

"Arrgghh," Thomas yelled and pulled Teddy into the snow beside him.

"Ohhh," she squealed before falling into a fit of laughter.

"I think your mother should have named you David," Thomas said.

"You certainly played the part of Goliath well. Shame on you for acting hurt. You were acting, weren't you?" Teddy turned her head in his direction. Those blue eyes shone with mirth in the moonlight, but he did not respond.

Thomas removed his glove and took her hand in his. "Your fingers must be frozen."

His touch warmed more than her fingers.

Thomas cleared his throat and tilted his chin up. "Would you look at that?"

Teddy followed his gaze. The moonlight showed their mingling breath. Teddy pulled her hand from the warmth of Thomas's and tucked it under her arm. "Beautiful. But if I'm right, there are several pairs of eyes brighter than those stars staring out the parlor window, and I can guarantee one pair is glowing red."

Thomas stood, wiping snow from his legs. He offered his hand and pulled her up with ease. He held her arm until she could unwrap her skirts from her legs. Teddy willed herself to breathe. "I need to gather the . . ." She swept her hand, not remembering the names of the items.

"Let me help." Thomas picked up the tin cups and wooden spoon and replaced the carrot that had been knocked off in the fight.

"Th . . . th . . . thank you." Teddy's teeth chattered, and her body followed.

"Let's get you inside and warmed up." Thomas placed his hand under her elbow.

Warming up was not the problem. Thawing out was more like it.

Chapter 15

New Year's Eve 1871
Thomas

Thomas arose early, dressed, and crept down the stairs. The parlor fire still provided warmth, as if someone had fed it recently. He added wood and placed his Bible on the table between the stuffed chairs. He knew what scripture he would read for this morning's gathering but thought a stout cup of coffee would help him plan his thoughts.

Light shone from under the kitchen door. He pushed it slowly so as not to disturb whoever was inside. Teddy's shoulders rose and fell. Her brown locks rested on her folded arms on the flour-laden table. The smell of yeast bread cooking made his stomach grumble loud enough to wake the sleeping form.

"Oh." Teddy jumped and hit her knee on the table, causing a white cloud to form around her.

"I'm sorry to wake you. I came for a cup of coffee."

"Not to worry. It should be hot still." Teddy covered a yawn.

"Still? How long have you been up?" Thomas poured a cup for himself and lifted the pot in her direction. She shook her head, her loose hair like waves, ready to drown him in their depths.

"It's the curse of working nights. I'm usually finishing up my shift about now. If I drink that coffee, I'll never get to sleep."

"You made bread?"

Teddy stood and stretched her back, hands encircling her slim waist, then peeked in the oven. "I hadn't planned on staying up all night, but the kitchen stayed so cold I couldn't get the yeast to rise. I just put the loaves in a while ago. It should be ready in about ten more minutes." She yawned again.

"You head on up to bed. I'm happy to take them out for you. Just give me a moment to grab my Bible." He watched her body relax.

"Are you sure?" She wiped her hand across her cheek and made the smear of flour worse.

He didn't have the heart to point out the mark. "Absolutely. I'm up anyway. I learned early on that if I wanted to eat something other than jerky or charcoal, I needed to keep a watch on the food cooking at our house. My mother is a horrible cook."

Teddy's yawn mixed with the laughter in her eyes. Thomas wanted to reach out and wipe the flour from her cheek. Instead, he reached for the coffee pot. The heat from the handle warmed his palm even through the dish cloth, reminding him of the briefest moment their hands had entwined last evening. Keeping his hands busy was a good idea, but he'd need to find a mug, or he'd scorch his palm.

"Here." Teddy rose on tip toes and pulled a mug from the cabinet.

He willed his hands not to shake as he poured, then quickly set the pot back on the stove. Steam rose from his cup as he held the warming mug.

Teddy covered another yawn. "Goodness. I believe I'll take you up on that offer, or bread bricks are what we'll have for breakfast, since I'm likely to fall back to sleep. I found a jar of apple butter and figured it would be enough to tide everyone over until lunch."

Thomas's stomach growled again, and his hand instinctively covered it.

"Well, except maybe you. You worked up an appetite with all that attacking last night."

He loved how her eyes sparkled when she teased him. "Attacking? More like self-preservation. You ladies didn't give fair warning, and you single-handedly slayed Goliath." He pointed to his forehead, then placed his unoccupied hand on his hip, trying to look stern.

She slapped his elbow as she grabbed the towel and wiped her hands. "All's fair in love and snowball fights."

She diverted her gaze, but Thomas glimpsed a pretty pink covering Teddy's cheeks. "Quoting John Lyly at this hour? Impressive. There is no limit to what one deems necessary to achieve one's ends and preserve one's reputation."

Her dark circles made her eyes shine even more. This time, the movement in his belly wasn't from hunger. This girl did something to his insides. She reached toward him, and he froze, his cup halfway to his mouth.

"Wash rag." She pointed behind him.

He was an idiot. "Right. I'll let you finish here, and I'll grab my Bible."

He set his cup down, not trusting himself to walk with it. The temperature in the parlor was rising like his own. He poked at the fire, moving a piece of wood farther back, then replaced the screen. The leather of his Bible was warm to the touch, and he held it to his chest.

"Help me remain focused, Father. I have no time for a woman, and Teddy has been clear she wants to buy a home and settle here while I want to return west. Thank you for her friendship. Help me keep it that way."

Streaks of flour and flecks of dough mingled with brown in her hair, now up in a mess of a bun on top of her head. The countertops and table were clean, and utensils sat in the sink. Teddy turned the water on and filled a pot to boil water for washing.

"I'll get those and take the bread out. You head on up to bed."

She released a deep sigh. "Thank you. There's butter on the table to melt on top after you take it out. Now to see if I can get a few hours of beauty sleep while my roommates are getting ready."

All he could do was nod. She didn't need sleep to do that. She was already beautiful.

Thomas closed his eyes as Reggie's harmonica expelled a deep, haunting sound while Merriweather sang the words of "Jesus, Lover of My Soul."

Merriweather's clear soprano was crisp compared to the flowing movement of the music. Thomas watched as Reggie embellished the sound with each movement of his cupped hand.

> *Plenteous grace with thee is found,*
> *grace to cover all my sin;*
> *let the healing streams abound;*
> *make and keep me pure within.* (Charles Wesley)

The music stopped. The crackle of the fire and the rustling of taffeta as Mrs. Jones wiped her nose were the only sounds. Thomas's throat was thick with emotion. He did not know the spiritual state of the souls in this room, but the song spoke to him. *Make and keep me pure within, Father*, he prayed.

When he lifted his head, expectancy filled most of the faces in the room. He lifted his Bible and placed it on his trembling knees. "Tomorrow is the start of a new year. It seems appropriate to read from Isaiah, chapter forty-three, verses eighteen and nineteen. 'Remember ye not the former things, neither consider the things of old. Behold, I will do a new thing; now it shall spring forth; shall ye not know it? I will even make a way in the wilderness, and rivers in the desert.'"

Thomas looked at each face in the room. Birdie already had the glassy-eyed stare of boredom. Josephina picked at her skirts. Only Teddy remained focused on her Bible, her finger tracing over the words. Thomas wondered how the pages of her Bible remained intact. Cracked leather peeked out from the edges of Teddy's skirt. Water stains marked the Bible's golden-painted foreedge, creating a unique pattern.

He ran a finger under the edge of his scratchy sweater. If he was going to keep the group's attention, he would need to move forward with enthusiasm. He marked his spot and closed his Bible, garnering the attention of all.

"I'm not a preacher," Thomas started.

"Amen," one girl muttered.

Thomas chuckled. "Amen is right. I've been called to save people another way."

Crocket chortled. "Well played, young man."

"Instead of a sermon, I'd like to tell you a story."

Birdie's shoulders visibly relaxed, and Merriweather brightened as she clasped her hands together.

"When I was a boy of four, my family traveled from South Carolina and headed west. I wasn't old enough to understand the reasons, but I trusted my father. He and my mother left behind far more than I did at my young age.

"I won't bore you with details of our travels, but all along the journey, I witnessed small instances of what I now call God-incidences. Some may say the stars aligned, the heavens smiled upon us, or even luck was on our side . . ." He had their attention and offered a quick prayer for succinct words. "But I knew it was God."

Birdie looked skeptical, but Merriweather scootched even farther onto the edge of her seat. Thomas dare not look at Teddy, or he'd lose his train of thought.

"We met a woman I named Grammie, and we became instant family. When I turned six, Grammie introduced me to Jesus. Technically, she'd shown him to me through her life every day up to that point, but on Christmas Day, she explained that this Jesus of the Bible, God's son, was a real man who came to take away the sins of the world. To wash away all my wrongdoings and cleanse me of all my sins.

"These verses in Isaiah from the Old Testament are that gospel story. We do not have to live in our past failures. Our brokenness, defeat, and pain no longer define who we are, condemn us, or hold power over us when we follow Christ. When the Spirit of God lives in us, He transforms us into a new creation."

Thomas swallowed the lump in his throat and brought his volume down. "This is the heart of the gospel. When you surrender your heart to Christ, the old you is washed clean, and a new you steps into a new beginning. Today is the last day of 1871. None of us know what the new year holds, but I pray you will allow God to be a part of a new start for you."

The crinkle of Mrs. Jones's sleeve pulled Thomas's gaze her way. Her red-rimmed eyes brimmed with tears. She dabbed at her nose. "Thank you, Thomas. You may not have been called to preach, but you certainly could do the job should God change His mind."

Reggie lifted the harmonica to his mouth. "Amazing Grace" poured from his soul through the mouthpiece. Teddy hummed, the rich sound a melodious harmony to that of the harmonica. She added words, but no one else sang. Thomas wasn't certain Teddy realized it was her voice alone filling the room. Merriweather joined in the second verse, her light soprano harmonizing. Crocket added a third layer before everyone else joined in.

It was a heavenly choir. Long after the song's last word,

the echoes of their voices filled Thomas's mind.

"Mr. Shankel, would you lead us in a closing prayer?" Mrs. Jones requested.

"It would be my honor. Lord, we praise You for being a God of new beginnings. We thank You for bringing us this far and trust You with our future. May we honor You in all we say and do. Amen."

Crocket slapped his knees. "Fine sermon. Best I've heard in a month of Sundays. Reggie, my friend. Wherever did you become master of the mouthpiece? Exceptional. And two harmonicas. I didn't realize they could be so different."

Reggie sat up taller and gave a quick glance at Merriweather. "Thank you. This diatonic was my first and given to me by Mr. Hohner himself during the war. The Hohner mouthpiece is American made, but I bought this German Seydel Classic Low when the war ended. It fit the more melancholy sounds of my mood." He relaxed his posture. A faint smile touched his lips as he dipped his head.

Merriweather's hand moved to her heart. Her voice was breathy. "Your sorrow after the war has brought joy. Your playing quite touched me."

Birdie stood. "That's my cue to start our afternoon meal. If you'll excuse me." The other women followed.

Crocket stood and peered out the window. "Quite the little family we have here."

Thomas detected emotion in the man's voice. "We are fortunate."

Reggie cleaned his harmonicas and put them in a

wooden box, then focused his attention on Thomas. "I believe you mentioned something about how it wasn't luck but a God —what did you call it?"

"God-incidence. And you're right. It's no coincidence we are all here. At this specific time. I can't imagine why, but perhaps the new year will shed light on that topic."

Reggie moved to the other window and pushed the curtain aside. "Speaking of light, would you look at that sun. With this cold weather and the cloudless skies, this snow won't be melting anytime soon. I doubt even the roads will be passable for a few days."

Crocket used his jacket sleeve to remove the haze from his breath. "Well, someone's braving the weather and blazing a path on a sleigh. Looks like he's stopping here." Crocket reached and opened the door before the man knocked.

"Message for a Mr. Thomas Shankel. I'm to wait for a reply."

Thomas's stomach quaked. Surely it wasn't a telegraph bringing bad news from home or Douglass or Harriet in need of him. Cold air rushed in, threatening to freeze him where he stood in the parlor entrance. He committed to do whatever was needed.

Crocket played host and closed the door. "Thank you, my man. Come in, and warm yourself. You must be frozen through. Might we offer you a cup of coffee?"

Thomas could see the man shivering from where he stood.

"Thank you kindly." He said to Thomas, "Are you Mr. Shankel?"

Thomas felt he was trudging through knee-deep snow. "I am." He reached for the cream envelope. A stamped wax seal with an embellished *W* sealed the paper. His nerves calmed. "Thank you. Excuse me while I read this and compose my reply."

Thomas moved to the now-empty parlor and stood at the window. Snow sparkled in the midmorning sunlight. One snowman leaned slightly, its nose askew from a direct hit by a snowball still lodged near the carrot. Footprints dotted the lawn, creating a haphazard pattern. A smile crept over Thomas's face. This may not be home, but these were his people. He fit here.

Thomas studied the flowing black script on the envelope that read, *Mr. Thomas Trexler Shankel.*

The paper crinkled as he opened the seal. The crisp linen paper, its edges frayed, felt stiff in his fingers. The same handwriting filled the page.

Thomas,

We request the honor of your company at this evening's grand New Year's Eve soiree as our daughter's special guest for her seventeenth birthday.

A driver will pick you up at seven o'clock.

Sincerely,

William T. Whitaker

The paper created a breeze as he opened and closed the note. The words may have said request, but the obvious message made his chest tighten. New Year's Eve and birthday. Perhaps Miss Whitaker's date could not attend because of snow or sickness.

Thomas felt a pang of awareness as he realized he hadn't been included in the earlier invitation. This sudden request could very well be a trial orchestrated by Dr. Whitaker to assess Thomas's dedication to assimilating into Philadelphia's elite circles. If this was a God-incident, he would prove himself worthy and inch closer to clinching the sought-after internship.

Now that his legs would carry him, Thomas headed toward his room. A quick glance let him know Crocket had things well in hand. His dramatic flair for storytelling kept the young man occupied, though the messenger seemed to only care for the steaming drink. The pleading eyes of the messenger met Thomas's.

"Let me pen my reply, and I'll return shortly." He lifted the note to the men and lumbered up the steps.

The desk chair creaked as he sat and placed his head in both hands. He'd looked forward to a night of games with his friends. If this was a birthday celebration, Miss Whitaker would have other friends in attendance. Why did she require his presence?

Her birthday. He'd need a gift. No stores were open on a Sunday, which meant he would need to be creative. Beside him sat his Christmas gift, *At the Back of the North Wind*. He'd read it twice, but it still looked new. "It is better to give than receive, right, Lord?"

Thomas pulled a pencil from his drawer and wrote an affirmative reply before he could change his mind.

Chapter 16

New Year's Eve 1871
Whitaker Home
Thomas

Thomas noted the lack of conveyances outside the Whitaker home. "Thank you, sir," he said to the driver as the man opened the door to the enclosed carriage. "Did I misunderstand the invitation? I thought this was . . ." He checked his pocket for the invitation with growing uncertainty.

"Cancelled due to inclement weather, sir."

Thomas stared at the man, who refused to make eye contact, then redirected his gaze to the now-open front door.

"Good evening, sir." The familiar toy soldier butler ushered Thomas into the home, taking his outerwear.

The coldness from the stone under Thomas's feet crept up his body. He'd expected hordes of people, but the empty foyer felt as cold as his limbs. Silence squeezed in on him. He tucked the wrapped package under his arm and awaited instructions. Footsteps overhead pulled his attention to the staircase. Emmaline's full golden skirts flowed down the steps like a shimmering waterfall in her descent.

Her ungloved hand hovered over the dark wood. Light

from the chandelier reflected off her buffed nails. Confidence flowed from her posture, making Thomas question his sanity in accepting the invitation. "Good evening, Miss Whitaker." His stiff words mimicked the butler's.

"Thomas, I thought we were past such formalities. Emmaline, please." She offered her hand.

He had no right to take it, no claim, no matter the thrill he felt at her touch. Her beauty and charm played tug-of-war with his resolve. He offered his arm. Her warmth emanated through his wool suit coat—or was that his own body heat reaching for connection with her fingertips?

"Father and Mother are indisposed. Care to lose another game of dominoes?" She leaned into him.

He took a step to provide distance and broke his resolve not to allow her gaze to pull him further under her spell. Her wink nearly made him stumble over the smooth marble tile. "It's your birthday. I suppose I should give you a chance to redeem yourself."

Her giggle was airy, like the ashes of the crackling fire warming the library.

Thomas moved them toward the leather chairs instead of the game table. "I'm sorry you had to cancel your party."

One creamy shoulder lifted her golden locks. "Mother nearly had the vapors when Father canceled. I'm glad you accepted my invitation."

Her invitation? "Let's sit for a moment." He needed to slow his beating heart.

A servant rounded the corner and stood sentry just inside

the library doors.

"First, your present." Thomas assisted her into the leather chair that nearly swallowed her slight frame.

"Oh, I adore presents. How very thoughtful." Emmaline clasped her hands together before opening them to receive the offering.

Thomas leaned back into the opposite seat, crossing his legs, and watched her. Gone was the proper young woman. In her place was a sparkling-eyed girl. Emmaline tore at the butcher block paper, and Thomas held back his mirth at the scene.

"Oh!" She turned the book over and back, running her fingertips across the edges.

Opening the front cover, she traced the words he'd written. He pulled in his toes, feeling the tension move up his calves. His stomach lurched, and he rubbed his finger and thumb over his clean-shaven jaw, pulling on his chin. He repeated the motion, then stilled when she lifted her shimmering eyes.

Emmaline placed her palm over his written words. "I adore George MacDonald's writing. Did you know he published this in installments in *Good Words for the Young*? I've read them all and had heard he'd published the serialized works as a book."

Thomas clasped his hands to keep from fidgeting. She mesmerized him with her loveliness and how she morphed from seductress to child to friend in mere breaths. Breaths that would not come out of his constricted throat. He stared at Emmaline's fingers, still tracing his chicken scratch as if reading braille.

"Thank you, Thomas. I appreciate the happy birthday sentiments. It's a very thoughtful gift."

"What gift?" Dr. Whitaker strode their way.

Thomas jumped to his feet. "Good evening, sir."

"Thomas, are you spoiling my daughter already?" Dr. Whitaker raised his eyebrows at Thomas, then turned and kissed his daughter on the top of her head, where soft yellow curls flowed down her back and over her shoulders.

She lifted the book in both hands. "*At the Back of the North Wind*, Father. The book I'd hoped to get for Christmas." She glared at the man as if the oversight was his fault.

Dr. Whitaker's boisterous laugh and hearty pat on Thomas's shoulder gave Thomas a moment to pull in a deep breath without anyone noticing.

"Fine choice, son. A man who knows the way to a woman's heart will reap all kinds of rewards." The hand tightened, then released.

Thomas blanched, working to swallow the dryness in his mouth. Something felt off. He looked to Emmaline for clues. Her chin dipped, and a single dimple formed with her coquettish smile. The clinking of glasses pulled his gaze across the room.

Dr. Whitaker lifted a highball glass and decanter. "Care for a drink?"

"No, thank you, sir," Thomas forced out. His stomach twisted, and his ears clogged. Emmaline's words sounded far away, and Thomas worked to grasp their meaning.

"Are you the boy?"

"The boy?" he squeaked.

Her giggle sounded like bubbles coming up from the deep.

"Diamond. The sweet little boy in the story who makes joy everywhere he goes."

Even though Thomas had read the story several times, he rifled through the recesses of his mind for an answer.

Dr. Whitaker lifted a glass to his lips. "Sounds like a children's story."

Emmaline turned in her chair. "Diamond fights despair and gloom and brings peace to his family. It's an adventure, father."

"Mm-hmm."

Thomas watched the exchange.

Emmaline closed the book and brought it to her chest. "One night, when Diamond is trying to sleep, the wind constantly comes through a hole in the wall and keeps him awake. He repeatedly plugs the hole but realizes he's keeping the North Wind from seeing through her window."

"Window? What is this woman doing in his bedroom?" Dr. Whitaker's tone held seriousness, but his eyes gave away his teasing.

"Father. Really. Diamond befriends North Wind, and she lets him fly with her, taking him on wondrous adventures."

"Like I said, children's book. Besides, Thomas here wouldn't dare entertain thoughts of another woman."

Thomas squeezed the back of his chair, the unease from earlier getting stronger. "Classic literature, sir. It holds many spiritual truths."

Dr. Whitaker downed the remainder of his drink, his expression and his tone going flat. "Your mother said dinner will be ready in ten minutes. I'll leave you two to your fantasies."

Thomas reclaimed his seat when the man left. "I see more sides of your father here than at school."

Emmaline placed the book in her lap and ran her fingers over the embossed wording. "He's more North Wind than Diamond. Sometimes gentle, other times harsh, but don't let him bother you."

Thomas thought of North Wind's words, "Sometimes they call me Bad Fortune, sometimes Evil Chance, sometimes Ruin," and wondered when fantasy and reality might collide. Emmaline's lyrical voice pulled him from his pondering.

"Thank you for your thoughtfulness."

Thomas leaned back, giving Emmaline his full attention. "You're most welcome. You read the weekly installments?"

"Oh, yes. What a treat it will be to read them in book format. What spiritual truths do you find in this story?" Emmaline remained at the edge of her seat, her perfect posture leaning in as if she were genuinely interested.

"Simply stated, suffering is a part of life that God uses."

"I hadn't considered that, but I see your point. Like when Diamond journeys to the back of the North Wind. Everything's perfect, but when he returns, he finds hardship. Yet, his unwavering joy and desire to help others shine brightly."

Thomas soaked in Emmaline's words. He had not seen this deeper side of her personality, which was more like Teddy's.

Emmaline ran her long fingers over the embossed writing on the cover. "I have to be honest and say I read it for pleasure— a story to be enjoyed. I didn't really think about the underlying meaning. What other spiritual truths did you uncover?"

Thomas liked this side of Emmaline over the pretentious, privileged daughter he'd noted when with her friends. "Death. It would take all night to cover that subject, but it seems we only have mere moments before the meal."

Emmaline pulled the book back to her chest. "George MacDonald is one of my favorites, but he can be quite wordy. If we're to discuss death, I prefer Emily Dickinson. She has a marvelous way of capturing the feelings but in far fewer words. 'That it will never come again is what makes life so sweet.'" Emmaline's sigh mimicked that of a gentle wind.

The servant cleared his throat. "Dinner is served."

Thomas stood, offering Emmaline his arm. "May I?" he asked.

She placed the gift in the chair on top of the torn wrapping. "After dinner, I'll be much too full to discuss such boring and profound subjects as death, but I'm confident in my ability to emerge victorious in a game of dominoes."

Thomas chuckled, a glimmer of playful challenge in his

voice. "Ah, no talk of death, only defeat. I believe we shall put your confidence to the test."

Emmaline placed her last tile. "I win."

Thomas leaned back and patted his overly full midsection. "Well played. It looks like I've underestimated you once again. That amazing meal must have slowed my brain." He'd watched her every move all evening. No one had mentioned missing guests or ruined plans because of the weather.

Emmaline turned her tiles facedown. "You give a worthwhile challenge. As for dinner, I asked for all my favorites since it is my special day."

Thomas put his thumb and finger on his chin. "My favorite was the dessert. I'm guessing it was almond cake?"

"You are correct. Venture a guess at the filling?"

"No seeds. The tangy flavor has me confused, but I'll guess raspberry."

"Close. Cranberry. Icing?"

"Lemon buttercream."

"Impressive." Emmaline cocked her head.

Thomas leaned back in his chair, a smirk tugging at the corner of his lips. "My hidden talents are many."

Emmaline's eyes sparkled with intrigue and a hint of danger. She leaned forward, her playful demeanor evident. "Sounds like a challenge I'm more than willing to accept." Emmaline trailed her fingers across the table, stopping just shy of Thomas's fingertips. "Care to play a different game?" Her voice dropped to a deeper tone.

Thomas quickly retracted his hand and ran it through his hair, raking his fingernails into his scalp while working to slow his racing heart. "As tempting as that sounds, I believe I'll stick to safer ground for now. My ego can only lose so many times in one evening."

Emmaline's lips curved into a teasing pout. "But it's my birthday."

He felt a prick in his spirit, and alarm bells sounded all manner of warning in his mind. His chair nearly toppled as he stood. "Emmaline. Miss Whitaker." His eyes darted around the room and landed on a piece of wrapping paper on the floor. "Presents. For your birthday. What did you receive?"

Emmaline sighed and shrugged nonchalantly. "Father isn't big on presents. He says he spoils me every day of the year, so he doesn't do much on birthdays and holidays. But this year, he got me exactly what I asked for." Her voice drew him in even as her hands smoothed her dress as she stood.

Thomas felt lost at sea, and Emmaline was a siren. *Help me, Lord.* If he thought he didn't understand the rules of high society, he was even more lost in understanding the underlying meanings of this woman's words.

"Who won?" Dr. Whitaker, his wife on his arm, entered.

Relief washed over Thomas, only to see a playful

exchange between the father and his daughter.

"I did, Father. To the victor belongs the spoils." Emmaline snaked her hand into the crook of Thomas's bent arm.

"Then you got your birthday wish." Dr. Whitaker winked at Thomas, then bent and kissed his daughter's cheek.

Frustration coursed through Thomas's veins. It was as if he were playing a game but didn't know the rules. Had he missed something? He put his free hand in his pocket and found the coin. He understood Jimmy's need for it now more than ever.

"Your mother has agreed to grace us with her music. Let's retire to the parlor." Dr. Whitaker gestured to the open door.

Thomas felt Emmaline's light tug and complied. He feared he might step on her skirt and sidestepped to give their girth more room.

"Practicing your dance moves so soon?" Emmaline whispered.

"Dance?"

"I'm hoping it's one of your hidden talents."

Dancing. His jacket felt overly warm. They passed a grandfather clock as it chimed the hour. Nine. Mrs. Jones locked the boarding house doors at ten. Where had the time gone? He was at the mercy of his hosts, and even though he had a key, he needed to get back.

The room they entered was bright, with ornate gold fixtures gracing the walls and covered in a large floral pattern of various shades of pink and green. The largest piano Thomas had ever seen sat open before floor-to-ceiling draperies of deep rose. Wind whistled through the covered windows, making the fabric look as if it were breathing—or the North Wind was moving about.

The piano bench creaked under Mrs. Whitaker's lithe frame. Emmaline's beauty and poise obviously came from this woman. Her fingers ran over the upper keys, making a tinkling sound.

"Mother, play something lively," Emmaline said.

Dr. Whitaker raised a glass. "The tango is all the rage."

Thomas blanched. "I'm afraid I'm not much of a dancer, sir."

"Then perhaps 'Haste to the Wedding' might be a better choice."

Emmaline giggled. "Father, there aren't enough of us for that dance."

"It only takes two, darling." The man downed his drink, setting the crystal with a bang on the tabletop nearby. "Come, let's give the boy a lesson in dancing. He seems a tad wet behind the ears."

Mrs. Whitaker's fingers deftly crossed the keys as the father twirled his daughter about the room. Thomas took two steps back, listening to Emmaline's childish laughter as they passed. Dr. Whitaker ceased moving, and Emmaline twirled and paraded around him as if trying to capture his attention.

"Ready to take my place?" the doctor asked.

Emmaline never missed a beat. She sashayed and began

what looked like an animal mating dance, her arms akimbo as she moved forward, back, then around Thomas. She took his hand in hers and moved his other to her waist, then began leading them around the room. Her hair swayed as they twirled.

Thomas recognized the movements of what they called a polka back home and quickly took over, causing Emmaline's smile to broaden. Her eyes stayed on him, allowing him complete control.

The music stopped, and he bowed to his partner. His heart beat wildly—and not only from exertion.

Dr. Whitaker clapped. "You make a marvelous couple."

Mrs. Whitaker moved to her daughter's side. "Emmaline, dearest. You've taken on a sheen. Let's leave these men to their discussions while we powder our noses."

Thomas felt the day of reckoning had come. He had a sneaking suspicion of what was going on, but he'd do just about anything for clarity.

"Drink?"

Except that. "Water or tea would be lovely. Thank you."

Dr. Whitaker lifted a finger, and a servant left the room. "Sit." He patted the cushioned seat beside him.

"Thank you for a lovely evening, sir. I'll need to head back to the boarding house soon. Strict rules and all." Thomas did his best to make his words light.

"Then I'll get right to the point. Do you want the internship position?"

"Of course. I mean, yes, sir. Very much so."

"I've been watching you. You have what it takes to become one of Philadelphia's finest surgeons. The new aim of medical education is to produce problem solvers and critical thinkers who know how to figure out and evaluate information for themselves. You already possess these characteristics. Add to that your work ethic, academic success, and desire to succeed, and you could go far. The only issue is a bit more convoluted." The doctor tapped his finger on his lips as if in deep thought.

"Thank you, sir. I always strive to do my best with the Lord's help." Thomas focused on the positive.

The man's demeanor changed to something dark.

"Medicine is a science, Thomas. We do not mix the supernatural with the scientific."

Thomas would not put his belief in Jesus Christ in the realm of the supernatural as if it were some mystical pagan religion but kept his mouth clamped.

"No, Thomas, the issue is much more complex. There are standards, societal expectations, to achieving the elevated position you seek."

Thomas felt his world crumbling. It was as Jimmy had said. If he couldn't break into Philadelphia's elite, he would never be afforded the opportunities he desired.

"But I believe I have a solution of sorts." Dr. Whitaker stood and poured himself another drink.

Thomas wiped his sweating palms on his trousers. "I'm listening." The servant handed him a drink, and he downed the cool, clear liquid before Dr. Whitaker turned around. He returned the glass, afraid he would drop it in his nervousness.

Dr. Whitaker's deliberate and controlled movements set the mood as he settled back into the chair. "It appears my daughter has taken a fancy to you. Of course, I did my homework well before the school approved your application. Although your family has an unusual breeding, your family is of proper standing."

Thomas's ears began ringing, and he ground his molars back and forth over each other. Thoughts of arranged marriages and dowries flitted through his mind. This man was not suggesting . . .

"Should you consider an alliance of sorts, we could make arrangements and adaptations." Dr. Whitaker ran his finger around the top of the glass before taking a drink.

Alliance? Arrangements? Adaptations? Was this a business proposition, and if so, were they equal partners, or was he a pawn?

The clock struck nine thirty.

"I'll give you some time to think it over, but I expect an answer when you return to school on Tuesday. If you're not interested, I'm sure Addison Blakeney would jump at the chance."

Surely the man would not give that pompous socialite the internship simply because of his bloodline and connections.

"Do you understand what I'm offering, Thomas?"

"I believe so, sir." He wasn't certain at all, but he wasn't about to ask for clarity since the servant was holding out Thomas's jacket to him. Thomas stood like a puppet and allowed the man to assist him in putting it on.

"I'll give the ladies your regards. Good night, son."

The man's final word hung in the air. Thomas's methodical movements carried him into the bitter wind and the stuffy confines of the carriage. The weight of the evening pressed in on him like the four walls of the moving conveyance.

"Father, what am I to do?" Thomas heard no reply and felt no peace. He raked his fingers through his damp hair, pulling on the ends until his scalp ached. "Think, Thomas."

The proposition of an alliance could mean many things. Business, courtship, marriage? They all seemed absurd. He desired to acquire the internship position on merit alone. Jimmy's words rang through his mind. Ability alone would not suffice.

"He doesn't even like me." Hair fell over Thomas's eye as he leaned his forearms on his knees. "Why would he want me as family?" A dip in the road jostled Thomas, and he grabbed the velvet cushioned seat. Perhaps this was only a business proposition. Playing the part of Emmaline's beau might provide Thomas with access to the social circles he needed to succeed and allow Dr. Whitaker the freedom to offer him the position.

But could he do it? Could he be a part of Emmaline's world and play the role of her suitor? Was she in on this plan? It raised the question as to whether the agreement was founded on attraction and the potential for a happy marriage or simply a strategic move on Dr. Whitaker's part. Thomas wasn't even certain how he felt about Emmaline other than the way she made his heart race.

He let his head rest against the back wall and looked at the dark ceiling. Had Emmaline meant he was the gift she'd wished for?

What was Dr. Whitaker to gain from this? And what was Thomas to lose?

Chapter 17

New Year's Day 1872
Boarding House
Teddy

T eddy covered her head, hoping to block out the noise around her. All she wanted was to sleep on this rare day when she didn't have to work either job.

As her roommates' even breaths had filled the room last night, Teddy had found herself wrestling with thoughts of Thomas spending New Year's Eve with Emmaline Whitaker. She'd spent hours trying to convince herself he couldn't be as wonderful as she thought. Yet, despite her efforts, his image persisted in her mind, weaving through her thoughts like a stubborn vine refusing to be pruned.

Now, as she finally succumbed to exhaustion, all she heard was Merriweather sounding like a chirping bird announcing the morning, a harsh reminder of the inner turmoil she couldn't escape.

"I haven't had so much fun since, well, I don't even know," Merriweather said. "Mother never let me play in the snow. She was fearful I'd catch a cold."

Teddy both felt and heard Josephine drop from the top bunk.

"All you did was hide. Birdie and I were warriors out there."

A herd of elephants crushing a village was quieter than these women. Teddy threw her arms over the pillow covering her head. Muffled giggles sounded before fingers attacked her from all sides.

"Stop," Teddy yelled. "I'll wet the bed." Laughter filled the room, and Teddy joined in.

Birdie plopped down, trapping Teddy's feet under the blanket. "About time you got up. We're going to ask Mrs. Jones if we can bake cookies today. Join us?"

Teddy pushed and pulled, finally extricating herself from her entrapment. "I'm afraid it's laundry day for me."

Merriweather gasped. "But Teddy, it's freezing outside, and your hands are already chapped and raw."

Teddy looked down at her red hands. "Even so, I work the next seven days straight, and today is the only opportunity I'll have."

Birdie bumped her with her elbow. "If David isn't here to help with the wash bin, let me know, and I'll help you carry it."

"Thank you, Birdie." Teddy wiped at the crust in the corners of her eyes and covered a yawn.

Birdie offered a smile and pushed off the bed. "Let's go, girls. This one needs a few more hours of beauty rest."

Teddy may need rest, but she needed the facilities more. When she returned to the quiet room, her Bible called to her.

"Good morning, Lord." She held the Bible tight as she climbed into the still-warm bed and wrapped the blankets around her legs. "What do You have for me today?"

She opened her Bible and lifted the ribbon holding her place. She closed her eyes and leaned against the pillow propped up behind her. "Lord, help me look past the words on the page. Invade my spirit, so I hear Your voice. Speak to me, and help me to have faith to trust in You and face whatever comes my way."

Teddy didn't offer an amen. Her eyes closed as she hummed, allowing the words to penetrate her mind.

My faith looks up to Thee,
Thou Lamb of Calvary,
Savior divine!
Now hear me while I pray,
take all my guilt away;
O let me from this day,
be wholly Thine. (Ray Palmer, "My Faith Looks Up to Thee")

Teddy woke to the smell of something sweet contrasting with something gamey. She wiped at her mouth, thankful no one saw the wetness she felt, then moved her hand to rub her neck.

"My spirit is willing, but my body is weak. I'm sorry, Lord." Goosebumps rose as the room's cool air covered her body. Teddy allowed herself to be uncomfortable and sat in the desk chair. She would have devotions even if it meant washing clothes until after dark.

One chair was empty at the table for the evening meal. Teddy rubbed the freshly applied beeswax on her rough hands, a futile attempt to distract herself from the disappointment gnawing at her. Just as she struggled with the roughness of her skin, she also grappled with the absence of Thomas, the void at the table mirroring the hollow ache in her heart.

"He's better off with Emmaline," she murmured under her breath. "I need to focus on my goals and being independent, not get sidetracked with a man who doesn't plan to stay in Philadelphia."

Josephine leaned in, her voice gentle yet firm. "He left early and hasn't returned. He was in work clothes if that helps."

Teddy raised an eyebrow. "Helps?"

"To wipe that forlorn look off your face and to assist in untangling whatever thoughts you're wrestling with," Josephine replied, her tone a mix of understanding and concern.

"I have no idea what you are referring to." Teddy snapped her napkin up and placed it on her lap.

"Right." Josephine chuckled.

The two men in the room stood as Mrs. Jones entered with a platter of meat. Teddy noted the color in Reggie's cheeks and followed the direction of his gaze. Merriweather blushed and looked down. Teddy fidgeted with her napkin throughout the prayer. It would be nice to have someone look at her that way. Not just anyone, but a specific someone. She shook her head. It was for the best that Thomas was with Emmaline now. Teddy would be able to focus on her goals and aspirations rather than succumb to ridiculous thoughts of the man.

Merriweather passed the beets, her voice more confident than usual. "Since we are short a player tonight, we should team up in groups of two."

Crocket placed a large scoop of potatoes on his plate. "Depends on the game. Without Thomas, Reggie and I are sure to lose every round."

Merriweather sat up straighter. "We can even out the odds, or odd out the—anyway, we can make it more equitable if we change up partners." She looked directly at Reggie.

Teddy sighed. She'd take one for the team. Neither Birdie nor Josephine would team up with Crocket. She forced a smile. "I think that's a marvelous idea, Merriweather. Why don't you and Reggie be on one team? Crocket and I can be on a team, and Birdie and Josephine can pair up."

Josephine's thank you came out surprisingly quiet.

Reggie placed his fork on his plate. "I'd be honored to be your partner, Miss Merriweather."

Mrs. Jones lifted her glass. "It sounds like you have a fun evening planned. Thank you, ladies, for making cookies and cleaning up your mess. Gentlemen, before games, would you consider assisting in the evening meal cleanup?"

"We can all help," Merriweather chirped.

"Speak for—" Josephine started, then went silent when Teddy kicked her under the table. Josephine cleared her throat. "Speaking of cookies, thank you for providing the ingredients,

Mrs. Jones."

Teddy moved her head in slow motion. Who was this girl beside her? A whisper and a compliment in one meal?

Cold air rushed in, and Teddy pulled her feet under her skirt.

Thomas appeared in the entryway. "Sorry I'm late, Mrs. Jones. Let me wash and change, and I'll be right down."

Teddy noted a smudge of what looked like dirt on Thomas's cheek before he turned to head upstairs. She wrinkled her nose, uncertain if the smell was from Thomas or the gamey meat shaped into a loaf on her plate. She chewed and allowed the texture of the cornmeal to keep her from thinking about what animal this ground-up meat might be. Sauteed onions and a brown gravy were not enough to mask the unique flavor.

"My apologies again, Mrs. Jones." Thomas took his seat, and Teddy welcomed the opportunity to put her fork down to pass a dish his way.

Crocket set his cup down, and Teddy watched his neck muscles strain. She wasn't the only one with an aversion to tonight's meal. He passed the meat platter to Thomas. "We were discussing partners for this evening's games. I've scored Miss Teddy."

Teddy winced at the pride in the man's voice.

Thomas heaped a large piece of meat onto his plate before Teddy could warn him.

"She's a formidable opponent. You made a wise choice in choosing her as your partner. I won't be able to join you this evening. I've neglected my studies all day, and we have a test tomorrow." He forked a large bite of meat into his mouth.

Teddy watched for his reaction.

"Ptarmigan or spruce grouse?" he asked of Mrs. Jones.

"I wondered if you'd recognize the flavor. In Pennsylvania, it is called the ruffled grouse. They were still warm when I purchased them this morning. It isn't often the Lord provides a manna of sorts right to your doorstep."

Teddy marveled as Thomas took another large bite. She shivered.

Merriweather placed her hand on Teddy's arm. "Are you cold? You slept most of the day away. I hope you're not getting sick."

Thomas's fork stopped mid-bite.

Teddy shook her head. "I'm not ill. I wasn't sleeping the entire time. I caught up on my laundry and devotions while you girls made cookies."

Teddy caught the resumed movement of Thomas's fork out of the corner of her eye.

Mrs. Jones placed her napkin beside her plate. "Staying in God's Word is virtuous. I've reread our Sunday passage several times."

The conversation changed to music, and Teddy listened as she pushed the meat around her plate, drawing streaks and swirls in the brown gravy. Thomas's deep voice pulled her from her artwork.

"Another exceptional meal, Mrs. Jones. I'm assuming you made this?" Thomas looked around as if Cook would appear.

Mrs. Jones dipped her chin. "I did. Thank you. I am ever so thankful that Bernadette helped clean the birds."

Birdie was showing a new side Teddy had not seen. She wasn't shying away from jobs no one else wanted and was proving to be a team player when allowed to use the giftedness God had given her.

"Would you young people enjoy having your cookies later in the parlor?" Mrs. Jones's face softened at the resounding yeses and thank-yous she received.

Reggie was the first to stand. "Gentlemen, let's get these dishes done, so we have more time to play games."

Teddy gathered her silverware and allowed Reggie to take them from her. "Thank you, Reggie. Josephine, I'll be in the parlor shortly. I need to check my laundry before it gets any darker."

Teddy grabbed her coat. A brisk wind blew at her hair as her feet broke through the crisp layer atop the snow. Her fingers ached as she removed the clothespins. Her clothing wasn't frozen stiff, but it would need a few more hours in the room to finish drying.

She may have hurried through putting it in the basket when outside, but she took her time hanging it on the wooden rack to dry in their room. She was in no hurry. Games wouldn't be as fun without Thomas. He always added an element of competition that even made Birdie sport the occasional smile.

"Game time!" a muffled yell carried up the stairs.

She opened the door and looked to see Birdie standing on the bottom step. "On my way. I have just two more things to hang."

Teddy looked across the hall at the closed door with light seeping through the crevice. "What is my problem?" She turned and gave the petticoat she held a good snap before laying it over the wooden rod.

How could one man disrupt her focus with such ease? Thomas Shankel was leagues ahead, destined for greatness as a future doctor—and heading back home to the West. She yearned for stability and tranquility. She dreamed of owning a home and settling down in the familiar embrace of the East. Her job was secure, her church was close, and her roommates had grown on her over the past few months. Teddy growled deep in her throat.

So, why did Thomas Shankel ignite a desire for something beyond her peaceful existence?

"Teddy!"

"Coming, Birdie." Teddy willed herself to keep from looking at his door.

Teddy's partner stood. "There's the other half of my team. We've decided to play word chain. Are you familiar with the game?"

"Remind me, please." Teddy took her place in the chair next to her partner.

"Mrs. Jones will choose a word," he started.

"Oh, no," Mrs. Jones said. "Let Theodora choose the word."

"Okay. You choose a word to start. We'll be team one. These two lovely ladies will be team two, and they must say a word that begins with the last letter of the word you chose. Team three, Reggie and Merriweather, must continue the list by again choosing a word that starts with the last letter of team two's word, and so on. The group with the most answers in one minute wins. Mrs. Jones will time us. Is that okay with you, Mrs. Jones?"

"Yes. Of course. Ready? Begin."

"Anesthesia." It was the first thing that came to Teddy's mind.

"Apple," Josephine quickly added.

"Ear." Merriweather beamed at Reggie, apparently pleased with her partner's answer.

"Raspberry," Crocket added.

"Yell."

Teddy laughed at the appropriate choice and matching volume from Birdie.

Merriweather clapped her hands in excitement. "Oh, L. Let's see. I know. Lemon."

"Needle," Teddy answered.

Josephine looked up as if for inspiration. "Eyeglasses."

"Spoon."

Merriweather leaned into Reggie. "Good answer."

Mrs. Jones chimed in. "Thirty seconds."

"Nougat," Crocket spat and wiped his mouth.

"Tummy." Birdie was on the edge of her seat.

"Yogurt," Merriweather blurted.

"Toothache." Could she think of nothing creative?

"Egg," Josephine added.

"Glasses," Reggie spat out.

"Someone already said glasses. You can't repeat a word," Birdie blurted.

Reggie straightened his spine. "It was eyeglasses, but fine. Gumdrop."

"Pickle."

Teddy may be stuck on medical terms, but her partner knew his food.

"Earnest."

Reggie challenged Birdie. "That's a name. Can we use proper nouns?" He looked to Crocket for a ruling.

Birdie's knees bounced. "It's not a name, you nincompoop."

Mrs. Jones's hand flew to her neck. "Bernadette. Language."

Birdie rolled her eyes before fixing them on Reggie. "Ernst is a single-syllable name. I said earnest, two syllables that mean doing everything needed to win the game."

"My apologies. I misheard your pronunciation. It's your turn, Merriweather."

"What letter are we on?" Merriweather asked.

A resounding "T" rang through the room.

Mrs. Jones lifted her hand. "Time."

Merriweather stuck out her bottom lip. "It's my turn."

Mrs. Jones lifted her fingers to her upturned lips. "I mean, time, as in the game is over."

"Oh. Who won?"

Mrs. Jones put the timer in her lap. "You all did. What fun. Let's make this next round harder. No proper nouns, and it must be a plant, animal, or food." She nodded to Reggie in acknowledgment.

Crocket leaned in Teddy's direction. "We'll win for sure."

"We make a good team." Teddy meant her words.

The companions gathered in this room were a true blessing, enriching her life. Friendship held immense significance, even though her heart longed for something more.

Chapter 18

January, 1872
University of Pennsylvania School of Medicine
Thomas

"Y ou aren't upset?" Thomas searched Jimmy's eyes for any hint of disappointment or jealousy but found none.

"Upset?"

The librarian cleared her throat and raised a finger to her lips. The two leaned closer.

Jimmy continued in hushed tones. "Why would I be upset? You've proven yourself to be the man for the job and have broken convention. Few around here ever accomplish that. I don't know what you did to secure a unanimous vote for the internship, but it worked."

"I'm just as baffled." Thomas went from worrying about his friendship with Jimmy because of securing the internship to feeling uncertain about what he had just agreed to do. Thomas didn't want to think about it. Like a riddle begging to be solved, the vote nagged at him. It felt as though he were attempting to unravel the enigma of x without all the necessary variables.

The familiar coin moved over Jimmy's fingers as they

rested on the library's worn wooden tabletop. "I have one question, though."

Thomas looked from the coin to the open books on the library table, then focused on his friend. "Anything."

"Addison is spreading a rumor. It's probably nothing, but, well..."

"Just say it, Jimmy. I rarely believe anything that comes out of that man's mouth."

"Emmaline. He says you got into Dr. Whitaker's graces through his daughter."

Truth hurt, but twisted truth hurt worse. Thomas rubbed his temples. Words would not form.

The coin moved faster. "Sorry. I shouldn't have brought it up. I just thought you might want to know."

"There is a shred of truth in his lie."

The coin hit the table, then clanged on the marble floor and rolled out of sight. The librarian held up two fingers. Three strikes, and they would be asked to leave.

Thomas put his hand around his lips to contain his whisper. "The truth is that Emmaline approached me. No, that sounds too forward. Emmaline let me know, in a roundabout way, that she'd set her hat on me. The odd thing is that I never expected Dr. Whitaker to see me as worthy of his daughter's hand."

Jimmy pulled out another coin. "So, you are courting her?"

The emphasis on *are* made Thomas's stomach sink. "Not exactly. Maybe. I don't know." Thomas's nervous laugh drew unpleasant looks from the students at the nearby table.

The librarian approached them, her gaze stern, possibly from the tightness of her bun. "Gentlemen, I'm afraid your time here is up for today."

Thomas was thankful for the break in the conversation. "Of course, ma'am. Sorry for the disturbance. We'll gather our things."

The librarian's expression didn't soften. "And please remember, gentlemen, this is a place of study, not idle chatter."

Thomas nodded, feeling a pang of guilt for allowing their conversation to stray when they needed to be studying. "Yes, ma'am."

Once they'd packed up and were outside the library, Jimmy turned to Thomas. "So, about Emmaline . . ."

Thomas fidgeted with the strap on his bag. "Let's talk about it as we walk. I could use some fresh air."

Jimmy didn't last two steps before returning to his earlier question. "How can you not know if you're courting her or not? I'm no expert on the entire relationship thing, but don't you kind of need an agreement or something?"

"That's just it. The agreement is between me and Dr. Whitaker. Not me and his daughter. I can't read her. We enjoy our time together, but . . ."

"No sparks?"

"Oh, there are sparks." Thomas felt heat rise in his cheeks.

"I know I should be flattered, but it all feels so contrived."

"Hmm."

"Hmm? Am I missing something? Help me out here. It feels like I'm being bought like a head of cattle."

The coin stilled, and Jimmy held it up. "What is the value of this coin?"

"What does that have to do with anything?"

"Play along." Jimmy turned the coin over.

"Okay. I suppose it depends on the context. In terms of currency, it has a face value of one cent. If we're being subjective, it could symbolize thriftiness, as in Benjamin Franklin's 'a penny saved is a penny earned.' If someone special gave it to you, it could have sentimental value. What are you getting at?"

"What about purchasing power? The penny has little value and is considered the lowest denomination of currency."

"I still don't understand." Thomas's frustration made his jaw tense.

"You are the coin. Comparing a coin's value to a person's self-worth is like comparing a drop of water to the ocean. This coin represents just a small part of one's wealth, external achievements, and possessions. Those aren't nearly as important as a person's inner qualities, experiences, and God-given abilities."

Thomas felt the words looking for a place to find a home in his mind.

Jimmy gingerly placed the coin in Thomas's hand, his voice soft and hesitant. "Don't doubt yourself too much. The internship—it's only one part of a bigger plan, you know? God's plan."

Thomas blinked and stopped walking, surprised at Jimmy's words. "That's the first time I've heard you mention God."

The tips of Jimmy's ears turned pink. "I'm not great at giving advice, especially about Emmaline, but I don't want to see you mess this up. You deserve that internship. Don't let anyone take that from you. If I listened to all your talk about God, and I don't often, I believe you once said, 'God is not the author of confusion but of peace.'"

"Peace. That's something I haven't felt recently."

But he knew where to find it.

My dearest Thomas,

Congratulations on being chosen for the internship. Medical Ambassador. What a distinguished title. It comes as no surprise that you've achieved this success. Your accomplishments bring us great joy and speak volumes about your character and work ethic.

Each of your sisters has included notes, so I'll let them tell you of their news. Clint says the cattle have fared well over this harsh winter thus far, but we are weeks away from warm weather. I look forward to seeing God's handiwork in the coming of spring. It feels like it will never come, yet I know God designed the seasons, and it will eventually arrive.

I'm stalling. Sharing negative news is never pleasant, but we eagerly seek your prayers. Gabe is worse in body and soul. Please do not let his poor choices affect your perseverance and determination to follow the path God has put you on. Gabe will return to his faith, but for now, I fear he is lost.

He received a warning at work for fighting. Robin says the foreman showed tremendous grace by only giving him a warning. Even so, he lost three days' pay and spent the weekend in a cell. Henry says the boy was like a rabid animal in his cell. I'm sorry. I should not have written those words, but now they are out, and I pray they help you know best how to pray for your friend.

We miss you but know your first year is nearly complete, bringing us closer to seeing you again. It saddened us to know you will not come home for summer break, but we understand the need to fulfill your new duties. Many men need work after the war, and your father is determined to ensure no man goes hungry. We will hire out what needs to be done on the farm.

Thank you for telling us about your friends. Jimmy seems like a kind soul, and your boarding housemates appear to be keeping a smile on your face. Please tell Harriet I tried the vinegar in the pie crust. I know she said just a splash, but my splash must have been bigger than hers. It ended up being a chicken pot pie without the pie. Thank the Lord Clint is easy to please.

Speaking of cooking, I need to get the beans on.

I love you, son.

Mama

February 1872

Bitter winter wind whipped through the Pennypackers' open barn doors. Thomas stood knee-deep in straw, his breath forming frosty clouds in the chilled air. With gloved hands, he vigorously mucked out the stalls, the muscles in his arms tensing with each pitchfork thrust.

The sharp tang of manure hung heavy in the air, mingling with the crisp scent of hay and the musty odor of damp straw. Despite the biting cold, sweat trickled down his brow, mixing with the stench as he worked.

Wheelbarrow loaded, he pushed the refuse into the pre-dawn light. The sound of his boots crunching on the frozen ground echoed against the expanse of the barn. He dropped the load and headed back in to continue his work.

The rhythmic scrape of the pitchfork against the stall floor mirrored his clenched jaw, each movement a reflection of the frustration simmering within him. Overhead, the rafters groaned and creaked under the burden of accumulated snow, a burden akin to the heaviness he felt in his weary body.

He'd not been able to sleep from worrying about Gabe and not knowing how to help his friend—or if he even should. Through the haze of his frustration, Thomas's vision blurred. He blinked away the moisture.

The sight of steaming piles of manure and the dark, empty stalls awaiting cleaning kept him going. His breath hitched with each exhale, his chest tightening with pent-up emotion.

Despite the numbing cold and the physical strain of his labor, Thomas found solace in the repetitive motions of his work. With each load of muck he removed from the stalls, he expelled a bit of the frustration that had been building inside him. And as he worked, the weight on his shoulders seemed to lessen, if only for a moment, in the quiet solitude of the winter barn.

"Since when did you start working here again—and so early in the morning?"

Thomas jumped, dropping the pitchfork with a loud clang. "Douglass, you scared the daylights out of me." Thomas leaned against the stall wall, catching his breath.

"Guess that's where it all went. Not a stitch of daylight out there." The man raised an eyebrow, his words light but his expression stoic. "It's always nice to have an extra hand helping out, but care to explain?"

Thomas picked up his tool and placed it against the wall. "I couldn't sleep and needed to burn off steam. I didn't know where else to go to do that but here. I hope you don't mind."

"Want to talk about it?" Douglass got right to the point.

More than anything, but if he hadn't talked to God about it on the long walk here or while he worked, he shouldn't burden his friend.

"At least have a cup of coffee and sit a spell."

Thomas obeyed, removing his gloves. Redness marred his skin. He was getting soft—and not just in body.

Thomas let out a weary sigh, grateful for Douglass's company despite his reluctance to burden his friend with his troubles. He leaned against the stall.

"Thanks, Douglass. I could use a break," Thomas admitted, rubbing his tired eyes.

Douglass poured two cups of steaming coffee from a battered thermos, the rich aroma mingling with the now-clean barn. Douglass handed it to Thomas, the heat seeping through the thick ceramic mug and into Thomas's chilled fingers.

"Here you go, son. Drink up," Douglass said, his voice gentle yet firm.

Thomas took a sip, the bitter brew offering a small comfort against the bitterness of his thoughts. "Thanks," he murmured, glancing up at Douglass.

Douglass settled on a nearby crate, his gaze steady as he regarded Thomas. "So, what's been weighing on your mind, son?"

Thomas hesitated, and the words caught in his throat. How could he explain the tangled mess of emotions swirling inside him? His voice came out low and hesitant.

"It's Gabe," he confessed, the name heavy on his tongue. "I'm torn between wanting to run home and help him and mad because I've always been the one to get him out of scrapes. I want him to grow up." Thomas spat the words, then lowered his head. "The thing is, he's sick, and I'm in no position to help him."

Douglass listened quietly, his expression sympathetic as Thomas spoke. "I can't imagine what you're going through, Thomas," Douglass said softly, his voice tinged with empathy, "but you can't carry the weight of the world on your shoulders alone. Sometimes, we have to accept that we can't fix everything."

Thomas swallowed hard, the lump in his throat threatening to choke him. "I know," he murmured, his voice barely above a whisper. "But it's hard not to rescue him and fix things, especially when he's my best friend."

Douglass placed a comforting hand on Thomas's shoulder, the warmth of his touch a silent reassurance. "You're doing the best you can by getting your medical degree. If Gabe's problem is physical, you're of no help to him yet. If it's spiritual, well, that's not up to you anyway."

Thomas nodded, his gaze fixed on the ground as he grappled with the weight of Gabe's illness and poor choices, and his own sense of helplessness. But with Douglass's steady presence and the reminder that God was the only one who could provide the ultimate healing, Thomas felt a glimmer of hope flicker to life in the darkness. And for now, that was enough.

Chapter 19

May 1872
Thomas

Thomas tried to ignore the laughter in the parlor below. He reviewed his comments on the patients assigned to him by Dr. Whitaker and made additional notes. Being thorough was necessary, but Dr. Whitaker expected perfection.

Since he'd accepted the internship, there had been little time for fun. He may not officially begin until the new school year, but Dr. Whitaker had him in rigorous training for the duties he would perform above his normal school workload and hospital rounds.

Thomas missed the physical activity of his Saturday position at Judge Pennypacker's but mourned the loss of time with Douglass and Harriet—and Teddy. She smiled and chatted amicably over dinners when he made it home in time, but they'd not shared the closeness he'd felt after their snowball fight last year.

Thomas dropped his head into his hands and pulled on his hair. "Hair. I have to have a haircut before tomorrow morning." He looked at his watch. Where would he find a place open this late or so early in the morning? Perhaps Cook could cut it for him.

Thomas tapped the stack of papers on his desk to even out the edges, then placed them in the folder for his morning meeting. He checked his suit and brushed at the shoulders before deeming it fit. Footsteps and laughter in the hall pulled at his heart, but he must remain focused on finishing well.

Thomas opened the door, and Merriweather squealed.

"Oh. You frightened me." Her hand flew to her throat.

Thomas watched as Reggie put a protective hand on her waist. When had that relationship happened?

"My apologies," Thomas offered. "I'm headed down to see Cook for a haircut."

Birdie pushed past, and Thomas watched Teddy take a step backward as if attempting to create distance between them. Her gaze flickered momentarily toward him, then darted away, almost as if she couldn't bear to meet his eyes.

Thomas was keenly aware of her presence, his senses heightened by her proximity. He couldn't help but notice the faint scent of beeswax lotion that wafted toward him, teasing his senses. Her presence filled the hallway, making it hard for him to think clearly.

Birdie slipped her key into the door and turned back, a sly smile on her lips. "Cook's already in bed with a headache. Teddy can do it. She cuts all of ours." Birdie disappeared into the room, followed by her roommates, except for the one dark-haired beauty whose mouth was slightly agape.

The silence stretched between them, punctuated only by the soft shuffling of feet. Thomas cleared his throat, struggling to find something to say that wouldn't sound awkward or forced. He took a tentative step forward, then hesitated, unsure whether to advance or retreat. Should he say something, acknowledge the tension simmering beneath the surface, or should he pretend everything was normal and they were just two acquaintances passing in the hall?

"I have a meeting tomorrow," he blurted out, his voice sounding strangely loud in the stillness of the hallway. "I have to defend my findings." He ran a hand over his tired face, the rough stubble scratching against his palm. He felt as though he hadn't slept in days, his exhaustion weighing him down like a lead weight.

He pushed the hair from his eyes and let it fall. "I'm sure you have better things to do on your night off."

"No. I mean, yes. It is my night off, but I have nothing else to do. I won't be able to sleep for hours. Hazards of working the night shift." She gave a half-hearted laugh.

Thomas couldn't help but notice the slight tremor in her laughter, the way her smile didn't quite reach her eyes, and how her words were tinged with a hint of uncertainty. Was she feeling as awkward as he was?

He swallowed hard, feeling the weight of her gaze on him, a tangible presence that seemed to press in on him from all sides. His hands trembled slightly as he forced them into his pockets, desperate to hide the nervous energy that coursed through him.

Teddy made the first move. "Let me get my scissors, and I'll meet you on the back porch. The weather is nice, and there should be enough light."

Thomas massaged the back of his neck, trying to release the tension. He grabbed a chair and followed the warmth from the stove as it spilled out into the crisp night air, then placed the chair on the landing. Thomas missed the wide-open space of Missouri. When he sat on his parents' porch, his gaze could roam freely across vast expanses of land. Here, however, the most prominent sight was the tangled growth of bushes obscuring the windows of the neighboring house just a short distance away.

Teddy stepped outside. "This is perfect. Just enough light."

Teddy wore an apron he had not seen before. The quilting was crude, and the faded colors blended together. A pair of scissors and a comb stuck out from a pocket. He took in a deep breath and let it go through puffed cheeks.

Teddy laughed, and the smile she gave seemed genuine. "That worried? I promise I've done this hundreds of times. You'll still have both your ears when I'm finished."

"But what about my eyebrows?" he teased, the familiarity of their easy banter so natural.

"That I can't promise."

It felt good to laugh. "I am at your mercy." He bowed, then sat. Lavender invaded his senses as Teddy placed a cloth over him and tied the ends behind his neck. He shivered at her nearness.

Teddy placed a hand on his shoulder. "If you're cold, we can move inside. I'll light a lamp."

"No. I'm fine. Overly tired and feeling a bit overwhelmed."

"What is your meeting about tomorrow?"

Thomas struggled to get words out of his mouth as Teddy ran a comb through his hair. The scratching motion was heavenly. If he wasn't careful, his tongue would hang out like his dog's. He laughed.

"What is so funny?" Teddy leaned over and attempted to make eye contact.

"You running that comb through my hair reminded me of petting my dog back home. He loved a good scratch. His tongue would loll, and he'd make these low moans that sounded like he was dying."

"Oh, dear. We can't have any of that." Teddy leaned close to his ear. "Mrs. Jones might hear and give us the stink eye for inappropriate behavior."

She resumed her combing, and he felt the first cut. Thomas watched small half-circles of hair slide down the cloth and onto the first step. His body warmed at her touch. "Tomorrow. . ." His voice creaked like it had in puberty.

"Yes. You were going to tell me what has you all worked up into a ball of knots. Lower those shoulders, or I'll have to take back my promise of keeping the ears."

"Right." He rolled his shoulders and tilted his head left and right before taking a deep breath in and releasing it—and the stress in his shoulders.

"Much better." Teddy resumed her work.

"The final grade for this semester is an accumulation of months of work. I have seven patients I monitor, each with unique issues. I've been tracking them since admittance and have kept detailed records. Most have been released from care. One is still hospitalized. Another died." Her sharp intake of breath made him flinch, but he continued.

"Tomorrow, I defend what I've learned."

"Defend?"

"I'm presenting my findings to eleven doctors, my professors, and will answer questions they have. Basically, the defense is to prove I've been paying attention to detail, researching deeper than they have, and that I meet the criteria they've set, granting me the honor of graduating from a lowly first-year to a second-year student with extra responsibilities." He laughed.

"That's wonderful, Thomas. I'm sure you'll do just fine. You've certainly put in the hours. All those missed meals and game nights are paying off," she remarked, her voice tinged with wistfulness.

He felt the change in her tone, recognizing the wistfulness that had crept into her voice even as she expressed her encouragement. The brief lightness of earlier turned heavy. "I suppose, but it will mean they'll expect even more of me. They haven't made the formal announcement, but I've been appointed as the new medical ambassador."

"Congratulations. What does that entail?"

"A more appropriate title is class representative and chief errand boy. It's basically an internship position with exclusive access to Dr. Whitaker. I'll be the primary liaison for our class, saving the professors' time from overbearing students. I'll also handle tasks the doctors either don't have time for or prefer not to do, such as grading papers. And, as if I have all the time in the world, I'll also provide support to struggling students during rounds and assist them with their studies."

She pressed his head forward, and he felt the cold steel against his neck.

"That is, if you don't sever a major artery."

Teddy laughed. "Just remember, I know my anatomy, too. I can make it look like an accident."

Thomas chortled and did his best not to move. A bat flew in his line of sight, and he focused on the light drawing others. Several moments passed with only the sound of scissors snipping hair.

Teddy broke the silence. "I understand you and Miss Whitaker are doing well. Congratulations on that accomplishment as well. She's quite the catch."

Time froze—his heart with it. "Emmaline? We're getting to know each other."

"Is that what you call it?"

"I mean, it's not like we're getting married or anything. Do you know Emmaline?"

"Our paths cross frequently." She pulled a little harder than necessary.

He turned in his chair, not caring about ears or eyebrows. Even in the dim light, he recognized the lines in her forehead. "Is she talking about me?"

Teddy put her scissors in her pocket and pulled out her comb. She ran it through his hair, then checked for unevenness, fixing one spot. "You could say that."

"Teddy. Please. I could use your help. Be a friend. What is

she saying?"

"Ask her yourself." Teddy pocketed the items and stepped to the side. He noted the crossed arms and stony expression.

He ran his fingers through his hair. "It's not like that."

"Like what?" Teddy leaned against the wall.

"Like . . . I don't know . . . like . . ."

"A relationship? Courtship? Engagement?" Her eyebrows went up.

"No. I mean. Ugh." He leaned forward and put his head in his hands.

Thomas wanted to talk to Teddy, but when he looked into her eyes, there was a vulnerability, or maybe hurt, in them.

She reached for him, and he felt the tension from earlier return.

"Let me get this apron off you."

Thomas couldn't determine if the trembling in her hands was from embarrassment, anger, or being cold. He opted for the latter. "Now you're the one who's cold."

"I'm fine. Let me sweep this up, and we can head into the parlor. The fire's still going. You take the chair back in."

He did as she asked, holding the door for her as she entered the kitchen. Teddy led them into the parlor, and they sat by the window.

"Teddy, I don't want to make you feel uncomfortable if

you don't want to share with me what Emmaline is saying, especially if it borders on gossip, but I'm truly at a loss." Thomas pushed down on his bouncing knee.

"Thank you. So, am I to understand there isn't anything between you and Emmaline?"

"Yes. No." He blew out a puff of air and leaned back. It would be better if he started at the beginning. "I'll give you the condensed version. I think Emmaline likes me, but I'm not even sure about that."

The sound Teddy made was not quite a laugh. "Oh, she likes you. Sorry. Please continue."

"Remember New Year's Eve? I thought I was attending a big party, but it was just me. Like when I went at Christmas, Emmaline and I played games. She's quite formidable, but unlike you, she's a sore loser." He winked and noticed a pretty flush fill Teddy's cheeks.

"I have to let you win every once in a while," Teddy teased.

"Right. Anyway, we talked, we ate, we played, we danced . . . " Thomas stopped when Teddy flinched. Was she upset? "Listen, it's not really important."

"Yes, it is, Thomas. Please continue. I'd like the big picture. It's hard to help without solid information."

"Emmaline left with her mother to powder her nose, and the next thing I know, I'm having a heart-to-heart with Dr. Whitaker. Essentially, he said if I wanted the internship, it would require some sacrifices on my part. I knew that, but I didn't understand it would also mean some compromises."

His chest tightened, and the room grew warm. He ran his

hand over the stubble on his jaw and leaned forward in his chair.

Teddy's voice was soft. "What compromises?"

When he looked at Teddy, her skin was pale. "Oh, nothing like that, if you mean—I mean, nothing improper."

Teddy nodded. Her clenched hands pulsed like his heart—hard and fast. "So, there is something to the rumors."

He felt utterly drained, like a punctured balloon losing its air, and slouched in the chair. "Which one? It seems like there are several. At this point, I'm not even sure what's true."

"Emmaline has insinuated that you two are more than a little close. She even hinted there may be a ring after graduation."

Thomas sat up straight. "What?"

Teddy sighed, her gaze focused on her hands. "I'm sorry. If she's not being truthful, maybe you should talk to her."

Thomas rubbed the back of his neck, feeling the weight of confusion and frustration settling in. "I didn't know it had gotten this far. Emmaline and I are just friends." That wasn't true, and he knew it.

"Talk to her. Clear things up."

Thomas felt trapped, and he'd walked right into the snare without thinking. Just last week, Dr. Whitaker had reminded him to never disappoint his daughter. Was marriage the expectation?

"Thomas?"

Teddy touched his forearm, and electricity shot up his arm. He stared at the rough skin, so unlike Emmaline's softness. He looked into Teddy's eyes and saw genuine compassion.

He pulled his arm into his lap. "I'll figure something out. Thanks for the haircut. Let me know how I can repay the favor." Nervous energy propelled him to his feet. "If I'm going to give my best tomorrow, I need to get some shut-eye. Thanks, Teddy."

"Anytime. I'll hold you to that favor." She smiled, but the sparkle didn't reach her eyes.

Thomas nodded in acknowledgment and headed toward his room. How would he ever sleep with so much to process—and the reality of the touch still burning his arm?

Chapter 20

Early August, 1872
Dr. Whitaker's Home
Thomas

Emmaline's light touch guided Thomas from one group of guests to another. Practiced greetings and shallow conversations wore on him, yet he kept up the pasted smile she'd instructed him to wear.

She directed him to three older ladies, all in mourning clothes. He couldn't face another round of pleasantries. "Emmaline, darling, you must be parched. Enjoy the company of these beautiful ladies, and I'll get some punch for you."

"Beautiful?" Emmaline raised an eyebrow.

Thomas couldn't tell if she was teasing or was truly offended. "Of course, but no one is more stunning than you." He pulled her hand to his mouth and brushed his lips over the soft skin. "Excuse me, ladies."

Whispers of "He's so handsome," "You're so fortunate, Emmaline," and "Those eyes remind me of my Stanley," filled the air as Thomas retreated.

Jimmy lifted a punch cup to him. Thomas moved quickly and emptied the contents in one long drink.

"You look wiped." Jimmy took the cup and refilled it.

"You have no idea."

Jimmy's laugh was uncharacteristic, making two ladies turn and stare. "Oh, I understand perfectly. That girl has you wrapped around her little finger. I thought my father was the only one who kowtowed that much, but . . ."

Thomas glared.

Jimmy's hands went up, nearly spilling the punch. "Okay, I get it. You're past the teasing. Need a break?"

"Yes, but I can't shirk my duties." Thomas rolled his eyes.

"Follow my lead." Jimmy breathed in what must have been confidence because his entire demeanor changed. He marched to Emmaline's side, though the coin moved fluidly in his hand behind his back.

"My fine ladies, you look lovely this evening." Jimmy's voice shook, and he swayed.

Thomas took hold of the wrist behind the man's back to steady him. Dampness covered the man's cool skin. Emmaline looked perturbed at the comment. Thomas squeezed Jimmy's wrist, and the contact seemed to bolster his friend.

"Miss Whitaker, might I borrow your man for a bit? School business. Dreadful, I know, but there is a matter of great importance we must settle. You understand Thomas's elevated position and responsibilities." He let his words hang.

Pride covered Emmaline like a dense fog. Thomas could no longer see the sweet girl, only the outline of a prominent woman enjoying her new power.

Emmaline spoke louder than necessary. "Of course. Thomas, dear, don't be too long. You are a host at this gathering."

Thomas dipped his head, then bowed. "Ladies."

He couldn't get out of there fast enough and followed Jimmy's short steps to the place they'd first talked a year ago. "That was amazing. Whatever came over you?" Thomas slapped his friend on the shoulder.

"There are some benefits to being a wallflower. I've heard all sorts of excuses men have used to escape the grasps of clinging women. I just didn't realize how difficult it would be once I started."

Was Emmaline clingy?

Jimmy pulled out his coin. "Actually, I was telling the truth. I have a small matter of importance to discuss, but it isn't anything urgent. I needed a breather from all those people."

They sat on the stone bench. Splashing water from the fountain did its best to calm Thomas's frayed nerves. The familiar scent of summer filled the air. Much had changed in one year, but not in Dr. Whitaker's gardens. They looked exactly the same. "Shoot."

"It's not that serious. You can keep your gun in the holster." Jimmy elbowed Thomas. "Lighten up. I'm the one who nearly fainted back there, and there wasn't even blood. You're wound as tight as a clock wire."

"I feel like one. You, on the other hand, are in a good mood and acting as if you don't have a care in the world. What's going on?"

223

"Acting is a good word. You grew up in South Carolina, right?" The coin moved fluidly over Jimmy's fingers.

"Until I was four. I have distant relatives there but have never been back. Why?"

"The University of South Carolina has a program I'm interested in. Pharmaceutical school."

"But you're going to be a doctor."

"I'd still be a doctor, just not one who cuts people open and hopes they survive." Jimmy wiped his brow.

"But you're nearly through. Surely you aren't thinking of giving up all your hard work to change paths at this point."

"That's the thing. I wouldn't be giving anything up. All my classes would transfer. I'd be behind in chemistry and a few other specific classes, but I think this is a better fit. I could use my love of botany."

The look on Jimmy's face was full of hope and a torture Thomas wanted to relieve. "What do your parents say?"

"I wanted to talk to you first."

Warmth spread over Thomas's heart. He would miss this friend. "What can I do to help you?"

Jimmy's face changed to that of pure joy. "Really? You don't think this is crazy?"

"I think it's the first time I've seen you this excited over something other than a ginkgo tree."

"Did you know laboratory studies have shown that

ginkgo improves blood circulation by opening up blood vessels and making blood less sticky? It's also an antioxidant."

The laugh Thomas released took all his stress with it. "My friend, I believe you have found your calling. My offer stands. What can I do to help?"

"Write a letter of recommendation."

"Me? It won't carry much weight."

"Maybe not with the university, but it will with the other professors I'm going to ask to support me in my decision. They think highly of you."

Thomas wasn't sure how to take the high praise but knew he'd do anything for this friend. "Sounds like you have a solid plan. What are the next steps?"

"Figuring out how to handle the heat and learning the lingo. What does 'bless your heart' mean?"

Thomas's entire body shook with mirth. "If you have to ask, it applies. Listen, don't worry about anything. If I can muddle my way through Philadelphia society, you can figure out the South's version."

The coin in Jimmy's fingers went still. "I hope my parents see my dreams as worthy."

Thomas pointed to the coin. "I believe a wise friend once told me I am that coin. This one decision does not change your worth. If anything, it will increase in value. We need men with your talents and desire to change the pharmaceutical industry. Where I come from, any snake oil salesman would run in your presence."

"Actually, I have another request."

"Name it."

"Some day, I'd like to meet your friend Gabe and his mother, Singing Bird. I've heard much about the Indian people's healing ways. I think I could learn from her if the stuff you spout off is any indicator of her knowledge."

"You have a standing invitation, my friend. You're welcome in my family home any time." A faint furrow creased his brow, and his back tightened. Thomas paused before continuing. "Now, I'm the one with the problem."

"Emmaline?"

"Exactly. She's been hinting at a ring after graduation, but she's given no indication of her willingness to return with me to Missouri."

"That puts a damper on your plans, or would you consider staying here?"

Thomas mulled over the question. He'd thought about it dozens of times but had never discussed it with someone else. Footsteps sounded along the gravel path. Thomas looked up into the stoic face of a young server.

"Excuse me, sirs. Mr. Shankel, sir. Dr. Whitaker requires your presence in the grand ballroom."

"Thank you. I'll be up straight away."

Jimmy pocketed the coin. "We can talk about this another day. It's time to welcome in the new recruits. Do you have your acceptance speech prepared?"

"I practiced it all week. I'm not one for public speaking in large groups."

Jimmy offered a hand and pulled Thomas to his feet. "Pretend it's a bunch of cows you're talking to."

"That I can do. If I break into song, please stop me."

"As a loyal friend should."

Thomas appreciated his friend and his ability to reduce the stress he felt.

When they reentered the home, he offered Emmaline his arm and paraded her up the stairs to the grand ballroom, where Dr. Whitaker stood on a raised platform waiting.

"Are you ready, son?"

The man placed a heavy hand on Thomas's shoulder. Thomas nodded, doing his best to swallow his nervousness.

"Good. Don't disappoint me."

Thomas felt Dr. Whitaker meant his statement for more than the speech.

The stringed instruments quieted as Dr. Whitaker raised his hand, the gesture silencing the crowd. Thomas scanned the gathering. A glowing Emmaline stood in front of the stage next to her mother, who looked to have more than her accustomed amount of powder on her face and heavy color on her cheeks and lips, accentuating her dull eyes. Addison Blakeney stood to her right; his goons flanked behind him as if guarding a treasure.

Dr. Whitaker spoke his name, and Thomas forced a smile,

willing himself to pay attention.

"One year ago, Mr. Shankel occupied the same position you new students do now. His consistent top-ranking performance in his class and achievements in the student intern position over the past months have exceeded the board's expectations. Mr. Shankel's commitment to serving his peers and the medical profession with dedication, integrity, and compassion, along with his exceptional ability and strong work ethic, have earned him the prestigious title of Medical Ambassador for the Class of 1873."

A roar of applause echoed through the room, and a surge of pride threatened to swell within him. Yet, as he glanced at Addison's measured applause and strained smile, a sense of humility washed over him. Not everyone in the room shared Dr. Whitaker's support for his position.

Thomas anchored his feet and relaxed his toes, allowing the noise to dissipate before beginning.

"Dr. Whitaker, esteemed faculty, fellow peers, and new students, I am truly grateful for your generous words and this tremendous honor. It is with a deep sense of humility that I accept this responsibility, fully aware of the trust and expectations placed upon me. Your guidance, Dr. Whitaker, and the collective mentorship of everyone present has helped shape me into the person standing before you now."

Thomas stole a glance at Emmaline. He wouldn't mention her by name but hoped she read the sentiments in his face for her help in acclimating him to Philadelphia society's elite.

"I pledge to approach this role with utmost dedication and integrity, striving to fulfill its duties to the best of my abilities. May I continue to learn and grow, drawing inspiration from the remarkable individuals around me."

Thomas looked at Jimmy, who nodded once in understanding.

"Together, let us work toward our shared goals of healing and easing suffering, providing compassionate care, and pursuing lifelong learning with unwavering determination and a steadfast commitment to excellence. Thank you."

This time, the applause did not affect him. He stood determined to fulfill his commitment to the future, no matter the cost.

Many hands reached for his as he stepped into the crowd. Hearty congratulations and well-wishes accompanied equally enthusiastic pats on the back. Judge Pennypacker wiped his eyes with a handkerchief and waited his turn.

"My boy." He blew his nose, then offered the wet hand to Thomas. "I couldn't be more proud if you were my flesh and blood."

Thomas ignored the hand and hugged the man, causing an animated response of rapid clapping from his wife. Thomas winked at her, stilling her hands, which moved to her now-flushed cheeks.

Thomas took a step back. "Thank you, sir."

The judge cleared his throat. "Quite proud." He wiped his eyes again.

A whiff of strong drink filled Thomas's senses as Dr. Whitaker joined the conversation. "Exceptional speech, Thomas. Perhaps you should run for office. Don't you think, Judge?"

Judge Pennypacker brightened. "Now, wouldn't that be something?"

Thomas interrupted before the conversation could continue. "I believe I have all the excitement I can handle at the moment."

Dr. Whitaker reached his hand out and pulled his daughter to his side. "Yes. Yes, you do. Emmaline, sweetheart, be a good girl, and get your Thomas something to drink."

"Yes, Father."

Thomas didn't miss the jerk in her smile that broadened into a forced full one.

She offered a curtsey to the Pennypackers. "Thank you both for coming. It's good to see you feeling well, ma'am." Emmaline touched Thomas's arm as she passed, her fingers trailing down his jacket sleeve like octopus tentacles seeking a meal.

Mrs. Pennypacker slipped her arm in the crook of her husband's. "What a precious daughter you have, William. She'll make someone a good wife."

Thomas could almost feel the weight of her gaze on him, causing a prickling sensation at the back of his neck. Her words seemed to hang in the air, heavy with implications Thomas wasn't ready to confront.

Dr. Whitaker took a glass offered to him by a servant. "She's young yet. Another year will tell. If you'll excuse me, I see someone I need to speak with."

Emmaline returned with a glass similar to her father's. Thomas stared at it.

"Father's best." She offered the amber liquid to him.

Thomas moved the glass away from his nose. "His best should be reserved for his finest guest." Thomas handed the drink to the judge, who took it greedily. "Thank you, sir, for taking a chance on me."

The man took a sip and licked his lips, making a guttural sound with the motion. "When my Martha told me about you, she had not only admiration in her words but also confidence. She believed in you. That's all it took for me. I'd do anything for my daughter. Most men would." The judge looked first at Emmaline, then Thomas. "To another fine year." The man raised his glass, then drained the contents.

Thomas's limbs felt as heavy as his heart. Expectations from all sides crushed in on him. Waves of emotion drained his final amount of energy, leaving him at the mercy of an ocean of responsibility.

He just had to stay afloat for one more year.

Chapter 21

Late August, 1872
Les Madeleines
Teddy

Teddy wiped at the powdered sugar covering her arm. She'd been a bundle of nerves all week. She'd heard rumors in the hospital halls of the severity of increased cases of yellow fever. Even last night, they'd begun moving patients to make room for a quarantine ward. Acid roiled in her stomach, and she cleared her throat from the burning sensation.

Teddy wasn't worried about herself. She'd contracted the disease as a small child. All her family had survived, though it had taken weeks to regain their strength.

Sam offered her a damp rag. "Here, this will work better than your hands. You certainly aren't yourself today. I've got six younger sisters, so I know a thing or two about that expression you're making. Want to talk about it?"

Teddy had to smile. "Six? Really? I heard you tell Pete you were the youngest of seven brothers and understood what it was like to get beaten up." She challenged him with her eyes.

"What? I've got a big family." He leaned against the wall beside her and bumped her arm. "Truth is, I'm an orphan, and the numbers aren't off by much."

Teddy knew her shocked expression showed when he laughed.

"I've worked in the kitchen of an orphanage since I was five. Hauling wood to start, but I eventually moved to cleaning, then cooking, and when I was old enough, to serving. Got a job here when I was fifteen. Going to open my own bakery one day."

"I'd be honored to be your first customer." She handed back the towel. "Did I get it all?"

He twirled his finger, and she turned in a full circle.

"Everywhere but here." He gestured to his right cheek.

Her hand flew to her face.

"Other side. Here." Sam's arm halted, then moved slowly forward until the cloth rubbed against her cheek. "That's better. I coulda spit on my thumb and rubbed, but . . ."

Teddy laughed. "You wouldn't dare. My mother used to do that. Drove me crazy." Teddy shivered at the thought, then calmed. "Thanks, Sam. I needed that."

The shift manager rushed by. "Whatever you needed isn't important. There are customers awaiting your services. Snap to it." She snapped her fingers for emphasis.

Teddy pushed the cart she'd loaded to her station. As if on cue, Emmaline Whitaker and her clutch of friends took their seats. Teddy waited until everyone was seated and then placed tea, a tiered tray of sandwiches, and crystal dishes of butter, cream, sugar, and a variety of jams on the tablecloth.

"Oh, I'm ever so thankful they still have the cranberry

orange relish. It's my favorite," Opal said when Teddy placed the item nearest her. The girl's yellow cotton print looked new and reminded Teddy of the child's dress she'd seen in the department store window. Only the grosgrain ribbon looked as if it might have been repurposed.

Teddy couldn't help herself. "Lovely outfit, miss," she whispered as she placed a crock of powdered sugar on her other side. The girl lifted kind eyes and mouthed a "thank you."

Emmaline tapped her finger on the table. "Quit talking with the help, Opal. For goodness's sake, if you want something, just say so."

Caroline placed her napkin in her lap. "You don't have to be cross, Emmaline. Just because you didn't get what you wanted at your father's start-of-school gala doesn't mean you can take it out on the rest of us." The girl set her jaw.

Louisa crossed her arms over her ruffled cream blouse, the linen navy in her jacket with ornate gold buttons making her look like a soldier ready for battle. "Oh, I just despise it when Mother makes us travel over the summer. I miss all the news."

Caroline smirked. "Emmaline wished for a ring and grand gesture, but the focus was on her beau receiving highest honors, not her receiving her wish."

Adeline's voice was barely above a whisper. "That is unkind."

Emmaline raised an eyebrow, her tone dripping with sarcasm. "Well, at least I'm not relying on Santa for my social life, Caroline. But I'll be certain to write a letter this Christmas and put in a good word for you."

Louisa snickered. "If she can stay off the naughty list."

Emmaline took her time stirring sugar into her tea, the spoon never making a sound. "If you must know, Father would like for Thomas and me to wait until I turn eighteen and prefers Thomas wait until after graduation to ask me, so he can focus on his studies. Thomas has shown tremendous restraint."

Teddy inwardly rolled her eyes.

Adeline passed the lemon curd before the leader asked. "I think he's being quite the gentleman." She lowered her gaze but not before Teddy saw a sheen of tears on the girl's lashes.

Emmaline's hand covered her friend's. "Adeline, I know your heart is broken over Jimmy, but he'll return from South Carolina in a year."

Opal's quiet voice joined the conversation. "They say absence makes the heart grow fonder."

Louisa coughed into her napkin. "Or go astray."

Caroline giggled.

Emmaline tapped a finger on the edge of her cup. "Ladies, we'll speak of this no more. We have pressing matters to attend to. It is our duty to help those less fortunate during this yellow fever epidemic. Father says educating the community is of utmost importance. I propose we devise a plan to prove ourselves worthy of the roles we were born into and hand out informational leaflets."

Adeline sat up straighter. "Will we have to talk to people?"

Emmaline took a measured breath and patted the girl's

hand. "You only need to smile and offer a leaflet."

Adeline's face turned ashen.

Opal raised her hand. "Couldn't we gather blankets or food or something?" She looked to Emmaline for a response.

"It's the middle of summer, Opal. Blankets aren't of great importance. The Ladies Auxiliary has a soup kitchen set up and graciously provided staff from their households to serve."

"What a tremendous sacrifice."

Caroline's monotone reply and deadpan expression made Teddy laugh. She turned and moved things around on her tray but not before seeing the pleased look from Caroline.

Teddy did her best to avoid eavesdropping. What she really wanted to do was set these girls straight. The dangers of contracting yellow fever were serious. She'd seen firsthand how the disease could take a man down in a matter of weeks.

But she had to admire these girls for wanting to help, and educating the community was important. Though neither a cause nor a cure had been found, the hospital encouraged frequent hand washing and improved sanitation procedures. Even the city had begun clearing streets of refuse and standing water.

Perhaps she could speak with Thomas, and he could warn Emmaline of the dangers. That wasn't likely. Teddy wasn't even sure if he was coming back to the boarding house for meals or if he was sleeping at all. The man had looked bone-tired when she'd last seen him.

Sam pushed a cart past her and nodded toward the lobby, a question in his eyes. Two uniformed officers conversed with the maître d'. Teddy wrinkled her brow, hoping Sam would understand she knew no more than he did.

"Pay attention to what you're doing," Caroline barked at Teddy.

"Sorry, miss." Teddy wiped up the spill on the tablecloth, turning her attention from the scene that now included the manager. She closed her eyes and offered a silent prayer. This could not be good.

Teddy's gaze followed the stiff form of the restaurant manager as he made his way to the piano player. The musician's wide eyes caused Teddy's already upset stomach to churn. The man played two jarring, discordant notes that reverberated throughout the elegant space. Hat feathers seemed to take flight as heads turned at the disruption.

The manager wiped his forehead with his handkerchief. "May I have your attention? Please?"

His voice sounded calm and confident, but Teddy saw his shaking hands even from this distance.

"Good afternoon, ladies. I regret to inform you that, due to health concerns, the City of Philadelphia is requiring us to close the restaurant for the foreseeable future. Your safety and well-being are our top priorities, and we apologize for any inconvenience this may cause."

High-pitched whispers and murmurs filled the room.

"Ladies, please. There is no cause for alarm. If you need assistance, your table staff is available."

The man looked at the officers still standing at the door before continuing. "We realize this news may be disappointing, and we sincerely appreciate your understanding and cooperation during this time. Please take care to retrieve your belongings and move slowly and safely to the door. May God be with us all."

A shiver ran down her spine, but Teddy would not give in to fear. She must stay composed. Her determination must override her anxiety. This was a time to be bold. "Miss Whitaker, how might I be of assistance to you and your friends? May I secure transportation?"

Emmaline stared at Teddy as if paralyzed by fear. "My father..."

Teddy could barely hear her over the increasing volume in the room. A woman tripped, causing more commotion. Teddy needed to help the woman. "Miss Whitaker, you are in no immediate danger. Would you ladies allow me to first help those who are of more advanced years?"

Tears shone in Adeline's eyes. "It's what Jimmy would do. And Thomas. They would think of others before themselves. Isn't that what we were just discussing? Handing out leaflets to help people? This is how we can help."

Caroline pushed her chair back. "Do what you want. I'm not staying."

"Sit down, Caroline." Emmaline's forceful words commanded attention. Caroline slid back into her chair. Emmaline softened her voice. "Thank you. And thank you, Adeline." Her words turned wistful.

Teddy needed to move, not just because she should help but also because she needed to do something to distract herself from the impact this decision would have on her income. Her head ached, and her eyes burned, but she would remain steady until Emmaline released her.

Emmaline clasped her hands in her lap. "We shall remain here. You may do what is needed."

"Thank you, miss." Teddy hated to admit it, but Emmaline would make a fine doctor's wife.

Teddy just had no idea what would become of herself.

Christmas Eve, 1872

University Hospital
Teddy

Teddy did not look forward to walking home in this weather. Bitter wind, heavy snow, and low temperatures had plagued Philadelphia all winter, but she supposed it was better than the heat of summer. Yellow fever had taken close to five thousand of the city's residents, but none had shocked her as much as the loss of her friend Sam. She would never get to taste one of his baked goods—but she pushed the thought from her mind.

Armilda removed her nurse's cap and set it in her oversized bag. She placed a shapely fur hat on her still perfectly styled hair. "I appreciate you taking my shift tomorrow."

"It's Christmas. I had both days off last year. I'm happy to work your shift this evening." Teddy gave her friend a hug.

"*Aitäh.* Thank you. My beau is taking me to meet his family for the evening meal."

"John is a lucky man. His family will adore you. What will you wear?"

"Something fabulous, but not too much. I don't want the outfit to overshadow the ring."

"The ring? Do you think he'll propose?"

"If he knows what's good for him, he will. Men need a little, how do you say, shovel?"

Teddy did her best not to laugh. "They do need a push now and again. I look forward to hearing all about it on our next shift together." Teddy helped Armilda into the ankle-length fur coat.

"It is quiet on the floor. You will be fine until my replacement arrives. I must hurry home to make Kringle." Armilda pushed through the door as if off on an important mission.

Armilda's matter-of-fact words, meant to be kind, always reminded Teddy how truly different cultures were around the world. She adored the vibrant tapestry of Philadelphia's melting pot. Yet, she wished others would see its diversity as a treasure rather than viewing individuals of different hues or languages as inferior.

"Nurse?" a feeble voice called.

Teddy's shoes clicked across the floor. "Yes, Mr. DuPlane. How may I assist you?"

"Where's the blond?" He stretched to look past Teddy.

"Her shift has ended. I'm happy to assist you until your new nurse arrives."

He flopped back on his pillow. "Never mind. Just get me some water, would you?"

"It would be my pleasure." Teddy tightened her jaw as she grabbed the empty water container beside the man's bed. Odd, she'd seen Armilda fill that earlier.

Teddy pulled the chart from outside the room. She was correct. He'd had a refill with his supper. She filled the container and returned to the patient. "How are you feeling, Mr. DuPlane?" She handed him the drink and watched him take long gulps.

"Been in this blasted bed so long my back hurts. When can I get out of here?"

"Let me take a quick peek at your legs."

"My legs? Woman, that's not where I had surgery. Are you daft?"

"Routine, Mr. DuPlane." She lifted the edge of the sheet and pressed on the swollen ankle. A dimple remained. She moved up a few inches and repeated the process. The skin did not bounce back.

"You want to cut my toenails while you're down there?"

"It's good to see your humor is still working well. Let me check with the attending physician before we get you out of bed."

"Great. I'll likely get one of those student doctors who do more poking and prodding than a cowhand."

Teddy pulled the curtain and marked her findings on the man's chart. Edema could mean something serious. She moved

241

on tiptoes to Head Nurse Callahan's office so as not to alert the patients of her hurry. The woman was not there. The room reeked of cigarette smoke, even with the window cracked. No wonder this ward was always so cold during the woman's shift.

"Think. No, pray. Lord, please send help."

The door at the end of the hall opened.

"Nurse . . ." Teddy started and then saw it was Thomas Shankel who moved in her direction.

He lifted one eyebrow. "Not exactly, but I can change a bedpan if necessary."

He wasn't whom she had expected, but who was she to question God? "What brings you here at such an early hour? Especially on Christmas Day?" Teddy's words failed to convey the professionalism she'd aimed for.

"I could ask the same of you, but I think we both know the answer. Were you in need of something?"

She could do this. "Please." She handed him Mr. DuPlane's chart, biting her tongue to keep from speaking until spoken to.

"Mmm. Edema." Thomas looked at her. "How long?"

She pointed to the three water refills since this morning and the two notations of urine output. "I only noticed it just now. I hadn't thought to check. I'm sorry . . ."

"No apologies. Let's take a look." He swept his arm, palm up.

"Right this way." Teddy led the way, then pulled back the curtain, allowing Thomas to enter first.

Thomas stepped in, then turned around and pulled at the curtain. "Quit worrying your lip like that. I'll call for you if needed."

Teddy felt the movement of air from the curtain as Thomas closed it the rest of the way. She listened to his easygoing discussion with the patient and moved to finish her duties, only to unexpectedly find herself standing before the head nurse.

"Oh, Nurse Callahan, I'm so sorry. I was looking for you and . . ." The nurse's steely gaze stopped her flow of words like a well-placed tourniquet.

"Really? From where I'm standing, you were flirting with the doctor."

"Oh, Thomas? He's not a doctor." The moment the words came out of her mouth, she wanted to pull them back in. Raised eyebrows spoke volumes.

"Nurse Morse, I'll take it from here. Your replacement arrived. You are relieved of your duties."

"Relieved?" Teddy stuttered, feeling the heat of tears surfacing. She could not lose this job, too.

"Go home, Miss Morse. I'll speak about your actions with Dr. Whitaker when I next see him."

"But I didn't do . . ." Teddy clamped her jaw tight at the steely look challenging her.

"Your reputation preceeds you, Miss Morse."

Teddy's stomach dropped. Her reputation?

Nurse Callahan's voice dipped low. "You don't think we all notice your attentions toward Dr. Whitaker?"

Teddy wanted to scream but balled her fists tighter. She was the victim of Dr. Whitaker's unwanted advances.

"Since it is the holiday and I have tomorrow off, as the good doctor does, I expect it will be a few days before any reprimand. A woman of your station has no business playing seductress."

Teddy shook with rage and sweaty uncertainty. "I'm scheduled to work again tonight. Should I come?" Teddy couldn't bear to disappoint Armilda.

Nurse Callahan exhaled heavily. "Fantastic. Absolutely fantastic. Finding a replacement on Christmas Day will be quite the challenge unless that heathen woman can work."

"Hea . . .?"

"Krill or whatever her name is."

"Nurse Kull?" Teddy wanted to slap the woman for her rudeness. "She has plans for Christmas." Teddy's nails bit farther into her palms.

"Don't be late," the woman spat out.

Thomas stepped from behind the curtain. "Is there a problem here?"

The corner of Nurse Callahan's mouth tipped up, showing yellowed teeth. "Not a thing, sir. Everything is handled."

"Very good. Nurse Morse, could you assist me for a moment?"

Nurse Callahan put her hand on Teddy's arm. "She was just leaving. I'll send someone to help you momentarily."

The woman squeezed hard enough to leave a bruise. Teddy wanted to cradle her forearm and cry but put on her brightest smile while not making contact with a pair of blue eyes that would be her ruin. Possibly literally.

Chapter 22

Late March, 1873
Philadelphia Hospital
Thomas

T homas jerked his head up. Gone were the days of lying awake for hours trying to get his mind to still enough to fall asleep. These days, he fell asleep standing. "Only another few minutes to my shift," he reminded himself.

A slender nurse with a purposeful stride approached, and Thomas pushed off the hallway wall. Dr. Whitaker would frown on leaning. "There's an urchin in the lobby requesting to see you, sir. He says he knows you." The nurse's curt tone held more disgust than no-nonsense professionalism.

"His name?"

"David, sir." Her voice dripped with disdain.

"Thank you. I'll be right there." Dr. Whitaker's reminder floated through Thomas's mind.

"Reputation, son. It's all about the image you portray. What you do behind closed doors is your business, but don't allow anyone, anyone, to see a single flaw in your character. Choose your friends and associates wisely, and stay within the boundaries of the social status you've achieved. Your standing, real or perceived, will take you far."

Thomas finished charting and shivered as he swallowed the final swig of now-cold coffee. Grounds remained in his mouth. He moved his tongue around until they were gone as he strode to the waiting area. Even amidst this crowd of people from a lower station, Thomas spotted David immediately. The boy had grown, his pant legs now touching the tops of his worn boots. The jacket Thomas had given him swallowed the boy but appeared to be keeping him warm and dry enough.

"David, it's good to see you. Is everything all right?" Thomas kept his hands entwined behind his back, a posture he'd seen Dr. Whitaker take when showing authority. All manner of individuals in varying states of need looked at the two.

"All's good, Mr. Thomas, I mean Dr. Shankel."

"I'm not a doctor yet," he whispered.

"Mrs. Jones sent me to check on you." The boy diverted his gaze, looking everywhere but at Thomas.

"Ah, rent. Right. Follow me." He was a disappointment to everyone. He couldn't even remember to pay his rent on time. Thomas led the boy to the stairs, and they climbed the multiple levels. His legs felt like water-logged grain sacks by the time they reached the storage area where Thomas had placed an old military cot and moth-ridden wool blanket. "Welcome to my home away from home."

David stared. "This is where you been staying? Why are you still paying rent when you got a castle like this?" The boy showed crooked teeth.

Thomas would have laughed, but he didn't have the energy. "I'm too tired to make the trek back to the boarding house and would only get a few hours of sleep anyway. This, at least, is quiet, if a bit stuffy."

David opened his jacket to reveal a paper-wrapped package. "Cook's more than a mite worried for you. She sent a loaf of bread, some cheese, and dried meat." David leaned in and whispered, "Just make sure you have plenty of water ready after the jerky. Oh, and Mrs. Jones sent this." The boy handed Thomas a letter with his mother's familiar handwriting.

"Thank you." Thomas dropped to his cot and invited David to join him. He tucked the letter in his pocket. He missed word from home but needed physical sustenance more. Thomas broke off a piece of bread and allowed the crispy exterior to meld with the soft center. The tang of sourdough aroused his senses.

"Good, huh? Ate a whole loaf myself this morning. Cook says I eat like a teenager but look like an upturned okra. I don't like okra."

Thomas coughed, wishing he'd brought a fresh cup of water with him. "Just so you know, it's one of her favorite vegetables, so take it as a compliment."

David scrunched up his face.

Thomas searched for the jerky, then thought better of it and unwrapped the cheese. "So, tell me news of home."

The boy brightened. "Mr. Ferret brought Miss Merriweather a bunch of prickly holly leaves with red berries. You'd a thought they were something special. Those two are all googly-eyed and sit so close on the parlor settee even Mr. Crocket could fit his wide self beside them." The boy dipped his head.

Thomas remembered himself at this young age, but he'd had a passel of women to help curb his improper outbursts. "Love does cause a body to act differently."

"Yeah. I heard Miss Josephine say you were probably staying over at your girl's house, but Miss Teddy—she wiped the smirk right off that girl's face. I thought I was gonna see a real brawl."

Thomas's jaw stilled. He wasn't sure what was more disturbing, Josephine's inappropriate accusation or Teddy having to come to his defense.

David sat taller. "But now that I know the truth, I'll set them straight."

"Thank you."

The boy looked around the room. "I gotta go. I'm supposed to stop at the butcher on the way back and use your rent money to pay the man." The boy picked at a loose string on his pants where his knees had worn the fabric thin.

"Certainly." Thomas moved to a metal cabinet, opened the door, and lifted a shelf. He grabbed his wallet, which was tucked underneath, and pulled out the required funds, plus an additional month's rent. These final months of schooling would be grueling, and he wasn't certain when he'd get back to the boarding house, even though he desperately wanted to soak in the deep tub.

He grabbed a few extra coins and handed them all to the boy. "You let Mrs. Jones know this is for this month and next. There are two coins in there for you."

The boy's eyes lit up and then squinted. "What for?"

"Can you get a message to my friend along with a load of laundry?"

"Sure."

Thomas removed the remainder of the food from the bag and filled it with a soiled set of clothing. "Let me write a quick note."

He pulled the pad and pen from his pocket and wrote in his best print. "Take this note and laundry to Douglass, the coachman at Judge Pennypacker's home. You'll find him in the stables."

Confusion lit the boy's face. "He ain't there no more."

Thomas stilled.

"I heard he got the fever real bad."

Thomas's heart ached, and he rubbed his chest to ease the pain. "Is he home?"

"Don't know. Just heard some other fellow with a bum leg took his place."

"David, this is very important. I can't leave, but I need you to get me word of my friends. Can you do that?"

"I can go when Cook heads to her second job. She don't need me there."

Thomas gave him directions, having to think hard about street names since it had been so long since he'd visited. "Forget about the laundry. I'll figure something out."

"Miss Teddy might do it for you. She started working

again at the fancy eating place but is looking for extra work."

Thomas had forgotten. He was dreadfully out of touch with the world around him and focused only on himself. Even Emmaline was unhappy with his lack of attention. He ran his fingers through his hair, wishing for a haircut. He felt Teddy's soft touch on his scalp.

David interrupted his thoughts. "You want me to ask her?"

"Ask her?" Exhaustion clouded his mind.

"Man, you really are tired. Do you want me to ask Miss Teddy if she'll do your laundry?"

He didn't, but his socks could stand on their own at this point, and he needed fresh ones. It embarrassed him to think of Teddy washing his undergarments, but as a nurse, she'd handled much worse.

Even so, it felt improper. "No. There's a laundry on Arch Street." He pulled another dollar from his wallet. He'd need to make time to go to the bank.

David stood and tucked the package under his arm and opened the heavy door. "I'll be back as soon as I can."

Thomas leaned back against the wall. Douglass and Harriet could be sick—or worse. He closed his eyes. "Lord, is this worth it? I'm so tired. The constant striving for perfection is wearing on me emotionally and physically, and I seem to disappoint people at every turn."

He slid onto the cot and rubbed the heels of his hands over his gritty eyes until he could no longer hold up his tired arms. They dropped to his chest, where he felt the letter from his mother. He didn't have the energy to read the words now even though he craved connection with the familiar, the stable.

Witnessing suffering and death sat like an anvil on his chest, and he struggled to take deep breaths. He'd lost so many patients. Some to the yellow fever he could do nothing for, but others to ailments he hadn't caught soon enough or infections he should have been able to prevent. Maybe he wasn't cut out for this work. Maybe he should have followed in Jimmy's footsteps.

"Lord," he cried out even as he felt the warmth of tears fill his ears. "Lord." When was the last time he'd called on that name? Tears came harder.

Thomas woke and checked his watch. He'd only slept his routine two hours. His feet hit the floor with a thud, and he realized that, not for the first time, he'd slept in his shoes. The weight of earlier remained, and Thomas splashed water from a bowl and dried his face with the scratchy towel. He should have given it to David as well.

What was he doing here? This was no way to live. Gone was the excitement of learning, the passion for healing, the sense of purpose that had once driven him forward. All that remained was a hollow shell of the person he used to be, trapped in a cycle of exhaustion and disillusionment.

Would dedicating so much of his life be worth it in the end? This wasn't the fulfilling career he had dreamed of.

Dreams. What even were those anymore? He only found disappointment wherever he turned.

Emmaline's scowl flashed through his mind as she'd reprimanded him for being tardy for the opera over a month ago. He'd used precious funds to get from the hospital to the boarding house to bathe and change into proper clothing. Nothing pleased the woman, and he'd not had to work hard to avoid her. There hadn't been time for such frivolities.

He didn't even measure up to the expectations Dr. Whitaker placed on him. What he wouldn't give to talk to his family and seek their guidance. He touched the letter in his pocket and pulled the wrinkled paper from the envelope. Only, the writing inside wasn't that of his mother. He scanned to the bottom to confirm Clint's name.

Son,

I pray you are well, especially with the news I am about to share. Henry and I continue our weekly Bible study at the jail, and this morning, after I lifted you to the Lord, he prayed for Gabe. Your mother says she told you of Gabe's fighting and subsequent jail time. What she didn't share was the extent of his misery.

Gabe suffers from headaches and what your sisters call brooding mood swings. The old Little Sun is nowhere to be found in those eyes of his, which are now usually red-rimmed. Henry says he doesn't believe the boy is prone to drink, but he complains of stomach aches similar to what the sheriff has seen in those who drink homemade gut rot.

Henry said Gabe spent his three days in the jail sleeping but never seemed to improve in his demeanor. The boy's as mad as a polecat and reeks of unhappiness. We last saw him three weeks ago when he ended up in jail again. Gabe lost his job in the mines. Sheriff says when he released Gabe, he was headed northeast, away from Rolla. When he left, he had nothing but the clothes on his back.

Pete headed to Rolla and gathered Gabe's things but found no clues to help him determine where his son had gone.

I've given a few medical details on purpose. Henry thinks it's spiritual, which I am certain is a factor, but your mother believes there is something else. She's heard word of many in the lead mine getting sick, though not exactly like Gabe.

I thought you should know. Perhaps you have found some new cure for unknown illnesses. I wouldn't put it past you. God has ordained your steps for His glory and good works in order to make his name known.

Sincerely,

Clint

They had more faith in him than he had in himself. What was he to do with this information? Even if he knew what was wrong, it was not like he could hop on a train and head home. Gabe wouldn't likely be there anyway.

"Where have you gone?" He knew Gabe wouldn't return to his Arapaho people. Reservation camps had less medical help and work than Shumard Oak Bend.

Thomas looked at the envelope stamped February 16. He reread Clint's words. If Gabe had left three weeks before this letter was written, that would mean his friend had left in late January. *Northeast.* Why? This time of year, travel by horse would be tough, but on foot?

Thomas crumpled the letter. "I do not have time for this, Gabe. I've pulled you out of more scrapes than I can count. I gave you to the Lord long ago. This time, I'm leaving you there." Thomas threw the paper on the floor and watched it roll, stepping on it as he walked out the door and back to work.

"There you are." Dr. Whitaker did not sound pleased. The man covered his mouth and an expletive Thomas was thankful he did not have to hear.

"Good day, sir." Thomas pasted on a smile.

Dr. Whitaker's scowl did not change as he looked from Thomas's shoes to his head. "I believe your Good Book says cleanliness is next to godliness. You'd do well to heed those words."

"Yes, sir." Thomas ran his fingers through his hair, getting stuck in a tangle and having to pull his fingers out.

"You can't represent the hospital, the university, your class, or the Whitaker name looking like that. There's no time for more than a cut and shave, but see that you get one. Now."

"Yes, sir." Thomas trudged his way back up the steps to get his wallet. He kicked the balled-up paper when he entered and watched it skid under the cot. He didn't have time for himself. How was he expected to fix Gabe's problems, too?

"Come unto me, all ye that labor and are heavy laden, and I will give you rest." The words from Matthew echoed in a faraway corner of his mind. He didn't even have time for God. His life was out of balance, leaving him feeling hopeless. He rubbed one shoulder, doing his best to relieve the tension. Maybe the barber could release the knots.

Thomas looked at the single remaining dollar and a few

coins. He'd have enough for the barber and something to eat from a street vendor, but he'd need to get to the bank. He hoped Dr. Whitaker wouldn't miss him for the few extra minutes he planned to take.

And, if he did, what did it matter? Everyone was disappointed in him. What was one more?

Chapter 23

April, 1873
Thomas

One more month, and he'd graduate.

If he survived that long.

The weight of exhaustion had become Thomas's constant companion, pressing down on him relentlessly. Yet, amidst the fatigue, the demand for swift, precise decision-making never relented. There were expectations, and he could not be found wanting.

It was bad enough a cleaner had discovered him squatting in the hospital attic. It had necessitated adjustments, and he'd found solace in returning to his room at the boarding house. The gift of lobbying for his fellow students and being granted a single day of respite each week for the remainder of the term made all the restless nights worth it.

The rain drummed against his window, a dreary accompaniment to his thoughts. Thomas had no desire to emerge from the warmth of his bed. Though fewer lecture classes alleviated some strain, the burden of responsibility remained unabated.

While a student of his caliber could easily forgo attending classes altogether, his role as ambassador obligated him to assist those persevering through the board's rigorous expectations to attain their degrees.

Knock, knock.

Thomas swung his feet to the floor. "Coming."

"It's David," the boy whispered into the wood.

Thomas opened the door to two brown paper-wrapped packages.

"Laundry's in this one. The lady said your clothes are dirtier than a miner's. At least, I think that's what she said. She's kinda hard to understand."

"Thank you, David. And the other?"

"Cook saved the innards from the chickens for your friends. Says liver, heart, and gizzards will get them feeling better soon. You want some breakfast? There's eggs, bacon, and bread left."

The clock struck eight. He'd lain around longer than usual. "I'll dress and be right down." He'd need to hurry if he planned to spend time with Douglass and Harriet and still make it in time for dinner at the Whitakers'. This time, he wouldn't be late.

Thomas washed, dressed, and grabbed his satchel on his way to the kitchen. The room was quiet as he swallowed rather than fully chewed his food. Over the past years, too many missed meals had taught him this skill. Eating food for the sake of sustenance was now ingrained. His mother would have a fit when he got home.

The house was quiet as he reached for his Mackintosh

on the coat tree. The rain jacket would be cumbersome and stuffy in this unusually warm spring weather. He opted for the umbrella tucked underneath but could not locate it. He bent farther under the hanging garments.

The front door swung open, colliding with his hip, and a coat covered his head as he stood up.

"Oh! I'm so . . ." The female on the other side burst into tears.

He hadn't meant to scare her and pulled the jacket away from his face. "Teddy?" He instinctively reached for her, but she recoiled.

"Don't. Don't." The frantic words rushed from her lips even as the umbrella went up, creating a barrier.

He hadn't frightened her; someone else had. The taste of metal filled his mouth even as the coolness of steel wrapped around his heart. "What happened?"

"N-n-nothing," she stuttered. "You frightened me; that's all. Too many ghost stories as a child." She swiped at her face. "I've made a mess. I need to clean this up." Her still-open umbrella dripped on her muddy shoes.

Trembling hands could be the result of the stress of being frightened, but the slight sheen of sweat on her brow didn't likely come from fast walking. Teddy stepped back, and Thomas watched her pupils dilate even more. Her sympathetic nervous system was in overdrive, and Thomas wasn't sure which response, fight or flight, was next. He stepped back, putting the coat tree between them, hung the jacket, then picked up the satchel he'd dropped.

Teddy didn't move. Like a statue in a storm, her taut

muscles still gripped the umbrella handle. Water continued to puddle at her feet. "Teddy, I'm going into the kitchen to get a towel." He backed away rather than turning until he reached the dining area, where he laid his satchel. "I'll be right back."

Teddy's gaze darted wildly around the room.

He spoke quietly. "You're safe." The words released something in her, and her body began to shake. This was going to require more than a towel to clean up.

Thomas strode to Cook's door and banged on it. "Cook?"

The woman's eyes went wide when she opened the door. "What is it? Is David hurt?"

"No, ma'am. I'm in need of towels, and—" Thomas rubbed his neck. "Teddy needs a woman's touch."

"Say no more." Cook grabbed a stack of clean towels and took deliberate steps. Thomas sank against the counter and listened to Cook's soothing words in the other room.

"Don't you be worrying none about the floor, child. May I take the umbrella for you?"

Thomas marveled at the woman's tone, the same one he'd used hundreds of times on a frightened animal that could be dangerous if not handled carefully. He rubbed his temples and remained in the kitchen until he heard the women heading up the stairs, Cook's soft words encouraging Teddy with each step.

What could have possibly happened to upset her so? Teddy had served as a war nurse. Perhaps some type of memory had surfaced. Only, she seemed to have an aversion to him, not Cook.

Him, a male.

Her, a female.

He felt the veins pop out in his neck. *If someone has been improper with her—* Thomas couldn't finish his statement.

The clock struck eight thirty. There was nothing more he could do here now, but he'd get to the bottom of this.

If she'd let him.

Harriet opened the door. Her hollow cheeks matched the slimness of her waist. The apron strings wrapped around and tied in the front in an uneven bow.

"Thomas. It's good to see you. Douglass isn't up quite yet, but the coffee's on."

He closed the door behind him, allowing fresh air to fill the stale room for a moment. "Is he feeling better?"

"Some. Every day is a new day. He's aged ten years in the past nine months."

Nine months. Had he really only visited a handful of times in that period? "I brought you something. Actually, Cook sent it." He handed her the waxed paper-wrapped package. "She's convinced chicken innards cure anything."

"She'd be just about right. I'll chop it up real fine and make giblet gravy. Douglass will like that over rice."

Gray hair and an unshaven face peered around the bedroom doorframe. "Did I hear my name?"

Thomas moved to where Douglass held the doorframe and offered his arm. Douglass's stooped form leaned on Thomas as he struggled to maintain balance. Every step was labored, and his legs wobbled as he turned to sit.

"Whew. These old bones ain't what they used to be." Douglass's veined hand shook as he wiped at his dry lips. Every motion was slow and looked painful.

"Are your joints bothering you with this rain?" Thomas slid the coffee Harriet placed before him to Douglass.

"Part of aging, son." He took a sip, the liquid spilling on the table when he replaced the heavy ceramic mug. "Tell me about you. You done with your schooling yet?"

"Classwork, yes, sir. But I have a few more hoops to jump through. Nothing is guaranteed until I hold that signed diploma in my hand."

"Fine. Fine." Douglass laid his hand flat on the table. His yellowed nails, which were full of ridges and cracks, looked odd next to the chalky brown skin. Thomas wanted to reach over and cover the hand to still the tremble.

Harriet joined them, setting two more cups on the table. The familiar spark of love passed between his two friends. Thomas had expected to feel something like that with Emmaline by this point, but all he saw in her eyes was disappointment and frustration.

"How's your girl?" Douglass asked.

"Emmaline? She's fine. I'm headed to the Whitakers' this

evening for dinner."

"Well, we won't keep you."

Thomas finished his coffee. "Oh, no. I'd planned to spend the morning here. I noticed you have a dead tree limb near the house. I thought I might take that down for you today."

The two exchanged glances, and Thomas quieted.

Harriet worried her napkin. "We were hoping you'd do something a little different today if you have the time." She looked at her husband.

"Anything."

Harriet laughed. "Don't be agreeing until you hear what Douglass is asking."

Thomas waited for Douglass to put his coffee mug down, but the man only stared at the liquid.

Harriet finally spoke. "If you won't ask, I will. I don't have the strength to get Douglass in and out of the tub, and he's sorely in need of a good soak in hot water."

Thomas was not prepared for that but didn't flinch. "Douglass, I'd be happy to assist you. No, don't go taking back the request. You shake that head all you want. I've already agreed. See, I'm already rolling up my sleeves." He stood. "I'll head to the shed and get the tub. Harriet, you may as well boil enough water for two." Her eyes went wide, and Thomas laughed. "You can get your own bath, but I'll change out the water for you."

"Well, isn't that just the most thoughtful thing? Did you hear that, Douglass?"

"I may be getting old, but I've still got my hearing." He winked at his wife.

Thomas sank into the boarding house tub and let out a sigh. It had been a good but draining day. The tree had proved hard work, but seeing Douglass's emaciated frame had been harder. Douglass wasn't long for this world. Thomas was all too aware of the final stages of life.

He'd tucked the man in bed, promising to be back the following week on his day off, but had said goodbye knowing it may be the final time. Harriet's side work seemed to be keeping food on the table, not that they were eating much, and he was thankful the woman had a source of income. But Thomas would pull from his savings if needed to ensure the comfort of his friends.

He dreaded the day Douglass would depart from this world, his heart heavy with the impending loss, almost as much as the thought of arriving late to the dinner party looming ahead if he didn't hasten his steps. He dunked under the water and rinsed the soap from his hair.

Back in his room, Thomas stared at his reflection. He almost didn't recognize himself. "What's the plan, Thomas?" The figure in the mirror didn't seem to have an answer either. He straightened his tie and opened the door. Whispered voices came from behind the door with the wreath. It had spring flowers in it now and was the only brightness at this moment.

Teddy didn't want his help. He couldn't fix everyone's

problems, especially if they didn't ask. Giving Douglass a bath hadn't been his idea of an enjoyable afternoon, but he would never say no to a friend's request. If Teddy wasn't willing to ask for assistance, there wasn't anything he could do.

Anger turned to resignation as Thomas accepted Teddy's reluctance to accept help. He couldn't force assistance onto someone unwilling to seek it themselves. While he might lack the energy to delve into the root of Teddy's struggles, he could still offer prayers for guidance and comfort.

He shut his door more forcefully than necessary and locked it. At the bottom of the stairs, he glanced into the parlor to find Reggie and Merriweather playing dominoes, unaware anyone was watching. They shared the same look he often saw pass between Harriet and Douglass. He heard a coach approach and stepped out into the damp Philadelphia evening, its moisture settling like a cloak around his mood.

Thomas opened his eyes and wiped at his mouth. He must have dozed. He ran his tongue over his teeth and took in a fortifying breath before descending the single step from the carriage. The toy soldier, forever at his post, did not speak but pointed to the library. Thomas was familiar with the sequence of events: drink, discussion, dinner, doldrums, and possibly dancing if Dr. Whitaker did not over-imbibe.

"Thomas, my boy. The women are running behind, giving us a chance to talk. Please join me." Dr. Whitaker's words slurred as he lifted his glass of amber liquid from where he sat in a leather chair.

At least there would be no dancing this evening. The man's leg, which was crossed over the other, bounced. Thomas was hypersensitive, and the motion scraped at his raw nerves. Maybe the evening would go better if he were hypnotized.

He stared at the up-and-down motion of the black leather. Although the man's shoes were buffed to a high shine, the sole was worn, showing the interior layers of leather.

He heard nothing the man droned on about and took in the curtains, faded by the sun. The vase of flowers was dried rather than fresh, a few of the stalks broken and silk flowers missing.

Had the house always been in this state of disrepair? Why hadn't he noticed the worn rug under his feet and cracked leather under his hand before? He watched Dr. Whitaker's animated hand motions as his lips moved, but Thomas heard nothing.

"Snap out of it, boy."

A shoe connected with Thomas's foot.

"Have you fallen asleep with your eyes open? So, what are your thoughts?"

Thomas had no idea what the man was talking about. From the recesses of his mind, he pulled a phrase he'd heard Jimmy use. "That is really something." He shook his head as if still processing the information.

"Exactly what I thought. I knew you'd think so as well. Fascinating, really. The marvels of medicine continue to amaze me. The future of medicine looks bright. Which brings me to the next subject—your future."

Thomas found it easy to focus now. "Sir?" he inquired.

"What are your thoughts on becoming the next general surgeon on staff? Upon graduation, naturally."

"Of course," Thomas replied, feeling his heart quicken.

"With a position like this, alongside Emmaline, you'll ascend rapidly in society's ranks. You've already established quite a remarkable reputation. We'd even consider you for an associate role on the new committee to the board. We'll soon discuss our fine hospital being the first teaching hospital in the East. You'd be at the forefront of a new era. Why, Emmaline, despite her youth, would assume the role of matriarch among incoming students."

Thomas let the man continue, the alcohol seemingly fueling the rambling discourse on the implications of having a son-in-law of high status.

Had this been the man's intention all along? To elevate his daughter, given his lack of sons? Or was it to bolster his own name and standing in Philadelphia society?

"Ah, there are my lovely wife and daughter."

The man stood and wobbled. Thomas reached out to catch the man, but Dr. Whitaker handed him the empty glass.

"That's a good boy. Already caring for your old man."

He'd cared for an old man today, but it wasn't this one.

"Dinner is served, darling." Mrs. Whitaker took her husband's offered hand.

Thomas followed the Whitakers into the dining room, his mind still reeling from Dr. Whitaker's proposal. He took his seat, trying to shake off the fog that enveloped him. The table was set with elaborate silverware and crystal glasses, but the air was heavy with tension.

Between courses, Mrs. Whitaker made small talk, but Thomas couldn't focus on the conversation. His thoughts kept drifting back to the offer Dr. Whitaker had hinted at. The position at the hospital was a prestigious opportunity, one that could significantly advance his career. And the offer of Dr. Whitaker's daughter's hand in marriage added another layer of complexity to the situation.

Thomas couldn't ignore the nagging feeling that something wasn't right. Why had Dr. Whitaker chosen this moment to make such a proposal? And why did it feel like there was more to the offer than met the eye?

The meal sat like a stone in his stomach. He needed to talk to Dr. Whitaker—but not with Emmaline in the room.

Emmaline's glass tipped. "Oh, how clumsy of me. And on my new dress." She locked eyes with Thomas.

Could Emmaline read his thoughts? Was she giving him the opportunity he desired?

Mrs. Whitaker stood. "Come, dear, let's get you changed. Gentlemen, we shall meet you in the music room momentarily."

This was his chance. "Dr. Whitaker, may I speak with you in private for a moment?" Thomas asked, trying to keep his tone casual despite the urgency he felt.

Dr. Whitaker looked pleased, as if he knew the outcome of this discussion. Rising from his seat, he motioned to the door. "Of course, Thomas. Shall we adjourn to the music room as instructed?"

They made their way down the hall. Dr. Whitaker turned to the servant. "Close the door, would you, Otis?"

Thomas wasted no time getting to the point. "Dr. Whitaker, I appreciate the offer you mentioned earlier, but I need to understand the full extent of what you're proposing." His voice was steady and firm, unlike his nerves.

Dr. Whitaker's expression turned sober, and he motioned for Thomas to take a seat. "What I'm offering you is a chance to excel in your career, to make a name for yourself in the medical community."

Thomas nodded, but his mind was racing. There was more to this offer than just professional advancement. Did the man expect him to marry his daughter and remain in Philadelphia forever?

Dr. Whitaker's foot bounced over his knee, showing his impatience.

"Sir, with all due respect, I was clear from the beginning that I would be returning to Shumard Oak Bend upon graduation."

"Ah, but all that has changed now. You have my daughter to consider. Your plans are no longer solely yours to decide. Your life has become intertwined with hers, and your future hinges on the decisions you make."

A subtle threat lingered beneath the man's words, a silent warning that hinted at consequences if Thomas didn't comply with his wishes.

Thomas's gaze hardened. He did not appreciate being bullied. "Indeed, sir. And I assure you, I will consider all aspects of your offer carefully. In due time."

"Don't wait too long, Mr. Shankel. Graduation is upon us, and every decision you make seals your fate."

It was a good thing Thomas didn't believe in fate.

Chapter 24

May 1873
Teddy

T eddy raised her water glass, its crystal surface catching the warm glow of the candlelight that danced around the room.

The chatter of the other boarders and friends quieted as all eyes turned to her. She could feel the silent support of their friendship enveloping her like a comforting embrace.

"To the new Dr. Thomas Trexler Shankel," Teddy began, her voice steady but ladened with emotion. "May we never need his services but always cherish his friendship."

"Hear, hear!" echoed around the table in a chorus of agreement. Glasses clinked in a symphony of celebration, but beneath Teddy's forced smile, a tumult of conflicting emotions churned within her.

Anger simmered just beneath the surface, a fiery resentment toward the man who had ensnared her friend in his clutches. Pity, too, tugged at her heartstrings for the choices Thomas had made and the consequences he would face. Yet, amidst the turmoil, there was a flicker of happiness for her friend's achievements and a twinge of regret for her own inaction, her silent involvement in his plight.

As Mrs. Jones clapped her hands with the pride of a doting parent, Teddy's gaze lingered on Thomas, noting the flush that crept up his neck, the humility etched in every line of his face. He'd always been one to shy away from the spotlight, to deflect praise with a self-effacing charm that endeared him to all who knew him.

Mrs. Jones spoke over the group. "Thomas, you must make a wish and blow out the candle," she urged, her voice gentle but insistent.

Thomas shook his head, his gratitude palpable even in the subtlest of gestures. "You've all done far too much already. Thank you," he murmured, his breath causing the flame to dance and sway.

Crocket held a match at the ready, a playful glint in his eye. "With purpose, man. Not by accident."

Thomas chuckled softly, a sound laced with warmth and genuine affection. "Right. I wish . . ."

Merriweather squealed. "You can't tell us your wish, or it won't come true!" she admonished in earnest.

"Very well," Thomas conceded with a good-natured grin. "Then, I pray I'll be blessed for the rest of my days with friendships equal to those gathered around this table."

Teddy was proud of Thomas and his accomplishments. Mrs. Jones, Cook, David, and the Douglasses sat at the table with them. So much had changed in two years—most for the better but not all.

Teddy busied herself handing out cake, refilling water glasses, and replacing dropped napkins—anything to keep her hands and mind busy.

Thomas wiped his mouth. "Cook, this may be the best cake you've made yet. You could open a bakery and make a fortune."

Cook pointed to Crocket. "Not me, a gift from your friend."

Crocket puffed out his chest. "Prune cake. My special ingredient adds a touch of texture to the cake and zip to the rich flavor. Would you care to venture a guess, Mrs. Douglass?"

Harriet worked her mouth as if taking in each individual flavor. "Buttermilk for your liquid, and"—she lifted the cake and studied it closely—"orange zest for the zip, as you called it."

"Well done."

Teddy had the perfect vantage point to study her friends as they conversed with each other. She continued around the table, taking her time pouring. Teddy felt eyes on her and looked to see Mr. Douglass scrutinizing her. She walked his way and leaned down.

"Is there anything I can get for you, sir?"

"Sir. Posh. My station's far below yours. Call me Douglass. And yes."

Teddy crouched to be close enough to hear his weak reply.

"Come care for me."

Teddy wasn't sure she'd heard him correctly over the hum of voices. She looked to his wife for confirmation, but the woman was still engaged in conversation with Crocket. Teddy placed the pitcher on the table, which allowed her to kneel before the man. "Care for you in what way?"

"I'm dying and an awful burden on my wife. My Thomas says you may have time during the day to ease some of my wife's burden."

Harriet turned her head, apparently able to take part in two conversations at once.

"You're no burden, but having some help a few hours a day would be a welcome gift. Let's talk later. Today, we focus on Thomas."

Teddy patted the man's wrinkled hand, and he covered hers with his other.

The man's voice was quiet. "We could help each other. I know a restless heart when I see one."

Teddy's throat tightened. By the looks of the man, she wouldn't have a job for long, but even a few extra cents a week would make a difference. The pain of not knowing her future weighed heavily on her mind.

"I'd be honored to assist you, Douglass. We'll make arrangements after the party."

She glanced at Thomas. He'd done this for her, but she'd not been the same kind of friend to him.

Mrs. Jones used her fork to tap on her glass. "Thomas, please share your plans with us. I certainly hope you desire to remain here, even though you're now a distinguished doctor."

"If you'll have me, there is no other place I'd rather be. I've been offered the position of general surgeon at the hospital. The powers that be haven't fully approved it. There are still a few hoops to go through, but I should start by the end of the month."

Reggie's brow furrowed with curiosity. "Ah, I see. So, instead of settling down in Missouri, you'll be honing your skills here. But why the change of heart? Wasn't Missouri where you intended to establish your practice?"

Thomas nodded, a hint of regret shadowing his expression. "Indeed. Missouri was my initial plan. However, circumstances have shifted. The opportunity at the hospital arose unexpectedly, presenting a chance to delve deeper into the medical field. It's not a decision made lightly, but it's one I believe will ultimately benefit both my career here and the community where I'm from when I return at some point in the future."

Teddy noticed a flicker of disappointment in Thomas's eyes.

Crocket joined in on the conversation. "Any idea which specialty you're leaning toward?"

Thomas paused. "Not yet. I'll need some time to assess the different departments at the hospital and determine where my interests and skills align best. But for now, I'll be serving as a floating general practitioner, lending my aid wherever it's required."

Teddy observed the subtle shift in Thomas's demeanor, recognizing the weight of his decision.

Mrs. Jones placed her napkin on the table. "It sounds like an exciting opportunity. I'm sure you'll excel in whatever path you choose."

Thomas offered a small smile, gratitude evident in his eyes. "Thank you. I appreciate your support. And, regardless of the specialty I pursue, my commitment to be here for Saturday evening game night is a priority."

Hearty cheers and laughter filled the room. Teddy knew his Saturday nights would not be spent with them. Not if Emmaline Whitaker had anything to say about it.

May 1873
Hospital

"Married? Armilda, that's wonderful." Teddy lowered her voice. "When? Where?"

"John is the quartermaster at the navy yard. He asked the chaplain to perform the ceremony on the ship they are committeeing."

Teddy wracked her brain for what Armilda was saying. "Commissioning. Yes. Oh, it must have been lovely. What did you wear?"

"Ladies." The gravelly voice of Head Nurse Callahan halted their conversation.

Teddy wanted to tuck tail and run, but Armilda's graceful turn and the hand on her arm kept Teddy in her place. Her friend held out the other hand to the woman, exposing the new gold band gracing her slender fingers.

"Thank you, Nurse Callahan. Nurse Morse and I were just enjoying a moment of friendship. Your ability to keep us on task is truly remarkable. It's a wonder you noticed since you stay so busy. As one who never takes a moment for herself, it's a challenge to measure up to the dedication you show to your job."

Teddy had no choice but to turn, or her expression would have given her away. Armilda may not always choose the right words, but she certainly knew the art of not mincing the ones she used. Teddy composed herself and chanced a glance back.

Nurse Callahan's expression hardened. "Nurse Morse, you will come to my office." The woman arched one side of her singular eyebrow and curled the corner of her thin lips into a smirk, her eyes narrowing slightly. Her look spoke volumes without uttering a word, dripping with contemptuous amusement. It was the kind of look that left a lingering sense of uncertainty in its wake.

"Yes, ma'am?" Teddy remained in the doorway, unable to stomach the stale smell of body odor and old cigarettes.

The head nurse riffled through the myriad papers on her desk, finally producing one. She picked up a pen, signed it, and placed it in an envelope. Her white tongue flicked in and out of her mouth as she licked the edge before sealing it tight. She held it out to Teddy, then shook it when Teddy didn't move.

"Nurse Morse, do you require that I walk it to you?"

"No, ma'am." Why couldn't she exude the same confidence as Armilda?

"You'll take this to Dr. Whitaker's office." The sly smile returned.

Teddy's breath caught in her throat. The room seemed to sway, and her vision blurred. Was she carrying Nurse Callahan's promised threat from earlier? Was this the document that could end her career?

Nurse Callahan wiggled the envelope again. "Take it. I'm not going to sit here all day. Deliver it to him. Personally."

Teddy took the envelope, the still-wet edge under her thumb causing her stomach to threaten mutiny. Her feet refused to move.

"I won't ask again." The chair creaked under the woman's weight. "And don't dawdle. You wouldn't want to be caught alone in the halls at this time of night."

She knew. Somehow, the woman knew. Nurse Callahan was intentionally putting her into a situation where Teddy felt vulnerable. Her knees went weak, and she forced herself out of the room, if only to get away from the wicked woman.

"And don't shirk your duties and ask Nurse Kull to do it for you. I have a way of finding things out," the woman yelled from her office.

Armilda popped her head out from behind a curtain. "Nurse Kress, now." When she saw Teddy's expression, she moved to her side. "What is it? Do I need to ruffle her up?" She lifted one fierce-looking fist.

Teddy couldn't laugh. "She—she—"

"Breathe." The word was a command.

Teddy obeyed and then showed her friend the envelope. "She wants me to deliver this to Dr. Whitaker."

Armilda's eyes narrowed. "Is he still bothering you?"

Still? Did she know the extent of what Teddy had endured, or was her friend making assumptions based on Teddy's behavioral changes? "Yes."

"I'll take it." Armilda snatched the envelope.

"No." Teddy looked at the open door, lowered her voice, and pointed to the office. "No. She said I had to do it."

"Then do it. That man is a bully, but you are strong. Now go." Armilda handed the envelope back, then pointed to the door as if the discussion was over.

Armilda would never throw her into the lion's den if she knew. "I'm not that strong."

"You are what you think you are. Now, unless you want us both in trouble, run the little errand and get back here."

Teddy knew Armilda's words weren't meant to be unkind. It was Armilda's nature to be matter-of-fact, and that was one thing Teddy admired in her.

"Right. I'll be back in a jiffy."

Teddy felt like she was wading through quicksand, each step an agonizing struggle dragging her down. The weight of her trauma bore down on her, suffocating her with every labored breath.

Her footsteps reverberated through the desolate corridors. The eerie silence amplified the pounding of her heart, each beat a thunderous echo in her ears. The faint creak of a door sent a shiver down her spine, her body instinctively recoiling in fear.

Wrapping her arms tightly around herself, Teddy tried to contain the tremors that wracked her frame, but her thin uniform provided little protection against the relentless grip of her anxiety. Her nails dug into the fabric in a futile attempt to anchor herself.

Summoning every ounce of courage, Teddy squared her shoulders and steeled herself against the encroaching dread. With a prayer on her lips, she clenched the envelope in her trembling hands, using it as a feeble shield against the man she loathed.

She turned the corner, and powerful arms grabbed hers, paralyzing her in fear. Gasping in shock, Teddy inwardly struggled to regain control of her emotions. The hands released her.

"Teddy?"

The sound of her name hung in the air, sending a chill down her spine. For a moment, she dared not open her eyes, afraid of what she might find.

When she finally summoned the courage to look, a pair of eyes brimming with concern looked into hers. Thomas stood before her, his features etched with a mixture of worry and determination, a silent sentinel ready to wage war on her behalf.

Unable to withstand the intensity of his gaze, Teddy felt her resolve crumble like sand slipping through her fingers. Tears welled in her eyes, blurring her vision as they spilled over onto her cheeks, a silent testament to the pain she had long suppressed.

She opened her mouth, but words would not come. She tried again. "I must deliver this to Dr. Whitaker," she choked out, her voice trembling.

Thomas's brow furrowed in confusion, but he made no move to take the envelope from her grasp. Instead, he stood before her, a beacon of unwavering support.

"Let me help you," he pleaded, his voice a gentle reassurance amidst the storm raging within her. "Whatever has happened, you don't have to face it alone."

Her head shook, and she lifted the envelope higher, trying to shield herself from taking on the pain she saw in his eyes.

"Hanky?"

With a trembling hand, Teddy reached out to accept the white flag he offered. She wiped at the torrent of tears.

"You're not alone," he said.

Teddy grasped at his words, desperate to cling to them like a lifeline. She knew she was not alone, but she could not place this burden on her friend.

This was one battle she needed to fight on her own.

Chapter 25

June 1873
Thomas

Thomas supported Harriet as she leaned over to throw the first handful of dirt on the wooden casket.

"Take me home, please, Thomas. There's no need for me to stay any longer. My Douglass isn't in that box. He's dancing at the feet of Jesus, just like I should be."

Thomas wasn't sure if she meant on Earth or in heaven beside her husband. "Of course." He led her to the carriage and helped her inside.

Harriet patted his hand. "He loved you." She used the other to dab at her eyes.

Thomas gazed out the window as he processed her words. Silence enveloped the carriage, and his heart filled with the weight of unspoken emotions. Harriet's hand remained on his, a gentle anchor in the midst of such loss. An unspoken understanding passed between them, conveying more than words ever could. "I know." The words came on a sob, and he cleared his throat. "What will you do?"

"For one, I plan on keeping Teddy on for as long as I can afford her."

"Don't worry about money, Harriet."

"No, son. You've done more than enough by paying for the burial."

Thomas wanted to do more. This woman was family.

Harriet turned in the seat to face him. "I hear those wheels turning in that head of yours. My Douglass wouldn't want you grieving his passing; he'd want you celebrating his going home. I had him nearly a year longer than expected. God gave me that. I can trust Him with the rest of my days."

Thomas wished he had the same confidence. He couldn't remember the last time he'd felt God's presence. Grammie would have told him he wouldn't hear God's voice if he wasn't in God's word. Thomas knew that was true but hadn't made time to commune with God in many months.

Two, to be exact.

Harriet squeezed his hand. "What has you all uptight? And don't tell me it's this." She swept her hand over her black dress.

"I like you better in blue." He winked.

"Oh, you. Good to see your humor isn't gone, just your spark. Where'd it go?"

"Harriet, if I knew that, I could cure the world of many ills." The words came out on one continuous breath.

"'These things I have spoken unto you, that in me ye might have peace. In the world ye shall have tribulation: but be of good cheer; I have overcome the world.' Don't allow the temporary troubles of this world to affect your eternal future."

"I suppose it's my earthly future giving me trouble."

"Your work or Miss Emmaline?"

"A good dose of both, but I don't want to burden you on this difficult day." He patted her hand.

"Burden? Son, seeing you like this is a greater burden than anything else I've faced today."

Thomas met her gaze.

"I'll always miss my Douglass. Impossible not to after thirty-eight years. But he's free from pain. Fully healed. You're the one needing care now. Let me help."

He'd said those words to Teddy recently, but she'd refused his help, and it was eating him alive. Thomas wouldn't allow Harriet to feel the same. The driver stopped, and Thomas helped Harriet down.

Thomas thanked and paid the driver, then assisted Harriet into the house. "If you're willing to listen, I'd like your advice."

"I'm all ears. Let me get out of these clothes, and we can chat."

"Mind if I make coffee?"

Her eyes misted over, but her smile was genuine. "I'd like that. And cut a slice of cake. People must think I need fattening up. I have enough cake and pie to feed an army."

Thomas removed his jacket and tie, then rolled up his sleeves. Little touches of Douglass were everywhere he looked. The stool he had crafted now rested in the corner by the fireplace. The shelving he had built held the tin of coffee Thomas pulled down. Even the worn imprint on the wooden handle of the coffee pot matched the size of Douglass's fingers.

Thomas wanted to turn back time. He'd known Douglass had been nearing death, yet rather than sacrifice time to be with him, he'd sent Teddy to help in the man's final days.

"Don't be dwelling on regrets."

Thomas laughed. "How'd you know?"

"You're slouching. Stand up tall."

Thomas did as she said and watched a smile spread over her face.

"I'm guessing you were wishing you had spent more time with Douglass in his final days."

Thomas nodded.

"What you may not know is Teddy needed to be here more than you."

He'd seen Teddy standing near the other boarders at the funeral but didn't remember speaking to her. "What do you mean?"

"That girl's dealing with a world of hurt and the weight she's carrying, well, Douglass helped lift some of it from her shoulders. He had that ability."

"Yes, ma'am, he did."

"She'll make someone a fine wife one day."

"Yes, ma'am, she will."

"Would have been a good one for you."

"Yes, ma'am, she would—" Thomas blinked.

Harriet's laughter filled the small room. "That's what I thought. You've liked that girl since you got here, but you got so caught up in working your way into Emmaline's world that you ignored your heart."

Thomas leaned his elbows on the table and hung his head.

"Is this what you want, Thomas?"

"Honestly? I don't know what I want."

"Well then, perhaps you should ask yourself if this is what God wants."

"I don't know what He wants, either."

"Starting there is a good idea. God desires to give you the desire of your heart, but if you don't know what that is, well . . ." Harriet sipped her coffee.

"My heart tells me one thing, and my head tells me another."

"Seems to me your head and your heart need about as much healing as Teddy's."

Thomas shifted in his chair. "She won't let me help her."

"Maybe not now, but in God's timing, you may be the only one who can."

My dearest Thomas,

Gabe has returned, at least in body. His mind is not the same. Pete found him in the same cave he'd rescued him from as a boy. They've done all they can and don't know where else to turn but to God for Gabe's healing.

Dr. Casey believes it to be gout and recommends eliminating organ meat and spirits, but there is no evidence Gabe has been imbibing in strong drink.

Thomas felt sick to his stomach. Had he returned to Shumard Oak Bend, he would have been there to help his friend.

A sturdy nurse with a military demeanor knocked on the door. "Dr. Shankel, you're needed in maternity."

Thomas refrained from saluting. "On my way." He folded the letter and placed it in his white coat pocket, then followed the sounds of a crying infant.

Thomas held the red-faced baby in his arms after giving the child a full exam. The boy's mouth puckered with each intake before wailing again.

"There's nothing wrong with your son that more milk won't cure. He's growing quickly, Mrs. Patterson. I recommend nursing more frequently. Every child is unique. Some children adapt easily to a set feeding schedule. This little guy may take a bit longer to get to a two-hour stretch."

287

He placed the child he'd brought into the world into the mother's arms. "You've healed nicely. I'll have your nurse begin preparations to send you home first thing in the morning."

Tears filled the woman's eyes. "Thank you for your excellent care, Dr. Shankel. Now, if you could make these ridiculous tears quit, that would be a bonus."

Thomas laughed. "Continue to rest, eat properly, and ask for help when needed." He looked at the father standing at the woman's shoulder. "Men can change diapers and clean dishes just fine."

The man put a hand on his wife's shoulder. "After what my wife went through, I'm hoping she'll let me do more than that. Thanks, Doc." He offered Thomas his hand.

The strong connection felt good. Thomas enjoyed interacting with his patients while they were coherent. He liked days in surgery, but the time with those patients felt as sterile as the room he operated in.

A nurse approached. "Excuse me, Dr. Shankel, you're needed elsewhere."

He handed the nurse the completed chart he held and followed her. "Where to now?"

"They sent word from recovery. One of your surgical patients opened up his stitches."

"On my way. You can release Mrs. Patterson in the morning. I've instructed her to increase her feedings. That's one hungry boy."

He could tell the old-school nurse did not agree, but she was wise enough to remain quiet.

"Please ensure she gets as much rest as possible tonight. Tomorrow, she'll be thankful for it."

The nurse gave a knowing smile. "Yes, Doctor."

Thomas was tired. Not the bone-weary tired he'd felt while in school, but a disheartening, disillusioned tired, if that was even a thing. He'd hoped to learn more and gain more experience while working these past few weeks, which he had, but nothing he did felt like it really mattered. Except for birthing that child. Maybe he should go into obstetrics, but doing that one thing for the rest of his life made him tired just thinking about it.

Thomas offered smiles to those he passed in the corridors but didn't recognize a single face. Images of familiar ones from home swam in his vision. He touched the letter in his pocket. He missed his family, Gabe, and the feeling of truly being a part of a community. Philadelphia was nice, but it wasn't his home.

He missed the wonder and excitement he'd once had about medicine. He no longer felt passionate about anything—or anyone.

Thomas slowed his steps. He suspected the reason he hadn't yet received his permanent position was that he was dragging his feet on proposing to Emmaline. There certainly was no passion there. She'd become tiresome and clingy, even a bit controlling—like her father.

Thomas knew he needed to make a decision. "Indecision is a decision." The words Douglass had once said to him echoed off the walls. He opened the door to the stairwell, the sound of it closing like a final drumbeat sealing his fate.

With each step he took, Thomas felt the weight of

Douglass's words pressing against his mind. *Indecision is a decision.* He couldn't afford to remain in the realm of indecision any longer.

As he descended the stairs, his resolve solidified. Today, he would make his choice, and whatever consequences it brought, he would face them head-on.

He opened the recovery ward door, nearly running into a commanding figure. "Pardon me."

"You are pardoned," the nurse said.

"I'm Dr. Shankel. Can you point me to Mr. Wellington? I understand his surgical site needs attention."

The nurse pointed with her pencil. "Three. But wash your hands first." She turned the pencil toward the lavatory before slipping into a patient area.

"Yes, ma'am," he said before thinking. There were a few nurses in this hospital who knew who was boss, and it wasn't him. Thomas swung open the door, only to freeze in horror at the sight that greeted him.

Teddy, usually vibrant and full of life, now looked like a ghost, her face drained of color, eyes wide with terror as she struggled against an assailant. Thomas clenched his fists, a surge of rage coursing through him, ready to unleash his fury on the man who had her pinned to the wall. But then the man turned, and Thomas's blood turned to ice.

"Dr. Whitaker," Thomas spat, the name heavy on his tongue. Suddenly, everything clicked into place, the missing pieces of the puzzle snapping together with chilling clarity.

Whitaker's face was a mask of malevolence, his features

contorted with a twisted satisfaction that sent shivers down Thomas's spine. He wiped his hand across his mouth and smoothed down the front of his jacket with deliberate, calculated movements. His eyes bored into Thomas's with a cold, unyielding gaze, devoid of any shred of humanity, like a stone gargoyle come to life.

In that moment, Thomas felt a surge of revulsion so potent it threatened to overwhelm him. He could scarcely believe what he was witnessing, the betrayal cutting deeper than any physical wound. This was the man he had trusted, the man he had looked up to—a monster masquerading as a mentor. The shock and horror of the realization washed over him in a sickening wave, leaving him shaken to his core.

"Thomas. Son. It appears your handiwork was less than desirable on your patient yesterday. Clean up, and get that taken care of," Whitaker said as if there were nothing untoward going on.

A frightening calm settled over Thomas as he surveyed the scene before him. Teddy's usually neat bun hung limp, her cap keeling to one side. Her arms covered her bodice, but the dress seemed intact.

Thomas replaced his initial surge of rage with a chilling resolve. He relaxed his fists, feeling the tension drain from his muscles as he lifted a hand toward Teddy.

"Teddy," he said softly, his voice barely above a whisper. His eyes locked with hers in a silent plea. "Come with me."

Teddy's response was not what Thomas expected. Instead of relief flooding her features at his offer of escape, her expression remained frozen in a mask of terror. Her breaths came in shallow, rapid gasps, her chest heaving.

Teddy's body trembled uncontrollably, and she leaned into the wall behind her as if trying to anchor herself to some semblance of reality. Her eyes, wide and dilated, darted frantically between Thomas and Dr. Whitaker.

Thomas could see the struggle playing out in Teddy's mind, the fear warring with the desperate desire to run. But fear held her captive, paralyzing her with its icy grip, leaving her unable to move, unable to speak, unable to do anything but tremble in silent terror.

Thomas held her frozen stare, a knot of dread twisting in his gut. He knew the decision he made in this moment would shape not only his own future but Teddy's as well. And as much as he longed to rescue her from the nightmare unfolding before them, he also knew that they were teetering on the edge of a precipice, with no way of knowing what lay on the other side.

Dr. Whitaker narrowed his eyes. "Choose wisely, Thomas. A decision like this will alter your future."

Dr. Whitaker's words hung in the air like a dark omen, a warning of the consequences that awaited him no matter which path he chose. But Thomas refused to let fear dictate his actions. With a steely determination, he reached out to Teddy once more, silently urging her to take his hand and trust him to lead her to safety.

Thomas's heart pounded in his chest as he stood resolute, his gaze unwavering.

Dr. Whitaker spat, "You would choose this strumpet over what I'm offering?"

The air crackled with tension as a surge of defiance rose

within Thomas. His gaze remained fixed on Teddy. Despite the palpable tension in the air and Whitaker's venomous words, Thomas's focus never wavered from the woman who stood before him, trembling and vulnerable.

A single tear slid down her ashen cheek.

The sneering face of Whitaker faded into the background. All that mattered was Teddy.

Thomas lifted his hand higher. Teddy met his gaze with a flicker of hope in her eyes. It was a small spark amidst the darkness, but it was enough to reignite the flame of defiance within him. When he repeated his words, his voice was steady despite the turmoil within.

"Teddy. I'm here for you." His eyes remained unwavering from Teddy's.

Dr. Whitaker's sneer only fueled Thomas's determination. He now saw the truth behind the facade. He'd witnessed first-hand the man's manipulation and disregard for others' well-being, including his own daughter's. Thomas's next steps became clear.

"What exactly is it you are offering?" Thomas asked, his tone laced with mock interest.

"Prestige. Power. Emmaline," Dr. Whitaker replied, his voice dripping with arrogance.

Thomas shook his head. Something flickered in Teddy's eyes. "I'm not interested in any of those. My friends mean more to me than anything you could offer."

Thomas watched Teddy's arms loosen. The Teddy he knew and loved was returning, gaining confidence with every breath.

A peace he'd not felt for months washed over him, and Thomas knew he had made the right choice—loyalty over ambition, friendship over prestige. A sense of clarity and purpose reinforced his resolve. He would stay true to himself no matter the consequences. His decision emboldened him, and he took a step forward.

"You do this, and you're finished, Shankel," the man said through a clenched jaw.

"Step out of the way." Thomas squared his shoulders and took another step toward the man.

"Don't threaten me." The man's anger was palpable, visible in the hard set of his jaw and the tense lines etched into his forehead. His eyes blazed with fury, daring Thomas to challenge him, but he stepped aside as if the trembling girl was of no significance to him.

Thomas offered Teddy his hand once more. This time, she moved quickly toward him and grasped his hand as if holding on for dear life. He moved her behind him. "Dr. Whitaker, I will have my resignation on the chief surgeon's desk in an hour."

The man shook with rage. "You are making a big mistake."

"The mistake was blindly following you rather than my heart." He squeezed Teddy's hand.

Thomas felt Teddy press up against his back. He didn't know if she was supporting his decision or if she needed him for support. "Nurse Morse is also tendering her resignation, effective immediately. You will ensure an extra two weeks' pay in her final check."

The man's sardonic laugh reverberated in the room. "Who are you to tell me what to do?" he sneered.

"The tables have turned. I'm the one who holds your future in my hands." Thomas didn't recognize the steel in his voice.

"No one would believe you," he scoffed.

The door opened, and Thomas heard the voice of the nurse from earlier, full of even more authority now. "Maybe not, but there's power in numbers."

Thomas missed Teddy's touch as she ran to her friend but knowing she was now safe gave him increased confidence. He took another step forward. This time, Dr. Whitaker's back pressed against the wall.

Thomas moved to the sink and peered into the mirror at the man who had yet to move, confronting the reflection of a man he had once admired. "I suggest you clean up. Spittle on one's face doesn't reflect well on the hospital or the university."

Slamming the door behind him felt good. He didn't see the women but heard whimpers coming from the head nurse's office.

Thomas would care for his patient—and then deliver on his promises. After that, only God knew—and he was perfectly fine with that.

Chapter 26

June 1873
Thomas

The birds chirped, announcing the morning's start, but Thomas did not feel their excitement. Dread filled his heart as he supported Teddy up the boarding house steps. Mrs. Jones greeted them at the door.

"What is the meaning of this?" Her words quieted as she took in the sagging form beside him. "Take her to her room. Then I will speak to you. In private."

He wanted nothing more than to sink onto the floor by his bed and seek God's guidance, but he knew this could not wait. He nodded and helped Teddy up the stairs, then knocked on the door.

"Who is it?" a gruff voice answered.

"Birdie, it's Thomas. And Teddy. Teddy requires assistance."

The girl flung open the door, her normally short, flat hair sticking up in all directions. Thomas heard Merriweather squeal and diverted his gaze.

"What happened?" Birdie demanded.

Thomas smiled in thanks for the words that did not include an accusation. "She's had a rough night and needs rest. I'll let her explain when she's ready." Thomas stood amazed as Birdie softened and pulled Teddy into a tender embrace.

"We'll take good care of her. Don't you worry."

Thomas nodded and stepped back as the door shut him out, possibly forever, from the girl he loved. He rubbed his chest. He'd known it all along, but that thick skull of his—no, he'd hardened his heart toward anything that might keep him from becoming a doctor. He'd accomplished that, but where had it left him?

Without a job. His stomach sank lower with each step down to the kitchen. He'd decided for Teddy as well. Now they were both unemployed. Thomas followed a waiting Mrs. Jones into the kitchen where Cook sat, wet hanky in hand. He held a chair for Mrs. Jones, then sat opposite them.

Mrs. Jones steepled her hands on the tabletop. "Dr. Shankel. Thomas . . ." She took a deep breath and whispered her next words as if they were painful to get out. "Is she compromised?"

Thomas's throat tightened. "Not in body, but most definitely in spirit."

Cook blew her nose.

Mrs. Jones remained stoic, but a single tear trailed down her cheek. "Is the perpetrator . . . ?"

"Teddy is safe." He would not reduce himself to gossip, no matter his feelings for the man. He wondered how the ladies had guessed the situation so quickly, but he'd learned women possessed an ability to sense these things.

"What can we do?" Cook asked.

"I don't know the answer to that question, but I'm trusting the Lord to provide it. What I know is this—I'll be returning to Missouri as soon as I've packed. Mrs. Jones, I'll pay you for my rent and Teddy's through the end of the month and next."

"Thank you, but that won't be necessary. Must you go?" Mrs. Jones wiped at a tear.

Thomas took the first full breath he'd had in hours. "Yes, and I'm praying Teddy will go with me, but she'll need someone to accompany her. I'll not be the cause of any more disgrace than she's already . . ." He could not finish.

Cook blew her nose again.

Mrs. Jones placed one hand over the other as if in prayer. "Perhaps one of the other girls will go."

"I'll go." A small voice came from the doorway, and all three turned.

Streaks ran down David's cheeks. He stepped in and stood beside Thomas.

"I'd miss you both awful if you left." David scrunched up his face.

Mrs. Jones's spine straightened. "It's impolite to eavesdrop."

David stood his ground. "It's wrong to hurt somebody, too. I don't know what happened, but I'll do anything to help Miss Teddy." His eyes pleaded with Thomas.

Thomas's heart went out to the boy, and he thought of the stories his mother had told of her and her younger brother Charlie setting out across the wilds of America to find refuge in the West. It could work.

Thomas put his hand on the boy's shoulder. "That's a fine offer, but your family might not appreciate it."

David turned to Cook. "Can I go?"

Thomas looked to Cook for understanding and watched as the woman pulled the boy to her side.

"I suppose I'm the closest thing to family you've got. But I'm not the one you should ask."

"Then who?" He looked at each face around the table.

Thomas felt more than heard from the Lord. "Teddy. You need to ask Teddy, but not today."

Mrs. Jones stood. "No more talk of this. We will give the girl all the time she needs to rest. David, wash your face, then head to the butcher for bones. Cook, we'll be making a stout broth for that girl. Nothing cures a weak heart like a hearty bone broth."

Thomas had known the women in his life were resilient, but he'd seen more examples today of strength in love than he'd thought possible. There'd been no condemnation of Teddy or him. These ladies cared deeply for their own. If Teddy would allow their ministrations, she'd recover, though Thomas was not the type of doctor to give a prognosis of how long that would be.

He slipped from the busy room and began the long walk to Harriet's, giving him plenty of time to process how and how much to share with the woman.

Thomas sipped his cup of coffee and waited for Harriet's response. She'd moved back and forth as if the kitchen chair rocked naturally while he'd shared an overview of the situation. He wasn't sure what to expect as a response.

Harriet met his gaze. "You could marry her."

He hadn't expected that. Thomas's mind whirled with a mix of surprise and consideration. Now that Harriet had voiced it, he found himself mulling over the possibility. Images of a shared future working together at their own clinic flashed through his mind, stirring a sense of warmth and excitement.

Yet, alongside that thought, doubts and uncertainties surfaced, reminding him of the complexities that such a commitment would entail. He couldn't deny the allure of the idea—until he remembered Teddy's fear-filled eyes. "She's not in a place where that discussion would come out favorably."

"Then, if she'll agree to go with you, you'll need a chaperone." Harriet stood and refilled their mugs.

"You could go with us," he pleaded.

"And leave Douglass?"

"You told me yourself he's not in that grave."

"That's true, but he is in this house. I feel his touch every time I run my hand over the smooth wood of the chair. I hear his voice in the crackling fire." Her eyes sparkled.

"I didn't think you believed in ghosts."

"Not ghosts, son. Memories. This house is full of them, and I can't leave those."

Thomas understood. He'd witnessed the same after the funeral. Douglass was everywhere in this home. "Then who? David offered. Apparently, he's an orphan. He could pass as Teddy's brother."

"Don't be rushing God. He'll provide in time. You book passage for three, and trust God with the details. And you let Teddy know I still want her coming each day. Often a body dealing with such a deep hurt needs a purpose to make them get out of bed and face the world."

"I'll do that," Thomas said.

"In the meantime, I believe we've some beseeching to do. Get my Bible."

As he walked to town later, Thomas carried Harriet's words in his heart—God would provide in due time. Their sweet communion in prayer had solidified his determination to convince Teddy to return with him to Shumard Oak Bend.

Each forward motion up the municipal building steps increased his resolve, and getting his affairs in order would be a good stewardship of his free time before heading home.

Home. He'd need to send a telegram letting them know of his upcoming return after he'd purchased the passage. So many details. And packing. He'd have more than the two crates he'd arrived with. The bookcase he'd added to his room had as many volumes lying on its surface as on its shelves. His magazine subscriptions would need to be redirected to his new address, as well as his final paycheck from the hospital.

Thomas held the door for a woman exiting the building. Her pert nose reminded him of Emmaline, as did the way she carried herself.

Emmaline. Speaking with her should be at the top of his list. His mother had always said to eat his brussels sprouts first to get them over with. He'd found it only ruined the rest of his meal, but like then, he'd tackle the distasteful chore as soon as he completed business with the clerk of court.

After completing his business, Thomas descended the stone steps and hailed a cab. He struggled to formulate the words to say to Emmaline but found none.

"Lord, may what I say be Your words. I harbor no ill will toward Emmaline or her family, though I trust Your Word and pray Your vengeance is carried out to the fullest extent of the law. I realize now that I should have sought Your guidance before acting on what I believed to be best for my future. I do not ask You to tidy up my mess, but to aid Emmaline in accepting the words You provide and to protect her heart from pain."

The tin soldier stood sentry at the door when Thomas alighted from the conveyance. "Good morning, sir. Might I enquire whom you wish to see?"

"Miss Emmaline."

The man looked at the sun. "This early?"

Thomas hadn't considered the time. "I can return at a more appropriate hour. Would you enquire when she might be available? I'll wait with my cab." Thomas needed the fresh air.

The man nodded once and slipped into the home. Thomas hadn't thought this through. He'd perfected the art of making snap decisions, but that didn't bode well when heeding the Holy Spirit's voice. Would he never learn to allow God to work in his timing?

The man opened the door. "She'll meet you in the library momentarily."

"Thank you." Thomas's stomach flipped. "Excuse me. Is Dr. Whitaker at home?"

"Not at present."

Thomas breathed a sigh of relief. He walked along the walls of the library, perusing titles and looking over his shoulder at every sound. He pulled a volume and opened it. The pages crackled with disuse. He turned at the sound of light footsteps.

Emmaline stood in the doorway. "Light reading this morning?"

Thomas replaced the book and bowed to the beauty before him. She was truly lovely, even with red-rimmed eyes. She knew. Maybe not the truth, but she knew something. He moved to the chairs.

"No need to sit. This visit will be quick." She stepped inside the door but stopped at the opposite edge of the worn rug.

"Emmaline," he started.

"Dr. Shankel. I wish to speak plainly."

Dr. Shankel. That spoke volumes.

She straightened her spine. "I wish to break our engagement."

Thomas wasn't sure which shocked him more—how God had handled the situation or that Emmaline considered them engaged when he'd never actually asked. He lowered his head and grasped his hands behind his back.

Emmaline spoke with unwavering resolve. "I hadn't fully understood your eagerness to return to the wilderness of the West. That was not part of the plan, and I refuse to accompany you."

Thomas's gaze snapped to her, but the sheen forming in her anguished eyes kept him silent.

"Father roused me early to relay your decision to relinquish the position he labored so generously and tirelessly to secure for you and our future."

Dr. Whitaker had done what? Thomas fought to maintain a stoic demeanor.

Emmaline pressed on. "Your choice simplifies mine. I do not harbor affection for you, Thomas. If I did, perhaps there would be room for forgiveness for this foolishness. Yet, I now realize you will forever remain the uncultured country dweller you were when you first arrived. I'm simply grateful I recognized it before committing the gravest mistake of my life."

Thomas stood dumbfounded. Could God really have made it this easy? As if taking the role of a patient receiving bad news, Thomas became resigned and lowered his gaze. "I understand."

"No hard feelings, darling. It's simply for the best."

"Of course, Miss Whitaker. I respect your decision and wish you all the best. I apologize for misleading you in my desires."

The toy soldier servant stepped into the room. "Your carriage has remained, sir."

Thomas nodded his thanks to the man, who displayed his first glimmer of emotion, which Thomas interpreted as a flicker of intrigue or perhaps a hint of bemusement.

Emmaline's usually poised and confident posture now seemed to wilt. Her eyes glistened with unshed tears, betraying the turmoil within.

Thomas watched Emmaline's lips press into a thin line, the tiny tremors betraying the effort it took to keep her emotions in check. Despite her best efforts, a flicker of pain flashed across her features, a fleeting glimpse of the heartache she fought so desperately to conceal. And yet, she held her ground, chin lifted in defiance, refusing to let him see the depth of her hurt.

She was struggling, and Thomas didn't want to add to her pain. "It has been my honor to know you, Emmaline. Thank you for your attempt to assimilate me into your world."

Thomas offered his hand in parting, and Emmaline allowed him to take hers. He pressed a kiss to her hand, noting the tremor that betrayed more than words ever could. One thing he had gleaned from his medical school experience was that the body revealed truths that even the most adept individuals endeavored to conceal.

Chapter 27

June 1873
Teddy

Teddy opened her eyes and blinked. The sheet covering her felt heavy. Panic worked its way into her mind. She clenched her teeth and pushed the thoughts away. Dr. Whitaker no longer had her in his grasp. She was safe. She turned and confirmed she was also not alone.

Birdie sat reading in a chair beside her. Teddy watched her friend's mouth move as if working to form an unknown word. Birdie's forehead wrinkled as she squinted and leaned closer to the page, chewing on the inside of her mouth.

A breathy sound escaped Teddy's mouth, and Birdie slammed the book closed.

Teddy smiled at her friend and leaned on one arm. "Whatever are you concentrating on so deeply?"

Birdie turned the book from front to back. "Your Bible. I hope you don't mind."

Teddy sat up, pulling the sheet to her neck. "I didn't know . . ."

"What? That I could read?"

Birdie's harsh response made Teddy flinch. "No. I didn't know you didn't have one of your own."

Birdie placed the Bible on the table with care. "How are you feeling today?"

Teddy yawned. "What time is it?"

"Three."

Teddy looked to the window. "In the afternoon? Why aren't you at work?"

"Sent word I was sick. Didn't lie. I'm sick of working." Birdie laughed at her own joke.

Tears surfaced, and Teddy struggled to speak. "For me?"

"Well, sure." Birdie's tone betrayed a hint of astonishment. "And I'll take down the guy who hurt you, too. Just say the word."

Teddy feared the girl meant it. "I'm fine, really. Just a bit shaken."

"Shaken is when you cut a tree, and it misses your baby brother by that much." Birdie made a short distance between her fingers. "You cried so hard and long you lost a day."

"A day? It's three in the afternoon tomorrow?"

Birdie's laughter filled the room. "And lost your mind to go with it." She sobered. "Thomas brought you home yesterday morning. Josephine put you in a hot tub and got you ready for bed. Merriweather fed you beef broth, and I stood guard. You've slept fifteen straight hours."

Teddy could not stop the tears.

"Knock, knock." Mrs. Jones poked her head in the door. "I heard laughter and hoped that meant you were up. I brought warm broth, and Cook made molasses cookies. She swears it's good for the blood."

"Thank you. Please, come in. You all have taken such good care of me. I'm sorry to have been a bother."

Mrs. Jones made a *tsk—tsk* sound. "No bother. Bernadette, if you need a break to stretch your legs, I'm happy to sit with Theodora while she eats."

Birdie hesitated until Teddy nodded at her. "Thanks, ma'am. Holler if you need me." Her expression left no doubt she was serious.

Mrs. Jones set the tray on the table and pulled out the chair. Teddy pushed off the bed, gave her legs a moment, then accepted the offered gift.

"Mrs. Jones?"

"Hmm?"

Teddy's arm felt too heavy to lift the spoon. "I may not have a job, but I have savings."

"If you're worried about rent, Dr. Shankel has taken care of that for you. As far as work goes, he left word that Mrs. Douglass still requires your help. He specifically said to wear something old. Harriet has canning to do."

Hard work sounded wonderful if she could get her strength back.

"You'll bounce back in no time. Eat your meal, and then Birdie can help you change. She's quite something. All that rough exterior, but a heart of gold."

Teddy took a sip of the broth, the taste both satisfying and nourishing. She realized how hungry she was. She pushed etiquette aside, picked up the bowl, and savored each sip.

Mrs. Jones tidied Teddy's bed and picked up Josephine's stockings from the floor, laying them on her bunk. "How you live with three women, I'll never know. It's worse than picking up after my Zebedee. That man could throw a penny across the room and into a mug but missed the laundry hamper every time."

The soup and the conversation warmed Teddy.

Mrs. Jones ran a finger under her eye. "But I wouldn't have changed him." She sat on Teddy's bunk and straightened the lace edge of her sleeve. "But he changed me." A noise like a small cough came from the woman's throat.

Teddy's curiosity got the better of her. "How long were you married?"

"Thirty-one years. I married him in a little church just down the road in 1839. I was a mere child of sixteen. All I wanted was to go to normal school and become a teacher, but I took one look at Zebedee and, well, that's all it took to change my mind."

Teddy took a bite of the molasses cookie and let the sharp tang fill her mouth. "How long has he been gone?"

"Soon to be four years."

"I thought he died in the war."

Mrs. Jones rubbed the fabric of her hanky between her finger and thumb. "In a way, he did. He never worked again, at least not in the traditional sense. We'd not had children, yet we had all these rooms, so we opened our home to boarders. Zebedee cooked all the meals. He could make a cake Crocket would salivate over."

Teddy realized the tension she'd been carrying was dissipating. "You said he changed you?"

"How my parents ever put up with me for sixteen years, I'll never know. I was such a precocious child and knew it. My father called me Cady Bug, saying I sounded like a cicada with my incessant noise. Which is ridiculous when you think about it because only the males make that buzzing noise to attract a mate."

Teddy covered her mouth to hide a giggle.

"But Zebedee would let me go on and on about every fact I knew. He'd ask me how to do something, or what type of bird that was, or, oh, any number of things."

She dabbed at her nose before continuing. "One day, he asked how to start the fire in the stove. My response? Zebedee Jones, we've been married for seven years. You know perfectly well how to start a fire. What are you asking me for?"

Mrs. Jones's laughter brought fresh tears down her sharp cheekbones. "He took me in his arms and told me he just liked to hear my voice." She folded her hanky and lifted her chin. "Such a silly story."

Teddy offered her most sincere smile. "It's a story of true love."

"Love? No, it's a story of devotion. I didn't fall in love with

Zebedee until after we buried our first child. He cared for me better than my mother could have had she been alive."

Mrs. Jones's laughter quickly turned to sorrow, her cheeks wet with fresh tears.

Teddy felt a pang of sorrow at the weight of Mrs. Jones's words. Teddy softened her features and offered a sincere smile. She extended her hand and squeezed Mrs. Jones's offered fingers. There were no words to properly express condolences for the gravity of the woman's loss, but Teddy offered a simple, "I'm sorry for your loss."

"Thank you. Things happen for a reason. We may not always understand God's ways, but look at all the children He's brought into my home. Technically, those under my roof are adults, but you'd never know it." Mrs. Jones pointed to Josephine's unmade bunk and the socks hanging over the edge.

Teddy let out a chuckle. "Thank you, Mrs. Jones."

"For what?"

"For being here for us. In some ways, we all still need mothering, and you're doing a fine job."

The woman blinked and lifted her chin. "Well"—her voice cracked—"what a nice thing to say."

Birdie pushed open the door with enough force to cause Mrs. Jones's hanky to flutter to the floor. "I'm back."

Mrs. Jones picked up the fabric. "So I see. Well, Theodora, you're in capable hands. If you're finished with your meal, I'll take your tray. I expect you to sit with us at the table this evening. None of this lying around all day." The woman winked when Birdie turned away.

"Yes, ma'am. I'll be down."

Birdie ran her fingers over the cracked leather of Teddy's Bible. "You need help getting dressed?"

"I'm feeling quite refreshed from my meal. I believe I can manage. Did you read something interesting while I slept?" Teddy asked her friend as she pulled her dress from the peg.

Birdie placed the worn leather book on her lap. "You had a ribbon in Matthew with lots of underlines. I thought writing in your Bible was a sin."

"The Bible is a precious gift. Those are God's inspired words and should be revered. But the paper they are printed on is just that—paper. I mark my Bible in different ways. There are underlines for emphasis, dates in the margins to remind me of a significant time God used that verse in my life, and even notes for clarity. It helps me. My Bible is my most cherished possession. I'm not defacing it with my writing."

Birdie ran her finger down the page. "Chapter six, verse eleven has me confused. I don't owe money to anybody, so why would I forgive a debt someone owes me?"

Teddy ran through the Lord's Prayer in her mind. "'And forgive us our debts, as we forgive our debtors.' Think of debts as wrongdoings. In this prayer, we're asking God to forgive us of those things that go against His laws and hurt His heart. We all need forgiveness, and in the same way, we are to forgive those who have wronged or hurt us."

"Do you forgive the man who hurt you?"

"He grievously wronged me," Teddy said, careful to choose the right words. "But yes, I do." Teddy meant those words, but it would be the forgetting that would take time.

"Help me with these buttons, will you?"

Birdie laid the Bible open on the table and secured the back of Teddy's dress. "I'm not sure I could. He doesn't deserve forgiveness—from me or God."

Teddy moved to her bunk and pulled out her shoes. "That's called grace."

"Grace?" Birdie ran one finger over the underlined section as if searching for the word.

"Yes. Grace isn't something that can be earned, but it is freely given, even when we don't deserve it. Just like we don't deserve love and forgiveness from our Heavenly Father, Jesus gave it anyway."

Birdie harrumphed. "Well, that man doesn't deserve any of it." She crossed her arms.

"That's why it's called grace. God's gift of grace and forgiveness is for everyone. No one deserves it. We didn't deserve His death on the cross for our sins—our wrongdoings, or debts. God wants us to forgive others, even when it's hard. We can't do it in our own strength."

Birdie tapped her foot. "But what if we can't forgive ourselves?" Her tone became reflective, and she diverted her gaze.

Teddy's compassion for this friend who had done so much for her in the past days increased. Birdie's hands were still tucked deep, or Teddy would have reached for one. She would have to connect with Birdie another way. She prayed her eyes conveyed understanding and kindness.

"Believe God's Word over your feelings." Teddy's gentle

words pulled Birdie's gaze back to hers. "When you ask, God not only forgives you but He also clears your guilty conscience. You may not feel it immediately, but God won't leave you as you walk beside Him. In 1 John 1:9, Jesus tells us: 'If we confess our sins, he is faithful and just to forgive us our sins, and to cleanse us from all unrighteousness.'"

Birdie leaned back in the chair. "Confess my sins to whom?" The girl's arms flailed.

"That is a question few ask, Birdie." Teddy saw a new interest in the girl's eyes. "Often, the biggest reason we can't easily accept God's forgiveness is because we haven't first asked for forgiveness from the ones we've wronged."

Birdie leaned on her forearms and blew out a breath. "Kinda hard when that person's dead."

Teddy wasn't certain how to respond. She closed her eyes and asked for help from above. "I'm not a Bible scholar, but I believe Psalm 51 addresses this. David knew the sacrifice God wanted more than anything was a broken spirit and a contrite heart. If you are truly sorry for your sin, the wrong you did to another, and there is no way to ask forgiveness from that individual, then repent your sin to the Lord and receive the forgiveness God offers you."

"What if it's hard?"

Teddy laughed. "It certainly isn't easy. If we had to forgive everyone we'd wronged before Jesus would accept us, we'd never come to Jesus. He does the work in us as we grow in Him."

Emotion filled Birdie's eyes. "That sounds good."

"You can have peace, Birdie. Jesus is waiting to wash away

your sins and give you new life in Him—a chance to start fresh and clean."

Teddy steadied her breathing. She needed to be patient and allow the Holy Spirit to work in Birdie's heart.

Birdie cocked her head and peeked out from one side as if embarrassed. "I don't know what to say. Will you help me?"

"Help you? That's the beauty of this, Birdie. You don't need my words. Jesus wants to hear words from your heart, not mine."

Birdie bowed her head. "I hope I get this right. Father in Heaven, hollow is your name."

Teddy tried to keep the mirth from escaping as she interrupted her friend's prayer and unique word choice. "You don't need to be formal. Just talk to God like you do me. Ask Him to forgive you of your sins and help you forgive others as you've been forgiven."

"God? I'm sorry for, well, you know what I did, and I shouldn't have, but I did, and I won't do it again." Birdie stopped.

Teddy looked up to see a light flush of color on her friend's cheeks.

Birdie held a pained look on her face. "Do I gotta say it out loud? Pray, I mean?"

"No, Birdie. It isn't me you're speaking to. It's God. He hears your thoughts and knows your heart. Confess your sin to Him, ask for His forgiveness, and accept His gift of new life."

Birdie bowed her head and clenched her hands so tightly

her fingers turned white. Her mouth moved and hands bobbed as she prayed. Teddy may not know what her friend was praying about, but she watched color return to Birdie's knuckles and her facial expression soften as the effects of what was happening in Birdie's heart shone in her countenance.

Birdie lifted her head. "I'm all done." A smile started on one side and spread to the other.

"That's a wonderful start. God desires all of your heart, Birdie. When you allow Him to direct your life, He will. Here." Teddy tenderly passed the girl her Bible. "This belongs to you now," she said softly, her voice carrying a gentle assurance. "May it guide you as you journey in obedience to Christ and deepen your understanding of Him."

The girl hesitated, her eyes wide with reverence before accepting the gift. Birdie swallowed hard.

A warm smile graced Teddy's lips as she shook her head gently. "It brings me great joy to entrust it to you, knowing it will be cherished and used to further your spiritual growth."

Birdie's smile lit up her face. "Thank you. It's the nicest gift I've ever gotten."

Teddy knew better. The gift of salvation was by far the best gift anyone would ever receive.

Teddy was thankful Thomas had rented an open carriage to transport her to Harriet's. The oppressive heat of the day and being so close to him in a confined space so soon after her ordeal would not have been easy.

He let out a low whoa to the horses. "I've errands to run. I'll be back this afternoon to pick you up. Does that work for you?"

Teddy nodded. "Yes. Please don't get down. I'm fine." She lifted her skirts and stepped to the ground, then turned back to him. "Thank you."

"My pleasure. Enjoy your day."

The *clip-clop* of hooves and scrape and grind of a poorly set wheel followed her all the way to Harriet's home. Teddy heard singing at the open door and stood motionless as she soaked in the words. Teddy knocked and stepped inside. "That was beautiful. I don't know that one."

"Teddy." Harriet wiped her hands on her soiled apron and opened her arms.

Teddy melted into the embrace. "I've missed you."

"I've missed you, too. Three days of canning, and I've sung every hymn in the book. That one was 'Lord, My Weak Thought in Vain Would Climb.'"

"Beautiful words, unusual tune."

Harriet laughed. "Some of that could have been on me, not the writer."

"What was the line about why this or that?"

"Ah, yes, I suppose that line would connect with your heart. 'Why that, or this, thou dost ordain'? We don't always understand God's ways, do we?"

"No, ma'am. As the song says, when the night is dark, and I can't rest, I can only lean on my Lord."

"Mmm-hmm, that I understand. There are some dark nights without my Douglass, but 'Thy sovereign wisdom I adore, and calmly, sweetly, trust thee still.' Next to the Bible, music always speaks most to my heart."

Teddy grabbed an apron from the peg on the wall and covered her dress. "What are we canning today?"

"I did the raspberries on Monday. Those couldn't wait. On Tuesday, I finished the blueberries. Yesterday was tomatoes. Today is sweet corn." Harriet pointed to the bushel baskets leaning against the wall outside the back door. "I made a trade with a farmer. His sweet corn is better than cash. Tomorrow starts the cucumbers. Our little store down the way says they'll buy all my pickles. They ran out last year. I care little for them. Those were Douglass's favorite."

Teddy hauled and shucked as Harriet rambled while standing over the hot stove. Even with the windows and doors open, the room was thick with steam.

"Did you do much canning growing up?" Harriet asked, taking a moment to wipe her apron over her face and neck.

"Yes, ma'am. I grew up on a farm. Dill pickles aren't my favorite either, but I can eat my weight in bread and butter pickles." Teddy pushed the husks and silks into the basket.

Harriet pulled the jars from the pressure cooker and prepared the next jars to go in. "We'll be making both if my feet can manage another day of standing."

"Switch jobs with me. You sit and cut this corn off the cob. I can handle the pressure cooker and throwing this mess out."

"Throw it out? Didn't your mama teach you to make corn broth?"

"I've heard of corn silk tea, but broth?"

"Absolutely. I'll take you up on your offer." Harriet sighed as she sat. "Now, get the stock pot off that shelf over there. Yes. That one. Fill it with all this goodness. Husks, too. Wait, cut the bad part off that cob. Good, now add enough water to cover them and let it cook for an hour."

The heavy pot clanged on the stove as Teddy struggled to set it down. "What do you do with it?" Teddy wiped the cabinet of the moisture.

"After straining it, that broth makes fine liquid to use with grits, rice, corn chowder, just about anything a woman needs to feed her family. It's a stock base and adds good flavor. Just don't be feeding it to your babies. Might bother their tummies."

"Family? Babies? Aren't you getting the cart before the horse?" Teddy laughed awkwardly. She added wood to the stove.

"It'll happen in God's timing." Harriet grew quiet, then began whistling. "You know, that Thomas will make someone a fine husband."

Teddy squirmed on the inside but kept her back to the woman and pushed the husks into the now-boiling water.

"Don't you agree?" Harriet asked but didn't give Teddy time to respond. "He'll need someone to be his helpmate back in Missouri. Lonely thing, serving people all day and night. Birthing others' babies. I hope they have a good eatery nearby. The man won't have a moment to fix his own meals. He'll probably hire out his laundry. Doing those things for my Douglass was pure joy. Every woman should have the privilege of partnering with a man."

"Partner? Sounds to me like you're describing a full-time job."

Harriet's laughter sounded good. "The full-time job is keeping them from killing themselves. Men do all kinds of ridiculous things for no good reason other than to take a year off our lives. They stop maturing after school age. If you're lucky, they mellow after a number of years, but they always keep you on your toes."

"It sounds like you and Douglass had a marvelous marriage." Teddy tried to play off the sigh that escaped her mouth as steam releasing from the pressure cooker. "These things always make me nervous."

"Sit here and shuck. I'll make tea. Yes, we did, but it wasn't always easy, and it certainly didn't start that way. Ours was an arranged marriage of sorts." Harriet wiped at her brow and poured water over the loose tea. "Phew. I'm plumb tuckered out, and it isn't even noon. We'll let that steep nice and strong. Now, where was I?"

"Arranged marriage." Teddy heard wistfulness and intrigue in her words. She took great pains to pick loose silks off the table as Harriet sat close enough to see the color on her face was not from the heat.

"Right. Not an easy story to tell, but one of great value. Douglass was a freedman working for Judge Pennypacker's father-in-law. He was eighteen years old and drove the man to Virginia to some important meeting. He was told to watch himself. Nasty business going on, people selling slaves right there in the market."

Teddy got up and poured the tea, then settled back into the story.

"Thank you. That's where he first saw me. I was thirteen, scrawny as all get out, and my skin as blue as it was black. I must have looked a fright with my swollen face." She dabbed at her eyes. "They left me until last. I figured they'd throw me in with the old ladies and broken men."

Teddy took a sip, doing her best not to make a sound. She wanted to hear every word. She couldn't imagine the life Harriet had led and the trauma she'd faced as a child.

"When the old judge came out, my Douglass asked the man to bid on his behalf. He said the judge asked him what he wanted with a girl like that. Douglass told the judge I was his family." Harriet lowered her head, shaking it back and forth. "That was a bald-faced lie for about two weeks until I married him."

"At thirteen?" Teddy felt her eyes widen.

"The judge didn't abide by slavery, and when he found out we weren't really kin, he told Douglass since he'd saved me, he needed to fulfill his duties. The judge gave me my freedom and a husband all in one fell swoop."

"Did you love him?" Her question felt personal, but she wanted to know. She was emotionally invested in this story and needed to know how to justify the loving couple she knew with this unusual and unconventional marriage.

"Eventually. Idolized him for a while, then loathed him. Felt like I'd escaped one type of slavery for another, like you said." Harriet winked. "Then, one day, I realized I was doing things for him because I wanted to, not because I had to. He was a good man."

Teddy was overcome by a profound sense of respect for Harriet's unwavering resilience and remarkable strength in the face of adversity. The depth of emotion stirring within Teddy was so overwhelming that tears welled up, mirroring Harriet's own. Despite the challenging circumstances surrounding Harriet's marriage, Teddy couldn't help but acknowledge the profound love that emanated from her, alongside her willingness to endure the distasteful until it had transformed into something joyful.

"Thomas is a good man, Teddy. A God-fearing man who would make a mighty fine husband."

Chapter 28

June 1873
Thomas

Thomas glanced over at the raw, red hands moving in Teddy's lap to the beat of the horse's hooves. She'd not said a word to him, but she was different somehow. "Did you finish the corn?"

"Yes."

"Pickles tomorrow?"

"Mmm-hmm."

"Sweet or sour?"

"Right."

"Marry me?"

"Of course. What?" Teddy's head jerked up. Her confused expression turned to shock.

"You agreed. Might want to start planning," he teased.

Teddy breathed a sigh that could be resignation, but she shook her head before playfully hitting his arm.

She looked straight ahead. "Don't be ridiculous."

Thomas pulled the carriage onto a side road.

"Where are you going?" Her voice shook, and all playfulness evaporated.

"You'll see." He watched her spine straighten and her hands tighten. It hadn't occurred to him a detour might make her nervous. "Just up there. I want you to see something. Do you mind?"

"No, of course not."

Thomas stopped in front of a small building with a large red cross on the front. "That's the medical facility for this side of town."

Teddy looked horror-struck. "One could barely call it a shed."

"These people are just thankful for educated medical care. Back home, I have an office waiting for me. The current doctor expected my return. That didn't happen, and he'd already moved south. My people need me. And I need them."

"You're doing the right thing." She turned away from him. "Do you think they'd hire me?"

"I already inquired."

"You did?" She swung back around.

He saw the excitement in her eyes. "They have no funds. The doctor works a full-time job to survive and provides care on weekends."

"I see." There was little inflection in her statement.

"Go with me to Missouri, Teddy. Be my nurse. We'd make a great team."

"It would be improper."

"Not if we were married." He let the words sink in. "I wasn't jesting. I have the means to provide for us. As my wife, you wouldn't be my employee. We'd share ownership and decision-making responsibilities. I respect you, Teddy, and admire your work ethic." He watched her eyes lose their sparkle with each word.

"How romantic." She lowered her gaze.

"I can do romantic if that's what it takes." He stood and put one hand over his heart and raised the other high. "I, Thomas—" The horse sidestepped.

"Sit down. Good grief, Harriet was right."

He plopped down and took the reins, stilling the horse. "About what? My good looks? Charming demeanor?"

"You're crazy and nearly took a year off my life." She pushed a strand of hair behind her ear.

Thomas sobered. "I understand your desire for a home of your own. Once we find a place, you can personalize it however you like to make it truly yours."

Teddy looked up, then at her folded hands. "The reality of owning a home dwindled months ago after losing several months of pay from my serving position. Now, with the loss of my nurse's job . . ."

"Resigning on your behalf without your permission was wrong of me. I'm sorry."

"I appreciate you saying so, but it was the right thing, and I thank you."

Thomas rubbed his thumb over the leather reins. "The problem now is I'm not sure you'll find a job close by, and I don't think Dr. Whitaker will give a favorable recommendation."

Teddy raised her eyebrows, a playful glint in her eyes. "So you're bullying me into going to Missouri?"

Relief at her teasing flooded Thomas. "I'm asking. I know you don't love me, but I believe we are a good match."

"Better than Emmaline?"

A mixture of curiosity, amusement, and perhaps a hint of skepticism shone on Teddy's face. And despite the lighthearted tone, Thomas noted a subtle undercurrent of vulnerability or perhaps insecurity.

"Anyone is better—sorry, that didn't come out right. Emmaline and I were not well suited for many reasons, the biggest being our faith."

She stared as if seeing something he could not. He watched her eyes move as if reading. She worried her lips, making her dimples deepen. Thomas nearly melted as she closed her eyes, and a single tear fell.

He was a fool. "Teddy, I'm sorry."

"When do we leave?" She lifted clear, bright eyes.

"What?" Had he heard correctly?

"I accept your proposal. But with stipulations."

A hesitant smile tugged at his lips at the mixture of joy and apprehension within him. "Anything."

"We marry before we leave but have a wedding when we arrive in Missouri."

"That's a wonderful idea. My parents—"

"Let me finish, please." Teddy once again folded her hands and squeezed them tight.

Thomas reined in his emotions. Teddy may have agreed, but the weight of the commitment they were about to undertake together was nothing to enter into lightly. "Of course. My apologies."

"I don't care where we live, but I want a garden, a horse, and a dog."

She was full of surprises. "Done, done, and big or small?"

"Big." Teddy's hands flew out, showing the enormity of the animal.

"Indoor or outdoor?"

"Both." She stared at him as if this was a deal breaker.

The twinkle in her eyes and matter-of-fact tone nearly did Thomas in. "You may reconsider when you see Missouri mud."

She raised her eyebrows in continued challenge.

"Done. Anything else?"

"My family. I'd like to stop on our way west and say goodbye."

"Where's home?"

"Western Pennsylvania. Farm country. Lots of dogs." The corner of her mouth lifted.

"Done. Anything else?" He was thinking he should have drawn the line at the dog.

Her playfulness turned serious. "Yes. I require a chaperone. Married or not, I—" She hesitated. "I need time."

"Would David do?"

"David? I don't understand."

"I'll explain on the way back."

July 23, 1873
Judge Horace Pennypacker's House

The heat of the day pressed in on Thomas as he stood in the judge's library. Even with the windows open, sweat trickled down his back, soaking his fresh shirt.

Judge Pennypacker wiped his brow, then ran the handkerchief under the high collar of his long, black robe. "Warm day for a wedding. Are you sure about this?"

"Absolutely." Thomas was hot, yet his toes and fingers felt cold.

"I suppose you are. Unusual circumstances, but your actions have kept that dear girl from scandal. You don't regret losing Emmaline?"

The man's eyes held something Thomas didn't comprehend. "No, sir. Emmaline is a wonderful young lady. Just not the one for me."

"Glad to hear it since Addison seems to have already laid claim to the spoils."

Thomas snorted, then wiped his nose. "I'm guessing you'll see more of Addison. I believe he aspires to politics since doctoring isn't his first love."

"The boy has connections. I'm just not sure Emmaline will have the same." The judge wiped at the sweat on his palms.

Thomas calmed his heart. "Is something going on?"

"Dr. Whitaker has resigned his post. I figured you would be aware of this, but since it happened the day after you left, perhaps not."

Thomas kept his voice steady. "Any idea what he'll do? Where he'll go?"

"Extended vacation to Europe, I believe. I'm not certain past that bit of information going around the gentleman's club." Harmonica music flowed through the window. "That's our cue."

The judge led the way to the garden, where the boarders sat on stone benches surrounding a rock waterfall that spilled into a small pond. Thomas looked across the yard. "Have you seen David?"

The judge blotted beads of sweat forming on his balding head with his nearly saturated handkerchief. "He's waiting for

Harriet, who's in the parlor with your bride. There he is now. Well, doesn't he clean up nicely."

The haircut and bath had done wonders for the boy, but the clean cotton pants and white shirt that fit his lean frame made him look less like a street urchin. The boy waved and pointed to Harriet on his arm.

Harriet looked resplendent in blue. A black lace bonnet covered her head. She'd honored him and Douglass today. She lifted a white hankie and waved it gently before dabbing her eyes, which shone.

Thomas moved to greet them. "You look lovely, Harriet." He leaned in and kissed her cheek. "You're not bad yourself." He reached to muss the boy's hair, then thought better of it and squeezed the thin shoulder.

David beamed. "Thanks. Mrs. Douglass made this for me." He pulled at his crisp shirt.

"How very kind. You look quite handsome." Thomas conveyed his thanks to Harriet with his eyes before looking back at David. "Please take Mrs. Douglass to the bench closest to the front. When she's seated, Judge Pennypacker will tell you where to stand."

Thomas took in the scene. He couldn't imagine a wedding back home being any better than this, but he'd honor his agreement. He greeted each of his friends as he moved to the front, then took his place.

Yellow fabric peeked out from the bottom edge of a set of French doors on the back of the house. Flowing white curtains kept the figure hidden from view. His heart raced, but an absolute peace covered him as his chest filled with emotion.

He only hoped one day this woman might return his deep affection.

Mrs. Jones, who had abandoned her usual attire of somber black, emerged from the doors in a navy-blue dress with a cream collar. A softer hairstyle from her usual tight bun gave her a look of youthfulness, but it was her radiant smile that transformed her countenance, making her almost pretty.

The woman extended her arm, and Teddy stepped out from the threshold. A burst of yellow enveloped her form like a ray of sunshine breaking through clouds. Her dress, the color of sun-kissed daisies, danced around her.

Teddy's hair hung in soft waves over the modest dress with small blue flowers imprinted on the fabric. Thomas willed himself to breathe. She was beautiful. He stood mesmerized, each step closer making his heart beat more wildly.

Mrs. Jones offered a smile, and he prayed the tenderness he felt for both the women before him showed in his.

Judge Pennypacker cleared his throat. "Dearly beloved. . . ."

Thomas marveled at God's goodness, this unusual group of friends supporting them, and the gift of the woman he was about to marry. God ordained. God had sifted every wonderful, difficult, traumatic, and blessed moment through His hand to land him at this spot.

"Who gives this woman to be married to this man?"

Mrs. Jones turned to Teddy. "In lieu of her blood family, her adopted family has this honor." The woman kissed Teddy on the cheek and placed the girl's trembling hand in Thomas's.

He waited to speak until she looked into his eyes. He expected resignation or even acceptance in her depths of blue, yet his heart registered something different. "Are you certain?"

"Yes."

Her firm reply relieved Thomas's jitters, and he squeezed her hand.

He was getting married.

A warm breeze blew a strand of Teddy's hair. He longed to touch it but knew giving into his desires would be a long time coming.

"Do you, Thomas . . ."

Thomas marveled at the depth of love he felt for this woman as they exchanged vows. Her response to the judge and the words she said were strong with conviction and certainty. He pulled a dainty gold band from his pocket and placed it on Teddy's finger, noting her trembling had vanished.

"You may kiss your bride."

She looked at him with what he could only hope was at least anticipation, since it could not yet be love, and marveled as she offered her lips to him. Despite the applause and laughter from the onlookers, Thomas was oblivious to it all, his focus entirely consumed by the woman before him. A surge of desire coursed through him, prompting him to press a second kiss gently upon her forehead, lingering there for a moment longer. As he withdrew, he watched Teddy's eyes flutter open, her serene expression filling him with hope.

In that suspended moment, the clamor of the crowd faded into the background, replaced by a spark that crackled between them. It was as if the world had paused, and God had granted them a private oasis amidst the chaos of the celebration. He felt her breath on his face before she pulled back and offered a tender smile.

Thomas knew this moment was just the beginning of a love story waiting to unfold. He would be patient and allow God to work out the timing.

"By the power vested in me by the great state of Pennsylvania, I pronounce you Dr. and Mrs. Thomas Shankel."

As cheers erupted around them, David let out a hearty whoop that echoed through the air. Thomas, sensing the moment was right, gently pulled the enthusiastic boy to his side.

"Are you ready?" Thomas asked.

David's eyes widened in surprise. "Now?" David looked to Teddy as if for approval.

Teddy offered her hand. "No time like the present," she replied.

With a determined nod, David agreed. Thomas guided him in front of him and his new wife and turned the boy to face the expectant crowd. Raising his hand, Thomas signaled for silence. The chatter gradually subsided as quizzical eyes watched them.

"We have a special announcement to make," Thomas declared, his voice carrying across the gathering. "Please join us in welcoming our son, David Yander Shankel, into our new family."

The announcement elicited a chorus of congratulations

among the guests.

Cook, her eyes widening in disbelief, clasped her hands under her chin, a radiant smile spreading across her face. "When did this happen?" she exclaimed, her voice tinged with astonishment.

Thomas nudged David, who eagerly ran into Cook's waiting embrace. "This morning, but it's official now that we're married. Instant family," Thomas explained, a mixture of excitement and joy evident in his tone.

Feeling Teddy's hand brush against his own, Thomas eagerly grasped it, intertwining their fingers with a gentle squeeze. She leaned into his side, a warmth spreading between them.

She tilted her face to him. "Family. I like the sound of that," she murmured softly.

His heart swelled with emotion, overwhelmed by the goodness of God and the promise of a future with this woman. "So do I," he whispered, his gaze moving to their intertwined hands.

With God as their foundation, Thomas knew their new little family could weather any storm that came their way.

Chapter 29

July 27, 1873
Thomas

Weathering storms was exactly what they'd endured since leaving Teddy's family farm. Storm clouds seemed to follow them on their trek through the central states, both literally and figuratively.

Teddy and David were enjoying each other's company, playing endless hours of games, balanced with schooling to get the boy caught up. Teddy bragged about how quickly the boy learned. Anyone would do their best with Teddy's encouragement.

The problem was him. A dark cloud loomed over his head, getting darker with each passing mile.

Teddy slid into the dining car seat across from him. "There you are. When I left David at your cabin, I expected to see you poring over your medical journals."

"Not today. I can't seem to focus." Thomas raised his hand to the waiter and indicated his wife's need for a cup.

"You're broody." Concern filled her eyes.

"I am no such thing."

"Sullen. Moody. Cross. All doom and despair." She wrinkled her brow. "Those lines are going to become permanent."

Thomas laughed at her ridiculous look. "Nathaniel Hawthorne would say broody men are irresistible."

Her laughter was like sunlight breaking through the dark clouds. "So, you agree?"

"No." He winked at her. "But you do find me irresistible."

She waved him off, accidentally hitting the server in the arm. "Oh. Pardon me."

"Not to worry, ma'am. Here is a cup and a fresh pot of tea. Might there be anything else?"

"No, thank you," she replied, then turned to Thomas. "Hawthorne often wrote of inner struggles in his male characters. Is that what's going on with you?"

Thomas sipped the tea she'd poured. "Perhaps. I'm not very good at sorting through my emotions."

"That's one benefit of being married."

"There's more than one?" He lifted both eyebrows and gave what he hoped was an irresistible grin.

She shook her head but otherwise ignored his comment. "Talk to me. You promised we would be partners. Start here, now. Let me help you work through what's bothering you."

Her words were a ray of sunshine poking a hole through the dark clouds and letting light and warmth shine through. "I don't know where to start."

Teddy put her cup down. "You've met my family and survived all my crazy sisters, their husbands, and all the children without incident, thankfully." She grew quiet.

"Don't forget the dogs. Lots of dogs." When she didn't respond, Thomas placed his hand over hers, pulling her from the view out the dining car window. "Now you're the brooding one. What just changed?"

She looked at their hands and flushed, slowly pulling hers away to pick up her cup. "Family."

Her cryptic response could mean anything. "Your family? Our family? My family we're headed to meet?"

She sighed and put the cup back down. "All of it. When my parents declined attending the wedding because of the crops, I understood. For farmers, these are long, busy days. But when I saw the state of things and the way my parents have aged, I better understood. I suppose that was the last time I'll see them this side of heaven."

"We could have stayed longer," Thomas started.

"No. Our short visit put them behind as it is."

"I could have—"

"Thomas, I'm fine. Really. Just a bit melancholy. I've spent years working to be independent of them and only now realize the consequences of my decisions. My parents are thankful I married a godly man. As with all my sisters, that has been their goal. They were afraid I'd end up an old maid, so they're quite happy."

Her laugh sounded forced, and Thomas wished he'd been more thoughtful. "What else?"

Teddy dropped her hands to her lap and lifted her shoulders, then dropped them. "Get used to moody, Thomas. It's something women cycle through. Now that you're married to one, you'll soon figure it out. As far as family? I'll miss our boarding house friends, Harriet, and my friend Armilda, but we can write. Do you miss Jimmy?"

"I do. I sent word but didn't receive a reply before we left. What about the family you are about to meet?"

"If they're anything like you, we'll get along just fine." Her smile was genuine and warm. "But as we get closer to seeing yours, it's your mood that has changed. You've told me of your parents and siblings and those who live on your parents' land. I know of Martha and her husband, the sheriff. Henry, right?"

Thomas nodded.

"The boarding house owners, the Kohornens—is that how you pronounce it?"

"Yes, he's from Finland. She's from Ireland. You'll like Katie. She should have her orphanage up and running by now. He's also the blacksmith and the pastor."

"Busy man. I look forward to meeting Robin and her husband, Pete, is it?"

"Impressive." His chest constricted.

"But I'm going to venture a guess by the change in your face just now that it's their son, your friend Gabe, that's causing you stress. Did you have an argument?"

"No. Not exactly." This woman was a marvel. A gift from above. Thomas reached over and placed his hand on hers and was pleased when she didn't pull away this time. He let the warmth of her skin melt whatever kept the angst from dissipating. "Gabe is ill, and my family expects me to figure out what's wrong with him. I haven't dedicated the time to research his condition until now. I've combed through the few medical journals I didn't pack." He ran his hand down his face.

"Have you prayed about it?"

He hadn't, nor had he prayed for Gabe in recent months. Thomas shifted his fingers and touched the soft underside of Teddy's. She turned her hand over and exposed her palm, allowing him to rub his thumb over her skin.

Her words came out breathy. "You are only a man, Thomas. This won't be the only time you'll need to allow the Great Physician to work in your stead."

"You're amazing. Do you know that?"

"I do." She laughed at his expression. "Thomas, I made a vow to you, and I intend to fulfill those promises."

"All of them?"

She pulled her hand away. "I'm adding incorrigible to your list of attributes."

A voice pulled Thomas's attention from the beauty before him.

"Incorrigible. I–N–C–O–R–R–I–G–I–B–L–E. Incorrigible." The boy grinned.

Teddy patted the seat beside her. "Well done. Hungry?"

"Always," David and Thomas said in unison.

A train attendant approached their table. "Excuse me, Dr. Shankel?"

"Yes?"

"We have a passenger who needs help." The man looked at David as he drew out the last word.

"Of course. Let me get my bag." Thomas stood. "Would you mind bringing something back to the cabin for me to eat, David?"

"Sure thing, Dad."

Thomas swallowed the rising responsibility.

The assistant cleared his voice. "Time is of the essence, sir."

The man followed Thomas to his cabin for his medical bag, then led the way to the back of the train, passing through several intermediate vestibules until arriving at what appeared to be only a cattle car with slatted sides for ventilation. Thomas recognized the quality of horseflesh secured in each stall.

"There, sir." The man pointed to a small child curled up in a pile of hay at the end of the car. "Found her this morning. She's breathing, but we can't get her to wake."

Thomas moved matted hair from the girl's face and gently shook the child. Her warm body curled into a tighter ball. He checked her breathing and pulse. Rapid, but with her dry tongue and cracked lips, she was likely only dehydrated.

"You say you found her? Has someone inquired as to a missing child?"

The assistant pulled a piece of paper from his pocket. "No, sir. I found this pinned to her shirt. I was afraid she'd stick herself, all curled up like that."

"Well done." Thomas took the note that revealed the child's name was Agnes, age eight. He turned the paper over. "That's it?" He looked around. "No bag? Nothing?"

"No, sir. It happens more than I'd like to say. Usually stowaways. When they get hungry enough, most get off, and we find evidence they were here. This one looks like someone put her on the train."

"I'm glad you found her. See if you can find a family with a child her size who might have extra clothing. I'll pay for the garments. Can you carry her to my wife's compartment? She'll care for the girl until we figure something out."

"Of course, sir."

The man lifted the limp form and turned his head. "Maybe a wash basin and towel are in order. I believe she started her journey at the wrong end of a horse."

Thomas held the door for the man. It looked like their little family had just gotten bigger. At least until they figured out who the girl belonged to.

Chapter 30

August 1873
Teddy

A knock sounded at Teddy's cabin door, and she trailed her hand along the edge of the overhead storage as she made her way to open the door. "Yes?"

The porter offered a polite smile. "Pardon the interruption, Mrs. Shankel. Your husband asked that I inform you he will be tardy for dinner. Might I escort you and your children to the dining car?"

Her children. What delightfully foreign words. "My son will assist us. Thank you. We'll be there momentarily."

"As you wish, madam."

Teddy turned to see Agnes still staring out the window in wonder, her nose pressed against the soot-covered glass. "Agnes, do you feel well enough to dine with us this evening?"

The child hopped down and offered her hand and a nod but didn't speak.

"Let's go see if David is finished with his studies, shall we?" Teddy knocked on the door beside hers. "David, dinner time."

"Coming, Mother."

Warmth filled Teddy. God had given her more than she could ever have asked for or imagined. "There you are. Hungry?"

David smirked. "You have to ask? Sorry. Yes, ma'am."

They maneuvered through the walkway to the dining car, Agnes holding on so tightly that Teddy's fingers went numb.

Agnes pulled on Teddy's sleeve. "May I sit by David?"

"Of course." The smells of roasted meat and vegetables filled the car, and Teddy glanced at her neighbor's table to confirm the menu.

She offered a brief prayer over their meal as they waited for the soup. Teddy marveled at the young girl's meticulous manners and exceptional posture. But then, compared to David's, anything was an improvement. Soup dripped from his overfilled spoon onto the table in his haste. He took a large bite from his dinner roll and placed it on the table just below his bread plate. Teddy counted to ten.

"When—"

Teddy held up one finger, and David chewed and swallowed before continuing.

"Sorry. When will we arrive?"

"Please place your roll on your bread plate." She waited for him to comply. "We will disembark tomorrow morning in Poplar Bluff, then secure a wagon and continue on to Shumard Oak Bend. We should be in our new home by the end of the day tomorrow."

Agnes lifted wide eyes to Teddy. "What about me?"

The words pulled at Teddy's heartstrings. "You will remain with us until we learn more of your circumstances. Dr. Shankel sent a telegram to the authorities back east. Don't you worry, Agnes. Dr. Shankel will sort this out."

Thomas strode up to the table. "Did I hear my name? All good, I hope."

"Thomas, wonderful. I was afraid you'd miss yet another meal." Teddy filled her husband's teacup, then placed her hands in her lap. She felt Thomas's knee brush up against her skirt and pulled the fabric in to give him more room. He caught her hand and gave it a gentle squeeze.

She missed his touch the moment he let go. Thomas was a kind man, attentive to her needs and those of the children. He cared deeply for helping anyone in need and was the most handsome man she'd ever seen. His startling blue eyes turned her way, and she blushed at having been caught staring at him.

Thomas placed his napkin on his lap. "David. Tell me about your day. What did you learn?"

"Did you know that in 1831, Dr. Thomas Latta used saline solution intraveinly—"

Teddy quietly corrected, "Intravenously."

"Right. Intravenously to treat cholera patients? Lots of people were dying from dehydration, and he rehydrated them, so they had the strength to beat the sickness."

"You're how old?" Thomas asked.

"Ten, I think. Why?"

"That's quite the reading material. At your age, I was more interested in *Robinson Crusoe*."

Teddy felt his leg bump into hers. "I was more of a *Swiss Family Robinson* girl myself. We will get copies of these for you, David. You're young to be reading medical journals."

Thomas looked across to Agnes. "And what about you, young lady?"

"I got dizzy," she proclaimed proudly.

Thomas tensed beside Teddy, and she placed her hand on his forearm. "From trying to count trees through a sooty pane in a moving train."

He relaxed. "I see. And how many were there?"

"I got so dizzy I lost count."

Teddy's heart flipped at Thomas's laughter. Having such a wonderful man as Thomas for her husband was a blessing. If God would allow the man to one day love her as much as she loved him, she would be the happiest woman in the world.

Teddy's legs wobbled on the wooden planking of the Poplar Bluff station. It wasn't fancy, but the town was bustling with activity. She stood with Agnes under a shade tree while Thomas and David ensured all their belongings were accounted for.

David came running. "We found all of them. Dad says he

may need to rent two wagons. Does that mean I get to drive one?"

"Have you driven a team before?" Would she ever tire of hearing the endearment he'd immediately given Thomas?

"A team?"

"That's what I thought. Where's your—where's Thomas?"

"He told me to come get you to stand by our things while he goes to the livery."

Teddy stepped over the dry ground, watching dust rise with every movement. The largest wagon she'd ever seen and an even larger man as dark as midnight, except for the gray tufts of hair over his eyes, drove past. She held Agnes's hand tighter.

Thomas ran like a boy at Christmas and helped the man down, then gave him a long hug. They patted each other's backs, even though Thomas had to stretch to reach the man's. She hurried their steps.

Thomas kept a hand on the man's massive arm. "Moses, it sure is good to see you. I heard you weren't feeling well, but you're looking right as rain to me." Thomas spoke loudly enough for her to hear, even from this distance.

"The Lord's been good to me. This your family?" The man turned, and Teddy felt Agnes move behind her skirts.

"This is my lovely bride, Teddy, my new son, David, and that little one peeking around the skirts is Agnes."

"Your mama said you were bringing a ready-made family. Good thing your daddy dreams big."

Teddy watched confusion cross Thomas's face and was thankful it wasn't just her who didn't understand. She offered her hand. "It's a pleasure . . ."

Thomas touched his ear and pointed up.

Teddy raised the volume of her voice. "It's a pleasure to meet you, Moses. Thomas speaks highly of you."

"Thank you kindly." His broad lips parted into a smile as large as he was.

"I'm David." The boy stuck out his hand. "You're big."

"That I am. That I am." The gray eyebrows moved up and down as the man's head bobbed.

Agnes moved farther out. "Are you Goliath?"

Teddy could tell Moses had not heard. "She's asking if you are Goliath from the Bible."

Moses's roar of a laugh caused the girl to again retreat behind Teddy's skirt.

"No, little missy, I'm not that big or that old." He turned to Thomas. "Let's get you loaded and head on home. Delphina fixed us a meal. You can thank her later. Rachel was going to cook it."

Teddy had heard enough stories about Rachel's cooking to laugh with the men. "Thomas, I'm going to go to the general store to see if they have a particular item Agnes requires. Do you three men need anything?"

She watched David square his shoulders and lift one end of a large crate with Thomas.

Thomas grunted. "Get what you need. We'll be ready to go in thirty minutes."

Now that the train was gone, the two crossed the street with ease.

The bell tinkled as they entered, and a female voice came from somewhere in the back. "Welcome. Be with you folks in a moment."

Teddy moved to the ready-made items and riffled through a haphazard array of undergarments until she found what appeared to be the right size. She fingered the dresses, but the cost astounded her, and she hurried on. Harriet had sent plenty of fabric, and she'd learn to sew—or swap her nursing skills in fair trade.

An elderly woman with a kind face approached them. "Are you finding everything to your satisfaction? What an adorable daughter. Looks just like you."

"Thank you," Teddy struggled to get out. She hadn't considered it before, but Agnes had her eyes and the same chestnut brown hair with just enough wave to make it unruly. "We only need these items, please."

The woman looked Agnes over from top to bottom, then moved behind the counter. "What brings you to these parts?"

"My husband—he'll be the new doctor in Shumard Oak Bend."

"You don't need any dresses or heavier boots for your girl? That kid leather won't last a Missouri winter."

Teddy didn't want to share too much information, but she decided staying as close to the truth without giving fodder for gossip was best. "The Lord will provide for our needs."

"Did you say doctor or preacher?" The woman laughed. "What's your name again?"

Teddy hadn't given it. The door opened, and Thomas walked in.

"You two pretty girls about ready?" He looked at the woman behind the counter. "How much do I owe you?"

The woman gave Thomas the once over as if determining if she approved of him as a match for Teddy and Agnes. "Are you the new doctor?"

"That I am. Thomas Shankel. Headed home to Shumard Oak Bend."

"Well, I'll be. Are you U.S. Marshal Clint Shankel's boy?"

"One and the same, though he retired many years ago."

The woman pulled a hanky from her pocket and dabbed at her eyes. "Your father saved my husband's life. It was back in . . ."

Agnes pulled Teddy's sleeve and whispered, "Mama, I need to use the—you know."

One simple word stopped Teddy's heart. Emotion filled her soul and overflowed into the rest of her being.

The woman stopped speaking to Thomas. "Where are my manners? You and your mama come with me."

She led a stunned Teddy and a wiggly Agnes through a curtain and out a back door.

"Right there. Let yourself back in when you're finished."

Teddy stood outside, trying to rein in the emotions that threatened to escape her eyes as Agnes took care of business. "Agnes, why did you call me mama?"

"She said I was your daughter; that makes you my new mama." The door creaked, and the girl came out. Teddy pulled at the bottom of Agnes's skirt, which was caught in her drawers.

"What about your real mama? You haven't spoken of her."

"She and Daddy are in heaven." The matter-of-fact statement didn't seem to bother the child.

Teddy was speechless as she walked back into the store. Thomas held a crate under his arm. His smile carried a hint of sheepishness. She lifted an eyebrow. "What in the world did you buy? Harriet gave us enough canned goods to last two winters."

"Not with David to feed. Mrs. Benton here gave Agnes a box of clothing."

Teddy turned to the woman. "Thank you."

"It's the least I can do to repay the marshal for his kindness."

Agnes offered a slight curtsy. "Thank you kindly, Mrs. Benton."

"What a sweet child. You are most welcome, dear."

"Ladies, time to go. Mrs. Benton, it's been a pleasure. I'll thank my father for you." Thomas held the door, then offered his free arm to Teddy.

A passing man raised his arm to them. "Best of luck to you, Doc," he said, then continued walking.

"Does everyone know you?" Teddy asked.

"Not me, but the Shankel name gets around. We've a long ride ahead of us. Ready?"

She was so tired of this train and eagerly anticipated a change of scenery. She yearned for something new beyond the repetitive views glimpsed from her train seat.

She was so done with this wagon travel. If she'd thought days on a train were tedious, the monotonous movement of the wagon was worse. At least on the train she'd been able to stretch her legs. Moses had only stopped for a cold lunch, a quick break, and a snack of apple turnovers late in the day before pressing on.

Agnes laid her head in Teddy's lap in the small section of the freight wagon not loaded with their belongings. Teddy was thankful they didn't also have furniture.

"How much longer, Mama?" Agnes asked.

Teddy caught Thomas's gaze and shrugged her shoulder at the name the child had given her. "How much longer? Agnes is pretty tired."

"Agnes, doll, we only have about thirty more minutes.

Would you like to crawl up here and sit with me?" Thomas offered.

The child scrambled from Teddy's lap, and Thomas lifted her over the crates. He mouthed to her, "Are you all right?"

"Just tired," she replied.

He winked at Teddy, and her insides melted.

With the space to herself, she moved her skirts around and bunched them under her knees for a cushion. As wrinkled as the fabric was now, doing this would make no difference in her appearance. She leaned her elbows on the crate in front of her, peered between Thomas and David, and listened as Moses's deep voice carried on the wind.

"We'll leave the wagon at the livery, then you'll spend the night at the boarding house. Tomorrow morning, it being Saturday, the local folk will help get you unpacked and settled. Church folk, including your family, will be here on Sunday. Your mama mentioned a wedding, and with the whole town here anyway, that'll be right after the service."

Thomas stole a glance at Teddy. She was so tired she didn't care what they'd planned. All she wanted was to stop moving. "That's fine," she whispered when he didn't turn back.

Thomas raised his voice. "That sounds like a marvelous plan. Agnes, do you see that? Up there on the hill. That's the church steeple. We're almost home."

Teddy didn't look at the church. She watched Thomas as he put one arm around David and, with the other, pulled the girl closer, her head resting on his chest. Where she wanted to be.

They pulled into Shumard Oak Bend as the sun was setting. Teddy remembered being introduced to Mr. Finch, the livery owner, but she couldn't have repeated what he looked like. It felt good to walk. Moses and Thomas led the family past faux-front buildings and one large stone structure, centrally located on the main street. Its front entrance was adorned with strategically placed rounded river rock, making the word "Bank" stand out in stark contrast to the lighter and larger rock completing the wall.

The setting sun drew Teddy's attention to the end of the thoroughfare, where a stately two-story building greeted them, its terracotta colors enhanced by the evening glow.

A sprite woman with red hair and freckles across her nose greeted them with a lilting Irish tone. "Welcome, you must be exhausted from your travels. I'm Katie. Everything's prepared for your stay. You've fresh linens in your room, and I'll bring hot water up straight away."

Teddy froze. She hadn't prepared for this. "Katie, Thomas and I—"

"Are in separate rooms. You and the girl can stay together."

"Thank you. How did you know?"

Katie pulled the boiling kettle from the stove. "Yer not getting married until Sunday. Come on with you." She led the way up a flight of stairs. "Truth is, I guessed. I'll not be making assumptions. Make yourself at home. If you get hungry, there's bread and butter on the counter. Help yourself."

Teddy thanked her and got Agnes ready for bed. Teddy hated getting into the crisp clean sheets without a proper bath but did her best with what she'd been given. She'd be dirtier tomorrow with all the unpacking. She snuggled next to an already-sleeping Agnes.

Teddy took a deep breath and relaxed into the bed. "Lord, I don't know what to expect tomorrow, but I certainly didn't expect all the wonderful things You've done so far. I'm looking forward to the surprise. Whatever is before me, I trust You to supply all my needs."

The need for sleep and desire to spend a quiet moment with the Lord fought with each other. Agnes mumbled in her sleep.

"And Lord, please help me understand Your ways if my desires are not yours." Teddy brushed a curl from the child's face. There were so many unknowns. Visions of a little shack of a doctor's office to work in and a house the size of Harriet's floated through her mind as she closed her eyes.

"Your will. Not mine."

Chapter 31

August, 1873
Teddy

Teddy dried the last breakfast dish. "Thank you, Katie, for the breakfast and good night's sleep. Both have done wonders for my attitude. I must confess, I don't care to sit in anything that moves more than a rocking chair for a good long while."

Katie wiped the counter. "Try months on a ship. I'll not be doing that again."

Teddy placed her folded towel alongside Katie's. "When did the men leave this morning?"

"Before first light. Hans fixed your husband and son ham and biscuits, so they'll be fine until we bring lunch. Care for a tour of your new home?"

"Do you have the time?" Teddy asked.

"Of course. I've no boarders and no orphans either. Speaking of which, I spoke to the magistrate before breakfast. He wants to speak with Agnes, but that can wait. Ready?"

Teddy's nerves were already frayed at the ends. The thought of losing Agnes was nearly her undoing. *Help me, Lord, not only with sweet Agnes but also help me be grateful for whatever You have provided for us here in our new home.*

Teddy reached her hand down to Agnes, who sat on the floor petting Marmalade. "Leave the cat be. Mrs. Korhonen is taking us to see our new home." Teddy's stomach lurched. *Let it be so, Lord. If she has no family, please let her stay with us.*

They walked back down the main street toward the livery at the opposite end of town. Agnes waved, and Teddy turned to see Moses shoeing a horse.

Katie stopped. "Here it is."

Teddy looked at the single-story building. A red gingham curtain blew in the breeze of the open window, which was surrounded by freshly sanded wood painted a deep brown. A red cross painted on a matching wooden sign swung in the breeze. The light creak it made was a homey sound.

Katie pushed the door into a large open area with several chairs and a small settee on gleaming wooden floors. "The Ladies Auxiliary cleaned. I hope it's to your satisfaction. There are three rooms down that hall on the left. The back door opens at the end, giving a nice cross breeze when needed. And this is the kitchen, if you can call it that." She pointed to a gas stove, small table, and ample counter and cabinet spaces.

God had provided the space she had requested, but she wouldn't be entertaining much. "I'm thankful for the gas stove."

"Good for boiling water, at least. Now, out back, you'll find a nice clothesline, though Doc Crosby didn't use it. His wife sent all their sheets and towels and such to the laundry down the row."

Teddy stepped out the back, Agnes on her heels. A large

tree shaded the area and would make a lovely place for a rope swing for the children.

Katie shut the door. "I hope it will be sufficient for your needs. Now let me show you the house."

Teddy stumbled over a root. "The house?"

"Of course. That was the clinic. The doc they built it for was single, so he lived and worked there. Doc Crosby and his wife had a little home just down there."

Teddy followed the woman's finger down the row of trees along the backs of the Main Street buildings.

Katie swatted at a bug. "Mr. Shankel, he dreams big. Real big. He designed the orphanage and donated the land. It should be finished next month. Here we are."

Teddy stared at a two-story house with a large front porch. "This is ours?"

"Like I said, he dreams big. Doc Crosby's house had one bedroom."

"Well, it certainly is bigger than any of my dreams."

Katie offered her hand to Agnes. "Come see the backyard. There's a swing."

"Can I, Mama?"

Teddy nodded and took the two wide steps up to the front door. All the windows were open, and she heard multiple voices inside. She peeked in and felt the tears prick.

To her right, a braided rag rug of blue covered the

darkly stained wooden floors. The parlor reminded her of the boarding house, complete with a fireplace. A spark of joy filled her at the thought of hosting game night with new friends and neighbors.

On the opposite side of the hall was the library and, evidently, Thomas's study, by the looks of the sturdy desk at one end. Crates of Thomas's books lay unopened near the window. Dark blue draperies danced in the breeze, creating an invitation to sit in the leather chairs and gaze out the windows while enjoying a lovely fire.

Overhead, a railing encircled the interior of the house, letting the grand chandelier hanging from the ceiling cast light on both levels. Teddy wiped at her eyes and caught a glimpse of David running up the stairs, his heels echoing in the hall around him.

"There you are." Thomas rounded the corner. "I had the same reaction."

He rubbed his thumb over her cheek. Teddy began to shake, and Thomas pulled her into his chest. She felt his beating heart in time with hers and heard his soft shushes in her hair. His breath was warm on her skin and penetrated to her soul.

His hand moved over her back as he spoke. "God has given us more than I could have ever imagined. I thought we'd be living in the clinic until I was able to build something for us."

Teddy giggled and stepped back. "I thought the same and would have gladly lived there. With you," she added and lifted her gaze to Thomas's questioning eyes.

He pulled a handkerchief from his pocket. "My thumb

was dirtier than I thought." He handed it to her and pointed. "Indoor plumbing. Praise the Lord. Philadelphia spoiled me with that."

"Thank you." She stepped into the small room with only a toilet and sink. Whoever had thought of putting a lavatory on the first floor?

Thomas offered his arm when she returned. "Come see the kitchen. I promise my mother had nothing to do with the design."

The walls were covered in a paper of light yellow with blue flowers. It would always remind her of her wedding day. A sigh escaped her as she watched the blue valances with yellow grosgrain ribbon at the hems flit in the breeze over the large cast iron sink. The polished wooden countertops and large butcher's block seemed to go on forever.

"David was in charge of unloading the box for the pantry, so you may need to do some reorganizing."

Teddy stepped inside the four walls and marveled at the space still available.

Thomas took her hand. "This is my favorite feature. Here, step back."

Teddy watched as he rolled up a four-by-six rag rug and placed it under the pantry's bottom shelf. He placed his hand in an indention and lifted to reveal an underground room. "What in the world is that? Please tell me it's not for Indian raids."

Thomas laughed as he descended the ladder. "You're safe here. Gather your skirts. I'll help you down."

Teddy's curiosity mixed with apprehension and intrigue. She scanned her surroundings with intent despite the fear fluttering in her chest. She couldn't resist the pull of curiosity driving her forward even when every instinct screamed at her to retreat.

She bunched her skirt in the front with one hand and used the other to steady herself on the rungs of the ladder. The heat of Thomas's hand hovering at her back felt like fire compared to the coolness of the underground room. She turned to find Thomas had not backed away.

She could not see his expression, but the whites of his eyes shone in the light coming down from above. They appeared to grow larger, and she felt his breath on her face.

"Mrs. Shankel, you are the most beautiful woman I've ever seen."

She lifted her hands to his chest to push him away, but he stepped closer, pinning them against his shirt. "Dr. Shankel, it's pitch black down here. I could be an old hag, and you'd never know it."

"Oh, I'd know."

His hand snaked around her waist, and she struggled to take a full breath. The absence of light, being confined, and his hold on her pulled her into a different kind of darkness. Her body shook.

Thomas stepped back but did not let go. "I will never intentionally hurt you, Teddy."

"I know. I'm so sorry." Her eyes had adjusted to the dimness, and she saw pain in Thomas's eyes. She lifted a hand to his face and felt wetness on his cheek. "It isn't you. I think it is being caught unaware. Give me time, and let me come to you on my terms. Please?"

He nodded, then took her hand from his face and kissed her palm.

A different type of shiver ran up her spine.

Footsteps sounded overhead. "Hey, that's really neat." David descended the ladder, making the space more crowded, but Teddy didn't feel the anxiety she'd felt moments before. "What is all this?"

Thomas pulled Teddy to the center of the room. "Root cellar. Good for keeping things cool in the summer and from freezing in the winter."

Teddy lifted a lid off a small box. She reached her hand into the sawdust. "Eggs? Thomas, where did these come from?"

"The townsfolk. It's their idea of a welcoming gift."

David pushed past them. "I see light."

"That would be the outside entrance."

Teddy marveled at the thoughtfulness. They must truly love Thomas. He had been right to come home. She only hoped she would measure up to their expectations.

"Yoo-hoo," a shrill voice called. "The wedding isn't until tomorrow. Do you need a chaperone?"

Teddy blushed, and David pushed past them once again.

"Nah, they're looking at all the food down there. It'll last weeks."

Teddy laughed and allowed Thomas to ascend, then help her up before he closed the door and replaced the rug. "David, those had better last months, not weeks." She turned to the heavyset woman. "Pardon my manners. I'm Teddy."

The woman pulled her into a fierce hug. Teddy shot a look at Thomas, but he lifted his hand and scooted around the woman, taking David with him.

"We're so pleased to have you here. I'm Magistrate Bill Marley's wife, Wilamena. You can call me Mena. My husband is speaking with that sweet child of yours. Agnes, is it? She's just a doll. Pity her circumstances. Left an orphan from the yellow fever, moved to live with her aunt, who died of consumption. Says she walked for days before climbing aboard that train to sleep. Next thing she knew, she was in Missouri."

The woman had garnered more information from Agnes in a few moments than they had in the entire trip. Teddy and Thomas had both questioned the child, but she'd always retreated, unwilling to share.

"My husband and yours will get to the bottom of this. Thank the Lord you took the child in." The woman shook her head as if it was a tragedy.

To Teddy, Agnes was pure joy.

The woman continued, "Have you seen your garden? I personally oversaw every detail. We expected you sooner and wanted to ensure your garden was started. When you were delayed, it became a community garden of sorts and has been a blessing to many. Until word gets out, you may find a few things missing here and there, so check your supply before starting your supper, or you'll have pepper steak on rice without the peppers."

Teddy walked as if in a daze, trying to keep up with the onslaught of words.

"We got a little heavy-handed on the tomatoes, but if you can, you'll have plenty to keep you busy in the coming days. Green peppers, like I said. That there light green starburst is a pattypan squash. My husband loves those. If you need a recipe, I've got just the one for a growing family like yours."

Teddy took in the cucumbers, several types of beans, okra, and a few cantaloupes. The garden was larger than the house. When would she ever find time to weed it, let alone can, dry, and cook everything?

"Now, like I said, if you're willing to share, the orphanage will need to be stocked. Mrs. Kilpatrick and her girls offered to help with canning, and there are others from the Auxiliary who will do the same."

Teddy hoped the ladies' group was a large one with hardworking women.

"Don't you go feeling overwhelmed by it all. And if it spoils, well, there's the goats and hogs to feed. And who is this striking young man?"

David approached, wide-eyed, at the woman's words.

"This is our son, David. David, this is Mrs. Marley, the magistrate's wife." Teddy gave the boy a nudge.

He bowed slightly. "It's a pleasure to meet you, ma'am." David turned to Teddy. "Dad needs your help deciding which wall to put the bed on."

"Thank you. Mena, it has been delightful chatting with you. Perhaps I'll see you in service tomorrow?"

"And the wedding. Don't forget the wedding."

The woman's chuckles followed Teddy all the way into the house. The wedding. How could she forget?

Chapter 32

August 1873
Thomas

Thomas woke to pounding at the door. Momentarily disoriented in his new home, he yelled down, "Coming," as he hopped into his trousers.

Thomas glanced at the clock. Almost midnight. He opened the door to a wild-haired man. "Yes, what is it?"

"Fight at the saloon. No gunshots, but there's lots of blood and a crazy man. Sheriff asked me to come get you."

"Let me grab my bag." Thank the Lord Teddy and the children had gone to the boarding house for the night. He slipped on his boots and grabbed his bag at the door. "Ready."

The man staggered but had a quick stride and seemed to know exactly where he was going even with the moon hidden behind dense clouds. Thomas had dealt with many emergencies in Philadelphia, but he knew rules were different here. Sounds of shouting and splintering wood filled the still night.

The man turned to Thomas. "Are you armed?"

"I'm here to heal, sir, not the other way around."

"Still might want to carry a gun. You can run up onto a bear just as easy as a drunken scoundrel."

Thomas wasn't about to argue. A loud crash followed by glass shattering had him wondering if he'd lost his senses.

The man stopped in front of the saloon. "Hey, Doc?"

"Yes?"

"Glad to have you in town, but I hope not to need your services."

Thomas hoped so, too, as the man tripped over his own feet when he turned toward Main Street. *Welcome back to the Wild West, Dr. Shankel,* Thomas said to himself as he climbed the steps and entered the saloon.

Men sat drinking in the back of the smoke-filled room as if nothing unusual was happening. The bartender cleaned glasses with a rag. It appeared this incident was a one-man fight.

Sheriff Adkins stood with his arms crossed, facing Thomas, but did not acknowledge his arrival. "Every chair you break adds to your bill. You sure you want to break that one, too?" he said to the man.

Thomas felt bile rise in his throat as he recognized the brown skin and lithe arms of his friend. Blood ran down the back of Gabe's filthy shirt as he held a chair over his greasy, matted hair. Thomas's heart broke as he assessed the situation. The head wound caused little worry. The real problem was him and his reaction to seeing Gabe like this.

Thomas thought through his options. Henry was the calm voice of reason, but that didn't seem to be working. Gabe was steady on his feet, not acting as if inebriated. He could be crazy, like the stranger said. Thomas had seen psychological issues many times in Philadelphia. People lost their minds, usually after a traumatic incident, but some struggled with their demons from birth. Neither seemed plausible in Gabe's case.

Thomas set his bag down quietly and pulled out a clean cloth and a bottle of chloroform. He took a quick look at the room and noted those smoking were in the back, away from the activity. The sweet smell saturated the cloth, and Thomas prepared himself to leap into action. He'd wrestled with Gabe enough over the years to know the element of surprise would be his friend.

Thomas said a quick prayer, then lunged while Gabe's steady and still-raised arms held the chair above his head. He covered his friend's nose and mouth with the cloth, then leaned and swept Gabe's legs out from under him. Gabe, the chair, and Thomas crashed to the floor, but Thomas never removed his hand. It was like capturing a mad pig.

Gabe writhed and kicked under Thomas's body weight, then stopped. Thomas pulled his hand and the cloth free, allowing the sheriff to put handcuffs on the now-silent figure before turning the motionless form over.

Under a mixture of blood, snot, and spit was the tortured face of his best friend, Gabe.

The sheriff looked pained when their eyes met. "Quick thinking, Doc. I'm sorry you had to see him like this." Henry called two of the men to help carry the limp body to the jail. "Gentlemen, I owe you a beer for your service," He turned to the owner. "Close her up, Bart. It's Sunday."

Thomas's hands shook, and he looked at the bruising beginning to show on his right hand. He repacked his bag and followed the group of men, leaving the establishment's patrons in different states of drunkenness. Thomas didn't miss this part of small-town living. He knew he'd see a few of those faces at service in the morning.

Thomas made his way to the jail to ensure his patient and friend didn't suffer any ill effects from the chloroform.

Henry removed the cuffs, and the men settled Gabe on the wooden shelf he'd call a bed for a few days. "Coffee?" Henry offered.

The smell of burned coffee met his nose. "I'll pass. Thanks."

Henry leaned against the cell opening as Thomas listened to Gabe's heartbeat. "How long will he sleep?"

Thomas checked Gabe's pulse. "Minutes. Maybe twenty. What happened tonight?"

"Same as the other times. Gabe went missing again, then showed up here looking for a fight. These men know him well enough to not engage. I heard the first chair break and tried to talk him down. Four chairs and a glass later, and here we are."

Thomas adjusted his position and checked Gabe's head. The wound still oozed.

Henry stepped inside. "Broke the first chair over his knee. A piece flew up. Thankfully, it hit his head and not an eye."

"Help me hold him, will you? I'd like to get this stitched before he wakes, but I'm not sure how much longer that will be."

Thomas washed his hands and returned to find Gabe back in handcuffs, though this time iron handles on either side of the wooden bed secured his arms and ankles. "Done this before?"

Henry's dry laugh ended in a heavy, released breath. "More times than I care to remember."

Thomas wasn't sure if it was for just Gabe or others as well and wasn't sure he wanted to know. He cut away some dark matted hair from around the wound, then cleaned the area before stitching. Gabe moaned, and Thomas clipped the tied end. He placed his used items in the cleaning cloth to boil when he got home.

Gabe's eyes popped open, and his body stiffened, pulling against the restraints. He turned his steely gaze to Thomas and spat.

Thomas wiped his cheek and forced a smile. "Your aim's off, but that's likely from the anesthesia." Thomas watched confusion, then recognition, fill Gabe's eyes.

Gabe growled, the sound guttural and hoarse like he'd either damaged his vocal cords or needed water.

"It's me, friend. Henry, can you pour some water for Gabe?"

"My name is Shadowed Spirit," the gravelly voice retorted, each word coated with a gritty edge.

Thomas's heart seized. What had happened to his friend, the Indian boy he'd loved since childhood? This new name Gabe had given himself evoked a sense of darkness in contrast to the brightness and optimism associated with his given Indian name, Little Sun.

"Gabe, it's me, Thomas."

"I know who you are. But I am Shadowed Spirit."

The name reflected the transformation of the man's current disposition. He'd changed from a boy full of light to a man overshadowed by despair or melancholy.

Thomas took the offered water and then looked at the shackles.

Gabe uttered another deep growl that bordered on a snarl. "I won't run. I could use a few nights' sleep and meals, even if they're barely edible."

Thomas didn't recognize the person in front of him. He stepped back to allow Henry to unlock the restraints, then handed the cup to Gabe, who gulped greedily, water spilling down his face and into his sweat-stained shirt.

Thomas's gaze focused on a leather strap around Gabe's neck that ended in a lump under his shirt. Had Gabe forsaken God and returned to the ways of his Arapaho people? Thomas offered a silent prayer.

"Gabe," Thomas started, then changed tactics when the look he received from the stranger in front of him made him quiver in his boots. "As your physician, I have a few questions."

Gabe sneered. "You always were the inquisitive one."

"Have you eaten any psilocybin-containing mushrooms or smoked cannabis recently?"

Gabe spat on the floor. "I may not have been smart enough for medical school, but I'm not an idiot."

Was that what he thought? "Smart enough? Not getting into medical school had nothing to do with your intelligence."

"Oh, that's right. It had everything to do with my blood. I guess mine doesn't run the same color as yours."

Thomas ignored the comment. "I understand you are experiencing lethargy, joint pain, and some confusion. Any swelling, redness, rash, or fever?"

Gabe leaned against the wall as if tired and exhaled as if giving up an unseen fight. He closed his eyes, then opened to show clear ones that remained focused on Thomas. "It's not gout."

"All right. Urine output?"

"Less, I guess."

Thomas noticed the cracked lips. Prolonged pain with the accompanied behavioral changes and extreme aggressiveness from this once fun, docile friend had him stumped. "Open your mouth."

Gabe did as asked, and Thomas stilled at the blue-black lines in the gums. "Lead poisoning," he said on an exhale. There was no cure, and in extreme cases, those affected often died.

"Makes sense. But if that's true, there are plenty of others working the mines who are affected. I just don't understand the extreme rage I feel. No one else seems to have that."

"Bowel habits?" Thomas inquired.

"Stopped up pretty good." The old Gabe shone through for an instant, then a shadow crossed his hardened face.

"Thanks to my son, I have an idea, but it won't be pleasant."

Gabe sat up straight. "You have a son?"

"And a wife. We have much to catch up on, friend." Thomas took a chance and placed his hand on Gabe's shoulder. "In fact, we're having our wedding tomorrow after service. It would be an honor to have you stand with me."

"You have a wife and a son, but you aren't married?"

It felt good to laugh. "It's a long story I'll share with you over coffee. For now, let's get you feeling better. Henry?"

"I heard. I'll make an exception since he didn't harm anyone but himself, but, Gabe, I want it in writing that you'll pay your debt to Bart."

Gabe rolled his eyes. "Whatever. I didn't even agree yet."

Thomas's heart sank. He couldn't imagine his special day without Gabe.

"But I'll do it if I don't have to attend service first."

Thomas realized the opportunity and seized it. "Sorry, that's part of the deal. Comes with the feast that follows. I hear a certain pretty schoolteacher made the cake." He had Gabe's attention now.

"I have nothing to wear."

Thomas watched Gabe's eyes flicker as if a war was battling inside his head.

"I've got you covered. What you need is a bath and a

haircut. Just be careful with those stitches. And sorry about the bald spot, I had to cut away some of that mop on your head."

Gabe gifted Thomas a smile. "At least you didn't scalp me." Gabe bumped his knee against Thomas's.

Thomas returned the gesture. "It crossed my mind."

All the well wishes from congregants delayed the start of worship. The pianist played the call to worship again, this time with more gusto. Surrounded by family and friends, Thomas offered praise to his Lord, and asked his heavenly Father to tune his heart to sing all praise.

The words of "Come, Thou Fount of Every Blessing" flowed through his mind. Thomas thanked God for helping him return safely home to the fold of God and to Shumard Oak Bend.

> *Jesus sought me when a stranger,*
> *wandering from the fold of God;*
> *He, to rescue me from danger,*
> *interposed his precious blood. (Robert Robinson)*

Thomas stole a glance across the aisle to where Gabe sat with his parents. Thomas noted the man's bouncing knee and prayed the conviction of the Holy Spirit caused the action and not another bout of aggressive behavior ready to be loosed on the congregants.

> *O to grace how great a debtor*

Daily I'm constrained to be!
Let that grace now, like a fetter,
Bind my wandering heart to thee.

Thomas prayed those words spoke to Gabe as much as they did to him.

Prone to wander, Lord, I feel it,
Prone to leave the God I love;
Here's my heart; O take and seal it;
Seal it for thy courts above.

Thomas glanced across the aisle to see Gabe's knee still. His friend steepled his fingers, leaning forward and remaining seated while the congregation stood for prayer.

Heal him, Father. Not just physically. Help Gabe leave his wandering ways and return to You—and to us. To all of us.

Thomas added his amen to the surrounding chorus.

Pastor Korhonen smiled down at his people. "Today we continue in 1 Kings. To follow up on last week's lesson, let me recap for those of you who are new to us today."

Hans smiled at several individuals. "The stage is set in a time of great spiritual conflict in Israel, under the reign of King Ahab and Queen Jezebel. Elijah, a prophet of God, emerges as a central figure in this narrative."

"Amen," a voice from the crowd exclaimed.

"Ahab and Jezebel have led Israel astray, promoting the worship of the pagan god Baal and suppressing the worship of Yahweh. This sets the backdrop for a dramatic confrontation between Elijah and the prophets of Baal to demonstrate the power of the one true God."

Thomas felt David sit up straighter. Hans had used the right words to capture his boy's attention.

"Our passage today tells the story where Elijah challenges the prophets of Baal in a dramatic showdown, proving God's power."

David leaned in.

"Yet Elijah's victory doesn't solve the ongoing struggle against evil. Threatened by Jezebel, Elijah falls into despair, seeking refuge in a cave."

"Lord, help us," someone offered from the back.

"But in a powerful display, God appears, reminding Elijah of His presence."

"Glory," an unfamiliar voice added.

"Despite Elijah's doubts, God reassures him and urges him to continue his mission."

Thomas felt the prick of the Holy Spirit in his heart. No matter his doubts, he knew God was encouraging him to move forward on the path He'd set before him.

"The story teaches the enduring battle against evil and the need to trust in God's power. Like Elijah, we're called to confront injustice, seek community, and remain steadfast in faith, even when faced with despair."

Thomas thought of Gabe. His friend had despair written all over him.

"We often view situations with limited, self-pitying lenses, but God's perspective encompasses a broader view.

While we may feel isolated, God is at work through others, accomplishing good things beyond our awareness."

"Thank you, Jesus," the now-familiar voice rang out.

"Even in moments of despair, God is preparing blessings beyond our sight. The lesson is to trust in God's mysterious ways, even when we can't perceive them. God reassures Elijah and us, saying, 'I'm in control.'"

Hans's volume increased. "Instead of telling God how big your problems are, tell your problems how big God is. Put yourself in the presence of God and feel his mighty power. You, my friend, are a child of the King."

A chorus of amens filled the room.

Thomas felt drawn to Gabe, and he watched in amazement as Gabe yanked the leather strap from his neck and threw it to the floor.

Chapter 33

August 1873
Thomas

T homas fidgeted like a restless child on the last day of school.

Gabe leaned in. "How in the world can you be nervous? You already married her once."

Thomas resisted the urge to elbow Gabe like he'd done in their growing up days. How could he explain how he felt? Yes, he was legally married, but this was different. Teddy and the children would move into his home tonight. It was more anticipation than nerves.

Hans gave the signal, and music played. The doors to the back of the church opened, allowing in a much-needed breeze. The congregation seemed to catch Thomas's anticipation, and the room quieted.

Thomas rocked forward and back on his feet, feeling Gabe's hand on his shoulder.

"Steady there, partner," Gabe whispered.

Thomas jutted his chin out, hoping to loosen the collar. He reached up and adjusted his tie. Agnes walked down the aisle, dropping petals from a basket, her smile lighting the way for what was to come.

The congregation stood, and Thomas took a step forward to see down the aisle. David offered his arm, and Teddy appeared in a gown of flowing white. Her graceful stride was purposeful, and her radiant smile outshone the sun coming in the doors behind her.

The two locked eyes, neither wavering until she finally stood before him. Thomas's heart swelled with love and awe of what God had done. Teddy bent and kissed David's cheek, then offered her hands to Thomas.

When Teddy looked into his eyes again, Thomas prayed she could read the promise of love and the declaration of devotion in his.

"Dearly beloved . . ." Hans began.

Thomas listened to the sacred words of love and commitment he vowed to follow all his days. God had given this woman to him, and he would treasure her for all time. Gabe nudged him and handed Thomas a ring.

Thomas's sly smile met Teddy's surprised one. He slipped his birth mother's gold band next to the one already on Teddy's finger, sealing their bond with the symbol of everlasting love and devotion.

Hans's voice was low and for their ears only. "You may now kiss your bride."

Thomas looked into Teddy's luminous eyes and bent to kiss her. He felt a surge of anticipation, ready to seal their vows with a tender gesture of affection. However, as her hands gently touched his cheeks, he remembered her earlier request not to push her, to allow her the space she needed. His smile faded into a gentle understanding, his eyes softening as they met hers. In that moment, he recognized the significance of her pause, realizing that this was Teddy's way of asserting herself, of taking control of a moment that was meant to be shared between them.

Thomas prayed his silent acknowledgment of accepting her boundaries and his deep respect for her wishes shone in his gaze. He heard nothing as they stood there. He would give her all the time she needed. Thomas knew that their bond was not just about grand gestures but also about the quiet moments of understanding and acceptance that made the love he had for her truly enduring.

Her voice was but a whisper. "On my terms." She winked and pulled his face to hers for a kiss that left no question she was his wife.

December 31, 1873

Thomas heard his wife's heels on the wooden floor.

"David," Teddy called from the bottom of the stairs. "Where is that boy?" Her exasperated tone made Thomas chuckle.

Thomas poked his head out of his study. "His nose is probably still in a book, living out adventures in *The Swiss Family Robinson*."

Teddy moved into his arms. Her warmth was better than any fireplace.

She lifted her hands to his chest and tugged on his sweater, pulling him into a kiss. "This time last year, you were engaged to a petite blond. Still happy with whom you ended up with?"

He pulled his wife closer, trapping her arms, which she wiggled until they wrapped around his neck. "I was never engaged." He kissed her forehead. "And you are the only one for me." He kissed her nose. "It just took me a while to figure that out." His lips caressed hers.

"Ew. That is so gross." David stood on the bottom stair, open book in hand.

Thomas grabbed Teddy's hand from behind his head and twirled her around. "Practicing our dancing. It's New Year's Eve."

Teddy flushed and brushed at Thomas's pant leg. "Now you have flour all over you."

David's eyes grew. "What are you making?"

Teddy pushed a wayward curl from her face. "Agnes's favorite. Gingerbread."

Agnes came down the hall, a cloud of flour trailing behind her. "Mama's about to put them in the oven. Do you want to help us decorate when they've cooled?"

Thomas watched the slow smile form on Teddy's face. His heart filled with thanksgiving to the Lord, who had seen fit to allow Agnes to become a permanent part of their family.

David looked first at Teddy. "Can I?"

"That depends. Have you finished cleaning your room? It

looked like whirligigs and marbles had exploded in there the last time I checked."

David looked sheepish and hid the book behind his back. "Hey, Agnes, want to play a game while they cook? It's called Who Can Clear the Floor the Fastest? I do it all the time, but it's a lot more fun with a second player."

"Sure," Agnes exclaimed. She untied her apron and handed it to Teddy, who patted the girl on the head before the child ran after her brother.

Thomas shook his head. "Maybe a different book would have been wiser. I believe Agnes has fallen to the fate of an older and wiser brother."

Teddy held out her hand. "Join me for a cup of tea while I put the cookies in?"

The now-smooth skin touched Thomas's rough hand. "I can do that." He wasn't prepared for the disaster that greeted him when he followed Teddy in.

Teddy filled the teapot. "Would you mind wiping down the table while I put this on?"

His laughter filled the room. "I'd say I'm now the one who's fallen victim to the older and wiser, but I'll just stick with wiser."

"I have no idea what you're talking about," Teddy said.

Thomas didn't miss the smirk but got to work. "So, Nurse Shankel, are you ready to join me at the clinic next week?"

Teddy spun around. "When? I so miss my days in the clinic with you. Don't get me wrong, I love being a wife and mother, but I'll be thankful when school resumes."

"Neither of us expected to have two children so soon. Besides Gabe's weekly treatments, I've only had the usual colds and flu, so you haven't missed much."

"How is Gabe?"

"I believe he's improved," Thomas began, his voice carrying a note of optimism. "His heart change has made the biggest difference in his healing."

Teddy's eyes brightened with hope. "Really? That's wonderful."

Thomas nodded. "It is, but I believe the upcoming date with Betsy has helped as well."

Teddy's hand found its way to Thomas's. "That's wonderful news. You're quite the healer."

Thomas leaned in, warmth and affection for this woman he loved filling him. "I don't know about that. But I know you healed my heart."

Teddy's eyes sparkled with emotion, reflecting the love that had grown between them. "And you healed mine."

In their shared moment of connection, amidst the challenges they faced and the triumphs they celebrated, they acknowledged the healing power of the Father above. For, in their union, they had found not only happiness but also the promise of a brighter future—a future built on love, guided by faith, and blessed with hope.

If you enjoyed Thomas and Teddy's story, preorder the next book, "Written on My Heart," coming May 2025.

Written On My Heart

It's hard to hear God's voice when you've already decided what you want him to say.

In the wilds of the rugged West, Betsy Smith discovers beauty in every corner—from the blazing sunsets to the wind murmuring secrets through the mountains. Yet, it's the magnetism of Gabe Manning, with his dark complexion and dashing demeanor, that draws her gaze. Having known him since childhood, Betsy sees in Gabe the embodiment of the heroes she admires from her novels: a stalwart protector of the innocent, a champion of justice, a man of unshakable integrity, and a paragon of honor, guided by principles as steadfast as the mountains themselves—all while reconciling with his Arapaho Indian heritage. Yet, amid her admiration, Betsy longs for God's reassurance that Gabe is the one for her.

As deputy of Shumard Oak Bend, Missouri, in 1875, Gabe "Little Sun" Manning sees the allure and harshness of frontier life. Amidst the chaos, he finds solace in the presence of Miss Betsy Smith, a compassionate schoolteacher whose independence and intellect captivate him as profoundly as her beauty. Yet, as their bond deepens, Gabe wrestles with doubts about his ability to fulfill the desires of her heart. He knows she's willing to forsake her career for a future with him, but can he offer her the family she seeks? Haunted by the secrets of his past and desperate for redemption, Gabe faces his most formidable challenge yet.

Written on My Heart is a powerful Christian historical romance full of resilience, redemption, and the enduring power of the human spirit. In award-winning author Heidi Gray McGill's fifth installment in the *Discerning God's Best* series, you'll be transported to a world of Wild West adventure and heartwarming romance.

For fans of Misty M. Beller, Lacy Williams, and Linda Ford, this standalone novel in the *Discerning God's Best* series will capture your heart and leave you breathless. You'll love this book if you enjoy gripping historical drama and compelling characters. Binge-read the entire series on Kindle Unlimited.

• Full-length Christian historical fiction
• A standalone novel in the *Discerning God's Best* series
• Includes discussion questions for book clubs
• Timeline: 1875–1876
• For fans of Misty M. Beller, Lacy Williams, and Linda Ford

Book One: *Desire of My Heart*
Book Two: *With All My Heart*
Companion Christmas Novella: *Stitched on My Heart*
Book Three: *Matters of the Heart*
Book Four: *Healing of the Heart*
Book Five: *Written on My Heart*
Prequel: *Deep in My Heart* – available for free with newsletter signup. Search Heidi Gray McGill to locate her website.

Acknowledgement

Dear Reader,

Thank you for embarking on this journey through the pages of my book. Your decision to delve into my world of words is the very essence of why I write - to share my faith, weaving its threads through the lives of my characters as a humble offering of praise to the King of Kings. Behind every word penned lies a tapestry of support and collaboration that brought this book to life.

To my remarkable team of editors, your dedication and insight have sculpted this work into its final form. Isabella Skellenger, with her keen eye as Development Editor, navigated the delicate task of suggesting cuts and guiding the narrative's development. Kathy McKinsey, my steadfast first-round editor, possesses an unparalleled ability to uncover the minutiae, ensuring the text's integrity. Jillian Claire Kohler's proofreading prowess and understanding of my voice enriched every page. Marbeth Skwarczynski, a fellow author and friend, lent her expertise in crafting the tagline, blurb, and book club questions. Any imperfections are solely my own, not a reflection of these ladies' remarkable talents. Stephanie Brank Leupp, librarian and confidante of over four decades, provided invaluable assistance with copyright citations and offered unwavering support.

To those who aided in research, your contributions were indispensable. Doug Winkleman's expertise as a train engineer added authenticity to the narrative. Mike Schmidt's insightful perspective and recitation of a poignant hymn breathed life into pivotal moments. Tom Doggart's knowledge of metallurgy enhanced the story's depth. Michelle Philpott's feedback on Teddy's message of salvation was invaluable.

A special acknowledgment is owed to Carissa Pastuch of the United States Library of Congress for her remarkable sleuthing in uncovering 19th-century maps of Philadelphia. Additionally, gratitude is extended to the Business Reference Services for their assistance in procuring historical train schedules and rail lines.

For technical guidance, I am indebted to Danica Lohmeyer for her unwavering support and expertise. My daughter, Jordan Gray Walker, expertly managed my social media presence and provided understanding during moments of intense focus.

My ACFW Critique group's unwavering encouragement, especially Tema Banner and Christine Boatwright, has been a source of strength.

Family support has been instrumental in this journey. To my husband, Bob McGill, whose unwavering support allowed for uninterrupted writing and editing time, and to Carol Kress McNeely and Barbara Kress McGill, whose insights and cheerleading bolstered my spirits.

Special thanks to Cheryl and Dave Maddox for their enduring friendship and willingness to offer constructive feedback, even years after a book's publication.

I am immensely grateful for the multitude of individuals who have made it possible for this story to reach your hands.

Heidi Gray McGill

More From This Author

All Books on Amazon and Kindle Unlimited

Discerning God's Best series

Sometimes, it's the unexpected twists that make life an exciting adventure. At other times, fear, trouble, and deep heartache make it feel perilous. But at all times, accepting God's will, even if it means losing the one you love, makes it worthwhile.

Embark on a journey from South Carolina to Missouri with characters who quickly become family, adventures that become real, and hope that becomes a promise.

Prequel: Deep in My Heart – *available for free with newsletter signup. Search Heidi Gray McGill to locate her website.*

Book One: Desire of My Heart

Book Two: With All My Heart

Companion Christmas Novella: Stitched On My Heart

Book Three: Matters of the Heart

Book Four: Healing of the Heart

Book Five: Written on My Heart – *Preorder now*

You Are On The Air Series

Finding love, repairing relationships, and healing broken hearts happen when you are on the air with your favorite radio station. Unique, clean, A-to-Z romance stories from fifteen authors make this a can't-put-down RomCom series.

Dial E for Endearment
Dial P for Perfect

The Proxy Bride series

A Bride for Harley
Available in Audiobook format at Store.HeidiGrayMcGill.com
La Elegida para Harley - *Coming soon*

Thank You

Thank you for reading *Healing of the Heart*. If you would like to read about Melvin's and Mary's journey in the Prequel, *Deep in My Heart*, it is available only to those who sign up for my newsletter at HeidiGrayMcGill.com.

I would be honored if you would follow me on Amazon, BookBub, Goodreads, Instagram, Facebook, and YouTube by searching Author Heidi Gray McGill.

DO YOU LIKE AUDIOBOOKS? Consider purchasing my audiobooks straight from my store at Store.HeidiGrayMcGill.com.

However you choose to connect (hopefully all the ways), I thank you. I value your support and look forward to getting to know you as we journey together!

About The Author

Heidi Gray Mcgill

Heidi Gray McGill is an award-winning, best-selling author known for infusing God's love into her Christian fiction works. Her Discerning God's Best series has garnered five NEST awards and widespread acclaim, while her book "Dial E for Endearment" was a finalist for the CIA Award. With over eight books in print, Heidi's Discerning God's Best series continues to dominate the best-seller lists, boasting over 1,000 five-star reviews for its first installment.

Despite facing challenges, including her blindness disability, Heidi embarked on her writing journey in March 2020 with unwavering determination. Both independently and traditionally published, Heidi's writing is characterized by its purposefulness. Through her masterfully crafted characters and meticulously woven narratives, she leads readers on journeys of faith, healing, and self-discovery, all while seamlessly integrating God's Word into the fabric of her stories.

Heidi resides in a small town south of Charlotte, NC, where she shares a loving bond with her husband of over thirty years. Beyond writing, she finds joy in spending time with her family, playing games, and exploring the world through the pages of books. Committed to inspiring and supporting fellow authors, Heidi pays forward the encouragement and mentorship she received at the outset of her career. Her speaking engagements aim to empower individuals to fulfill their calling through the written word and to overcome obstacles with resilience and faith.

Join Heidi on her inspiring journey and discover the transformative power of God's love woven intricately into the fabric of her award-winning Christian fiction works. To glimpse her world and claim your free book, visit her website and sign up for her newsletter today at heidigraymcgill.com.

Made in United States
Troutdale, OR
09/24/2024

23112794R00224